P9-CQW-247

Also by Len Deighton

NONFICTION

Fighter: The True Story of the Battle of Britain

Airshipwreck

*Blitzkrieg: From the Rise of Hitler
to the Fall of Dunkirk*

FICTION

The Ipcress File

Horse Under Water

Funeral in Berlin

Billion-Dollar Brain

An Expensive Place to Die

Only When I Larf

Bomber

Declarations of War

Close-Up

Spy Story

Yesterday's Spy

Catch a Falling Spy

SS-GB

XPD

Goodbye, Mickey Mouse

Berlin Game

Mexico Set

MEXICO SET

LEN DEIGHTON

ALFRED A. KNOPF

NEW YORK

1985

Library of Congress Cataloging in Publication Data

Deighton, Len [*date*]   Mexico set.

I. Title.
PR6054.E37M4   1985   823'.914   84-48500
ISBN 0-394-53525-1

Manufactured in the United States of America

FIRST AMERICAN EDITION

Mexico Set

Chapter 1

"SOME OF these people *want* to get killed," said Dicky Cruyer as he jabbed the brake pedal to avoid hitting a newsboy. The kid grinned as he slid between the slowly moving cars, flourishing his newspapers with the controlled abandon of a fan dancer. SIX FACE FIRING SQUAD; the headlines were huge and shiny black. HURRICANE THREATENS VERACRUZ. A smudgy photo of street fighting in San Salvador covered the whole front of a tabloid.

It was late afternoon. The streets shone with that curiously bright shadowless light that precedes a storm. All six lanes of traffic crawling along Insurgentes halted, and more newsboys danced into the road, together with a woman selling flowers and a kid with lottery tickets trailing from a roll like toilet paper.

Picking his way between the cars came a handsome man in old jeans and checked shirt. He was accompanied by a small child. The man had a Coca-Cola bottle in his fist. He swigged at it and then tilted his head back looking up into the heavens. He stood erect and immobile, like a bronze statue, before igniting his breath so that a great ball of fire burst from his mouth.

"Bloody hell!" said Dicky. "That's dangerous."

"It's a living," I said. I'd seen the fire-eaters before. There was always one of them performing somewhere in the big traffic jams. I switched on the car radio but electricity in the air blotted out the music with the sounds of static. The city was very hot

3

that year. I opened the window but the sudden stink of diesel fumes made me close it again. I held my hand against the air-conditioning outlet but the air was warm.

Again the fire-eater blew a huge orange balloon of flame into the air.

"For us," explained Dicky. "Dangerous for people in the cars. Flames like that, with all these petrol fumes . . . can you imagine?" There was a slow roll of thunder. "If only it would rain," said Dicky. I looked at the sky, the low black clouds trimmed with gold. The huge sun was colored bright red by the city's ever present blanket of smog, and squeezed tight between the glass buildings that dripped with its light.

"Who got this car for us?" I said. A motorcycle, its pillion piled high with cases of beer, weaved precariously between the cars, narrowly missing the flower seller.

"One of the embassy people," said Dicky. He released the brake and the big blue Chevrolet rolled forward a few feet and then all the traffic stopped again. In any town north of the border this factory-fresh car would not have drawn a second glance. But Mexico City is the place old cars go to die. Most of those around us were dented and rusty, or they were crudely repainted in bright primary colors. "A friend of mine lent it to us."

"I might have guessed," I said.

"It was short notice. They didn't know we were coming until the day before yesterday. Henry Tiptree—the one who met us at the airport—let us have it. It was a special favor because I knew him at Oxford."

"I wish you hadn't known him at Oxford; then we could have rented one from Hertz—with air-conditioning that worked."

"So what can we do . . . ," said Dicky irritably, "take it back and tell him it's not good enough for us?"

We watched the fire-eater blow another balloon of flame while the small boy hurried from driver to driver collecting a peso here and there for his father's performance.

Dicky took some Mexican coins from the slash pocket of his denim jacket and gave them to the child. It was Dicky's faded work suit, his cowboy boots and curly hair that had attracted the attention of the tough-looking lady immigration officer at Mexico City airport. It was only the first-class labels on his expensive baggage and the fast talking of Dicky's counselor friend from the embassy that saved him from the indignity of a body search.

Dicky Cruyer was a curious mixture of scholarship and ruthless ambition, but he was insensitive and this was often his undoing. His insensitivity to people, place, and atmosphere could make him seem a clown instead of the cool sophisticate that was his own image of himself. But that didn't make him any less terrifying as friend or foe.

The flower seller bent down, tapped on the window glass, and waved at Dicky. He shouted, *"Vamos!"* It was almost impossible to see her face behind the unwieldy armful of flowers. Here were blossoms of all colors, shapes, and sizes. Flowers for weddings and flowers for dinner hostesses, flowers for mistresses and flowers for suspicious wives.

The traffic began moving again. Dicky shouted *"Vamos!"* much louder.

The woman saw me reaching into my pocket for money and separated a dozen long-stem pink roses from the less expensive marigolds and asters. "Maybe some flowers would be something to give to Werner's wife," I said.

Dicky ignored my suggestion. "Get out of the way," he shouted at the old woman and the car leaped forward. The old woman jumped clear.

"Take it easy, Dicky, you nearly knocked her over."

"Vamos! I told her; *vamos.* They shouldn't be in the road. Are they all crazy? She heard me all right."

"Vamos means 'okay, lets go,' " I said. "She thought you wanted to buy some."

"In Mexico it also means 'scram,' " said Dicky, driving up close to a white VW bus in front of us. It was full of people and boxes of tomatoes and its dented bodywork was caked with mud in the way that cars become when they venture onto country roads at this rainy time of year. Its exhaust pipe was newly bound up with wire and the rear panel had been removed to help cool the engine. The sound of its fan made a very loud whine so that Dicky had to speak loudly to make himself heard. "*Vamos;* scram. They say it in cowboy films."

"Maybe she doesn't go to cowboy films," I said.

"Just keep looking at the street map."

"It's not a street map, it's just a map. It only shows the main streets."

"We'll find it all right. It's off Insurgentes."

"Do you know how big Mexico City is? Insurgentes is about thirty-five miles long," I said.

"You look on your side and I'll look this side. Volkmann said it's in the center of town." He sniffed. "Mexico they call it. No one here says Mexico City. They call the town Mexico."

I didn't answer; I put away the little colored town plan and stared out at the crowded streets. I was quite happy to be driven round the town for an hour or two if that's what Dicky wanted.

Dicky said, " 'Somewhere in the center of town' would mean the Paseo de la Reforma near the column with the golden angel. At least that's what it would mean to any tourist coming here for the first time. And Werner Volkmann and his wife Zena are here for the first time. Right?"

"Werner said it was going to be a second honeymoon."

"With Zena I would have thought one honeymoon would be enough," said Dicky.

"More than enough," I said.

Dicky said, "I'll kill your bloody Werner if he's brought us out from London on a wild goose chase."

"It's a break from the office," I said. Werner had become "my" Werner, I noticed, and would remain so if things went wrong.

"For you it is," said Dicky. "You've got nothing to lose. Your desk will be waiting for you when you get back. But there's a dozen people in that building scrambling round for my job. This will give Bret just the chance he needs to take over my work. You realize that, don't you?"

"How could Bret want to take your job, Dicky? Bret is senior to you."

The traffic was moving at about five miles an hour. A small dirty-faced child in the back of the VW bus was staring at Dicky with great interest. The insolent stare seemed to disconcert him. Dicky turned to look at me. "Bret is looking for a job that would suit him; and my job would suit him. Bret will have nothing to do, now that his committee is being wound up. There's already an argument about who's to have his office space. And about who's to have that tall blonde typist who wears the white sweaters."

"Gloria?" I said.

"Oh? Don't say you've been there?"

"Us workers stick together, Dicky," I said.

"Very funny," said Dicky. "If Bret takes over my job, he'll chase your ass. Working for me will seem like a holiday. I hope you realize that, old pal."

I didn't know that the brilliant career of Bret was taking a downturn to the point where Dicky was running scared. But Dicky had taken a Ph.D. in office politics so I was prepared to believe him. "This is the Pink Zone," I said. "Why don't you park in one of these hotels and get a cab?"

Dicky seemed relieved at the idea of letting a cab driver find Werner Volkmann's apartment but, being Dicky, he had to argue against it for a couple of minutes. As he pulled into the slow lane, the dirty child in the VW smiled and then made a terrible face at us. Dicky said, "Are you pulling faces at that child? For God's sake, act your age, Bernard." Dicky was in a bad mood and talking about his job had made him more touchy.

He turned off Insurgentes onto a side street and cruised eastwards until we found a car park under one of the big hotels. As we went down the ramp into the darkness he switched the headlights on. This was a different world. This was where the

Mercedes, Cadillacs, and Porsches lived in comfort, shiny with health, smelling of new leather and guarded by two armed security men. One of them pushed a ticket under a wiper and lifted the barrier so that we could drive through.

"So your school chum Werner spots a KGB heavy here in town. Why did Controller Europe insist that I come out here at this stinking time of year?" Dicky was cruising very slowly round the dark garage looking for a place to park.

"Werner didn't spot Erich Stinnes," I said. "Werner's wife spotted him. And we have a departmental alert out for him. There's a space."

"Too small, this is a big car. Alert? You don't have to tell me that, old boy. I signed the alert, remember me? Controller of German Stations? But I've never seen Erich Stinnes. I wouldn't know Erich Stinnes from the man in the moon. You're the one who can identify him. Why do I have to come?"

"You're here to decide what we do. I'm not senior enough or reliable enough to make decisions. What about there, next to the white Mercedes?"

"Ummmmm," said Dicky. He had trouble parking the car in the space marked out by the white lines. One of the security guards—a big poker-faced man in starched khakis and carefully polished high boots—came over to watch us. He stood staring, arms akimbo, while Dicky went backwards and forwards trying to squeeze between the white convertible and a concrete stanchion that bore brightly colored patches of enamel from other cars. "Did you really make out with that blonde in Bret's office?" said Dicky as he abandoned his task and reversed into another space, marked RESERVED.

"Gloria? I thought everyone knew about me and Gloria," I said. In fact I knew her no better than Dicky did but I couldn't resist the chance to needle him. "My wife's left me. I'm a free man again."

"Your wife defected," said Dicky spitefully. "Your wife is working for the bloody Russkies."

"That's over and done with," I said. I didn't want to talk

about my wife or my children or any of my other problems. And
if I did want to talk about them, Dicky would be the last person
I'd choose to confide in.

"You and Fiona were very close," said Dicky accusingly.

"It's not a crime to be in love with your wife," I said.

"Taboo subject, eh?" It pleased Dicky to touch a nerve and
get a reaction. I should have known better than to respond to
his taunts. I was guilty by association. I'd become a probationer
once more and I'd remain one until I proved my loyalty all over
again. Nothing had been said to me officially, but Dicky's little
flash of temper was not the first indication of what the Department really felt.

"I didn't come on this trip to discuss Fiona," I said.

"Don't keep bickering," said Dicky. "Let's go and talk to
your friend Werner and get it finished. I can't wait to be out of
this filthy hellhole. January or February; that's the time when
people who know what's what go to Mexico. Not in the middle
of the rainy season."

Dicky opened the door of the car and I slid across the seat
to get out his side. *"Prohibido aparcar,"* said the security guard
and, with arms folded, he planted himself in our path.

"What's that?" said Dicky and the man said it again. Dicky
smiled and explained, in his schoolboy Spanish, that we were
residents of the hotel, we would only be leaving the car there
for half an hour, and that we were engaged on very important
business.

"Prohibido aparcar," said the guard stolidly.

"Give him some money, Dicky," I said. "That's all he
wants."

The security guard looked from Dicky to me and stroked his
large black mustache with the ball of his thumb. He was a big
man, as tall as Dicky and twice as wide.

"I'm not going to give him anything," said Dicky. "I'm not
going to pay twice."

"Let me do it," I said. "I've got small money here."

"Stay out of this," said Dicky. "You've got to know how to

handle these people." He stared at the guard, *"Nada! Nada! Nada! Entiende?"*

The guard looked down at our Chevrolet and then plucked the wiper between finger and thumb and let it fall back against the glass with a thump. "He'll wreck the car," I said. "This is not the time to get into a hassle you can't win."

"I'm not frightened of him," said Dicky.

"I know you're not, but I am." I got in front of him before he took a swing at the guard. There was a hard, almost vicious, streak under Dicky's superficial charm, and he was a keen member of the Foreign Office Judo Club. Dicky wasn't frightened of anything; that's why I didn't like working with him. I folded some paper money into the guard's ready hand and pushed Dicky towards the sign that said ELEVATOR TO HOTEL LOBBY. The guard watched us go, his face still without emotion. Dicky wasn't pleased either. He thought I'd tried to protect him against the guard and he felt belittled by my interference.

The hotel lobby was that same ubiquitous combination of tinted mirror, plastic marble, and spongy carpet underlay that international travelers are reputed to admire. We sat down under a huge display of plastic flowers and looked at the fountain.

"Machismo," said Dicky sadly. We were waiting for the top-hatted hotel doorman to find a taxi driver who would take us to Werner's apartment. "Machismo," he said again reflectively. "Every last one of them is obsessed by it. It's why you can't get anything done here. I'm going to report that bastard downstairs to the manager."

"Wait until after we've collected the car," I advised.

"At least the embassy sent a counselor to meet us. That means that London has told them to give us full diplomatic backup."

"Or it means Mexico City embassy staff—including your pal Tiptree—have a lot of time on their hands."

Dicky looked up from counting his traveler's checks. "What do I have to do, Bernard, to make you remember that it's Mexico? Not Mexico City; Mexico!"

Chapter 2

THIS WAS a new Werner Volkmann. This was not the introverted Jewish orphan I'd been at school with, nor the lugubrious teenager I'd grown up with in Berlin. Nor the affluent overweight banker who was welcome on both sides of the Wall. This new Werner was a tough, muscular figure in short-sleeve cotton shirt and well-fitting Madras trousers. His big droopy mustache had been trimmed and so had his black bushy hair. Being on holiday with his twenty-two-year-old wife had rejuvenated him.

He was standing on the sixth-floor balcony of a small block of luxury apartments in downtown Mexico City. From here was a view across this immense city, with the mountains a dark backdrop. The dying sun was turning the world pink now that the storm clouds had passed over. Long ragged strips of orange and gold cloud were torn across the sky, like a poster advertising a smog-reddened sun that had been ripped by a passing vandal.

The balcony was large enough to hold a lot of expensive white garden furniture as well as big pots of tropical flowers. Green leafy plants climbed overhead to provide shade while a collection of cacti were arrayed on shelves like books. Werner poured a pink concoction from a glass jug. It was like a watery fruit salad, the sort of thing they pressed on you at parties where no one got drunk. It didn't look tempting but I was hot and I took one gratefully.

Dicky Cruyer was flushed; his cowboy shirt bore dark patches of sweat. He had his blue denim jacket slung over his shoulder. He tossed it onto a chair and reached out to take a drink from Werner.

11

Werner's wife, Zena, held out her glass for a refill. She was full-length on a reclining chair. She was wearing a sheer rainbow-striped dress through which her sun-tanned limbs shone darkly. As she moved to sip her drink, German fashion magazines, balanced on her belly, slid to the ground and flapped open. Zena cursed softly. It was the strange flat-accented speech of eastern lands that were no longer German. It was probably the only thing she'd inherited from her impoverished parents and I had the feeling she would sometimes have been happier without it.

"What's in this drink?" I said.

Werner recovered the magazines from the floor and gave them to his wife. In business he could be tough, in friendships outspoken, but with Zena he was always indulgent.

Werner raised money from Western banks to pay exporters to East Germany, and then eventually collected the money from the East German government. "Avalizing" it was called, with Werner taking a tiny percentage on every deal. But it wasn't a banker's business; it was a free-for-all in which many got their fingers burned. Werner had to be tough to survive.

"In the drink? Fruit juices," said Werner. "It's too early for alcohol in this sort of climate."

"Not for me it isn't," I said. Werner smiled but he didn't go anywhere to get me a proper drink. He was my oldest and closest friend, the sort of close friend who gives you the excoriating criticism that new enemies hesitate about. Zena didn't look up; she was still pretending to read her magazines.

Dicky had stepped into the jungle of flowers to get a clearer view of the city. I looked over his shoulder to see the traffic still moving sluggishly. In the street below there were flashing red lights and sirens as two police cars mounted the pavement to get around the traffic. In a city of fifteen million people there is said to be a crime committed every two minutes. The noise of the streets never ceased. As the flow of homegoing office workers ended, the influx of people to the Zona Rosa's restaurants and cinemas began. "What a madhouse," said Dicky.

A malevolent-looking black cat awoke and jumped softly down from its position on the footstool. It went over to Dicky and sank a claw into his leg and looked up at him to see how he'd take it. "Hell," shouted Dicky. "Get away, you brute." Dicky aimed a blow at the cat but missed. The cat moved very fast, as if it had done the same thing before to other gringos.

Wincing with pain and rubbing his leg, Dicky moved well away from the cat and went to the other end of the balcony to look inside the large lounge with its locally made tiles, old masks, and Mexican textiles. It looked like an arts and crafts shop, but obviously a lot of money had been spent getting it that way. "Nice place you've got here," said Dicky. There was more than a hint of sarcasm in his remark. This was not Dicky's style. Anything that departed much from Harrods furniture department was too foreign for him.

"It belongs to Zena's uncle and aunt," explained Werner. "We're taking care of it while they're in Europe." That explained the notebook I'd seen near the telephone. Zena had neatly entered "wine glass," "tumbler," "wine glass," "small china bowl with blue flowers." It was a list of breakages, an example of Zena's sense of order and rectitude.

"You chose a bad time of year," complained Dicky. "Or rather Zena's uncle chose a good one." He drained the glass, tipping it up until the ice cubes, cucumber, and pieces of lemon slid down the glass and rested against his lips.

"Zena doesn't mind it," said Werner as if his own opinions were of no importance.

Zena, still concentrating on her magazine, said, "I love the sun." She said it twice and continued to read without losing her place.

"If only it would rain," said Werner. "It's this buildup to the storms that make it so unbearable."

"So you saw this chap Stinnes?" said Dicky very casually as if that wasn't the reason the two of us had dragged four thousand miles to talk to them.

"At the Kronprinz," said Werner.

"What's the Kronprinz?" said Dicky. He put down his glass and used a paper napkin to dry his lips.

"A club."

"What sort of club?" Dicky stuck his thumbs into the back of his leather belt and looked down at the toes of his cowboy boots reflectively. The cat had followed Dicky and looked as if it was about to reach up above his boot to put a claw into his thin calf again. Dicky aimed a vicious little kick at it but the cat was too quick for him. "Get away," said Dicky, more loudly this time.

"I'm sorry about the cat," said Werner. "But I think Zena's aunt only let us use the place because we'd be company for Cherubino. It's your jeans. Cats like to claw at denim."

"It bloody hurts," said Dicky rubbing his leg. "You should get its claws clipped or something. In this part of the world cats carry all kinds of diseases."

"What's it matter what sort of club?" said Zena suddenly. She closed the magazine and pushed her hair back. She looked different with her hair loose; no longer the tough little career girl, more the lady of leisure. Her hair was long and jet black and held with a silver Mexican comb which she brandished before tossing the hair back and fixing it again.

"A club for German businessmen. Its been going since 1902," said Werner. "Zena likes the buffet and dance they have on Friday nights. There's a big German colony here in the city. There always has been."

"Werner said there would be a cash payment for finding Stinnes," said Zena.

"There usually is," said Dicky slyly, although he knew there would be no chance of a cash payment for such a routine report. It must have been Werner's way of encouraging Zena to cooperate with us. I looked at Werner and he looked back at me without changing his expression.

"How do you know it really is Stinnes?" said Dicky.

"It's Stinnes all right," said Werner stoically. "His name is on his membership card and his credit at the bar is in that name."

"And his checkbook," said Zena. "His name is printed on his checks."

"What bank?" I asked.

"Bank of America," said Zena. "A branch in San Diego, California."

"Names mean nothing," said Dicky. "How do you know this fellow is a KGB man? And even if he is, what makes you so sure that this is the johnny who interrogated Bernard in East Berlin?" A brief movement of the hand in my direction. "It might be someone using the same cover name. We've known KGB people do that. Right, Bernard?"

"It has been known," I said, although I was damned if I could recall any examples of such sloppy tactics by the plodding but thorough bureaucrats of the KGB.

"How much?" said Zena. And, when Dicky looked at her and raised his eyebrows, she said, "How much are you going to give us for reporting Stinnes? Werner said you want him badly. Werner said he was very important."

"Steady on," said Dicky. "We don't have him yet. We haven't even positively identified him."

"Erich Stinnes," said Zena as if repeating a prepared lesson. "Fortyish, thinning hair, cheap specs, smokes like a chimney. Berlin accent."

"Beard?"

"No beard," said Zena. Hastily she added, "He must have shaved it off." She did not readily abandon her claims.

"So you've spoken with him," I said.

"He's there every Friday," said Werner. "He's a regular. He works at the Soviet Embassy, he told Zena that. He says he's just a driver."

"They're always drivers," I said. "That's how they account for their nice big cars and going wherever they want to go." I poured myself some more of Werner's fruit punch. There was not much of it left, and the bottom of the jug was a tangle of greenery and soggy bits of lemon. "Did he talk about books or American films, Zena?"

She swung her legs out of the reclining chair with a display of tanned thigh. I saw the look in Dicky Cruyer's face as she smoothed her dress. She had that sexy appeal that goes with youth and health and boundless energy. And now she knew she had the right Stinnes, her pearly gray eyes sparkled. "That's right. He loves old Hollywood musicals and English detective stories . . ."

"Then that's him," I said without much enthusiasm. Secretly I'd hoped it would all come to nothing and I'd be able to go straight back to London and my home and my children. "Yes, that's 'Lenin,' that's the one who took me down to Checkpoint Charlie when they released me."

"What will happen now?" said Zena. She was short; she only came up to Dicky's shoulder. Some say short people are aggressive to compensate for their small stature, but look at Zena Volkmann and you might start to think that aggressive people are made short lest they take over the whole world. Either way, Zena was short and the aggression inside her was always bubbling along the edges of the pan like milk before it boils over. "What will you do about him?"

"Don't ask," Werner told her.

But Dicky answered her. "We want to talk to him, Mrs. Volkmann. No rough stuff, if that's what you are afraid of."

I swallowed my fruit punch and got a mouthful of tiny pieces of ice and some lemon pips.

Zena smiled. She wasn't frightened of any rough stuff; she was frightened of not getting the money for arranging it. She stood up and twisted her shoulders, slowly stretching her arms above her head one after the other in a lazy display of overt sexuality. "Do you want my help?" she said.

Dicky didn't answer directly. He looked from Zena to Werner and back again and said, "Stinnes is a KGB major. That's too low a rank for the computer to offer much on him. Most of what we know about him came from Bernard, who was interrogated by him." A glance at me to stress the unreliability of uncorroborated intelligence from any source. "But he's senior staff in Berlin. So what is he doing in Mexico? Must be a Russian national. What's his game? What's he doing in this German club of yours?"

Zena laughed. "You think he should have joined Perovsky's?" She laughed again.

Werner said, "Zena knows this town very well, Dicky. She has aunts and uncles, cousins and a nephew here. She lived here for six months when she first left school."

"Where, what, how, or why is Perovsky's?" said Dicky. He was German Stations Controller. He didn't like being laughed at, and I could see he was taking a little time getting used to Werner's calling him Dicky.

"Zena is joking," explained Werner. "Perovsky's is a big, rather run-down club for Russians near the National Palace. The ground floor is a restaurant open to anyone. It was started after the Revolution. The members used to be dukes and counts and people who'd escaped from the Bolsheviks. Now it's a pretty mixed crowd, but the anti-Communist line is still de rigueur. The people from the Soviet Embassy give it a wide berth. If a man such as Stinnes went in there and spoke out of turn he might never get out."

"Really never get out?" I asked.

Werner turned to look at me. "It's a rough town, Bernie. It's not all margaritas and mariachis like the travel posters."

"But the Kronprinz Club is not so particular about its membership?" persisted Dicky.

"No one goes there to talk politics. It's the only place in town where you can get real German draft beer and good German food," explained Werner. "It's very popular. It's a social club; you get a very mixed crowd there. A lot of them are transients—airline pilots, salesmen, ship's engineers, businessmen. Priests even."

"And KGB men?"

"You Englishmen avoid each other when you are abroad,"

said Werner. "We Germans like to be together. East Germans, West Germans, exiles, expatriates, men avoiding tax, men avoiding their wives, men avoiding their debtors, men avoiding the police. Nazis, monarchists, Communists, even Jews like me. We like to be together because we are Germans."

"Such Germans as Stinnes?" said Dicky sarcastically.

"He must have lived in Berlin. His German is as good as Bernie's," said Werner looking at me. "Even more convincing in a way, because he has the sort of strong Berlin accent you seldom hear except in some workers' bar in the city. It was only when I began to listen to him really carefully that I could detect something not quite right in the background of his voice. I'll bet everyone in the club thinks he's German."

"He's not here to get a tan," said Dicky. "A man like that is sent here only for something special. What's your guess, Bernard?"

"Stinnes was in Cuba," I said. "He told me that when we talked together. Security Police. I went back to the continuity files and began to guess he was there to give the Cubans some advice when they purged some of the bigwigs in 1970. It was a big shake-up. Stinnes must have been some kind of Latin America expert even then."

"Never mind old history," said Dicky. "What's he doing now?"

"Running agents, I suppose. Guatemala is a KGB priority, and it's not so far from here. Anyone can walk through; the border is just jungle."

"I don't think that's it," said Werner.

I said, "The East Germans backed the Sandinist National Liberation Front long before it looked like winning and forming a government."

"The East Germans back anybody who might be a thorn in the flesh of the Americans," said Werner.

"But what do you think he's really doing?" Dicky asked me.

I was stalling because I didn't know how much Dicky would want me to say in front of Zena and Werner. I kept stalling. I said, "Stinnes speaks good English. Unless the checkbook is a deliberate way of throwing us off the scent, he might be running agents into California. Handling data stolen from electronics and software research firms perhaps." I was improvising. I didn't have the slightest idea of what Stinnes might be doing.

"Why would London give a damn about that sort of caper?" said Werner, who knew me well enough to guess that I was bluffing. "Don't tell me London Central put out an urgent call for Stinnes because he's stealing computer secrets from the Americans."

"It's the only reason I can think of," I said.

"Don't treat me like a child, Bernard," said Werner. "If you don't want to tell me, just say so."

As if in response to Werner's acrimony, Zena went across to the fireplace and pressed a hidden bellpush. From somewhere in the labyrinth of the apartment there came the sound of footsteps, and an Indian woman appeared. She had that chin-up stance that makes so many Mexicans look as if they are ready to balance a water jug on their head, and her eyes were half closed. "I knew you'd want to sample some Mexican food," said Zena. Personally it was the last thing I'd ever want to sample, but without waiting to hear our response she told the woman we would sit down immediately. Zena used her poor Spanish with a fluent confidence that made it sound better. Zena did everything like that.

"She can understand German perfectly and a certain amount of English too," said Zena after the woman had gone. It was a warning to guard our tongues. "Maria has worked for my aunt for over ten years."

"But you don't talk to her in German," said Dicky.

Zena smiled at him. "By the time you've said tortillas, tacos, guacamole, and quesadillas and so on, you might as well add *por favor* and get it over with."

It was an elegant table, shining with solid silver cutlery, hand-embroidered linen, and fine cut glass. The meal had obviously been planned and prepared as part of Zena's pitch for a cash payment. It was a good meal, and not too damned ethnic, thank God. I have a very limited capacity for the primitive permutations of tortillas, bean mush, and chili that numb the palate and sear the insides from Dallas to Cape Horn. But we started with grilled lobster and cold white wine, with not a refried bean in sight.

The curtains were drawn back so that air could come in through the open windows, but the air was not cool. The cyclone out in the Gulf had not moved nearer the coast, so the threatened storms had not come, but neither had much drop in temperature. By now the sun had gone down behind the mountains that surround the city on every side, and the sky was mauve. Pinpointed like stars in a planetarium were the lights of the city; they stretched all the way to the foothills of the distant mountains until like a galaxy they became a milky blur. The dining room was dark; the only light came from tall candles that burned brightly in the still air.

"Sometimes London Central can get in ahead of our American friends," said Dicky, suddenly spearing another grilled lobster tail. Had he really spent so long thinking up a reply for Werner? "It would give us negotiating power in Washington if we had some good material about KGB penetration of anywhere in Uncle Sam's backyard."

Werner reached across the table to pour more wine for his wife. "This is Chilean wine," said Werner. He poured some for Dicky and for me and then refilled his own glass. It was Werner's way of telling Dicky he didn't believe a word of it, but I'm not sure Dicky understood that.

"It's not bad," said Dicky, sipping, closing his eyes and tilting his head back to concentrate all his attention on the taste. Dicky fancied his wine expertise. He'd already made a great show of sniffing the cork. "I suppose with the peso collapsing, it will be more and more difficult to get any sort of imported wine. And Mexican wine is a bit of an acquired taste."

"Stinnes only arrived here two or three weeks ago," said Werner doggedly. "If London Central is interested in Stinnes, it won't be on account of anything he might be planning to do in Silicon Valley or in the Guatemala rain forest; it will be on account of all the things he did in Berlin during the last two years."

"Do you think so?" said Dicky, looking at Werner with friendly and respectful interest, like a man who wanted to learn something. But Werner could see through him.

"I'm not an idiot," said Werner, using the unemotional tone but exaggerated clarity with which a man might specify decaffeinated coffee to an inattentive waiter. "I was dodging KGB men when I was ten years old. Bernie and I were working for the Department when the Wall was built in 1961, and you were still at school."

"Point taken, old boy," said Dicky with a smile. He could afford to smile; he was two years younger than either of us, with years less time in the Department, but he'd got the coveted job of German Stations Controller against tough competition. And —despite rumors about an imminent reshuffle in London Central—he was still holding on to it. "But the fact is that the people in London don't tell me every last thing they have in mind. I'm just the chap chipping away at the coal face, right? They don't consult me about building new nuclear power stations." He poured some warm butter over his last piece of lobster with a care that suggested he had no other concern in his mind.

"Tell me about Stinnes," I said to Werner. "Does he come along to the Kronprinz Club trailing a string of KGB zombies? Or does he come on his own? Does he sit in the corner with his big glass of *Berliner Weisse mit Schuss,* or does he sniff round to see what he can ferret out? How does he behave, Werner?"

"He's a loner," said Werner. "He probably would never have spoken to us in the first place except that he mistook Zena for one of the Biedermann girls."

"Who are the Biedermann girls?" said Dicky. After the remains of the lobster course had been removed, the Indian servant brought an elaborate array of Mexican dishes: refried beans, whole chilis, and the tortilla in its various disguises—enchiladas, tacos, tostadas, and quesadillas. Dicky paused for long enough to have each one identified and described, but he took only a tiny portion on his plate.

"Here in Mexico the chili has sexual significance," said Zena, directing the remark to Dicky. "The man who eats hot chilis is thought to be virile and strong."

"Oh, I love chilis," said Dicky, his tone of voice picking up the hint of mockery in Zena's. "Always have had a weakness for chilis," he said as he reached for a plate on which many different ones were arranged. I glanced at Werner, who was watching Dicky with interest. Dicky looked up to see Werner's face. "It's the tiny, dark-colored ones that blow your head off," Dicky explained. He took a large pale-green cayenne and smiled at our doubting faces before biting a section from it.

There was a silence after Dicky's mouth closed upon the chili. Everyone except Dicky knew he'd mistaken the cayenne for one of the very mild *aji* chilis from the eastern provinces. And soon Dicky knew it too. His face went red, his mouth half opened, and tears shone in his eyes. He fought against the pain but he had to take it from his mouth. Then he fed himself lots and lots of plain rice.

"The Biedermanns are a wealthy Berlin family," said Zena, carrying on as if she'd not noticed Dicky's desperate discomfort. "They are well known in Germany. They have interests in German travel companies. The newspapers said the company had borrowed millions of dollars to build a holiday village in the Yucatán peninsula. It's never been finished. Erich Stinnes thought I looked just like the younger sister, Poppy, who's always in the newspaper gossip columns."

There was a silence as we all waited for Dicky to recover. Finally he leaned back in his chair and managed a rueful smile. There was perspiration on his forehead and he was breathing with his mouth open. "Do you know these Biedermann people, Bernard?" said Dicky. He sounded hoarse.

"Have an avocado," said Werner. "They are very sooth-ing." Dicky took an avocado pear from the bowl and began to eat some.

I said, "When my father was attached to the military government in Berlin he gave old Biedermann a license to start up his bus service again. It was one of the first after the war; it started the family fortune, I suppose. Yes, I know them. Poppy Biedermann was having dinner at Frank Harrington's the last time I was in Berlin."

Dicky was eating the avocado pear quickly with his teaspoon, using it to heal the burning in his mouth. "That was bloody hot," he confessed finally.

"There's no way you can be sure which are hot and which are mild," said Zena in a gentle tone that surprised me. "They cross-pollinate; even on the same plant you can get fiery ones and mild ones." She smiled.

"Could these Biedermann people be interesting to Stinnes?" said Dicky. "For instance, might they own a factory that's making computer software in California? Or something like that? What do you know about that, Bernard?"

"Even if that was the case, no point of making contact with the boss," I said. I could see that Dicky had focused on the idea of Silicon Valley and it was not going to be easy to shake him off it. "The approach would be made to someone in the microchip laboratory. Or someone doing the programs for the software."

"We need to know the current situation from the California end," said Dicky with a sigh. I knew that sigh. Dicky was just getting me prepared for a sweaty week in Mexico City while he went off to swan around in Southern California.

"Talk to the Biedermanns," I said. "It's easier."

"Stinnes asked about the Biedermanns," said Werner. "He asked if I knew them. I used to know Paul very well, but I told Stinnes I knew the family only from the newspapers."

"Werner! You didn't tell me you know the Biedermanns," Zena interjected excitedly. "They are always in the gossip columns. Poppy Biedermann is beautiful. She just got divorced from a millionaire."

Dicky looked at me and said, "Better you talk to Biedermann. No sense in me showing my face. Keep it informal. Find out where he is; go and see him. Would you do that, Bernard?" It was an order in the American style; disguised to sound like a polite inquiry.

"I can try."

Dicky said, "I don't want to channel this through London, or get Frank Harrington to introduce us, or the whole world will know we're interested." He poured himself some iced water and sipped a little. He was recovering some of his composure until he screamed, "You bastard," his eyes fixed on poor Werner and his head thrust forward low over the table. Werner looked perplexed until Dicky, still leaning forward with his head almost on his plate, yelled, "That bloody cat."

"Cherubino, you're very naughty," said Zena mildly as she bent down to disengage the cat's claws from Dicky's leg. But by that time Dicky had delivered a kick that sent Cherubino across the room with a howl of pain.

Zena stood up flushed and furious. "You've hurt her," she said angrily.

"I'm awfully sorry," said Dicky. "Just gave way to a reflex action, I'm afraid."

Zena said nothing. She nodded and left the room in search of the cat.

"Paul Biedermann is approachable," said Werner to cover the awkward silence. "He arranged a bank guarantee for me last year. It cost too much but he came through when I needed him. He has an office in town and a house on the coast at Tcumazán." Werner looked at the door but there was no sign of Zena.

"There you are then," said Dicky. "Get onto him, Bernard."

I knew Paul Biedermann too; I'd exchanged hellos with him recently in Berlin and hardly recognized him. He'd smashed himself up driving a brand-new Ferrari back to Mexico from a drunken party in Guatemala City. At one hundred and twenty miles an hour the car had gone deep into the roadside jungle. It took the rescuers a long time to find him, and a long time to cut him free. The girl with him had been killed, but the inquiry had glossed over it. Whatever the truth of it, now one of his legs was shorter than the other and his face bore the scar tissue of over a hundred neat stitches. These infirmities didn't help me overcome my dislike of Paul Biedermann.

"Just a verbal report. Nothing in writing for the time being. Not you, not me, not Biedermann." Dicky was keeping all the exits covered. Nothing in writing until Dicky heard the results and arranged the blames and the credits with God-like impartiality.

Werner shot me a glance. "Sure thing, Dicky," I said. Dicky Cruyer was such a clown at times, but there was another very clever Dicky who knew exactly what he wanted and how to get it. Even if it did sometimes mean giving way to one of those nasty little reflex actions.

Chapter 3

THE JUNGLE stinks. Under the shiny greenery and the brightly colored tropical flowers that line the roadsides like the endless window displays of expensive florists, there is a squelchy mess of putrefaction that smells like a sewer. Sometimes the road was darkened by vegetation that met overhead, and strands of creeper fingered the car's roof. I wound the window closed for a moment even though the air-conditioning didn't work.

Dicky wasn't with me. Dicky had flown to Los Angeles giving me a contact phone number that was an office in the Federal

Building. It was not far from the shops and restaurants of Beverly Hills where by now he would no doubt be sitting beside a bright blue pool, clasping an iced drink, and studying a long menu with that kind of unstinting dedication that Dicky always gave to his own welfare.

The big blue Chevy he'd left for me was not the right sort of car for these miserable winding jungle tracks. Imported duty-free by Tiptree, Dicky's embassy chum, it didn't have the hard suspension and reinforced chassis of locally bought cars. It bounced me up and down like a yo-yo in the potholes, and there were ominous scraping sounds when it hit the bumps. And the road to Tcumazán was all potholes and bumps.

I'd started very early that morning, intending to cross the Sierra Madre mountain range and be in a restaurant lingering over a late lunch to miss the hottest part of the day. In fact I spent the hottest part of the day crouched on a dusty road, with an audience of three children and a chicken, while I changed the wheel of a flat tire and cursed Dicky, Henry Tiptree and his car, London Central, and Paul Biedermann, particularly Biedermann for having chosen to live in such a godforsaken spot as Tcumazán, Michoacán, on Mexico's Pacific coast. It was a place to go only for those equipped with private planes or luxury yachts. Getting there from Mexico City in Tiptree's Chevy was not recommended.

It was early evening when I reached the ocean at a village variously called Little San Pedro or Santiago, according to who directed you. It was not on the map under either name; even the road leading there was no more than a broken red line. Santiago consisted only of a rubbish heap, some two dozen huts constructed of mud and old corrugated iron, a prefabricated building surmounted with a large cross, and a cantina with a green tin roof. The cantina was held together by enameled advertisements for beer and soft drinks. They had been nailed, sometimes upside down and sideways, wherever cracks had appeared in the walls. More adverts were urgently needed.

The village of Santiago is not a tourist resort. There were

no discarded film packets, paper tissues, or vitamin containers to be seen littering the streets or even on the dump. From the village there was not even a view of the ocean; the waterfront was out of sight beyond a flight of wide stone steps that led nowhere. There were no people in sight, just animals: cats, dogs, a few goats, and some fluttering hens.

Alongside the cantina a faded red Ford sedan was parked. Only after I pulled in alongside did I see that the Ford was propped up on bricks and its inside gutted. There were more hens inside it. As I locked up the Chevy, people appeared. They were coming from the rubbish heap, a honeycomb of tiny cells made from boxes, flattened cans, and oil drums. It was a rubbish heap, but not exclusively so. No women or children emerged from the heap, just short, dark-skinned men with those calm inscrutable faces that are to be seen in Aztec sculpture, an art form obsessed with brutality and death.

The smell of the jungle was still there, but now there was also the stink of human ordure. Dogs—their coats patchy with the symptoms of mange—smelled each other and prowled around the garbage. One outside wall of the cantina was entirely covered with a crudely painted mural. The colors had faded, but the outline of a red tractor carving a path through tall grass, with smiling peasants waving their hands, suggested that it was part of the propaganda for some long-forgotten government agricultural plan.

It was still very hot and my damp shirt clung to me. The sun was sinking and long shadows patterned the dusty street, and the electric bulbs that marked the cantina doorway made yellow blobs in the blue air. I stepped over a large mongrel dog that was asleep in the doorway and pushed aside the small swing doors. There was a fat mustachioed man behind the bar. He sat on a high stool, his head tipped forward onto his chest as if he were sleeping. His feet were propped high on the counter, the soles of his boots pushed against the drawer of the cash register. When I entered the bar he looked up, wiped his face with a dirty handkerchief, and nodded without smiling.

There was an unexpected clutter inside, a random assortment of Mexican aspirations. There were sepia-colored family photos, the frames cracked and worm-eaten. Two very old Pan American Airways posters depicted the Swiss Alps and downtown Chicago. Even the girlie pictures revealed the ambivalent nature of machismo: Mexican film stars in decorous swim suits and raunchy *gringas* torn from American porno magazines. In one corner there was a magnificent old jukebox, but it was for decoration only; there was no machinery inside it. In the other corner there was an old oil drum used as a urinal. The sound of Mexican music came quietly from a radio balanced over the shelf of tequila bottles that, despite their varying labels, looked as if they'd been refilled many times from the same jug.

I ordered a beer and told the *cantinero* to have one himself. He got two bottles from the refrigerator and poured them both together, holding two bottles in one hand and two glasses in the other. I drank some beer. It was dark, strong, and very cold. "*Salud y pesetas,*" said the bartender.

I drank to health and money and asked him if he knew anyone who could mend my punctured tire. He didn't answer immediately. He looked me up and down and then craned his neck to see my Chevy, although I had no doubt he'd watched me arrive. There was a man who could do such work, he said after giving the matter some careful thought. It might be arranged, but the materials for doing such jobs were expensive and difficult to obtain. Many of the people who claimed such expertise were clumsy inexpert men who would fix patches that, in the hot sun and on the bad roads, would leak air and leave a traveler stranded. The brakes, the steering, and the tires—these were the vital parts of a motor car. He himself did not own a car, but one of his cousins had a car and so he knew about such things. And on these roads a stranded traveler could meet bad people, even *bandidos.* For a punctured tire I needed someone who could make such a vital repair properly.

I drank my beer and nodded sympathetically. In Mexico this was the way things were done; there was nothing to be gained in interrupting his explanation. It was for this that he got his percentage. He shouted loudly at the faces looking in through the doorway and they went away. No doubt they went to tell the man who fixed flats that his lucky day had finally come.

We each had another beer. The *cantinero*'s name was Domingo. Awakened by the sound of the cash register, Pedro looked up and growled. "Be quiet, Pedro," said the bartender and edged a small plate of chilis across the counter towards me. I declined. I left some money on the counter in front of me when I asked him how far it was to the Biedermann house. He looked at me quizzically before answering. It was a long, long way by road, and the road was very bad. Rain had washed it out in places. It always did at this time of year. On a motorcycle or even a Jeep it was possible. But in my Chevy, which Domingo called my double bed—*cama matrimonial*—there would be no chance of driving there. Better to take the track and go on foot, the way the villagers went. It would take no more than five minutes, maybe ten. Fifteen minutes at the most. If I was going up to the Biedermann house everything was okay.

Mr. Biedermann owed me some money, I explained. Might I encounter trouble collecting it?

Domingo looked at me as if I'd just arrived from Mars. Didn't I know that Señor Biedermann was *"muy rico, muy, muy rico."*

"How rich?" I asked.

"For no one does what he gives seem little, or what he has seem much," said the bartender, quoting a Spanish proverb. "How much does he owe you?"

I ignored his question. "Is he up at the house now?" I fiddled with the money on the counter.

"He's not an easy man to get along with," said Domingo. "Yes, he's up at the house. He's there all alone. He can't get anyone to work for him anymore and his wife is seldom with him nowadays. He even does his own laundry. No one round here will work for him."

"Why?"

Domingo put the tip of his thumb in his mouth and upended his fist to show me that Biedermann was a heavy drinker. "He can get through two or three bottles of it when he's on one of his rages. Tequila, mezcal, aguardiente, or imported whiskey, it's all the same to him once he starts guzzling. Then he gets rough with anyone who won't drink with him. He hit one of the workmen mending the floor; the youngster had to go to the dispensary. Now the men refuse to finish the work."

"Does he get rough with people who collect money?" I asked.

Domingo didn't smile. "When he is not drinking he is a good man. Maybe he has troubles; who knows?"

We went back to talking about the car. Domingo would arrange for the repair of my tire and look after the car. If the beer delivery truck arrived, it would perhaps be possible to deliver the car to the Biedermann house. No, I said, it was better if the car remained where it was; I'd seen a few beer delivery drivers on the road.

"Is the track to the Biedermann house a good one?" I asked. I pushed some money to him.

"Whatever path you take, there is a league of bad road," said Domingo solemnly. I hoped it was just another proverb.

I got my shoulder bag from the car. It contained a clean shirt and underclothes, swimming trunks and towel, shaving kit, a big plastic bag, some string, a flashlight, some antibiotics, Lomatil, and a half bottle of rum for putting on wounds. No gun. Mexico is not a good place for gringos carrying guns.

I took the path that Domingo had shown me. It was a narrow track made by workers going between the crops and the village. It climbed steeply past the flight of stone steps that Domingo said was all that remained of an Aztec temple. It was sunny up here while the valleys were swallowed in shadow. I looked back to see the villagers standing round the Chevy, Domingo parading before it in a proprietorial manner. Pedro cocked his leg to pee on the front wheel. Domingo looked up, as if sensing that I was watching, but he didn't wave. He wasn't a friendly man; just talkative.

I rolled down my shirt sleeves against the mosquitoes. The track led along the crest of a scrub-covered hill. The path skirted huge rocks and clumps of yucca, sharp leaves that thrust into the skyline like swords. It was hard going on the stony path, and I stopped frequently to catch my breath. Through the scrub oak and pines I could see the purple mountains over which I'd driven. There were more mountains to the north. They were big and volcanic-looking, their distance—and thus their exact size—unresolved, but in the clear evening air everything looked sharp and hard, and nearer than it really was. Now and again, as I walked, I caught sight of the motor road that skirted the spur and came in a long detour up the coast. It looked like a damned bad road; I suppose only the Bieder-manns ever used it.

It took me nearly an hour to get to the Biedermann house. I was almost there before I came over the ridge and caught sight of it. It was a small house of modern design. It was built of decorative woods and matte black steel, its foundations set into the rocks upon which the Pacific Ocean dashed huge breakers. One side of the house was close to a patch of jungle that went right to the water's edge. There was a little pocket of sandy beach there, and from it ran a short wooden pier. There was no boat in sight, no cars anywhere, and the house was dark.

A chain-link fence that surrounded the grounds of the house had been damaged by a landslide, and the wire was cut and bent up to provide a gap big enough to get through. The makeshift track continued after the damaged fence and ended in a steep scramble up to a patch of grass. There were flowers here—white and pink camellias and floribunda and the inevita-ble purple bougainvillea. Everything had been landscaped to hide the place where a new macadam road ended at the double garage and shaded carport. But there were no cars to be seen and wooden crates blocked the white garage doors.

So Paul Biedermann had taken flight despite the appoint-ment I'd made with him. I was not surprised. There had always been a streak of cowardice in him.

I had no difficulty getting inside the house. The front door was locked, but a ladder left on the grass reached to one of the balconies. The sliding window, secured only by a plastic clip, was easy enough to force.

There was still enough daylight coming through the window for me to see that the master bedroom had been tidied and cleaned with that rigorous care that is the sign of leave-taking. The huge double bed was stripped of linen and covered with clear plastic covers. Two small carpets were rolled up and sealed into bags that would protect them from termites. Torn up in the wastepaper basket I found half a dozen Mexico City airport luggage tags dating from some previous journey, and three new and unused airline shoulder bags not required for the next. The sort of airline bags that come free with airline tickets were not something that the Biedermanns let their servants carry. I stood listening, but the house was completely silent. There was only the sound of the big Pacific Ocean waves battering against the rocks below the house and roaring their displeasure.

I opened one of the wardrobes. It smelled of moth repellent. There were clothes there: a man's cream-colored linen suits, brightly colored pants and sweaters, handmade shoes—treed and in shoe bags embroidered *P.B.*—and drawers filled with shirts and underclothes.

In the other wardrobe: a woman's dresses, expensive lingerie folded into tissue paper, and a multitude of shoes of every type and color. On the dressing table there was a photo of Mr. and Mrs. Biedermann in swimsuits standing on a diving board and smiling self-consciously. It had been taken before the car accident.

The three guest bedrooms on the top floor—each with separate balcony overlooking the ocean, and private bathroom—had all been stripped bare. Inside the house, a gallery that gave access to the bedrooms was open on one side to overlook the big lounge downstairs. All the furniture was covered in dust sheets, and to one side of the lounge there was a bucket of dirty water, a trowel, some adhesive and dirty rags marking a place where a large section of flooring was being retiled.

Only when I got to Biedermann's study, built to provide a view of the whole coastline, was there any sign of recent occupancy. It was an office; or more exactly it was a room furnished with that special sort of luxury furniture that can be tax-deducted as office equipment. There was a big puffy armchair, a drinks cabinet, and a magnificent wood-inlay desk. In the corner was the sort of daybed that Hollywood calls a casting couch. On it there were blankets roughly folded and a soiled pillow. A big waste bin contained computer printout and some copies of the *Wall Street Journal.* More confidential printout was now a tangle of paper worms in the clear plastic bag of the shredder. But the note pads were blank, and the expensive desk diary—the flowers of South America, one for every week of the year in full color printed in Rio de Janeiro—had never been used. There were no books apart from business reference books and phone and telex directories. Paul Biedermann had never been much of a reader at school, but he'd always been good at counting.

I tried the electric light again but it didn't work. A house built out here on the edge of nowhere would be dependent upon a generator going only when the house was occupied. By the time I had searched the house and found no one, the daylight was going fast. The sea had turned the darkest of purples and the western skyline had almost vanished.

I went back up to the top floor and chose the last guest room along the gallery as a place to spend the night. I found a blanket in the wardrobe, and choosing one of the plastic-covered beds, I covered myself against the cold mist that rolled in off the sea. It soon became too dark to read and, as my interest in the *Wall Street Journal* waned, I drifted off to sleep, lulled by the sound of the waves.

It was two thirty-five when I was awakened by the car. I saw the lights of it flashing over the ceiling long before I heard its engine. At first I thought it was just a disturbed dream, but then the bright patch of light flashed across the ceiling again and I heard the diesel engine. It never struck me that it might be Paul Biedermann or any of the family coming home. I knew instinctively that there was danger.

I slid open the glass door and went outside onto the balcony. The weather had become stormy. Thin ragged clouds raced across the moon, and the wind had risen so that its roar was confused with the sound of the breakers on the rocks below. I watched the car. The headlights were high and close together, a configuration that suggested some Jeep-like vehicle, as did the way it negotiated the bad road. It was still going at speed as it swung round the back to the garage area. The driver had been here before.

There were two voices; one of the men had a key to the front door. I went through the guest bedroom and crouched on the interior gallery so that I could hear them speaking in the lounge below.

"He's run away," said one voice.

"Perhaps," said the other as if he didn't care. They were speaking in German. There was no mistaking the Berlin accent of Erich Stinnes, but the other man's German had a strong Russian accent.

"His car is not here," said the first man. "What if the Englishmen arrived before us and took him off with them?"

"We would have passed them on the road," said Stinnes. He was perfectly calm. I heard the sound of him putting his weight onto the big sofa. "That's better." A sigh. "Take a drink if you want it. It's in the cabinet in his study."

"That stinking jungle road. I could do with a bath."

"You call that jungle?" said Stinnes mildly. "Wait till you go over to the east coast. Wait until you go across to the camp where the freedom fighters are trained, and cut your way through some real tropical rain forest with a machete, and spend half the night digging chiggers out of your backside. You'll find out what a jungle is like."

"What we came through will do for me," said the first man.

I raised my head over the edge of the gallery until I could see them. They were standing in the moonlight by the tall window. They were wearing dark suits and white shirts and trying to look like Mexican businessmen. Stinnes was about forty years old: my age. He had shaved off the little Lenin-style beard he'd had when I last saw him, but there was no mistaking his accent or the hard eyes glittering behind the circular gold-rimmed spectacles.

The other man was much older, fifty at least. But he was not frail. He had shoulders like a wrestler, cropped head, and the restless energy of the athlete. He looked at his watch and then out of the window and then walked over to the place where the tiles were being repaired. He kicked the trowel so that it went skidding across the floor and hit the wall with a loud noise.

"I told you to have a drink," said Stinnes. He did not defer to the other man.

"I said you should frighten Biedermann. Well, you've frightened him all right. It looks as if you've frightened him so much that he's cleared out of here. That's not what they wanted you to do."

"I didn't frighten him at all," said Stinnes calmly. "I didn't take your advice. He's already too frightened. He needs reassurance. But he'll surface sooner or later."

"Sooner or later," repeated the elder man. "You mean he'll surface after you've gone back to Europe and be someone else's problem. If it was left to me, I'd make Biedermann a number-one priority. I'd alert every last KGB team in Central America. I'd teach him that an order is an order."

"Yes, I know," said Stinnes. "It's all so easy for you people who sit at desks all your life. But Biedermann is just one small part of a complicated plan . . . and neither of us knows exactly what the plan is."

It was a patronizing reproach and the elder man's soft voice did not conceal the anger in him. "I say he's the weak link in the chain, my friend."

"Perhaps he is supposed to be just that," said Stinnes complacently. "One day maybe the Englishwoman will put you in charge of one of her crazy schemes, and then you'll be able to ignore orders and show everyone what a clever man you are in the field. But until that time you'll do things the way you're ordered to do them, no matter how stupid it all seems." He got to his feet. "I'll have a drink even if you don't want one. Biedermann has good brandy."

Stinnes passed below me out of sight and I heard him go into the study and pour drinks. When he returned he was carrying two glasses. "It will calm you, Pavel. Have patience; it will work out all right. You can't rush these things. You'll have to get used to that. It's not like chasing Moscow dissidents." He gave the elder man a glass and they both drank. "French brandy. Schnapps and beer are not worth drinking unless they come from a refrigerator." He drank. "Ah, that's better. I'll be glad to be back in Berlin if only for a brief spell."

"I was in Berlin in 1953," said the elder man. "Did you know that?"

"So was I," said Stinnes.

"In 'fifty-three? Doing what?"

Stinnes chuckled. "I was only ten years old. My father was a soldier. My mother was in the army too. We were all kept in the barracks during the disturbances."

"Then you know nothing. I was in the thick of it. The bricklayers and builders working on those Stalinallee sites started all the trouble. It began as a protest against a ten percent increase in work norms. They marched on the House of Ministries in Leipzigerstrasse and demanded to see Party Leader Ulbricht." He laughed. It was a low manly laugh. "But it was the poor old mining minister who was sent out to face them. I was twenty. I was with the Soviet Control Commission. My chief dressed me up like a German building worker and sent me out to mix with the mob. I was never so frightened in all my life."

"With your accent you had every cause to be frightened," said Stinnes.

His colleague was not amused. "I kept my mouth shut; but

I kept my ears open. That night the strikers marched across to the RIAS radio station in West Berlin and wanted their demands to be transmitted over the Western radio. Treacherous German swine."

"What were their demands?" asked Stinnes.

"The usual: free and secret elections, cuts in the work norms, no punishment for the troublemakers." The elder man drank some more. He was calmer now that he'd had a drink. "I advised my people to bring our boys out to clear the streets the way we'd cleared them in 1945. I told them to announce an immediate curfew and give the army shoot-on-sight orders."

"But they didn't," said Stinnes.

"I was only twenty years old. The men who'd fought in the war had no time for kids like me. The Control Commission was not taken seriously. So they sat up all night hoping that everything would be all right in the morning."

"The disturbances spread next day."

"By eleven a.m. on June seventeenth they were tearing the red flag down from the Brandenburg Gate and ransacking the Party offices."

"But the army sat on it, didn't they?"

"Eventually they had to. There were strikes all over the country—Dresden, Leipzig, Jena, and Gera, even in Rostock and the Baltic island of Rügen. It took a long time before things settled down. They should have acted immediately. Since then I've had no sympathy for people who tell me to have patience because everything will come out all right."

"And that's what you'd like me to do now?" asked Stinnes mockingly. "Bring our boys out to clear the streets the way we cleared them in 1945? Announce an immediate curfew and give the army shoot-on-sight orders?"

"You know what I mean."

"You have no idea what this business is all about, Pavel. You've spent your career running typewriters, I've spent mine running people."

"What do you mean?"

"You scream like a rapist when we're in the middle of a seduction. Do you really think you can march agents up and down like Prussian infantry? Don't you understand that men such as Biedermann have to be romanced?"

"We should never use agents who are not politically dedicated to us," said Pavel.

Stinnes went to the window and I could see him clearly in the moonlight as he looked at the sea. Outside, the wind was roaring through the trees and making thumping noises against the glass windows. Stinnes held his drink up high and swirled it round to see the expensive brandy cling to the glass. "You've still got that passion that I once had," said Stinnes. "How do you hang on to all your illusions, Pavel?"

"You're a cynic," said the elder man. "I might as well ask how you continue doing your job without believing in it."

"Believing?" said Stinnes, drinking some of the brandy and turning back to face his companion. "Believing what? Believing in my job or believing in the socialist revolution?"

"You talk as if the two beliefs are incompatible."

"Are they compatible? Can a 'workers' and peasants' state' need so many secret policemen like us?"

"There is a threat from without," said the elder man, using the standard Party cliché.

"Do you know what Brecht wrote after the seventeenth of June uprising? Brecht I'm talking about, not some Western reactionary. Brecht wrote a poem called 'The Solution.' Did you ever read it?"

"I've no time for poetry."

"Brecht asked wouldn't it be easier for the government to dissolve the people, and vote itself another?"

"Do you know what they say about you in Moscow?" the elder man asked. "They say, Is this man a Russian or is he a German?"

"And what do you say when people ask that question of you, Pavel?"

"I had never met you," said the elder man. "I knew you only by reputation."

"And now? Now that you've met me?"

"You like speaking German so much that sometimes I think you've forgotten how to speak Russian."

"I haven't forgotten my mother tongue, Pavel. But it's good for you to practice German. Even more you need Spanish, but your appalling Spanish hurts my ears."

"You use your German name so much that I wonder if you are ashamed of your father's name."

"I'm not ashamed, Pavel. Stinnes was my operational name and I have retained it. Many others have done the same."

"You take a German wife and I wonder if Russian girls weren't good enough for you."

"I was on active service when I married, Pavel. There were no objections then, as I remember."

"And now I hear you talk of the June 'fifty-three uprising as if you sympathized with the German terrorists. What about our Russian boys whose blood was spilled restoring law and order?"

"My loyalty is not in question, Pavel. My record is better than yours and you know that."

"But you don't believe anymore."

"Perhaps I never did believe in the way that you believe," said Stinnes. "Perhaps that's the answer."

"There's no halfway," said the elder man. "Either you accept the Party Congress and its interpretation of Marxist-Leninism or you are a heretic."

"A heretic?" said Stinnes, feigning interest. *"Extra ecclesiam nulla salas*—no salvation is possible outside the Church. Is that it, Pavel? Well, perhaps I am a heretic. And it's your misfortune that the Party prefers it that way, and so does the service. A heretic like me can't lose his faith."

"You don't care about the struggle," said the elder man. "You can't even be bothered to search the house."

"There's no car, and no boat at the dock. Do you think a man such as Biedermann would come on foot through the jungle that frightens you so much?"

"You knew he wouldn't be here."

"He's a thousand miles away by now," said Stinnes. "He's rich. A man like that can go anywhere at a moment's notice. Perhaps you haven't been in the West long enough to understand how difficult that makes our job."

"Then why did we drag out here through that disgusting jungle?"

"You know why we came. We came because Biedermann told us the Englishman phoned and said he was coming here. We came because the stupid woman in Berlin sent a priority telex last night telling us to come here."

"And you wanted to prove Berlin was wrong. You wanted to prove you know better than she knows."

"Biedermann is a liar. We have found that over and over again."

"Then let's get on the road back," said the elder man. "You've proved your point, now let's get back to Mexico City, back to electric light and hot water."

"The house must be searched. You are right, Pavel. Take a look around. I will wait here."

"I have no gun."

"If anyone kills you, Pavel, I will get them."

The elder man hesitated as if he might argue, but then he went about his task, nervously poking around with his flashlight, while Stinnes watched him with ill-concealed contempt. He came upstairs too, but he was an amateur. I stepped outside on the balcony to avoid him. I needn't have bothered to do even that, for he did little more than shine a light through the doorway to see if the bed was occupied. After no more than ten minutes he was back in the lounge telling Stinnes that the house was empty. "Now can we go back?"

"You've gone soft, Pavel. Is that why Moscow sent you here to be my assistant?"

"You know why Moscow sent me here," the elder man grumbled.

Stinnes laughed briefly and I heard him put his glass down on the table. "Yes, I read your personal file. For 'political realignment.' Whatever did you do in Moscow that the department thinks you aren't politically reliable?"

"Nothing. You know very well that that bastard got rid of me because I discovered he was taking bribes. One day his turn will come. A criminal like that can't survive forever."

"But meanwhile, Pavel, you suit me fine. You are politically unreliable and so the one man I can be sure will not report my unconventional views."

"You are my superior officer, Major Stinnes," said the older man stuffily.

"That's right. Well, let's head back. You'll drive for the first couple of hours. I will drive when we reach the mountains. If you see anything in the road, drive over it. Too many people get killed on these roads swerving to avoid eyes they see shining in the headlights."

Chapter 4

I DIDN'T sleep again after they departed. I dozed fitfully but imagined I could hear their diesel car returning, with the alternate roars and screams that a really bad surface racks from a small engine. But it was just the wind, and then, as dawn came and the storm passed over, I was kept awake by the screeching and chattering of the animals. They came right down to the water through the thick undergrowth that bordered one side of the house. There was a stream there; it passed close by a window of Paul Biedermann's study. I suppose he liked to watch the animals. It was an aspect of Biedermann's character that I'd not yet encountered.

Dawn shone its hard gray light and made the sea look like

granite. I went down to the kitchen and found some canned food; beans and tomatoes. I could find no way of warming the mixture so I ate a plateful cold. I was hungry.

From the kitchen window there was a view back towards the village. That way the sky was light pink. I counted seven vultures, circling very high and looking for breakfast. Nearer to the house there were birds in the trees making a lot of noise, and monkeys scrambling about in the lower branches with occasional forays into the garden.

I would have given a lot for a cup of coffee but instant powder stirred into cold tinned milk did not appeal. I made do with a shot of Biedermann's brandy. It was everything Stinnes said about it—so good, in fact, that I took another.

Fortified by the strong drink and one of Biedermann's fancy striped sweaters chosen from his wardrobe, I went outside. The sky was overcast to give a cold shadowless light and, although the black clouds had gone, there was still a cold wind from the ocean. The tire marks of the "Jeep" were to be seen on the roadway. I followed the new macadam road to the entrance gate. It was open, its chain freshly cut. Despite the borrowed sweater I was cold, and colder still as I circled the house completely, crossed the patio that was sheltered from the wind, and climbed up the hill at the back to the highest point of rock. I couldn't see the road or the village, but there was a haze of wood smoke rising from where I guessed the village must be. I couldn't see any sign of Biedermann or his car. That was the first time I'd noticed the swimming pool. It was about two hundred meters from the house and hidden by a line of junipers planted by some landscape gardener for that purpose.

The pool was big, and very blue. And full length on the bottom, at the deep end, was a man. At first I thought he was drowned. Wrapped in cheap gray blankets the figure made a shapeless bundle that almost disappeared in the dark depths of blue shade. It was only when I got past the wooden building that housed four changing rooms and filtering and heating equipment, that I was sure the pool was dry and drained.

"Hey," I shouted at the inert figure. *"Tu que haces?"*

Very slowly the blankets became unraveled to reveal a man dressed in badly wrinkled white trousers and a T-shirt advertising Underberg. One of his bare sunburned arms bore a lacework of neat white scar tissue, and so did one side of his face. He blinked and squinted into the light, trying to see me against the glaring sky.

"Paul Biedermann," I shouted. "What the hell are you doing in the pool?"

"You came," he said. His voice was hoarse and he coughed to clear his throat. "The others have gone? How did you get here?"

"Its Bernd," I said. "We spoke on the phone—Bernd Samson. I walked. Yes, the other two drove away hours ago." He must have been watching the road. My approach along the track had gone unobserved from wherever he'd been hiding.

Wrapped into his blanket I could see a hunting rifle. Biedermann pushed it away as he bent his head forward almost to his knees and stretched his arms. Then he rubbed his legs and arms, trying to restore his circulation. It must have been very uncomfortable on the hard cold surface of the concrete pool all night. He looked up and then smiled as he recognized me. It was a severe smile, twisted by the puckered scars that marked one side of his face.

"Bernd. Are you alone?" he said, trying to make it sound as if it meant no more to him than how many cups of coffee to order. His face and arms were blue; it was the light reflected from the painted sides of the pool.

"They've gone," I said. "Come and switch the electricity on, and make me a cup of coffee."

He slung the rifle on his shoulder and climbed up the ladder of the empty pool. He left the blanket where it was. I wondered if he intended to spend another uncomfortable night there.

He moved about like an automaton. Once inside the house he showed me all the things I should have found for myself. There was bottled gas for cooking, a generator for lighting, and a battery-powered Sony shortwave radio. He boiled water and measured out coffee in silence. It was as if he wanted to take as long as he could to defer the start of the conversation. Even when we were both seated in his study, hands clasped round cups of strong black coffee, he still didn't offer any explanation about his curious behavior. I said nothing. I waited for him to speak. It was usually better that way; I wanted to see how he would start and, even more important, what he would avoid.

"I've got everything," said Paul Biedermann. "Plenty of money, my health, and a wife who stood by me after the accident. Even after that girl was killed in my car." It was hard to believe that this was the nervous schoolboy I'd known in Berlin. It was not just the strong American accent he'd acquired at his expensive East Coast school but something in his poise and his manner too. Paul Biedermann had become unreservedly American in a way that only Germans are able to do.

"That was a nasty business," I said.

"I was unconscious three days. I was in hospital almost six months altogether, counting the convalescence. Six months, and I hate hospitals." He drank some coffee. It was a heavy Mexican coffee that Biedermann had turned into a devil's brew that made my teeth tingle. "But then I got entangled with those bastards and I haven't slept properly ever since. Do you know that, Bernd? It's the literal truth that I haven't slept really well since the start of it."

"Is that so," I said. I didn't want to sit there with my tongue hanging out. I wanted to sound casual; bored almost. But I wanted to know, especially after I'd heard Stinnes and his pal talking about Biedermann as if he was a KGB agent.

"The Russians," said Biedermann, "spies and all that. You know what I'm talking about, don't you?" He was looking over my shoulder as if he wanted to see the animals and birds in the trees outside.

"I know what you're talking about, Paul," I said.

"Because you're in all that, aren't you?"

"In a manner of speaking," I said.

"I was talking to my sister Poppy. She met you at a dinner party at the house of one of the big Berlin spy chiefs. You're one of them, Bernd. You probably always have been. Was that why your father sent you to school in Berlin, instead of sending you back to England the way the other British families sent their kids back there to go to school?"

"Who were they, Paul? Who were those men who came in the night?"

"I didn't see you arrive. I was out with the gun, shooting lizards. I hate lizards, don't you? Those Russkies are like lizards, aren't they? Especially the one with glasses. I knew they would come, and I was right."

"How well do you know them?"

"They pass me around like a parcel. I've dealt with so many different Russians that I've almost lost count. These two were sent from Berlin. The one with the strong Berlin accent calls himself Stinnes, but he's not really a German he's a Russian. The other one calls himself Pavel Moskvin. It sounds like a phony name, doesn't it? I still haven't figured out if they work from Moscow or are part of the East German intelligence service. What do you think, Bernd?"

"Moskvin; means 'man from Moscow.' It could be a genuine name. Do they have diplomatic cover?"

"They said they do."

"Then they're Russians. The KGB give almost all their people diplomatic cover. The East Germans don't. They work mostly in West Germany and infiltrate their agents into the refugees going there."

"Why?"

"It's part of the overall contingency plan. East German agents in West Germany are hard to find. They don't need the cover. And in other parts of the world, East German networks survive after Russians with diplomatic cover are discovered and kicked out."

"They never answer any questions. I thought they'd leave me alone now that I spend most of the year in Mexico." Not most of the time, but most of the year. Most of the financial year; it was a fiscal measurement of time.

"How did you get entangled with the Russians, Paul?" I asked, carefully using his own words.

"What am I supposed to do? I've got half my family still living over there in Rostock. Am I supposed to tell them to go to hell so that they take it out on my aunts and uncles?"

"Yes, that's what you're supposed to do," I said.

"Well, I didn't," said Biedermann. "I played along with them. I told them I'd do nothing serious, but I played along when they asked for run-of-the-mill jobs."

"What did they get you to do?"

"Launder money. They never asked me to give them money —they seem to have plenty of that to throw around—but they wanted Deutschemark changed into dollars, Swedish kronor changed into Mexican pesos and vice versa, Latin American currencies changed into Dutch guilders."

"They could have done all that at a money exchange in West Berlin."

He smiled and stared at something beyond me and drank his coffee. "*Ja,*" he said, forgetting for a moment that we were speaking English. He touched the side of his face as if discovering the terrible scars for the first time. "There was a difference; the money was sent to me in large cash transfers and I had to pass it on in small contributions and donations."

"Pass it on how?"

"By mail."

"In small amounts?"

"One hundred dollars, two hundred dollars. Never more than five hundred dollars—or the equivalent amount in whatever currency."

"Cash?"

"Oh yes, cash. Strictly no checks." He shifted uneasily in his seat and I had the feeling that he now regretted this confession. "High-denomination notes in plain envelopes. No registered letters; that would mean a lot of names and addresses and post office forms. Too risky that sort of thing, they said."

"And where has all this money been going to?"

He put his coffee on the table and began searching the pockets of his pants as if looking for a cigarette. Then he stood up and looked round. Eventually he found a silver box on the table. He took one for himself. Then he offered the open box to me. It was of course that sort of evasive temporizing that armchair psychologists call displacement activity. Before he could repeat the whole performance in pursuit of matches I threw him mine. He lit his cigarette and then nervously waved the smoke away from his face. "You know where it's been going to, Bernd. Trade unions, peace movements, ban the bomb groups. Moscow can't be seen making donations to them. The money has to come from 'little people' all over the world. You weren't born yesterday, Bernd. We all know the way it's done."

"Yes, we all know the way it's done, Paul." I swung around to see him. On the side table there was the bottle of brandy that Stinnes and I had plundered. I wondered if that was what had attracted his gaze when he had stared over my shoulder. He wasn't looking at it now; he was looking at me.

"Don't damn well sneer at me. I've got my relatives to worry about. And if I hadn't koshered their bloody contributions, someone else would do it for them. It's not going to change the history of the world, is it?" He was still moving around the room looking at the furnishings as if seeing them for the first time.

"I don't know what it's going to do, Paul. You're the one that had the expensive education—schools in Switzerland, schools in America, and two years postgraduate studies at Yale. You tell me if it's going to change the history of the world."

"You weren't so high and mighty in the old days," said Biedermann. "You weren't so superior when you sold me that old Ferrari that kept breaking down."

"It was a good car. I had no trouble with it," I said. "I only sold it because I went to London. You should have looked after it better." What a memory he had; I'd quite forgotten selling him that car. Maybe that's how the rich got richer, by remembering in resentful detail every transaction they made.

He kept his cigarette in his mouth and, still standing, fingered the keys of the computer as if about to use it. "It's getting more and more difficult," he said. He turned to look at me, the smoke of the cigarette rising across his face like a fine veil and going into his eyes so that he was squinting. "Now that the Mexicans have nationalized the banks, and the peso has dropped through the floor, there are endless regulations about foreign exchange. It's not so easy to handle these transactions without attracting attention."

"So tell your Russians that," I suggested.

"I don't want them to solve my problems. I want to get out of the whole business."

"Tell them that."

"And risk what happens to my relatives?"

"You talk as though you're some sort of master spy," I said. "If you tell them you've had enough, that will be the end of it."

"They'd kill me," he said.

"Rubbish," I said. "You're not important enough for them to waste time or effort on."

"They'd make an example of me. They'd cut my throat and make sure everyone knew why."

"They would not make an example of you," I said. "How could they? The last thing they want to do is to draw attention to their secret financing network. No, as long as they thought you'd keep their secrets, they'd let you go, Paul. They'd huff and puff and shout and threaten in the hope you'd get frightened enough to keep going. But once they saw you were determined to end it, they'd reconcile themselves to that."

"If only I could believe it." He blew a lot of smoke. "One of the new clerks in my Mexico City office—a German fellow—has been asking me questions about some of the money I sent out. It's just a matter of time . . ."

"You don't let the staff in your office address the envelopes, do you?"

"No, of course not. But I do the envelopes on the addressing machine. I can't sit up all night writing out envelopes."

"You're a fool, Paul."

"I know," he said sadly. "This German kid was updating the address lists and he noticed these charities and trade unions that were all coded in the same way. It was a different code from all the other addresses. I said it was part of my Christmas charity list, but I'm not sure he believed me."

"You'd better transfer him to one of your other offices," I said.

"I'm going to send him to Caracas, but it won't really solve the problem. Some other clerk will notice. I can't address the envelopes by hand and have handwritten evidence all over the place, can I?"

"Why are you telling me all this, Paul?"

"I've got to talk it over with someone."

"Don't give me that," I said.

He stubbed out his cigarette and said, "I told the Russians that the British secret service was becoming suspicious. I invented stories about strangers making inquiries at various offices."

"Did they believe that?"

"Phone calls, I always said the inquiries were phone calls. So I didn't have to describe anyone's physical appearance." He went over to the side table and picked up the bottle of brandy. He put it into a cupboard and shut the door. It looked like the simple action of a tidy man who didn't want to see bottles of booze standing around in his office.

"That was clever," I said, although I thought such a device would sound very unconvincing to any experienced case officer.

"I knew they'd have to give me a respite if I was under surveillance."

"And talking to me is a part of that scheme? Did you tell them about my phone call? Was it that that gave you the idea? Is that why they came here last night?"

He didn't answer my question and that convinced me my guess was right. Biedermann had thought up all this nonsense about the British becoming suspicious only after I'd phoned him. He said, "You're something in the espionage business, you've admitted that. I realize you're not in any sort of senior position, but you must know people who are. And you're the only contact I have."

I grunted. I didn't know whether that was Paul Biedermann's sincere opinion or whether he was hoping to provoke me into claiming power and influence.

"Does that mean you can help?" he said.

I finished the coffee and got to my feet. "You copy that list of addresses for me, London might be interested in that, and I'll make sure that Bonn is told that we are investigating you. You'll become what NATO intelligence call sacred. None of the other security teams will investigate you without informing us. That will get back to your masters quickly enough."

"Wait a moment, Bernd. I don't want Bonn restricting my movements or opening my mail."

"You can't have it both ways, Paul. 'Sacred' is the lowest category we have. There's not much chance that Bonn will find that interesting enough to do anything; they'll leave you to us."

Biedermann didn't look too pleased at the idea of his reputation suffering, but he realized it was the best offer he was likely to get. "Don't double-cross me," he said.

"How would I do that?"

"I'm not up for sale to the highest bidder. I want out. I don't want to exchange a master in Moscow for a master in London."

"You make me laugh, Paul," I said. "You really think you're a master spy, don't you? Are you sure you want to get out, or do you really want to get in deeper?"

"I need help, Bernd."

"Where did you hide your car?"

"You can drive along the beach when the tide is out."

I should have thought of that one. The tide comes in and washes away the tire tracks. It fooled Stinnes and his pal too. Sometimes amateurs can teach the pros a trick or two. "The tide is out now," I said. "Get it and give me a lift into the village, will you, before someone starts renting my Chevy out as a bijou residence."

"Keep the sweater," he said. "It looks good on you."

Chapter 5

M UY COMPLICADO," said Dicky. We were elbowing our way through a huge cobbled plaza that twice a week became one of Mexico City's busiest street markets, and he was listening to my account of the trip to Paul Biedermann's house. It was what Dicky called combining business with pleasure. "*Muy* bloody *complicado,*" he said reflectively. That was Dicky's way of saying he didn't understand.

"Not *very* complicated," I said. I'd found Biedermann's story depressingly simple—too simple perhaps to be the whole truth—but not complicated.

"Biedermann hiding in the bloody pool all night clasping a gun?" said Dicky with heavy irony. "No, not complicated at all, of course." He'd been chewing the nail of his little finger and now he inspected it. "You're not telling me you believed all that stuff?"

The sun was hot. Towering cumulus clouds were building up to the east and the humidity was becoming intolerable. We were walking down a line of vendors selling secondhand hardware that varied from ancient spark plugs to fake Nazi medals. Dicky stopped to look at some broken pottery figurines that a handwritten notice said were ancient Olmec. Dicky picked one up and looked at it. It looked too new to be genuine, but then so did many of the fragments in the National Museum.

Dicky passed it to me and walked on. I put it back on the

ground with the other junk. I had too many broken fragments in my life already. I found Dicky looking at a basketful of silver-plated bracelets. "I must get some little presents to take back to London," he said.

"Which parts of Biedermann's story do you think were not true?" I asked him.

"Never mind the exam questions," snapped Dicky. He didn't want to be in Mexico; he wanted to be in London making sure his job was secure. In some perverse way he blamed me for his situation, although, God knows, no one would have waved good-bye to him with more pleasure.

He started bargaining with the Indian squatting behind the folk-art jewelry. After a series of offers and counteroffers, Dicky agreed to buy six of them. He crouched down and solemnly began to sort through all of them to find the best six.

"I'm asking you what you believe and what you don't believe," I said. "Hell, Dicky. You're in charge. I need to know."

Still crouched down, he looked at me from under the eyelashes that made him the heartthrob of the typing pool. He knew I was goading him. "You think I've been swanning around in Los Angeles wasting my time and the Department's money, don't you?" Dicky was looking very Hollywood since his return from California. The faded jeans had gone, replaced by striped seersucker trousers and a short-sleeve green safari shirt with loops to hold rhino bullets.

"Why would I think that?"

Satisfied with his choice of bracelets, he sorted out his Mexican money and paid for them. He smiled and put the bracelets in the pocket of his shirt. "I saw Frank Harrington in L.A. You didn't know I was going to see Frank, did you?"

Frank Harrington headed the Berlin Field Unit. He was an old experienced Whitehall warrior with influence where it really counted—at the very top. I didn't like the idea of Dicky's sliding off to meetings with him, especially meetings from which I was deliberately excluded. "No, I didn't know."

"Frank was attending some CIA powwow and I buttonholed

him to talk about Stinnes." We'd got to the end of the line and Dicky turned to go up the next row of stalls: brightly colored fruit and vegetables on one side and broken furniture on the other. "This is not just another Mexican street market," said Dicky, who'd insisted that we come here. "This is a *tiangui*—an Indian market. Not many tourists get to see them."

"It might have been better to have come earlier. It's always so damned hot by lunchtime."

Dicky chuckled scornfully. "If I don't jog and have a decent breakfast I can't get going."

"Perhaps we should have found a hotel right here in town. Going backwards and forwards to Cuernavaca eats up a lot of time."

"A couple of miles jogging every morning would do you good, Bernard. You're putting on a lot of weight. It's all that stodge you eat."

"I like stodge," I said.

"Don't be ridiculous. Look at all these wonderful fresh vegetables and delicious fruits. Look at those great heaps of chilis. There must be fifty different kinds. I wish I'd brought the camera with me now."

"Does Frank know anything about Stinnes?"

"Ye gods. Frank knows everyone in Berlin, you know that, Bernard. Frank says Stinnes is one of their brightest people. Frank has a fat file on him and all his activities from one end of the world to the other."

I nodded. Frank always claimed to have fat files on everything when he was away from his office. It was only when you were with him in Berlin that the "fat file" turned out to be a small pink card with "refer to Data Centre" scribbled on it. "Good old Frank," I said.

This end of the market beyond the vegetables was occupied by food stalls. Almost everyone in the market seemed to be eating. They were eating and buying, eating and selling, eating and chatting, and even eating as they smoked and drank. Some of the more dedicated were sitting down to eat, and for these aficionados seats were provided. There were chairs and stools of every kind, age, and size, with nothing in common but their infirmity.

Most of the stalls had steaming pots from which stewed mixtures of rice, chicken, pork, and every variety of beans were being served. There were charcoal grills too, laden with pieces of scorching meat that filled the air with smoke and appetizing smells. And the ever present tortillas were being eaten as fast as they could be kneaded, rolled out, and cooked. An old lady came up to Dicky and handed him a tortilla. Dicky was disconcerted and tried to argue with her.

"She wants you to feel the texture and admire the color," I said.

Dicky gave her one of his big smiles, fingered it as if he were going to have it made up into a three-piece suit, and handed it back with a lot of *"Gracias, adios."*

"Stinnes speaks excellent Spanish," I said. "Did Frank tell you anything about that?"

"You were right about Stinnes. He went to Cuba to sort out some of their security problems. He did so well that he became the KGB's Caribbean troubleshooter all through the early seventies. He's been to just about all the places where the Cubans have sent soldiers—and that's a lot of traveling."

"Does Frank know why Stinnes is here?"

"I think you've answered that already," said Dicky. "He's here running your friend Biedermann." He looked at me and, when I didn't respond, said, "Don't you think so, Bernard?"

"Arranging a little money to prop up a trade union or finance an anti-nuke demo? Not exactly something for one of the KGB's brightest people, is it?"

"I'm not so sure," said Dicky. "Central America is a top KGB priority, you can't deny that, Bernard."

"Let me put it another way," I said. "Covert financing of that sort is an administration job. It's not something for Stinnes with his languages and years of field experience."

"Ho ho," said Dicky. "Hint, hint, eh? You mean, you chaps

with field experience and fluent languages are wasted on the
sort of job that administrators like me can manage?"

It was exactly what I thought, but since it wasn't what I'd
intended to say, I denied it. "Why the German name?" I said.
"And why does a man like that work out of Berlin? He must be
forty years old—a crucial age for an ambitious man. Why isn't
he in Moscow where the really big decisions are made?"

"Si, maestro," said Dicky very slowly. He looked at me quizzically and ran a fingertip along his thin bloodless lips as if trying
to prevent himself from smiling. Instead of concealing my own
feelings, I'd subconsciously identified with Stinnes. For I was
also forty years old and I wanted to be where the big decisions
are made. Dicky nodded solemnly. He might be a little slow on
languages and fieldwork, but in the game of office politics he
was seeded number one. "Frank Harrington had an answer for
that one. Stinnes—real name Nikolai Sadoff—married a German girl who couldn't master the Russian language. They lived
in Moscow for some time but she was miserable there. Stinnes
finally asked for a transfer. They live in East Berlin. Frank
Harrington thinks a Mexico City assignment will probably be a
quick in and out for Stinnes."

"Yes, he talked as if he was going soon—'when I've gone
back to Europe,' he said."

"He said the Englishwoman had put him in charge of one
of her crazy schemes, didn't he?"

"More or less," I said.

"And we both know who the Englishwoman is, don't we?
Your wife is running this operation. It was your wife who sent
the telex from Berlin that they grudgingly obeyed. Right?"

I said nothing.

Dicky stared at me, his mouth pursed, his eyes narrowed. "Is
it right or not?" He smiled. "Or do you think they might have
some other Englishwoman running the KGB office in Berlin?"

"Probably Fiona," I said.

"Well, I'm glad we agree on that one," said Dicky sarcastically. It was only when I heard the contempt in his voice that

I realized that he hated working this job with me as much as I did with him. In the London office our relationship was tolerable, but on this type of job every little difference became abrasive. Dicky turned away from me and took a great interest in the various pots of stew. One of the stall holders opened the lids so that we could sniff. "Smell that," I said. "There's enough chili in there to put you into orbit."

"Obit, you mean," said Dicky, moving on quickly. "Put you into *The Times* obit column." His dinner with the Volkmanns had lessened his appetite for the chili. "Our friend Paul Biedermann is going soggy on them. He starts making up stories about British spies telephoning him, and who knows what other sort of nonsense he's been telling them. So they get nervous and Stinnes is sent over here to kick ass and get Biedermann back into line."

"Is that also what Frank says?"

"No, that's what *I'm* saying. It's obvious. I don't know why you are being so baroque about it. Maybe it's not a very big deal, but these KGB people like a nice little jaunt to Mexico—fresh lobster salad and a swim in the Pacific to brighten up their working days. Stinnes is no different."

"It doesn't feel right. Biedermann is rich and successful; he's woolly-minded and flabby too. He doesn't have the motivation, and he certainly doesn't need the money."

"So what? Biedermann was frightened for his family. Shall we eat here? Some of this food look really good. Look at that." He read the sign. "What are *carnitas*?"

"Stewed pork. He's serving it on *chicharrones:* pork crackling. You eat the meat, then eat the plate. Biedermann wouldn't give that plate of pork for his family, and especially not for distant relatives in Rostock."

"We'll walk to the end and see what else there is and then come back here and try some," Dicky suggested. Dicky could always surprise me. Just as I had decided he was the archetype gringo tourist, he wanted to have lunch at a *fonda*. "So what's your theory?"

"I have no theory," I said. "Agents come in many shapes and sizes. Some are waiting for the socialist millennium, some hate their parents, some get angry after being ripped off by a loan company. Some simply want more money. But usually it begins with opportunity. A man finds himself handling something secret and valuable. He starts thinking about using that opportunity to get more money. Only then does he become a dedicated Communist. So how does Biedermann fit into that? Where are his secrets? What's his motivation?"

"Guilt," said Dicky. "He feels guilty about his wealth."

"If you'd ever met Paul Biedermann you'd know what a good joke that is."

"Blackmail then?"

"About what?"

"Sex."

"Paul Biedermann would pay to have people say he was a sex maniac. He thinks of himself as a rich playboy."

"You let your acute dislike of Paul Biedermann spill over into your judgments, Bernard. The fact of the matter is that Biedermann is an agent. You heard the two KGB people talking. He is an agent; it's no good you trying to convince yourself he's not."

"Oh, he's an agent," I said. "But he's not the sort of agent that a man such as Stinnes would be running. That's what puzzles me."

"Your experience makes you overestimate what qualities an agent needs. Try and see it from their point of view: rich U.S. businessman—someone the local cops would be reluctant to upset—isolated house on a lonely stretch of beach in western Mexico, not too far by road from the capital. And not too far by sea from Vladivostok."

"Landing guns, you mean?"

"A man with a reputation for drinking who gets so rough with his servants that he's left all alone in the house. Wife and children often away. Convenient beach, pier big enough for a big motorboat."

"Come along, Dicky," I said. "This is just a holiday cottage by Biedermann's standards. This is just a place he goes to read the *Wall Street Journal* and spend the weekend dreaming up a quick way to make a million or two."

"So for half the year the house is completely empty. Then Stinnes and his pals have the place all to themselves. We know guns go from Cuba to Mexico's east coast and onwards by light plane. So why not bring them across the Pacific from the country where they're manufactured?" We'd got to the end of the food stalls and Dicky became interested in a stall selling pictures. There were family group photos and colored litho portraits of generals and presidents. All of the pictures were in fine old frames.

"It doesn't smell right," I said. But Dicky had put together a convincing scenario. If it was the house they were interested in, it didn't matter what kind of aptitude Biedermann had for being a field agent. Yes, London Central would love a report along those lines. It had the drama they liked. It had the geopolitic that called for maps and colored diagrams. And, as a bottom line, it could be true.

"If it doesn't smell right," said Dicky with heavy irony, "I'll tell London to forget the whole thing." He stood up straight as he looked at the selection of pictures on sale and I realized he was studying his reflection in the glass-fronted pictures. He was too thin for the large bright green safari shirt; it made him look like a lollipop. "Is it going to rain?" he said, looking at the time. He'd bought a new wristwatch too. It was a multidial black chronometer that kept perfect time at fifty fathoms.

"It seldom rains in the morning, even during the rainy season."

"It will bucket down on the stroke of noon then," said Dicky, looking up at the clouds that were now turning yellowish.

"I'm still not sure what London wants with Stinnes," I said.

"London want Stinnes enrolled," he said as if he'd just

remembered it. "Shall we walk back to where the pork is? What did you say it's called, *carnitas?*"

"Enrolled?" It could mean a lot of things, from persuaded to defect to knocked on the head and rolled in a carpet. "That would be difficult."

"The bigger they are, the harder they fall," said Dicky. "You said yourself that he's forty years old and passed over for promotion. He's been stuck in East Berlin for ages. West Berlin is a plum job for Western intelligence, but it's the boondocks for their people. A smart KGB major left to rot in East Berlin is sure to be fretting."

"I suppose his wife likes it there," I said.

"What's that got to do with it?" said Dicky. "Would I take an intelligence job in Canada because my wife likes ice hockey?"

"No, Dicky, you wouldn't."

"And this fellow Stinnes will see what's good for him. Frank Harrington thought the chances were good."

"You talked about all this with Frank?"

"Sure. Frank has to be in on it because Stinnes is based in Big B. Stinnes is very much in his territory, Bernard." A nervous movement of fingers through curly hair. "The worst difficulty is that the Data Centre showed that Stinnes has an eighteen-year-old son. That might prove sticky."

"Christ, Dicky," I said, as I came to terms with this bombshell. "Did you know all this when we left London?"

"Enrolling Stinnes, you mean?"

"Yes, enrolling Stinnes, I mean."

"It looked as if it might go that way." That was Dicky on the defensive. He'd known all along, that was obvious. I wondered what else he knew that he was not going to tell me about until it happened. "London Central put out a departmental alert for him, didn't they?" We had reached the *carnitas* stand by now. He selected a chair that didn't wobble and sat down. "I'll have mine wrapped in a tortilla. Pork skin is very fattening."

"London Central put out departmental alerts for clerks who make off with the petty cash."

"But they don't send senior staff, like us, to identify them when they are spotted," said Dicky.

"Enrolled," I said, considering all the implications. "A hotshot like Stinnes. You and me? It's madness."

"Only if you start thinking it's madness," said Dicky. "My own opinion"—pause—"for what's it's worth"—a modest smile—"is that we stand an excellent chance."

"And when did you last enroll a KGB major?"

Dicky bit his lip. We both knew the answer to that one. Dicky was a pen pusher. Stinnes was the first KGB officer Dicky had ever come this close to, and he hadn't seen Stinnes yet.

"Isn't London proposing to send someone over here to help? This is a complicated job, Dicky. We need someone who has experience."

"Nonsense. We can do it. I don't want Bret Rensselaer breathing down my neck. If we can pull this one off, it will be a real coup." He smiled. "I didn't expect you to start asking London for help, Bernard. I thought you were the one who always liked to do everything on his own."

"I'm not on my own," I said. "I'm with you." The stall holder was stirring his cauldron of pork and arranging suitable pieces on a large metal platter.

"And you'd prefer to work with your friend Werner, eh?"

I could hear danger signals. "We were at school together," I said. "I've known him a long time."

"Werner Volkmann isn't even employed by the Department. He hasn't been employed by us for years."

"Officially that's right," I said. "But he's worked for us from time to time."

"Because you give him jobs to do," said Dicky. "Don't try to make it sound as if the Department employs him."

"Werner knows Berlin," I said.

"You know Berlin. Frank Harrington knows Berlin. Our friend Stinnes knows Berlin. There is no great shortage of people who know Berlin. That's no reason for employing Werner."

"Werner is a Jew. He was born in Berlin when the Nazis were running things. Werner instinctively sees things in people that you and I have to learn about. You can't compare his knowledge of Berlin and Berliners with anything I know."

"Calm down. Everyone knows Werner is your alter ego, and so mustn't be criticized."

"What do you want? You can have 'lean meat,' 'pure meat,' 'meat without fat,' or 'a bit of everything'?"

"What's the difference between . . ."

"Don't let's get into semantics," I said. "Try *surtido*, that's a bit of everything." Dicky nodded his agreement.

Dicky, who always showed a remarkable aptitude for feeding himself, now discovered that a *carnitas* stand is always conveniently close to those that sell the necessary accompaniments. He provided us with *salsas* and marinated cactus, and was now discovering that tortillas are sold by the kilo. "A kilo," he said as the tortilla lady disappeared with the payment and left him with a huge pile of them. "Do you think they'll keep if I take them back for Daphne?" He wrapped some of the pork into the top tortilla. "Delicious," he said as he ate the first one and took a second tortilla to begin making another. "What are all those pieces?"

"That's ear, and those pieces are intestine," I said.

"You just wait until Daphne hears what I've been eating, she'll throw up. Our neighbors came out to Mexico last year and stayed in the Sheraton. They wouldn't even clean their teeth unless they had bottled water. I wish I had my camera so you could photograph me eating here in the market. Now, what is it again—*carnitas*? I want to get it exactly right when I tell them."

"*Carnitas,*" I said. "*Surtido.*"

Dicky wiped his mouth on his handkerchief and stood up and looked round the market square. Just from where we were sitting I could see people selling plastic toys, antique tables and gilt mirrors, cheap shirts, brass bedsteads, dog-eared American film magazines, and a selection of cut-glass stoppers that always survive long after the decanters. "Yes," said Dicky, "it's really quite a place, isn't it? Fifteen million people perched at seven thousand feet altitude with high mountaintops all round them and thick smog permanently overhead. Where else could you find a capital city with no river, no coastline, and such lousy roads? And yet this is one of the oldest cities the world has ever known. If that doesn't prove that the human race is stone raving mad, nothing will."

"I hope you don't think I'm going to walk right up to Stinnes and offer him a chance to defect," I said.

"I've been thinking about that," said Dicky. "The Volkmanns already know him. Shall we let them make the first overtures?"

"Werner doesn't work for the Department. You just told me that."

"Correction," said Dicky. "I said that Werner's knowledge of Berlin is not sufficient reason for using him in Berlin. Let's remember that Werner has had a 'noncritical employment only' tag on his file."

"You can be a spiteful bastard, Dicky," I said. "You're talking about that signals leak in 1978. You know very well that Werner was completely cleared of suspicion."

"It was your wife who did it," said Dicky. Suddenly he was angry. He was angry because he'd never suspected Fiona of leaking secrets, and now I realized that Dicky saw me as someone who had helped to deceive him rather than as Fiona's principal victim.

The sky was darkening with clouds now and there was the movement of air that precedes a storm. I never got used to the speedy effects of the heat and humidity. The sweet smell of fresh fruits and vegetables had filled the air when we first arrived at the market. Now it was already giving way to the smells of putrefaction as the spoiled, squashed, and broken produce went bad.

"Yes, it was my wife who did it. Werner was innocent."

"And if you'd listened, you'd have heard me say that Werner 'has had' a noncrit tag on his file. I didn't say it was still there."

"And now you're going to ask Werner to enroll Stinnes for you?"

"I think you'd better put it to him, Bernard."

"He's on holiday," I said. "It's a sort of second honeymoon."

"So you told me," said Dicky. "But my guess is that they are both getting a bit bored with each other. If you were on your honeymoon—first, second, or third—you wouldn't want to spend the evenings in some broken-down German club in a seedy part of town, would you?"

"We haven't seen the club yet," I reminded him. "Perhaps it's tremendous."

"I love the way you said that, Bernard. I wish I could have recorded the way you said 'tremendous.' Yes, it might be Mexico's answer to Caesar's Palace in Vegas, or the Paris Lido, but don't bank on it. You see, if it was me on a second honeymoon with that delectable little Zena, I'd be in Acapulco, or maybe finding some sandy little beach where we could be undisturbed. I wouldn't be taking her along to the Kronprinz Club to see who's winning the bridge tournament."

"The way it's turned out," I said, "you're not taking the delectable little Zena anywhere. I thought I heard you saying you didn't like her. I remember you saying that one honeymoon with Zena would be enough for you." From the sulphurous yellow sky there came a steady drumroll of thunder, an overture for a big storm.

Dicky laughed. "I admit I was a little hasty," he said. "I hadn't been away from home for very long when I said that. The way I feel now, Zena is looking sexier and sexier every day."

"And you think talking to Stinnes about Western democracy and the free world will give the Volkmanns a new interest in life," I said.

"Even allowing for your sarcasm—yes. Why don't you put it to them and see what they say?"

"Why don't *you* put it to them and see what they say?"

"Look at those children and the donkey and the old man with the sombrero. That would make the sort of photo that wins prizes at the photo club. I was stupid not to bring a camera, but have you seen the sort of price you have to pay for a camera in this country? The Americans are really putting the squeeze on the peso. No, I think you should put it to them, Bernard. You get hold of Werner and talk with him and then he could go along to the Kronprinz Club tonight and see if Stinnes is there." He stopped at a stall to watch a man making *chiles rellenos*, putting meat fillings into large peppers. Each one got a big spoonful of chopped chilis before being deep-fried and put in a garlicky tomato sauce. Just looking at it made me feel queasy.

"You'll have to let Werner know what London is prepared to offer Stinnes. I assume there will be a big first payment, a salary, and contractual provisions about the size of the house they'll get and what sort of car and so on."

"Is that the way it's done? It sounds like a marriage contract."

"They like it defined that way because you can't buy houses in East Europe and they don't know the prices of cars and so on. They usually want to have a clear idea of what they're getting."

"London will pay," said Dicky. "They want Stinnes; they really want him. That's just between us, of course; that's not for Werner Volkmann to know." He touched the side of his nose in a conspiratorial gesture. "No reasonable demand will be refused."

"So what does Werner say to Stinnes?" On the cobbled ground there were shiny black spots appearing one after the other in the gray dust. The rain had come.

"Let's keep it all very soft-sell, shall we?" said Dicky. His wife, Daphne, worked in a small advertising agency. Dicky told me that it had very aggressive methods with really up-to-date selling techniques. Sometimes I got the feeling that Dicky would like to see the Department being run on the same lines. Preferably by him.

"You mean we don't brief Werner?"

"Let's see how the cookie crumbles," said Dicky. It was an old advertising expression that meant put your head in the sand, your ass in the air, and wait for the explosion.

MY PREDICTION that the rain came only in the afternoons was only just right. It was a few minutes after one o'clock when the rain started. Dicky took me in the car as far as the university, where he was to see one of his Oxford friends, and there—on the open plaza—let me out into steady rain. I cursed him, but there was no hostility in Dicky's self-interest; he would have done the same thing to almost anyone.

It was not easy to get a cab, but eventually an old white VW beetle stopped for me. The car's interior was battered and dirty, but the driver's position was equipped like the flight deck of a Boeing jet. The dashboard was veneered in walnut and there was an array of small spanners and screwdrivers and a pen-shaped flashlight as well as a large colored medallion of the shrine of the Virgin of Guadalupe. In contrast to the derelict bodywork of the little car, the young driver was dressed in a freshly starched white shirt with a dark gray tie and looked more like a stockbroker than a cab driver. But Mexico is like that.

The traffic moved slowly through the heavy rain, but it didn't make less noise. There were two-stroke motorcycles and cars with broken mufflers and giant trucks—some so carefully painted up that every bolt head, rivet, and wheel nut was picked out in a different color. Here on the city's outskirts, the wide boulevard was lined with a chaos of broken walls, goats grazing on waste ground, adobe huts, rubbish tips, crudely painted shop fronts in primary colors, and corrugated iron fences defaced with political slogans and ribaldry. Despite the rain, drunks sprawled full-length on the pavement and the barbecue fires hissed and flared at the taco counters.

By the time we got near to Werner Volkmann's apartment, the rainstorm was flooding the gutters and making great lakes through which the traffic splashed and in which it sometimes stalled. There was a constant racket of car horns and engines being overrevved by nervous drivers. The cab moved slowly and I watched drenched and dirty kids offering dry, clean lottery tickets that were protected inside clear plastic bags. And plenty of well-dressed shoppers had chauffeurs who could hold an umbrella in one hand and open the door of a limousine with the other. I couldn't imagine Zena Volkmann anywhere but here in the Zona Rosa. Within the area contained by Insurgentes, Sevilla, and Chapultepec there are the big international hotels, smart restaurants, the shops with branches in Paris and New York. And in the crowded cafés that spill out onto the pavement are to be heard every new rumor, joke, and scandal that this outrageous town provides in abundance.

Zena Volkmann could live anywhere, of course. But she preferred to live in comfort. She'd learned to respect wealth, and the wealthy, in a way that only a poverty-stricken childhood teaches. She was a survivor who'd climbed up the ladder without benefit of any education beyond reading and writing and painting her face, plus a natural ability to count. Perhaps I did her an injustice, but sometimes I had the feeling that she would do anything if the price was high enough, for she still had that fundamental insecurity that one bout of poverty can inflict for a lifetime and no amount of money remedy.

She made no secret of her feelings. Even amid the contrasts of Mexico she showed no great interest in the plight of the hungry. And like so many poor people she had only contempt for socialism in any of its various forms, for it is only the rich and guilty who can afford the subtle delights of egalitarian philosophies.

Zena Volkmann was only twenty-two years old, but she'd

lived with her grandparents for much of her childhood. From them she'd inherited a nostalgia for a Germany of long ago. It was a Protestant Germany of aristocrats and *Handküsse,* silvery Zeppelins and student duels. It was a *Kultiviertes* Germany of music, industry, science, and literature; an Imperial Germany ruled from the great cosmopolitan city of Berlin by efficient incorruptible Prussians. It was a Germany she'd never seen, a Germany that had never existed.

The elaborate afternoon *Kaffee-Trinken* that she'd prepared was a manifestation of her nostalgia. The delicate chinaware into which she poured the coffee, and the solid silver forks with which we ate the fruit tart, and the tiny damask napkins with which we dabbed our lips were all parts of ceremony that was typically German. It was a scene to be found in the prosperous suburbs of any one of a hundred West German towns.

Zena's brown silk afternoon dress, with embroidered collar and hem below the knee, made her look like a dedicated hausfrau. Her long dark hair was in two plaits and rolled to make the old-fashioned "earphone" hairstyle virtually unknown outside Germany. And Werner, sitting there like an amiable gorilla, had gone to the extent of putting on his tan-colored tropical suit and a striped tie. I was only too aware that my old rain-wet open-neck shirt was not the required dress code, as I balanced the coffee cup on the knee of my mud-splashed nylon pants.

While Zena had been in the kitchen I'd told Werner about my trip to Biedermann's house, about the Russians I'd seen there and Biedermann's confession to me. Werner took his time to answer. He turned to look out of the window. On a side table the broken fragments of a cup and saucer had been arranged in a large ashtray. Werner moved the ashtray to the trolley that held the TV. From this sixth-floor apartment there was a view across the city. The sky was low and dark now, and the rain was beating down in great shimmering sheets, the way it does only in such tropical storms. He still hadn't answered by the time Zena returned from the kitchen.

"Biedermann always was a loner," said Werner. "He has two brothers, but Paul makes all the business decisions. Did you know that?"

It was small talk, but now Zena was with us and I was undecided about how much to say in front of her. "Are both his brothers in the business?"

Werner said, "Old Biedermann gave equal shares to all five of them—two girls and three boys. But the others leave all the decisions to Paul."

"And why not," said Zena, cutting a slice of fruit tart for me. "He knows how to make money. The other four have nothing to do but spend it."

"You never liked him, did you, Bernie?" said Werner. "You never liked Paul."

"I hardly knew him," I said. "He went off to some fancy school. I remember his father. His father used to let me steer the trucks round their yard while he operated the accelerator and brakes. I was only a tiny child. I really liked the old man."

"It was a filthy old yard," said Werner. He was telling Zena rather than me. Or perhaps he was retelling it to himself. "Full of junk and rubbish. What a wonderland it was for us children who played there. We had such fun." He took a piece of tart from Zena. His slice was small; she was trying to slim him down. "Paul was a scholar. The old man was proud of him, but they didn't have much in common when Paul came back with all those college degrees and qualifications. Old Mr. Biedermann had had no proper education. He left school when he was fourteen."

"He was a real Berliner," I said. "He ran the transport business like a despot. He knew the names of all his workers. He swore at them when he was angry and got drunk with them when there was something to celebrate. They invited him to their marriages and their christenings, and he never missed a funeral. When the union organized a weekend outing each year they always invited him along. No one would have wanted to go without the old man."

"You're talking about the road transport business," said Werner. "But that was only a tiny part of their setup."

"It was the business the old man started, and the only part of the Biedermann empire he ever really liked." A timer began to ping somewhere in the kitchen, but Zena didn't move. Eventually it stopped. I guessed the Indian woman was there, but banished to the back room.

"It was losing money," said Werner.

"So when Paul Biedermann came back from his American business management course, the first thing he did was to sell the transport company and pension his father off."

"You sound very bitter, Bernie. That couldn't be why you hate Paul so much, could it?"

I drank some more coffee. I began to have the feeling that Zena didn't intend to leave us alone to talk about the things we had to talk about. I kept the small talk going. "It killed old Biedermann," I said. "He had nothing to live for after the yard closed and the company was being run from New York. Do you remember how he used to sit in Leuschner's café all day, talking about old times to anyone who would listen, even to us kids?"

"It's the way things are now," said Werner. "Companies are run by computers. Profit margins are sliced thin. And no manager dare raise his eyes from his accounts long enough to learn the names of his staff. It's the price we pay for progress."

Zena picked up the ashtray containing the broken cup and saucer. I could tell that Werner had broken it by the way she averted her eyes from him. She took the coffeepot too and went to the kitchen. I said, "Dicky saw Frank Harrington in L.A. Apparently London have decided to try enrolling Erich Stinnes." I had tried to make it unhurried but it came out in a rush.

"Enrolling him?" I was interested to see that Werner was as dismayed and surprised as I had been. "Is there any background?"

"You mean, have there been discussions with Stinnes before? I was wondering the same thing myself, but from what I got out of Dicky, I think the idea is to go in cold."

Werner leaned his considerable weight back in the armchair and blew through his pursed lips. "Who's going to try that?"

"Dicky wants you to try," I said. I drank some of my strong coffee and tried to sound very casual. I could see that Werner was torn between indignation and delight. Werner desperately wanted to become a regular departmental employee again. But he knew that being chosen for this job was no tribute to his skills; he was simply the man closest to Stinnes. "It's a great opportunity," said Werner resentfully, "a great opportunity for failure. So Frank Harrington, and all those people who've been slandering me all these years, can have a new excuse and start slandering me all over again."

"They must know the chances are slim," I said. "But if Stinnes went for it, you'd be the talk of the town, Werner."

Werner gave me a wry smile. "You mean both East and West sides of it?"

"What are you talking about?" said Zena returning with the coffee. "Is this something to do with Erich Stinnes?"

Werner glanced at me. He knew I didn't want to discuss it in front of Zena. "If I'm going to try, Zena will have to know, Bernie," he said apologetically. I nodded. The reality was that Werner told her everything I told him, so she might as well hear it from me.

Zena poured more coffee and offered us a selection of *Spritzgebäck,* little German biscuits that Werner liked. "It is about Stinnes, isn't it?" she said as she picked up her own coffee—she drank it strong and black—and sat down. Even in this severe dress she looked very beautiful; her big eyes, very white teeth, and the high cheekbones in that lightly tanned face made her look like the work of some Aztec goldsmith.

"London want to enroll him," said Werner.

"Recruit him to work for London, do you mean?" said Zena.

"You recruit ordinary people to become spies," Werner

explained patiently. "But an enemy security officer, especially one who might help you break his own networks, is 'enrolled.' "

"It's the same sort of thing," said Zena brightly.

"It's very different," said Werner. "When you recruit someone, and start them spying, you paint romantic pictures for them. You show them the glamour and make them feel courageous and important. But the agent you enroll knows all the answers already. Enrollment is tricky. You are telling lies to highly skilled liars. They're cynical and demanding. It's easy to start it off but it usually goes sour some way along the line and everyone ends up mad at everyone else."

"You make it sound like getting a divorce," said Zena.

"It's a bit like that," I said. "But it can get more violent."

"More violent than a divorce?" Zena fluttered her eyelashes. "You're only going to offer Erich Stinnes a chance to defect to the West. Can't he do that any time he wants? He's in Mexico. Why go back to Russia if he doesn't want to?" There was something deliciously feminine about Zena and her view of the world about her.

"It's not as easy as that," said Werner. "Not many countries will allow East European nationals to defect. Seamen who jump ship, passengers or Aeroflot crew who leave their planes at refueling stops, or Soviet delegates who walk into foreign police stations and ask for asylum find it's not so easy. Even right-wing governments send them right back to Russia to face the music." He bit into a biscuit. "Good *Spritzgebäck*, darling," he said.

"I couldn't get hazelnuts but I tried this other sort, with honey. They're not bad, are they? Why won't they let them defect? They send them back to Russia? That's disgusting," said Zena.

"Encouraging defectors upsets the Russians, for one thing," said Werner. "If Stinnes said he wanted to stay in Mexico, the Soviet ambassador would go running along to the foreign secretary and start pressuring the Mexican authorities to hand him back."

"In which case doesn't Stinnes just say go to hell?" said Zena.

"The ambassador then says that Stinnes has stolen the cash box or that he's wanted to face criminal charges in Moscow. The Mexicans then find themselves accused of harboring a criminal. And don't forget that someone has to pay the defector a salary or find him a job." Werner reached for another biscuit.

"This is Mexico," said Zena. "What do they care about the Russians?"

Werner was fully occupied with the biscuits. I said, "The Russians have a lot of clout in this part of the world, Mrs. Volkmann. They can stir up trouble by getting neighboring countries to apply pressure. Cuba will always oblige, since its economy depends totally on Soviet money. They can apply economic sanctions. They can influence United Nations committees and all the rigmarole of UNESCO and so on. And all of these countries have to contend with a domestic Communist Party organization ready to do whatever the Russians want done. Governments don't offend the Soviet Union without very good reason. Providing asylum for a defector is seldom reason enough."

"There are still plenty of defectors though," persisted Zena.

"Yes," I said. "Many defectors are sponsored by the U.S.A., the way that famous musicians or performers are, because of the bad publicity their escapes make for the Communist system. And they can earn their own living easily enough. The remainder have to bring something worthwhile with them as the price of entry."

"Secrets?"

"That depends what you call secrets. Usually a country provides asylum to someone bringing information about the way the Soviets have been spying on the host country. For that sort of information, a government is usually prepared to withstand Russian pressures."

"And for that reason," said Werner, "most of the decent Russians can't defect and the KGB bastards can. Put all the defectors together and you'd have a ballet company and orchestra, some sports stars, and a vast army of secret policemen."

Zena looked at me with her big gray eyes and said archly, "But if you two are right about Erich Stinnes, he's a KGB man. So he could provide some secrets about spying on Mexico. So he would be allowed to stay here without your help."

"Would you like to live in Mexico for the remainder of your life, Mrs. Volkmann?" I said.

She paused for a moment as if thinking the idea over. "Perhaps not," she admitted.

"No, a man such as Stinnes would want a British passport."

"Or a U.S. passport?" said Zena.

"American citizenship provides no right to travel abroad. A British passport identifies a British subject, and they have the right to leave the country any time they wish. Stinnes will give us quite a list of requirements if he decides to defect. He'd need a lot of paperwork so that he has a completely new identity. I mean an identity that is recorded in such a way that it will withstand investigation."

"What sort of things?" said Zena.

I said, "Things that require the cooperation of many different government departments. For instance, he'll need a driving license. And we don't want that to materialize out of nowhere, not for a forty-year-old with no other driving experience on file and no record of passing a driving test. He'd need to have some innocuous-looking file in his local tax office. He'll want a credit card; what does he put on the application? Then there are documents for traveling. He'll probably want some freedom of movement, and that's always a headache. Incidentally, he must give us some identity photos for his passport and so on. One good full-face picture will be enough. A picture of his wife too. I'll get the copies done at the embassy."

Werner nodded. He realized that this was his briefing. I was talking around the sort of offer he would be able to make to

Stinnes. "You're assuming that he would live in England?" said Werner.

"Certainly for the first year," I said. "It will be a long debriefing. Would that be a problem?"

"He's always spoken of Germany as the only place he'd ever want to be. Isn't that true, Zena?"

"That's what he's always said," Zena agreed. "But it's the sort of thing everyone says at the Kronprinz Club. Everyone is drinking German beer and exchanging news of the old country. It is natural to talk of Germany with great affection. We all do. But when you are offering someone a chance to retire in comfort, England wouldn't be too bad I think." She smiled.

I said, "Dicky thinks Stinnes will jump at any decent offer."

"Does he?" said Werner doubtfully.

"London think Stinnes has been passed over for promotion. They think he's been stuck away in East Berlin to rot."

"So why is he here in Mexico?" said Werner.

"Dicky thinks it's just a nice little jaunt for him."

"It's a convenient thing to say when you can't think of any convincing answer," said Werner. "What do you think, Bernie?"

"I'm convinced he's here in connection with Paul Biedermann," I said cautiously. "But why the hell would he be?"

Werner nodded. He didn't take me seriously. He knew I disliked Biedermann and thought this was clouding my judgment. "What makes you think that, Bernie?" he said.

"Stinnes and his pal didn't know I was listening to them out at the Biedermann house. They said they were running Biedermann, and I believe it."

"Paul Biedermann has been koshering cash for the KGB," Werner told Zena. "And sending it off for them too."

"What a bastard," said Zena. The family property in East Prussia, which Zena had failed to inherit because it was now a part of the USSR, made her unsympathetic to people who helped the KGB. But she didn't put much venom into her condemnation of Biedermann; her mind was on Stinnes. "What's so special about Stinnes?" she asked me.

"London want him," I said. "And London Central move in strange and unaccountable ways."

"It's all Dicky Cruyer's idea," she said as if she'd had a sudden insight. "I'll bet it's not London at all. Dicky Cruyer went off to Los Angeles and had a meeting with Frank Harrington. Then he returned with the electrifying news that London want Erich Stinnes, and he's to be coaxed into defection."

"He couldn't do that," said Werner, who hated to have his faith in London Central undermined. "It's a London order, isn't it, Bernie? It must be."

"Don't be silly, Werner," his wife argued. "It was probably made official afterwards. You know that anyone could talk Frank Harrington into anything."

Werner grunted. Zena's brief love affair with the elderly Frank Harrington was something that was never referred to, but I could see it was not forgotten.

Zena turned to me. "I'm right. You know I am."

"A successful enrollment would do wonders for Dicky's chances of holding onto the German desk," I said. I got up and walked over to the window. I had almost forgotten that we were in Mexico City, but the mountains just visible behind a veil of mist, the dark ceiling of clouds, the flashes of lightning, and the tropical storm that was thrashing the city were not like anything to be seen in Europe.

"When do we get the money for finding him?" Zena said. My back was to her, and I pretended to think that she was asking Werner.

It was Werner who replied. "It will work out, darling. These things take time."

Zena came across to the window and said to me, "We'll not do any more to help until we've been paid some money."

"I don't know anything about the money," I said.

"No, no one knows anything about the money. That's how you people work, isn't it?"

Werner was still sitting heavily in his chair munching his biscuits. "It's not Bernie's fault, darling. Bernie would give us the crown jewels if it was only up to him." The crown jewels had always been Werner's idea of ultimate wealth. I remembered how, when we were at school, various prized possessions of his had all been things he wouldn't exchange for the crown jewels.

"I'm not asking for the crown jewels," said Zena demurely. I turned to look her in the face. My God, but she was tough and yet the toughness did not mar her beauty. I suddenly saw the fatal attraction she had for poor Werner. It was like having pet piranhas in the bath, or a silky rock python in the linen cupboard. You could never tame them, but it was fun to see what effect they had on your friends. "I'm asking to be paid for finding Erich Stinnes." She picked up a note pad by the phone and entered the cup and saucer onto her list of breakages.

I looked at Werner but he was trying on some new inscrutable faces, so I said, "I don't know who told you that there was a cash payment for reporting the whereabouts of Erich Stinnes, but it certainly wasn't me. The truth is, Mrs. Volkmann, that the Department never pay any sort of bounty. At least I've never heard of such a payment being made." She stared at me with enough calm dispassionate interest to make me worry whether my coffee was poisoned. "But I probably could sign a couple of vouchers that would reimburse you for air fares, first class, return trip."

"I don't want any charity," she said. "I want what is due to me." It wasn't "us," I noticed.

"What sort of fee would you think appropriate?" I asked.

"It must be worth sixteen thousand American dollars," she said. So she'd decided what she wanted. At first I wondered how she'd come to such an exact figure, but I then realized that it had not been quantified by the job she'd done; it was the specific amount of money she wanted for something or other. That was the way Zena's mind worked—every step she took was on the way to somewhere else.

"That's a lot of money, Mrs. Volkmann," I said. I looked at Werner. He was pouring himself more coffee and concentrating on the task as if oblivious of everything around him. It suited him to have Zena giving me hell. I suppose she was voicing the resentment that had been building up in Werner in all the years he'd suffered from the insensitive double-dealing of the birdbrains at London Central. But I didn't enjoy having Zena bawl me out. I was angry with him and he knew it. "I will see that your request is passed on to London."

"And tell them this," she said. She was still speaking softly and smiling, so that a casual observer might have thought we were chatting amicably. "You tell them unless I get my money, I'll make sure that Erich Stinnes never trusts a word you say."

"How would you achieve that, Mrs. Volkmann?" I asked.

"No, Zena . . ." said Werner, but he'd left it too late.

"I'd tell him exactly what you're up to," she said. "I'd tell him that you'll cheat him just as you've cheated me."

I laughed scornfully. She seemed surprised. "Have you been sitting in on this conversation and still not understood what Werner and I are talking about, Mrs. Volkmann? Your husband earns his money from avalizing. He borrows money from Western banks to pay in advance for goods shipped to East Germany. The way he does it requires him to spend a lot of time in the German Democratic Republic. It's natural that the British government might use someone such as Werner to talk to Stinnes about defecting. The KGB wouldn't like that, of course, but they'd swallow it, the same way we swallow it when they use trade delegates to contact troublemakers and float some ideas we don't like."

I glanced at Werner. He was standing behind Zena now, his hands clasped together and a frown on his face. He'd been about to interrupt but now he was looking at me, waiting to hear what I was going to say. I said, "Everyone likes a sportsman who can walk out into the middle of a soccer field, exchange a joke with the linesmen, and flip a coin for the two team captains. But 'enrolling' doesn't just mean offering a man money to come to the other side; it can mean beating him over the head and shipping him off in a crate. I don't say that's going to happen, but Werner and I both know it's a possibility. And if it does happen, I want to make sure that the people on the other team keep thinking that Werner is an innocent bystander who paid the full price of admission. Because if they suspect that Werner is the kind who climbs the fence and throws beer cans at the goalkeeper, they might get rough, Mrs. Volkmann. And when the KGB get rough, they get very rough. So I advise you most sincerely not to start talking to Erich Stinnes in a way that makes it sound as if Werner is closely connected with the Department, or there's a real risk that they'll do something nasty to you both."

Werner knew I was going to spell it out for her. I suppose he didn't want her to understand the implications in case she worried.

I looked at her. She nodded. "If Werner wants to talk to Stinnes, I won't screw it up for you," she promised. "But don't ask me to help."

"I won't ask you to help," I said.

Werner went over to her and put his arm around her shoulder to comfort her. But she didn't look very worried about him. She still looked very angry about not getting the money.

Chapter 6

IF ZENA ever left me, I don't know what I'd do," said Werner. "I think I'd die, I really would." He fanned away a fly with his straw hat.

This was Werner in his lugubrious mood. I nodded, but I felt like reminding him that Zena had left him several times in the past, and he was still alive. He'd even survived the very recent time when she'd set up house with Frank Harrington— a married man more than old enough to be her father—and had looked all set to make it permanent. Except that Zena was never going to make anything permanent, except perhaps eventually make Werner permanently unhappy.

"But Zena is very ambitious," said Werner. "I think you realize that, don't you, Bernie?"

"She's very young, Werner."

"Too young for me, you mean?"

I worded my answer carefully. "Too young to know what the real world is like, Werner."

"Yes, poor Zena."

"Yes, poor Zena," I said. Werner looked at me to see if I was being sarcastic. I smiled.

"This is a beautiful hotel," said Werner. We were sitting on the balcony having breakfast. It was still early in the morning, and the air was cool. The town was behind us and we were looking across gently rolling green hills that disappeared into gauzy curtains of morning mist. It could have been England—except for the sound of the insects, the heavy scent of the tropical flowers, and the vultures that endlessly circled high in the clear blue sky.

"Dicky found it," I said.

Zena had let Werner off his lead for the day, and he'd come to Cuernavaca—a short drive west from Mexico City—to tell me about his encounter with Stinnes at the Kronprinz Club. Dicky had decided to "make our headquarters" in this sprawling resort town where so many Americans came to spend their old age and their cheap pesos. "Where's Dicky now?" said Werner.

"He's at a meeting," I said.

Werner nodded. "You're smart to stay here in Cuernavaca. This side of the mountains it's always cooler and you don't have to breathe that smog all day and all night."

"On the other hand," I said, "I do have Dicky next door."

"Dicky's all right," said Werner. "But you make him nervous."

"I make him nervous?" I said incredulously.

"It must be difficult for him," said Werner. "You know the German desk better than he'll ever know it."

"But he got it," I said.

"So did you expect him to turn a job like that down?" said Werner. "You should give him a break, Bernie."

"Dicky does all right," I said. "He doesn't need any help. Not from you, not from me. Dicky is having a lovely time."

Dicky had lined up meetings with a retired American CIA executive named Miller and an Englishman who claimed to have great influence with the Mexican security service. In fact, of course, Dicky was just trying out some of the best local restaurants at the taxpayers' expense, while extending his wide circle of friends and acquaintances. Dicky had once shown me his card index files of contacts throughout the world. It was quite unofficial of course—Dicky kept them in his desk at home. He noted the names of their wives and their children and what restaurants they preferred and what sort of houses they lived in. On the other side of each card Dicky wrote a short résumé of what he estimated to be their wealth, power, and influence. He joked about his file cards: "He'll be a lovely card for me," he'd say when someone influential crossed his path. Sometimes I wondered if there was a card there with my name on it, and if so, what he'd written on it.

Dicky was a keen traveler and his choice of bars, restaurants, and hotels was the result of intensive research through guidebooks and travel magazines. The Hacienda Margarita, an old ranch house on the outskirts of town, was proof of the benefits that could come from such dedicated research. It was a charming old hotel, its cool stone colonnades surrounding a courtyard with palmettos and pepper trees and tall palms. The high-ceilinged bedrooms were lined with wonderful old tiles and there were big windows and cool balconies, for this place was built long before air-conditioning was ever contemplated—built at the time of the conquistadores, if you could bring yourself to believe the plaque over the cashier's desk.

Meanwhile I was enjoying the sort of breakfast that Dicky

insisted was the only healthy way to start the day. There was a jug of freshly pressed orange juice, a vacuum flask of hot coffee, canned milk—Dicky didn't trust Mexican milk—freshly baked rolls, and a pot of local honey. The tray was decorated with an orchid and held a copy of *The News,* the local English-language newspaper. Werner drank orange juice and coffee but declined the rolls and honey. "I promised Zena that I'd lose weight."

"Then I'll have yours," I said.

"You're overweight too," said Werner.

"But I didn't make any promises to Zena," I said, digging into the honey.

"He was there last night," said Werner.

"Did he go for it, Werner? Did Stinnes go for it?"

"How can you tell with a man like Stinnes?" said Werner. "I told him that I'd met a man here in Mexico whom I'd known in Berlin. I said he had provided East German refugees with all the necessary papers to go and live in England. Stinnes said did I mean genuine papers or false papers. I said genuine papers: passports and identity papers and permission to reside in London or one of the big towns."

"The British don't have any sort of identity papers," I said. "And they don't have to get anyone's permission to go and live in any town they like."

"Well, I don't know things like that," said Werner huffily. "I've never lived in England, have I? If the English don't need papers, what the hell are we offering him?"

"Never mind all that, Werner. What did Stinnes say?"

"He said that refugees were never happy. He'd known a lot of exiles and they'd always regretted leaving their homeland. He said they never properly mastered the language, and never integrated with the local people. Worst of all, he said, their children grew up in the new country and treated their parents like strangers. He was playing for time, of course."

"He knew what you were getting at?"

"Perhaps he wasn't sure at first, but I persisted and Zena

helped. I know she said she wouldn't help, Bernie, but she did help."

"What did she do?"

"She told him that a little money solves all kinds of problems. Zena said that friends of hers had gone to live in England and loved every minute of it. She told him that everyone likes living in England. These friends of hers had a big house in Hampshire with a huge garden. And they had a language teacher to help them with their English. She told him that these were all problems that could be solved if there was help and money available."

"He must have been getting the message by that time," I said.

"Yes, he became cautious," said Werner. "I suppose he was frightened in case I was trying to make a fool of him."

"And?"

"I had to make it a little more specific. I said that this friend of mine could always arrange a job in England for anyone with experience in security work. He'd just come down here for a couple of weeks' holiday in Mexico after traveling through the U.S., recruiting security experts for a very big British corporation, a company that did work for the British government. The pay is very good, I told him, with a long contract optional both sides."

"I wish you really did have a friend like that, Werner," I said. "I'd want to meet him myself. How did Stinnes react?"

"What's he going to say, Bernie? I mean, what would you or I say, in his place, faced with the same proposition?"

"He said maybe?"

"He said yes . . . or as near as he dare go to yes. But he's frightened it's a trap. Anyone would be frightened of its being a trap. He said he wanted more details, and a chance to think about it. He'd have to meet the man doing the recruiting. I said I was just a go-between, of course . . ."

"And he believed you are just the go-between?"

"I suppose so," said Werner. He picked up the orchid and examined it as if seeing one for the first time. "You can't grow

orchids in Mexico City, but here in C
No one knows why. Maybe its the sm

"Don't just suppose so, Werner." I
he avoided important questions by
conversation. "I wasn't kidding last n
Zena. I wasn't kidding about them get

"He believed me," said Werner in a
he was just trying to calm me down.

"Stinnes is no amateur," I said. "He's the one they assigned
to me when I was arrested over there. He had me taken to the
Normannenstrasse building and sat with me half the night chatting and smoking and making it clear that if he was in charge
of things they'd be kicking shit out of me."

"We've both seen a lot of KGB specimens like Erich
Stinnes," said Werner. "He's affable enough over a stein of
beer, but in other circumstances he could be a nasty piece of
work. And not to be trusted, Bernie. I kept my distance from
him. I'm no hero, you know that."

"Was there anyone with him?"

"An older man—fifty or so—built like a tank, cropped hair,
can't seem to speak any language without a strong Russian
accent."

"Sounds like the one who went with him to the Biedermann
house. Pavel, he called him. I told you what they said, didn't I?"

"I guessed it was him. Luckily Pavel isn't really fluent in
German, especially when Stinnes and I got going. Stinnes got
rid of him as soon as he realized the drift my conversation was
taking. I thought that might have been a good sign."

"I can use all the good signs we can get, Werner." I drank
some coffee. "It's all right telling him about language lessons
in Hampshire, but he knows the real score would be him sitting
in some lousy little safe house blowing KGB networks. And
drinking half a bottle of Scotch every night in an effort to forget
what damage he's doing to his own people, and that he's going
to have to start doing it all over again next morning. Hey, don't
look so worried, Werner."

He looked at me, biting his lip. "He knows you're here,

sure he does." There was a note of anxiety now.
ed if I knew an Englishman who was a friend of Paul
rmann. I said Paul knew lots of Englishmen. He said yes,
t this one knew all the Biedermann family and had done for
years."

"That description fits lots of people," I said.

"But it doesn't fit anyone else who's in Mexico City," said Werner. "I think Stinnes knows you're here. And if he knows you're here, that's bad."

"Why is it bad?" I said, although I knew what he was going to say. I'd known Werner so long that our minds ran on the same track.

"Because it sounds like he got it from Paul Biedermann."

"Maybe," I said.

"If Stinnes was worried about Biedermann, the way he sounded worried from that conversation you overheard, then he's likely to put him through the wringer. You know, and I know, that Biedermann couldn't take much punishment before he started to recount everything he knows, plus a few things he only guesses at."

"So what could Biedermann tell them? That I sell second-hand Ferraris that keep breaking down?"

"You're smiling. But Biedermann could tell them quite a lot. He could tell them about you working for the SIS. He could tell them about Frank Harrington in Berlin and the people Frank sees."

"Don't be ridiculous, Werner. The KGB know all about Frank Harrington. He's been Berlin Resident for a long time, and he was no stranger to Berlin before he took the job. As for knowing who I work for, we were discussing rates of pay that night Stinnes had me in Normannenstrasse."

"I think he wants to talk to you, Bernie. He did everything except spell out your name."

"Eventually he'll have to see me. And he'll recognize me. Then he'll telex Moscow and have them send a computer print-out of whatever they know about me. That's the way it is, Werner. There's nothing we can do about that."

"I don't like it, Bernie."

"So what am I going to do—glue on a false beard and put a stone in my shoe to make me limp?"

"Let Dicky do it."

"Dicky? Are you joking? Dicky enroll Stinnes? Stinnes would run a mile."

"He'll probably run a mile when you try," said Werner. "But Dicky has no record of work as a field agent. It's very unlikely that they'd do anything really nasty to Dicky."

"Well, that's another reason," I said.

"It's not something to joke about, Bernie. I know you were painting a rosy picture for Zena yesterday. And I appreciate you trying to set her mind at rest. But we both know that the best way to prevent an enrollment is to kill the enroller . . . and we both know that Moscow shares that feeling."

"Did you fix a time and place?"

"I still don't like it, Bernie."

"What can happen? I tell him how lovely it is living in Hampshire. And he tells me to get stuffed."

Music started from the big patio below our balcony. Some of the hotel staff were erecting a stage, arranging folding chairs, and decorating the columns with colored lanterns in preparation for the concert I'd seen advertised in the lobby. Sitting under the tall spiky palmetto trees on the far side of the patio there were six men and a flashy-looking girl. One of the men was strumming a guitar and tuning it. The girl was smiling and humming the tune but the other men sat very still and completely impassive as the natives of very hot countries learn to do.

Werner followed the direction of my gaze and leaned over to see what was happening. The man strumming the guitar picked out a melody everyone in Mexico knows, and quietly sang:

> *"Life is worth nothing, life is worth nothing,*
> *It always starts with crying and with crying ends.*
> *And thats why, in this world, life is worth nothing."*

Werner said, "Stinnes says he's frightened of this man Pavel. He says Pavel is desperate to get back to Moscow and that his only way of doing that is to get back into favor. Stinnes is frightened that Pavel will make trouble at the first opportunity."

"It sounds like a cozy chat, Werner. He said he's frightened?" Stinnes was not the type who was easily frightened, and certainly not the type to say so.

"Not like I'm telling you," said Werner. "It was all wrapped up in euphemisms and double meanings, but the message was clear."

"What's the end result?"

"He wants to talk to you, but it's got to be somewhere completely safe. Somewhere that can't be bugged or have witnesses hidden."

"For instance?"

"Biedermann's boat. He'll meet my contact on Biedermann's boat, he says."

"That sounds sensible," I said. "You did well, Werner."

"Sensible for him, but not so sensible for you."

"Why?"

"Are you crazy? He's sure to have Biedermann with him. They'll cruise out into the Pacific and dump you over the side. They'll say you had cramp while swimming. The local cops are sure to be in Biedermann's pocket, and so is the local doctor who'll issue a death certificate, if that's the way they decide to play it."

"You've got my demise all worked out, haven't you, Werner?"

"If you're too stupid to see the danger for yourself, then it's as well I spell it out for you."

"I don't see them going to all that trouble to do something that can be more easily achieved by a hit-and-run traffic accident as I hurry across the Reforma one morning."

"Of course, I don't know what kind of backup you'll be arranging. For all I know you'll have a Royal Navy frigate out there, with a chopper keeping you on radar. I realize you don't tell me everything."

There were times when Werner could drive me to the point of frenzy. "You know as well as I do that I tell you all you need to know. And if I'm going out to meet Stinnes on this bloody boat, I won't even be carrying my Swiss Army knife . . . Royal Navy frigate . . . Good God, Werner, the ideas you come up with!" Below us the guitar player sang,

> ". . . *Only the winner is respected.*
> *That's why life is worth nothing in Guanajuato . . .*"

"Do whatever you want," said Werner mournfully. "I know you won't take my advice. You never have in the past."

I seem to have spent half my life listening to Werner handing out advice. And engraved on my memory there was a long list of times when I heartily regretted taking it. But I didn't tell him this. I said, "I'll be all right, Werner."

"You *think* you're all right," said Werner. "You think you're all right because your wife defected to the Russians. But that doesn't make you any safer, Bernie."

I didn't understand what he was getting at. "Make me safer? What do you mean?"

"I never got along with Fiona, I'll admit that anytime. But it was more because of her attitude than because of mine. When you married her I was ready to be friends. You know that, Bernie."

"What are you trying to say, Werner?"

"Fiona works for the KGB nowadays. Well, I'm not saying she's going to send a KGB hit team after the father of her children. But don't imagine you will enjoy complete immunity forever and ever. That's not the way the KGB work, you know that, Bernie."

"Isn't it?"

"You're on different sides now, you and Fiona. She's working against you, Bernie. Remember that always. She'll always be working against you."

"You're not saying that Fiona sent Stinnes to Mexico in the hope that you might come here on holiday? Instead of going to Spain for which you'd already booked tickets when you read in *Time* magazine about Mexico being even cheaper. That she did that because she hoped you would spot Stinnes and report it to London Central. Then she figured that they would send me here with an offer to enroll him. I mean that would be a lot of ifs, wouldn't it? She'd have to be a magician to work that one out in advance, wouldn't she?"

"You like to make me sound ridiculous," said Werner. "It makes you feel good, doesn't it?"

"Yes, it does. And since you like to feel sorry for yourself, we have the perfect symbiotic relationship." It was getting warmer in the morning sunshine, and the sweet scents of the flowers hung in the air. And yet these were not the light fresh smells of Europe's countryside. The flowers were big and brightly colored, the sort of blooms that eat insects in slow motion in nature films on TV. And the heavy cloying perfumes smelled like an airport duty-free lounge.

"I'm simply saying what's obvious. That you mustn't think that you'll continue to have a charmed life just because Fiona is working for them."

"Continue to have? What do you mean?"

Werner leaned forward. "Fiona made sure nothing happened to you during all those years when she was an active agent inside London Central. That's what you said yourself. It's no good denying it, you told me that, Bernard. You told me just after they let you go."

"I said *maybe* she had a deal like that."

"But she's not going to be doing that anymore. She's running Stinnes—and whatever he's doing with Biedermann— from a desk in East Berlin. Moscow is going to be watching every move she makes, and she's got to show them that she's on their side. Even if she wanted to protect you she'd not be allowed to. If you go out on Paul Biedermann's boat with the idea that nothing can happen to you because the KGB will play it the way Fiona wants, you might not come back."

"Well, perhaps this would be a good chance to find out what the score is," I said. "I'll go out on the boat with Stinnes and see what happens."

"Well, don't say you weren't told," said Werner.

I didn't want to argue, especially not with Werner—he was worried for my safety even if he was clucking like a mother hen. But I was nervous about what Stinnes could have in store for me. And Werner, voicing my fears, was making me twitchy. My argument with Werner was an attempt to allay my own fears, but the more we argued the less convincing I sounded. "Put yourself in his place, Werner," I said. "Stinnes is doing exactly what you or I would do. He is reserving his position, asking for more information, and playing it very safe. He doesn't care whether we will find it easy or convenient to rendezvous on Biedermann's boat. If we don't overcome our reservations, our fears, and our difficulties, he'll know we're not serious."

Werner pushed his lower lip forward as if in thought. And then, to consolidate this reflective pose, he pinched his nose between thumb and forefinger while closing his eyes. It was a more elaborate version of the faces he'd pulled at school when trying to remember theorems. "I'll go with you," he said. It was a noble concession; Werner hated boats of any shape or size.

"Would Stinnes permit that?"

"I'll just turn up there. We'll say you had trouble with the traffic cops. We'll say they wanted a notarized affidavit from the legal owner of the car you're using—that's the law here. We'll say you couldn't get one, so I had to drive you in my car."

"Will he believe that?" I said.

"He'll think the cops were trying to wring a big bribe from you—it's common for cops to stop cars with foreigners and demand a bribe from the driver—and he'll think you were too dumb to understand what they really wanted."

"When is this meeting to be?"

"Tomorrow. Okay?"

"Fine."

"Very early."

"I said okay, Werner."

"Because I have to phone him and confirm."

"Codes or anything?"

"No, he just wants me to phone and say if my friend will be able to go on the fishing trip."

"Good. A lot of mumbo jumbo with codes would have made me uneasy. It's the way the Moscow deskmen would want it done."

Werner nodded. The guitar player was still singing the catchy melody:

"... *Christ on your hill, on the mountain ridge of Cubilete,*
Console those who suffer, you're worshiped by the people,
Christ on your hill, on the mountain ridge of Cubilete."

"It's a popular song," said Werner. "Did you know that the Cubilete is a mountain ridge shaped like a dice cup? But why is life worth nothing?"

"It means life is cheap," I said. "The song is about the way that people are killed for nothing in this part of the world."

"By the way," said Werner. "If you could let us have the return air fares you mentioned, I'd appreciate it."

"Sure," I said. "I can do that on my own authority. Two first-class air tickets Berlin to Mexico City and return. I'll give you a voucher that any big airline will cash."

"It would be useful," said Werner. "The peso is cheap, but we get through a lot of money one way and the other."

Chapter 7

I<small>T WAS</small> still night when we got to Santiago, but there was enough moonlight to see that Biedermann's gate was locked. I noticed that a new chain had been found to replace the one that had been sawn through on my previous visit. There was no response to my pressing the button of the speaker-phone.

"If that bastard doesn't turn up . . ." I said and kicked the gate.

"Calm down," said Werner. "We're early. Let's stroll along the beach."

We left Werner's pickup truck at the entrance and walked to the beach to watch the ocean. The storms had cleared and the weather was calm, but close to, the noise of the ocean was thunderous. The waves hitting the beach exploded across the sand in great galaxies of sparkling phosphorescence. Every-where the coast was littered with flotsam, broken pieces of timber from boats and huts and limbs of trees torn apart by the great winds.

Over the salty putrefaction that is the smell of the ocean there came a whiff of wood smoke. Along the water's edge, at the place where a piece of jungly undergrowth came almost to the sand, there was a flickering light of a fire. Werner and I walked along to see it, and round the corner of the rocks we saw blanketed shapes huddled around a dying fire.

Here in the shelter of the rocks and vegetation there was less noise from the sea, but I could feel the pounding surf underfoot, and the spray in the air made beads of moisture on my spectacles.

Nearer to the fire, perched with his back against a rock, there was a man. Now and then the fire flared enough to show his bearded face and the hair tied in a ponytail. He was a muscular youth, darkly tanned, wearing old swimming trunks and a clean T-shirt that was too small for him. He was smoking and staring into the fire. He seemed not to see us until we were almost on top of him.

"Who's that?" he called in English. His voice was high-pitched; he sounded nervous.

"We live nearby," I said. "We're going out fishing. We're waiting for the boat."

There was a snuffling sound coming from one of the huddled shapes. At first it was a soft warbling muffled by the blankets. "Shut up, Betty," said the bearded boy. But the sound didn't cease. It became more nasal, almost stertorous, until it was recognizably a girl sobbing. "Shut up, I say. There are people here. Try and go back to sleep." The bearded boy inhaled deeply on his cigarette. There was the sweet smell of marijuana smoke in the air.

But the girl sat up. She was about eighteen years old, pretty if you made allowances for the spots on her face that might have been a sign of adolescence or bad diet. Her hair was cut short, shorter in fact than that of the bearded boy. As the blanket fell away from her shoulders, I could see that she was wearing only a bra. Her body was badly sunburned. She stopped sobbing and wiped the tears from her eyes with her fingertips. "Have you got a cigarette?" she asked me. "An American cigarette?"

I offered her my packet. "Can I take two?" she whispered.

"Keep the packet," I said. "I'm trying to give it up."

She lit the cigarette immediately and passed the packet to the bearded boy, who used the joint he'd been smoking to light up a Camel instead. Behind him one of the other sleepers moved. I had the feeling that all of them were awake and listening to us.

"Have you just arrived?" I said. "I don't remember you being here last week."

The boy seemed to feel that some explanation was necessary. "There were seven of us, four guys and three girls." He leaned forward and used a piece of wood to prod the fire. There were tiny burned fragments of unprocessed film there and the boy poked them into the ashes until they burned. "We met and got together waiting for a bus way north of here in Mazatlán. We're backpacking along the coast, and heading down towards Acapulco. But one of the guys—Theo—slept under a manzanillo tree the night before last, and the sap is poisonous. That was at our previous camp a long way up the coast from here; we made good mileage since then. But Theo was shook. He cut away inland to look for a clinic." The bearded boy rubbed his arm where the dark suntan was made even darker by a long stain of iodine that had treated a bad cut on his forearm.

"Have you seen a powerboat in the last few hours?" I asked.

"Sure," said the bearded boy. "She's anchored on the other side of the headland. We were watching it earlier. It's a ritzy son of a bitch. Is that the one you're going on? She came up the coast and tried to get into the little pier, but I guess the tide was wrong or something because finally they had to use the dinghy to land a couple of guys." He turned his head to look at the waves striking the beach. They came racing towards us, making a huge shimmering sheet of polished steel until the water lost its impetus and sank into the darkened sand.

"We haven't seen her yet," I said. "A good boat, is it?"

"That boat's a ship, man," he said. "What are you going after—marlin or sailfish or something?"

"We're after anything that's out there," I said. "Are you hiking all the way?"

"We thumb a ride now and again. And twice we took a Mexican second-class bus, but along this piece of coast the highway runs too far inland. We like to keep near the ocean. We like to swim, and catching fish to eat saves dough. But it's heavy going along this section. We've chopped our way through for the last five miles or so."

They were all obviously awake now, all six of them. But they remained very still so that they heard everything being said. I could see that they'd made a little encampment here in the shelter of a rocky outcrop. There were seven backpacks perched up on the rocks and kept fastened against rats and monkeys. Someone had tried to build a *palapas,* the hut that local people make as a temporary shelter using the coconut palms. But making them is not so easy as it looks, and this one had fallen to pieces. The wood framework had collapsed at one end, and split palm fronds were scattered across the beach. Laundry was hanging to dry on some bushes—a man's T-shirt, a pair of jeans, and a set of underpants. A yellow plastic jug was rigged up in a tree to make a shower bath. Two tin plates were bent almost double.

"Someone's tried to eat their plate," I said.

"Yeah," said the bearded boy. "We tried to dig a well without a spade. It's tough going. There's no water here, we'll have to move on tomorrow."

"Where will you meet your friend?" I said.

The boy looked at me long enough to let me know I was asking too many questions, but he answered. "Theo decided to head back home. He left his backpack with us. He didn't want to go on down to Acapulco."

"That's tough," I said.

"Those manzanillo trees really burn a piece out of you, man."

"I'll watch out for them," I said.

"Do that," said the boy. The rocks here were volcanic, teeth riddled with cavities so that the sea gurgled and gulped and vented spray that hissed before falling back, in a flash of fluorescent light, onto the sharp black molars.

"Thanks for the cigarettes," the girl said very quietly as we moved away. There was another girl alongside her. She put her arm round the girl who'd been crying and, as we moved away, she said, "Try and go to sleep, Betty. Tomorrow we have to move on."

Werner and I strolled back along the beach and then got

into the little pickup truck. It had four-wheel drive and had managed the final section of road without much trouble. Werner had borrowed it. He had an amazing ability to get almost anything at anytime anywhere. I didn't ask where it had come from. He looked at his watch. "Stinnes should be here any minute," he said.

"A man like that is usually early," I said.

"If you've got any doubts . . ."

"No, we'll hang on."

"Did you wonder who those people were on the beach? Did you guess they were hippies?"

"I'm still wondering," I said. I could taste the salt spray on my lips and I polished my glasses again to get rid of the marks.

"What the girl was crying about? Is that what you're wondering?"

"Six people backpacking through miles of scrub but there's seven packs?"

"One belongs to the kid who went looking for the clinic. Hell, you know the crazy things people do."

"An injured kid abandons his backpack? That's like saying he's abandoned all his belongings."

"It's possible," said Werner.

"And the other six carry an extra backpack? How do you do that, Werner? Never mind cutting your way through the scrub at the same time. How do you carry a backpack when you're already wearing one? Try it some time."

"So what are you saying?"

"If those kids had an extra pack to carry, they would take it to pieces and distribute it. More likely—seeing those kids—they would sell it in the local village where a decent pack would get them some stores or something to smoke or whatever they wanted."

"And the boy had a bad cut on his arm," said Werner.

"A bad cut in exactly the right place, Werner, the left forearm. And there were cuts on his hand too. Maybe more cuts under the borrowed T-shirt. The girl was sobbing as if her heart was broken. And the other girl was comforting her."

"Someone had taken a shower bath."

"Yes, and washed one set of clothes," I said. "Four men and three girls, sleeping on the beach each night. It's a recipe for trouble."

"Why dig for water? There must be water in the village," said Werner.

"Sure. And you can bet that Biedermann didn't start building his house until he found water there."

"If we're guessing right, we should tell the police," said Werner.

"Oh, sure," I said. "That's all we need, the local cops quizzing us all night and walking all over Stinnes and Biedermann too. I can't think of any surer way of ending any chance of enrolling Stinnes than having him walk into a murder investigation that we've made sure coincided exactly with his expected time of arrival."

"I don't like the idea of just doing nothing about it," said Werner.

"Sometimes, Werner, you amaze me."

He didn't answer. I'd seen him like this before. Werner was in a self-righteous sulk. He thought I should report my suspicions to the police and I had no doubt that he was preparing a lecture to which I would be subjected when he had it word perfect. We sat in the car watching the eastern sky lighten and thinking our own thoughts, until, half an hour later, we saw the headlights of two cars bumping along the track towards us.

Stinnes was in one car and Paul Biedermann in the other. One of the cars had got stuck on the final stretch of bad road. Biedermann opened the gate without more than a mumbled greeting and we all drove up to the house.

"I'm sorry about the locked gate," said Biedermann. There had been no formal introductions. It was as if by tacit consent this was to be a meeting that never took place. "The servants must have forgot what I told them."

The "servants" were a man and boy who, judging by the state of their boots, had recently arrived by the footpath that I had taken on the previous visit. They gave us mugs of the very sweet coffee made from the sugar-coated coffee beans that Mexicans like. They wore checked shirts and jeans. The boy was little more than a child. I guessed they were also the crew of Biedermann's motorboat. They treated Biedermann with a surly deference that might have been the result of the drunken rages that he was reputed to indulge in. But now Biedermann was sober and withdrawn. The four of us stood on the patio looking at the sun-streaked dawn sky and down to where a forty-foot cabin cruiser was at anchor a hundred meters off-shore.

I took this opportunity to look at Stinnes and I suppose he was making the most of this chance to study me. It was only his perfect German and the Berlin accent that made it possible for Stinnes to be mistaken for a native Berliner. Such thin wiry bodies and Slavic faces are common on the streets of Moscow. He'd removed his straw hat and revealed a tall forehead and hair that was thinning enough to show the shape of his skull. His eyes glittered behind small circular gold-rimmed eye-glasses that he now took off to polish while he looked around. He'd been in the sun and the chin from which he'd shaved a small beard was darkened, but his complexion was sallow and without pigment enough to tan evenly. In the Mexican sun his cheekbones and nose had turned a yellowish brown like the nicotine-stained fingers of a heavy smoker. And his cotton suit —so light in color as to be almost white—was ill-fitting and wrinkled by the car journey. And yet for all that, Stinnes had the quick intelligent eyes and tough self-confidence that make a man attractive to his fellow humans.

"Let's get going," said Biedermann impatiently. He was nervous. He made sure he never met my gaze. "Leave the coffee. Pedro and his son will make more on the boat if you want it. We're taking food aboard." He fussed about us like a tour guide, leading the way as we went down to the pier. He was telling us to mind the steps and watch out for the mud or the slippery wooden boards. I looked along the coast to see the hippies on the beach, but it was too far and they were hidden by the rocks. I looked back over my shoulder. Stinnes was at the very rear, picking his way down the steps with exaggerated care, his straw hat, old-fashioned spectacles, and creased white suit making him look like a character from Chekhov. Not the muddled avuncular Chekhov of the Western stage, but the cold arid class enemy that the Soviet theatre depicts.

The sun was coming through the haze now, its yellowish glare like a melted blob of butter oozing through a tissue paper wrapping. No one had commented on Werner's presence and I was grateful to him for being there. Either they didn't plan to get rough, or they planned to get so rough that one extra victim would make no difference.

IT WAS named *Maelstrom* and was the sort of boat that the Paul Biedermanns of this world love. It stood high out of the water with a top deck used for spotting and an awning-covered stern with a big "dentist's chair" for the man who was fishing. The lounge was lined with expensive veneering and had a stereo hi-fi, a big TV, and a wet bar with refrigerator. Steps up from there gave on to a big bridge, where a swivel seat provided the captain with a panoramic view through the wraparound windscreen. There was even a yachting cap with the word "Captain" entwined in crossed anchors and embroidered in fine gold wire. But Pedro the Mexican didn't wear the captain's hat; his long greasy hair would have stained it. He sat at the controls like a long-distance bus driver waiting at a depot. He rested on the wheel, toying with a wrapped cheroot that he never lit. There was a cheap transistor radio jammed behind the sun visor. He tuned it to a local station that played only Mexican music, and then turned the volume down so that it couldn't be heard in the lounge.

The big engines throbbed with a note so low that the sound

was less apparent than the vibrations through the soles of my shoes. Stinnes looked round without much sign of delight or admiration. I suppose it was everything a Communist hated. Even a lapsed fascist like me found it a bit too rich.

"Now, who would like a drink?" asked Biedermann in a voice that had the cheerful vibrancy of the perfect host. He had unlocked the bar and was pulling various bottles of drink from the cupboard. "Scotch. Brandy. English gin." He held up a bottle and shook it. "Robert Brown—that's Mexican whiskey, and if you've never tried it, it's quite an experience."

Stinnes walked across the lounge and very quietly said, "Better if you took Mr. Volkmann back up to the house, Paul. If Pedro shows me the controls I can handle the boat." It was a typical KGB trick, carefully planned but unexpected. They could not learn spontaneity, but they contrived ways to do without it.

Paul Biedermann looked up at him and blinked. "Sure. If that's the way you want it."

"It's the way I want it," said Stinnes. He took off his straw hat and smoothed his sparse hair by pressing the flat of his hand against his skull.

"And I'll take Pedro and his kid too. Or do you want them with you?" When Stinnes didn't reply, Biedermann gave a nervous smile and got to his feet. "Pedro. Show Mr. Stinnes how to manage the boat."

I was sitting on the far side of the lounge watching Biedermann carefully. Either he was scared of Stinnes or it was a very good act. Werner was watching the whole scene too. Typically he was hunched in an armchair with his eyes half closed. It was always like that with Werner, he liked to know everything that was going on and guess the things he didn't know. But he liked to look half asleep. Werner would have made a very successful gossip columnist, except that he would have missed a lot of deadlines.

Stinnes looked at me and, although his expression didn't change, he waited for me to nod before going up to take over the controls. "And, Paul," said Stinnes. "No drinking, Paul. Better we all keep clear heads."

"Oh, sure," said Paul Biedermann. "I just thought somebody . . ."

"Better lock it away," said Stinnes. "You take Mr. Volkmann up to the house and have more coffee."

"Before you lock it away," I said, "leave a little something to one side, would you?"

I poured myself a good measure of malt whiskey from the bottle Biedermann had put aside for me and sipped it neat. I never really trust drinking water anywhere but Scotland, and I've never been to Scotland.

I heard the whine of the electric motor that brought the anchor up and felt the boat wallow as the current took hold. Through the porthole I could see the dinghy containing Werner and Paul Biedermann and the two Mexicans returning to the pier. It was being tossed about. I wondered if Werner was feeling okay. He hated the sea in any shape or form. It was a notable gesture of friendship that he should have offered to come along.

The engines vibrated right through the boat as Stinnes—sitting upstairs at the controls—increased the revs and engaged the screws. The sound of waves pounding against the hull changed to the noise of water rushing past it and a large patch of sunlight raced across the veneered bulkhead as Stinnes turned the wheel and headed the boat out to the open sea.

I let Stinnes play with the controls while I continued to drink my malt and ask myself what I was doing out at sea in this floating Cadillac in the hurricane season with a KGB major at the helm. He pushed up the revs after a few minutes, and soon there was the crash of shipped water spewing across the deck, and the boat heeled over so that green ocean dashed against the glass for long enough to darken the cabin. Stinnes corrected the steering, more gently this time. He was learning. Best to leave him alone for a few minutes.

I left him for what seemed a long time. By the time I went

across the cabin to pour myself a second drink I had to plant my feet wide apart because the boat was reeling. We'd reached the point where the cool equatorial stream of the Pacific was affected by the very warm summer currents that follow the coast. I held tight to my drink as I went upstairs to where Stinnes was at the controls. The sunlight was behind him, making his sparse hair into a bright halo and edging his white cotton jacket with a rim of gold. There was the muffled sound of Mexican music coming from the little plastic radio.

"Suppose I take you seriously?" said Stinnes, greeting my appearance on the bridge. "Suppose I say, 'Yes I'd like to defect.' Is it some kind of joke? Or are you really able to negotiate?"

"Where are you taking us?" I said with some alarm. "We're out of sight of land." I had to talk loudly to be heard over the noise of the sea and the music from the radio.

"I know what I'm doing," said Stinnes. "Biedermann has radar and sonar and depth-finding gear and every other luxury."

"Does he have anything to cure a fatal drowning?" I said.

"Volkmann says you have some sort of deal," said Stinnes. He glanced down at the instruments and rapped the barometer with his knuckles.

"Are you just crazy about Mexican music, or are you waiting for a hurricane warning?" I said. He turned down the volume of the little radio until it was only a whisper heard faintly against the sound of the wind and the throb of the engines. "There is a deal," I said. "Ready and waiting."

"Why me?" said Stinnes.

I'd asked myself that already and got no answer. "Why not?" I said.

"Your government has not sent you all this way without a motive; a good motive."

No mention of Dicky Cruyer, I noticed. Did that mean that Dicky was unknown to him? It could be useful. "There were other reasons for my being here."

He looked at me and his face was blank, but I knew he didn't believe me. He was suspicious, just as I would have been in his place. There could be no half measures. I would have to work very hard to land this one. He was like me—too damned old and too damned cynical—to fall for anything but innocent sincerity or a cynicism even more profound than his own. "You are targeted," I said. "Starred by London as an exceptional enemy agent."

The sun was brighter now, coming over his shoulder and falling on the instrument panel so that I could see the controls reflected in the lenses of his eyeglasses. "Is that so?" His voice was flat, but I had the feeling he believed me and was proud to be starred by London. This was probably the right way to tackle him. It would be like a love affair, and Stinnes had reached that dangerous age when a man was only susceptible to an innocent little cutie or to an experienced floozy. And the stock in trade of both was flattery.

"London are like that sometimes," I said. "They decide they want someone and then it's rush, rush, rush. I hate this sort of job."

"I want no mention of all this in your signals traffic," said Stinnes. "Especially not in your embassy signals from Mexico City. I insist on that right from the start."

I didn't want him to think London was *too* keen. If Stinnes said no, we might have to snatch him, and I didn't want him prepared for that sort of development. I kept it very cool. "We'll have to act quickly," I said. "If we don't get everything settled in the next week or so, London might lose interest and drop the idea. It's the way they are."

It was fully daylight now and, although the sun had still to eat through the morning haze, there were no clouds. It was going to be a very hot day. The wind was at about eight to ten knots, so that the waves were lengthening and breaking here and there to make scattered white horses. On the westerly horizon I could see two ships. I watched the compass. Was Stinnes going to turn the tables on me? Were they Russian trawlers, waiting for Stinnes to deliver me to the ship's side, with a KGB interrogation team leaning over the rails? Perhaps Stinnes understood what was going through my mind, for he swung the wheel gently to head well south of them. As he changed the heading, an extra big wave broke over the bow and dashed spray so that the air was full of the taste of it. "Your people are clever, Samson . . . is that your true name, Samson?"

"It's my name. Are they clever?"

He smiled a humorless little smile. "I'm forty, and still a major. Slim chance now for a colonel's badges. I'm not a *Wunderkind,* Samson. I won't end up a general with a department to myself and a nice big office in Moscow, and a big car and driver who takes me home each night. Even I have begun to admit that to myself."

"I thought you liked Berlin," I said.

"I've been there long enough. I've had enough of Berlin. I've had enough of sitting in my cramped little house watching West German television advertise all the things my wife wants and can't get." Another wave broke across the bow. He throttled back so that the boat just rode the waves with enough power to hold the heading. The boat slid about, tossed from wave to wave, and I had to grab a rail to hold myself steady. "I'm going to get a divorce," he said, suddenly occupying himself with the controls so that it seemed to be an aside without importance. "Did London know anything about that?"

"No," I said.

"No, of course not. Even my own people don't know yet. The Directorate don't like divorce . . . instability, they call it. Domestic instability. Anything that goes wrong in a marriage is categorized as 'domestic instability'—it can be child beating, wife beating, keeping a mistress, or habitual drunkenness. It's called domestic instability and it gets a black mark. It gets you the sort of black mark that results in long talks with investigating officers, and sometimes leads to a short 'leadership course' with political indoctrination and physical training. Wives of KGB officers get to depend on it, Samson."

"I don't like physical training," I said. Perhaps London are clever, I thought. Perhaps they did know. That's why they were in such a hurry. I wondered if Dicky had been told. I wondered too how many of those black marks Stinnes was eligible for: not child beating—wife beating, possibly, mistress keeping highly likely. He was the sort of man who would attract some women. I looked at that hard unyielding face, smooth like a carefully carved *netsuke* handled by generations of collectors, and darkening as elephant tusk darkens when locked away and deprived of light.

"You wouldn't like this sort of physical training," said Stinnes. "The KGB Field Officers Leadership School is nearly one hundred miles from the nearest town on Sakhalin Island in the Sea of Okhotsk. I went there once when I was a young lieutenant. I was part of a two-man armed escort. It was in September 1964; a captain from my unit had been assigned to the school for the four-month course. He was sent there because when very drunk one night he told a roomful of officers that Nikita Khrushchev was not fit to be prime minister and certainly should not be first secretary of the Soviet Communist Party. It's a grim place, Samson. I was only there two hours, but that was enough for me. Unheated rooms, cold water showers, and 'candidates' have to run everywhere. Only the staff are permitted to walk. Not the sort of place that you or I like. The funny thing was, that a few weeks later Khrushchev was denounced in far stronger terms and replaced by Brezhnev and ousted." Stinnes gave a brief humorless smile. "But the captain wasn't released. He served his full sentence . . . that is to say, he did the whole leadership course. I wouldn't like to be sent there."

"It sounds like a strong argument for marital fidelity," I said.

"Yes, I haven't officially asked for a divorce. I was only thinking about it. But everyone knows that I no longer get along so well with my wife, Inge. I am bored with her and she is bored with me and there is nothing to be done except that

I must get out before I begin to loathe her. Do you understand?" He looked at me. We both knew what had happened
to my wife: she'd become his boss. And he didn't seem like a
man who would enjoy working for a woman boss. I wondered
if that was a part of the real story.

"Have you got any other children?" I asked.

"No, just the boy, eighteen years old. He is at an age when
he realizes how I fall short of the Daddy he once revered. At
first it made me angry, then it made me sad. Now I've come to
see it as the natural progress of youth."

"You married a German," I said.

"I was lonely. Inge was only a few months younger than me.
You know that special sort of magic Berlin girls can wield.
Sunshine, strong beer, short skirts, long lazy evenings, sailing
boats on the Muggelsee. It shouldn't be allowed." Stinnes
laughed, a short dry bitter laugh, as if he still was in love with
her and resented it.

"Coming to the West would solve all your problems," I said.
I didn't want to rush him, any suggestion of haste now could
make him change his mind. Maybe he would come to us, maybe
he was just humoring me, but I knew it was important to keep
pressing forwards. I knew what sort of ideas must be going
through his mind. There would be so many things he would
have to do. There would be good people he'd want to transfer
away so they weren't tainted by his treachery.

"What a wonderful offer. How could anyone resist a future
without problems!"

"It's your life," I said. For a moment I didn't care what he
did, but immediately my professionalism overcame my anger.
It was my job to enroll Erich Stinnes and I would do everything
I could to land him. "But say no and I doubt if London will
come back to you again. It's now or never."

"Very well," said Stinnes. "You tell your people that I said
no. I want that to go to London through your Mexico City
embassy in the usual coding." I nodded and tried not to show
my surprise that the Russians had broken our codes. In future

we'd have to make sure that everything important went to London via Washington and used the NSA's crypto-ciph B machines.

He waited until I grunted my assent.

"I will report an approach. I won't identify you, Samson. I'll make it vague enough for Moscow to think it's some low-grade local agent trying to make a name for himself. But you go back to London and tell whoever is the deskman on this one that they've got a deal."

"What will the timing be?"

"There are things I have to do. I'll need a month."

"Yes," I said. He'd want to get his hands on some secret paperwork, so that he'd have something to bring. He'd want some time with his wife, a last talk with his son, a meal with his family, a drink with his secretary, an evening with old friends. He'd want to imprint them upon his memory. "I understand."

I felt the hot sun on my arm; it was on the starboard bow. Only now did I notice that he'd been turning the helm in tiny expert movements that had brought the boat round until it was heading back home again. Stinnes did everything with that same professional stealth. It made me uneasy.

"My people will be impatient," I warned.

"We all know what deskmen are like. You'll keep them warm?"

"I'll try," I promised. "But you'd better bring something good with you."

"I'm not a beginner, Samson. That's what I need a month to arrange." He got a small black cigar from his top pocket and took his time lighting it. Once he got it well alight he took the cheroot from his mouth and nodded as if confirming something to himself.

If he really intended to come to us, he'd be grabbing as many secret documents as he could find and locking them away somewhere, a Swiss bank vault perhaps. Only a fool would come without having some extras tucked away somewhere. And Stinnes was no fool.

"What sort of material are they looking for?" he asked.

"They'll expect you to break a network," I said.

He thought about it. "Is that what London say?"

"It's what I'm saying. You know they'll expect it. It's what you'd want if you had me in Moscow."

"Yes."

"I'll give you a word of advice," I said. "Don't withdraw a net and then come over to us with a list of people who have left no forwarding address. That would just make everyone bad-tempered, and they'll start to think you're still on salary from Moscow. Understand?"

He blew evil-smelling cigar smoke. "It's a pleasure to do business with you, Samson. You make everything very clear."

"So let me make this clear too. If you try to turn me around, if you try any tricks at all, I'll blow you away."

Chapter 8

BY MIDDAY we'd been waiting nearly three hours, and our plane had still not arrived. Other departures were also delayed. The official explanation was the hurricanes. Mexico City airport was packed with people. There were Indian women clasping sacks of flour and a sequin-suited rock group guarding their amplifiers. All found some way to deal with the interminable delay: mothers suckled babies, boys raced through the concourse on roller skates, a rug peddler—burdened under his wares—systematically pitched his captive audience, tour guides paced resolutely, airline staff yawned, footsore hikers snored, nuns told their rosaries, a tall black man listening to a Sony Walkman swayed rhythmically, and some Swedish school kids were gambling away their last few pesos.

Dicky Cruyer had excess baggage and a parcel of cheap tin decorative masks that he insisted must go as cabin baggage. From where I sat I could see him, focusing all his charm on the girl at the check-in desk. There were no seats available. I was propped on one of Dicky's suitcases talking to Werner. I watched Dicky gesturing at the girl and running his hands back through his curly hair in the way he did when he was being shy and boyish.

"Don't trust him," said Werner.

"Dicky? Don't worry, I won't."

"You know who I mean," said Werner. "Don't trust Stinnes." Werner was sitting on another of Dicky's many cases. He was wearing a *guyavera,* the traditional Mexican shirt that is all pleats and buttons, and with it linen trousers and expensive-looking leather shoes patterned with ventilation holes. Although Werner complained of Mexico's heat and humidity, the climate seemed to suit him. His complexion was such that he tanned easily and he was more relaxed in the sunshine than ever he'd seemed to be in Europe.

"There's nothing to lose," I said.

"For London Central, you mean? Or nothing to lose for you?"

"I'm just doing what London want me to do, Werner . . . 'Theirs not to make reply/ Theirs not to reason why/ Theirs but to do and die . . .' You know how London expect us to work."

"Yes," said Werner who'd had this same conversation with me many times before. "It's always *easier* to do and die than it is to reason why."

"I don't trust him, I don't distrust him," I said as I thought about Werner's warning. "I don't give a damn about Stinnes. I don't begrudge him his opportunity to squeeze a bigger cash payment from the Department than any loyal employee ever got. More money, I'd guess, than the wife and kids of any of the Department's casualties ever collected. But it makes me wonder, Werner. It makes me wonder what the hell it's all about."

"It's the game," said Werner. He too was slumped back against the wall with a plastic cup of warm weak coffee in his hand. "It's nothing to do with virtue and evil, or effort and reward, it's just a game. You know that, Bernie."

"And Stinnes knows how to play it better than we do?"

"It's not a game of skill," said Werner, "it's a game of chance."

"Is there nothing that lights up and says 'tilt' when you cheat?"

"Stinnes isn't cheating. He's just a man in the right place at the right time. He's done nothing to entice London to enroll him."

"What do you make of him, Werner?"

"He's a career KGB officer. We've both seen a million of them. Stinnes holds no surprises for me, Bernie. And, providing you don't trust him, no surprises for you either."

"He didn't ask enough questions," I said. "I've been thinking of that ever since the boat trip. Stinnes didn't ask me any important questions. Not the sort of questions I'd be asking in his place."

"He's a robot," said Werner. "Did you expect him to engage you in a political argument? Did you expect a detailed discussion about the deprivation of the third world?"

"I suppose I did," I admitted.

"Well, this is the right country for anyone looking for political arguments," said Werner. "If ever there was a country poised on the brink of revolution, this is it. Look around; two-thirds of the Mexican population—about fifty million people—are living at starvation level. You've seen the *campesinos* struggling to grow crops in volcanic ash or rock, and bringing to market half a dozen onions or some such pathetic little crop. You've seen them scratching a living here in the city in slums as bad as anywhere in the world. Four out of ten Mexicans never drink milk, two out of ten never eat meat, eggs, or bread. But the Mexican government subsidizes Coca-Cola sales. The official explanation is that Coca-Cola is nutritious." Werner drank some of the disgusting coffee. "And now that the IMF have forced Mexico to devalue the peso, big U.S. companies—such as Xerox and Sheraton—can build factories and hotels here at rock-bottom prices, but sell to hard-currency customers. Inflation goes up. Unemployment figures go up. Taxes go up. Prices go up. But wages go down. How would you like it if you were Mexican?" It was quite a speech for Werner.

"Did Stinnes say that?"

"Haven't you been listening to me? Stinnes is a career KGB officer. Stinnes doesn't give a damn about the Mexicans and their problems, except how and when it affects his career prospects. I started talking about all this to him at the club one evening. Stinnes knows nothing about Mexico. He hasn't even had the regular briefing that all East European diplomatic services give to their personnel."

"Why?" I said.

"Why?" said Werner irritably, thinking I merely wanted to change the subject. "How could I know?"

"Think about it, Werner. The first thing it indicates is that he came here at short notice. Even then, knowing the KGB, they would have arranged for him to have political indoctrination here in Mexico City."

Werner shifted his weight uncomfortably on Dicky's suitcase and looked around to see if there was anywhere else to sit. There wasn't—in fact, the whole place was getting more and more crowded. Now there was a large group of young people carrying bright orange shoulder bags that announced them to be a choir from New Zealand. They were seating themselves all along the corridor. I hoped they wouldn't start singing. "I suppose you're right," said Werner.

"I am right," I said. "And I'll tell you something else. The complete absence of political indoctrination suggests to me that Stinnes is not here to run agents into California, nor to supervise Biedermann's funneling of Moscow money to local organizations."

"Don't keep me in suspense," said Werner wearily.

"I haven't got the answer, Werner. I don't know what Stinnes is doing here. I don't even know what *I'm* doing here. Stinnes could be positively identified without having me along."

"London didn't send you along so that you could identify Stinnes," said Werner. "London sent you along so that Stinnes could identify you."

"No anagrams, Werner. Keep it simple for me."

"What do you think was the first thing that came into his mind the other night when I started telling him about freezers, videos, and the acceleration a Porsche 924 turbo gives you from a standing start?"

"Entrapment?"

"Well, of course. He was terrified that I was a KGB employee who was going to provide the evidence that would put him into a Siberian penal battalion for twenty years."

"Ummm. But he could be sure that I was an SIS agent from London because he'd actually had me under arrest in East Berlin. I suppose you're right, Werner. I suppose Bret had that all figured out."

"Bret Rensselaer, was it? Of all the people in London Central, he's the most cunning one. And right now he's very keen to prove the Department needs him."

"Dicky is frightened that Bret will get the German desk," I said.

"*Stuhlpolonaise,*" said Werner.

"Exactly. Musical chairs." Werner's use of the German word called to mind the prim formality and the slow rhythm of the promenading couples that exactly described London Central's dance when some big reshuffle was due. "And Bret has sent Dicky marching four thousand miles away from the only chair, and Dicky wants to get back to London before the music stops."

"But he doesn't want to return without news of a great success," said Werner.

"You see that, do you," I said admiringly. Werner didn't

miss much. "Yes, Bret has contrived a quandary that alarms even Dicky. If he waits here long enough to land Stinnes, Bret will be the man who congratulates him and sends him off on another assignment. On the other hand, if Dicky rushes back there without a conclusion to the Stinnes operation, someone is going to say that Dicky is not up to the job."

"But you're both going back," said Werner. He looked round the crowded lounge. Outside, the apron was empty and the regular afternoon rainstorm was in full fury. There was not much evidence that anyone was going anywhere.

"I'm now the file officer. Dicky is writing a report that will explain the way in which he has brought the Stinnes operation to the brink of a successful conclusion before handing everything over to me."

"He is a crafty little bastard," said Werner.

"Now tell me something I don't know."

"And if Stinnes doesn't come over, Dicky will say you messed it up."

"Go to the top of the class, Werner. You're really getting the hang of it."

"But I think there's only a slight chance that we'll get Stinnes over."

"Why?" I agreed with Werner but I wanted to hear his views.

"He's still frightened, for one thing. If Stinnes really trusted you, he wouldn't tell you to send a negative signal to London. He'd let you tell London anything you liked."

"Don't tell Dicky I told you about the compromised signal traffic," I said. "He'll say it's a breach of security."

"It is a breach of security," said Werner. "Strictly speaking, I shouldn't be told that sort of top-grade item unless it's directly concerned with my work."

"My God, Werner, am I glad you don't have the German desk in London! I think you'd shop me if you thought I was breaking security."

"Maybe I would," said Werner complacently. I grabbed

him by the throat and pretended to throttle him. It was a spectacle that interested one of the nuns enough for her to nudge her companion and nod towards me. I gave them both a sinister scowl and Werner put his tongue out and rolled his eyes.

After I'd released Werner and let him drink some more of that awful coffee, I said, "You said Stinnes knows I'm kosher on account of interrogating me."

"That could be a double ploy," said Werner. "If you were really working for Moscow then you would be quite happy to let yourself get arrested in East Berlin. Then you'd be perfectly placed to trap Stinnes."

"But Stinnes isn't important enough for Moscow to play out that sort of operetta."

"Stinnes probably thinks he is important enough. It's human, isn't it? We all think we're important enough for anything."

Werner could be exasperating. "That's what Hollywood calls 'moronic logic,' Werner. It's the sort of nit-picking insanity that can't be faulted but is only too obviously stupid."

"So explain why it's stupid."

I took a deep breath and said, "Because if Moscow had a well-placed agent in London whose identity was so closely guarded that Stinnes could not possibly suspect him, then Moscow would not bring him to Berlin and get him arrested just to get the confidence of Stinnes so that months later in Mexico City he could be enticed into agreeing to a defection plan. I mean . . . ask yourself, Werner."

He smiled self-consciously. "You're right, Bernie. But Stinnes will continue to be suspicious, you mark my words."

"Sure, but he'll be suspicious of London and whether those tricky deskmen will keep their promises. He won't be worrying if I'm a KGB plant. A man like Stinnes can probably recognize a KGB operator at one hundred paces just as we can recognize one of our people."

"Talking of recognizing one of our own at one hundred

paces, Dicky is heading this way," said Werner. "Is the man with him SIS?"

Dicky Cruyer was still wearing his Hollywood clothes; today it was blue-striped seersucker trousers, sea island cotton sport shirt, and patent Gucci shoes. He was carrying a small leather pouch that was not, Dicky said, a handbag, or anything like one.

Dicky had his friend from the embassy in tow. They'd been at Balliol together and they made no secret of their intense rivalry. Despite their being the same age, Henry Tiptree looked younger than Dicky. Perhaps this was because of the small and rather sparse mustache that he was growing, or his thin neck, bony chin, and the awkward figure he cut in his Hong Kong tropical suit and the tightly knotted old school tie.

Dicky told me how his friend Henry had been made counselor at the very early age of thirty-eight and was now working hard to reach Grade 3. But the diplomatic service is littered with brilliant counselors of all ages, and a large proportion of them get shunted off to the Institute for Strategic Studies or given a fellowship at All Souls, Oxford, where they can write a lot of twaddle about Soviet aims and intentions in East Europe, while people like me and Werner actually deal with them.

"Henry has arranged everything about the baggage," said Dicky.

"There was nothing to arrange about my baggage," I said. "I checked it through when we first got here."

Dicky ignored my retort and said, "It will go air freight. But because we have first-class tickets they'll put it on the same plane we're on."

"And which plane is that?" I asked.

Henry looked at his watch and said, "They say it's coming in now."

"You don't believe that, do you?" said Dicky. "Ye gods, these airline buggers tell lies more glibly than even the diplomatic service."

"Haw, haw," said Henry dutifully. "But I think this time it's probably true. There are lots of delays at this time of year, but eventually they come lumbering in. Three hours is about par for the course. That's why I thought I'd better be here to see you off." Henry pronounced it "orrf"; he had that sort of ripe English accent that he'd need for becoming an ambassador.

"Plus the fact that you had to be here because it's bag day," said Dicky. Henry smiled.

Werner said, "Bag day?"

"The courier with the diplomatic bag is coming in on this plane," I explained.

"Even so, your presence is much appreciated, Henry," Dicky told him. "I'll make sure the prime minister's private secretary hears about the cooperation you gave us." They both laughed at Dicky's little joke, but there was a promise of some undefined help when the opportunity came. Balliol men were like that; or so Dicky always said.

I could see that Werner was eyeing Henry with interest, trying to decide whether he was actually employed by the SIS within the embassy staff. It seemed possible. I winked at Werner. He grinned as he realized that I'd known what was in his mind. But we untutored men were like that; or so I always said.

"Dicky says that you're the man who holds the Department together," said Henry.

"It's not easy," I said.

Dicky, who had expected me to deny that I held the Department together, said, "Henry loaned us the car."

"Thanks, Henry," I said.

"I don't know how you managed with that damned air-conditioning not working," said Henry. "But I suspect you chaps are going to charge full Hertz rates on your expenses, eh?"

"Not Dicky," I said.

"Haw, haw," said Henry.

Dicky changed the subject hurriedly. "Strawberries and freshly caught salmon," said Dicky. "This is the time to be in England, Henry. You can keep the land of tacos and refried beans."

"Don't be a sadist, Dicky," said the man from the embassy. "I'm hoping my transfer comes through. Else I might be stuck here until Christmas or New Year. I have no chance of leave."

"You shouldn't have joined," said Dicky.

"I mustn't complain. I had an enjoyable six months learning the lingo and I get up to Los Angeles now and again. Mind you, these Mexicans are a rum crowd. It doesn't take much to make them awfully cross." Henry said "crorss."

"No matter. You won't be here forever. And now you're Grade 4 you're certain to end your career with a K," said Dicky enviously. It was Dicky's special grievance that equivalently graded SIS employees could not count on such knighthoods or even lesser honors. Everything depended upon where you ended up.

"As long as I don't spill drinks over the president's wife or start a war or something." He laughed again.

Quietly I asked Dicky if he'd told the embassy about their intercepted signals.

"Ye gods," said Dicky. "Bernie has just reminded me of something for your very private ear. Something for your Head of Station's very private ear, in fact."

Henry raised an eyebrow. Head of Station was the senior SIS officer in the embassy.

Dicky said, "Strictly off the record, Henry old bean, we have reason to believe that the Russians are listening to your Piccolo machinery and have learned to read the music."

"I say," said Henry.

"I suggest he tells your Head of Mission immediately. But he must make it clear that it's only a suspicion."

"I don't get to talk to the boss all that often, Dicky. The top brass stagger off to Acapulco every chance they get." He went to the window and said, "It's coming in now. She'll turn round quickly. Better get your luggage checked through."

"It might be a hoax," said Dicky. "But we hope to be in a position to confirm or deny within a couple of weeks. If there's

anything to it, you'll hear officially through the normal channels."

"You London Central people really do see life," said Henry.
"Have you really been doing a James Bond caper, Dicky? Have
you been crossing swords with the local Russkies?"

"Mum's the word," said Dicky. "We'd better get some of
these airline chappies to haul this baggage over to the check-
in."

"But where will we sit then?" said ever practical Werner.

Dicky ignored this question and snapped his fingers at a
passing slave, who readily and instantly responded by tipping
Werner off his perch and grabbing Dicky's other cases to swing
onto his shoulder.

Dicky stroked his expensive baggage as if he didn't like to
see it go. "Those three are very fragile—*muy frágil. Comprende
usted?*"

"Sure thing," said the porter. "No problem, buddy."

"So those Russian buggers are reading the Piccolo radio
traffic," mused Henry. "Well, that might explain a lot of
things."

"For instance?" said Dicky, counting his cases as the porter
heaved them onto a trolley.

"Just little things," said Henry vaguely. "But I'd say your
tip-off is no hoax."

"One up for Mr. Stinnes," said Werner.

The TV monitor flashed a gate number for our flight, and
we hurriedly said good-bye to Henry and Werner so that Dicky
could follow closely behind the porter to be sure his cases
didn't go astray.

"HENRY did Modern Languages," said Dicky once we were
airborne and heading home with a glass of champagne in our
fists and a smiling stewardess offering us small circular pieces
of cold toast adorned with fish eggs. "He was a damned fine bat,
and Henry's parties were famous, but he's not very brainy and

he wasn't exactly a hard worker. He got this job because he knows all the right people. To tell you the truth, I never thought he'd stick to the old diplomatic grind. It's not like Henry to have a regular job and say yes sir and no sir to everyone in sight. Poor sod, sweating out his time in that hellhole."

"Yes, poor Henry," I said.

"He's desperately keen to get into our show, but quite honestly, Bernard, I don't think he's right for us, do you?"

"From what you say I think he's exactly right for us."

"Do you?" said Dicky.

Dicky had arranged everything the way he liked it. He'd put his three fragile parcels onto a vacant seat and secured them with the safety belt. He'd taken off his shoes and put on the slippers he'd taken from his briefcase. He'd swallowed his motion sickness tablets and made sure the Alka-Seltzer and aspirin were where he could find them easily. He'd read the safety leaflet and checked the position of the emergency exits and reached under his seat to be sure that the advertised life jacket was really there. "These airline blighters speak their own language," said Dicky. "Have you noticed that? Stewardesses are hostesses; it makes you wonder whether to call the stewards 'hosts.' Safety belts are lap straps, and emergency exits are safety exits. Who thought up all that double-talk?"

"It must have been the same PR man who renamed the War Office the Ministry of Defence."

I held up my glass so that the stewardess could pour more champagne. Dicky put his hand over his glass. "We've a long journey ahead," he said with an admonitory note in his voice.

"Sounds like a good reason to have another glass of champagne," I said.

Dicky put down his glass and slapped his thigh lightly, like a chairman bringing a meeting to order, and said, "Well, now I've got you to myself at last, perhaps we can talk shop."

The only reason we'd not spent a lot of time talking shop was because Dicky had spent every available moment eating, drinking, shopping, sight-seeing, and extending his influence.

Now he was going to find out what work I'd been doing so that he'd be able to persuade his superiors that he'd been working his butt off. "What do you want to know, Dicky?"

"What are the chances that comrade Stinnes will come over to us?"

"You're skipping the easy ones, are you?"

"I know you hate making guesses, but what do you think will happen? You've actually met with Stinnes. What sort of fellow is he? You've handled this sort of defection business before, haven't you."

I didn't hate making guesses at all; I just hated confiding them to Dicky since he so enjoyed reminding me of the ones I got wrong. I said, "Not with a really experienced KGB official, I haven't. The defectors I've dealt with have been less important."

"Stinnes is only a major. You're making him sound like a member of the Politburo. I seem to remember you were involved with that colonel . . . the air attaché who dithered and dithered and finally got deported before we could get him."

"Rank for rank, you're right. But Stinnes is very experienced and very tough. If we get him we'll have a very good source. He will keep the debriefing panel scribbling notes for months and months and give us some good data and first-class assessments. But our chances of getting him are not good."

"You told me he said yes," said Dicky.

"He's bound to say yes just to hear what we say."

"Is it money?" said Dicky.

"I can't believe that money will play a big part in his decision. Men such as Stinnes are very thoroughly indoctrinated. It's always very difficult for such people to make the change over to our sort of society."

"He's a hard-nose Communist, you mean?"

"Only inasmuch as he knows he mustn't rock the boat. I'd be surprised to find he's a real believer." I drank my champagne. Dicky waited for me to speak again. I said, "Stinnes is a narrow-minded bigot. He's one of a top-level elite in a totalitarian state where there are no agonizing discussions about capital punishment, or demos about pollution of the environment or the moral uncertainties of having atomic weapons. A KGB major like Stinnes can barge into the office of a commanding general without knocking. Here in the West no one has the sort of power that he enjoys."

"But we're offering him a nice comfortable life. And from what you say about him wanting a divorce, the offer comes at exactly the right time."

"Giving up such power will not be easy. As a defector he'll be a nobody. He's probably seen defectors and the way they live in the Soviet Union. He'll have no illusions about what it will be like."

"How can you compare the life of a defector going to the East with that of a defector coming to the West? All they have to offer is a perverted ideology and a medieval social system based on privilege and obedience. We have a free society; a free press, freedom to protest, freedom to say anything we like."

"Stinnes has spent a long time in the upper layers of an authoritarian society. He won't want to protest or demonstrate against government—whatever its creed—and he'll have precious little sympathy for those who do."

"Then give him a handful of cash and take him round the shops and show him the material benefits that come from free enterprise and competition."

"Stinnes isn't the sort of man who will sell his soul for a mess of hi-fi components and a microwave oven," I said.

"Sell his soul?" said Dicky indignantly.

"Don't turn this into a political debate, Dicky. You asked me what chance do we stand, and I'm telling you what I think is in his mind."

"So what sort of chance *do* we stand?" persisted Dicky. "Fifty-fifty?"

"Not better anyway," I said.

"I'll tell the old man fifty-fifty," said Dicky as he mentally ticked off that question. I don't know why I tried to explain things to Dicky. He preferred yes or no answers. Explanations confused him.

"And what about this Biedermann chap?"

"I don't know."

"He's as rich as Croesus. I looked him up when I got to Los Angeles."

"I can't see how he can be important to us, so how can he be important to Stinnes? That's what puzzles me."

"I'll put him into my report," said Dicky. Although it sounded like a statement of intent, it was Dicky's way of asking me to okay it.

"By all means. I've got the list of people he forwarded the money to. You could probably get one of the bright young probationers to build that into something that sounded impressive."

"Are we going to do anything about Biedermann?"

"There's not much we can do," I said doubtfully, "except keep an eye on him, and rough him up from time to time to let him know he's not forgotten."

"Gently does it," said Dicky. "A man like that could make trouble for us."

"I've known him since I was a kid," I said. "He's not going to make trouble for us unless he thinks he can get away with it."

"Getting Stinnes is the important thing," said Dicky. "Biedermann is nothing compared with the chance of bringing Stinnes over to us."

"I'll stroke my lucky rabbit's foot," I said.

"If we do manage to land Stinnes, you'll get all the credit for it."

"Will I?" I said. It seemed unlikely.

"That's one of the things I told Bret before we left London. I told him that this was really your operation. You let Bernard handle things his way, I told him. Bernard's got a lot riding on this one."

"And what did Bret say to that?" I found that if you scraped the ancient airline caviar off the little discs of toast, the toast didn't taste too bad.

"Have you upset Bret?"

"I'm always upsetting him."

"You've got a lot riding on this one, Bernard. You need Bret. You need all the help you can get. I'm right behind you all the way, of course, but if Bret takes over my desk you'll get no support from him."

"Thanks, Dicky," I said doubtfully. It was just Dicky's way of getting me to help him in his power struggle against Bret, but I was flattered to think that Dicky thought I had enough clout to make any difference.

"You know what I'm talking about, don't you, Bernard?"

"Sure," I said, although in fact I didn't know. I settled back in my seat and looked at the menu. But from the corner of my eye I could see Dicky wrapping his fountain pen in a Kleenex tissue although we were already at 35,000 feet and if his pen was going to leak it would have leaked already.

"Yes," said Dicky. "This one will be make or break for you, Bernard." He laid the bandaged pen to rest in his handbag, like a little Egyptian mummy that was to stay in its tomb for a thousand years. "Thank God there's no in-flight movie," he said. "I hate in-flight movies, don't you?"

"Yes," I said. It was one of the very few things upon which Dicky and I could have unreserved agreement.

Now that we were above the clouds, the sunlight was blinding. Dicky, seated at the window, pulled down the tinted shield. "You don't want to read or anything, do you?"

I looked at Dicky and shook my head. He smiled, and I wondered what sort of game he was playing with all his talk of this being my operation. He'd certainly taken his time before revealing this remarkable aspect of our jaunt to me.

WE REACHED London midmorning. The sun was shining in a clear blue sky, but there was a chilly wind blowing. It was

Sunday and in response to two telex messages and a phone call he'd made from Mexico, Dicky had arranged for a car to meet us. We loaded it to the point where its suspension was groaning and went to Dicky's house. Once there I accepted Dicky's offer to go inside for a drink.

Dicky's wife was waiting for us with a chilled bottle of Sancerre in the ice bucket and coffee on the warmer. Daphne was an energetic woman in her early thirties. I found her especially attractive standing there in the kitchen surrounded by wine and food. Daphne had radically changed her image; floral pinafores and granny glasses were out, and pale yellow boiler suits were in. Her hairstyle had changed too, cut in a severe pageboy style with fringe so that she looked like the art student Dicky had married so long ago. "And Bernard darling. What a lovely surprise." She had the loud voice and upper-class accent that go with weekends in large unheated country houses, where everyone talks about horses and reads Dick Francis paperbacks.

Daphne was in the middle of preparing lunch. She had a big bowl on the table in front of her and a spring scale upon which half a pound of warm butter was being weighed. Her hands were covered in flour and she was wiping them on a towel that bore a printed picture of the Eiffel Tower. She picked up a collection of bracelets and bangles and slipped them all onto her wrist before embracing Dicky.

"You're early, darling," she said as she kissed him and gave me a peck too.

Dicky brushed flour from his shirt and said, "The plane arrived on time. I didn't allow for that."

She asked Dicky if he wanted coffee or wine, but she didn't ask me. She took a glass from the cupboard and the opened bottle of chilled wine from the ice bucket and poured me a generous measure. It was delicious.

Dicky, rummaging through the kitchen cupboard, said, "Where are the blue Spode cups and saucers?"

"They're in the dishwasher. We only have three left now. You'll have to use a mug."

Dicky sighed the way he did when one of the clerks returned to him top-secret papers he'd left in the copying machine. Then he poured himself a mug of black coffee and we sat down round the kitchen table.

"I'm sorry we can't go into the lounge," said Daphne. "It's out of use for the time being." She looked up at the kitchen clock before deciding it was okay to pour a glass of wine for herself.

"Daphne's left her ad agency," said Dicky. "I didn't tell you, did I? They lost the breakfast food account and had to cut staff. They offered Daphne a golden handshake—five thousand pounds. Not bad, eh?" Dicky was pressing his ears and gulping, the way he always did after a flight.

"What are you doing now, Daphne?" I asked.

Dicky answered for her. "She's stripping. She's gone into it with another girl from the agency." Daphne smiled the sort of smile that showed she'd heard this joke before, but she let Dicky squeeze it dry. "There's money in stripping, Daphne says." Dicky smiled broadly and put his arm on his wife's shoulder.

"Furniture," said Dicky. "The lounge is stacked to the ceiling with antique furniture. They'll strip the paint off it and polish it up and sell it for a fortune."

"Not *antique* furniture," said Daphne. "Bernard already regards us as philistines. I don't want him to think I'm a complete barbarian, ruining antiques. It's secondhand odds and ends, kitchen chairs and tables and so on. No use going round the little shops in Camden Town looking for it. Liz and I go off into the country banging on doors. It's rather fun. You meet the oddest people. Apparently you just dip the furniture into caustic soda and the paint falls off. We're starting that next week when I've got some gloves to protect my hands."

"I tried it once," I said. "It was a wooden fireplace. It fell to pieces. It was only fifty years of paintwork that was holding it together."

"Oh, don't say that, Bernard," said Daphne. She laughed. "You're discouraging me." She poured more wine for me. She didn't seem at all discouraged.

"Take no notice of Bernard," said Dicky. "He can't fix an electric plug without fusing all the lights."

"We won't be selling the furniture as perfect," said Daphne.

"It's what all the newlyweds are looking for," said Dicky. "At least it's one of the things." He gave his wife a wink and an affectionate hug. "And it looks good. I mean that. It looks very good. Once the girls get decent premises, they'll make a fortune, you mark my words. They were going to call the shop The Strip Joint, but now we hear someone is using that already."

"You're not very tanned, Dicky," she said, looking closely at his face. "Considering where you've been. I thought you'd come back much more tanned than that. Neither is Bernard," she added, glancing at me.

"We've been working, old thing, not sunning. Right, Bernard?" He picked up the cork from the wine Daphne had served me and sniffed at it.

"Right, Dicky."

"And I saw Henry Tiptree, darling. You remember Henry. He was at Balliol with me."

"The one who left the BBC because they were all poofs?"

"No, darling—Henry. Tall, thin, reddish hair. Looks a bit of a twit. His cousin is a Duke. Henry's the one who always used to bring you those huge boxes of Belgian handmade chocolates, remember?"

"No," said Daphne.

"And you always took the chocolates to your mother. Then Henry was posted off somewhere and you made me buy them for her. Belgian chocolates. They cost me a fortune."

"Yes, and then when we got married you told her the shop didn't sell them anymore and you got her Black Magic instead."

"Well, they cost an absolute fortune," said Dicky. "Anyway, Henry is in Mexico now and let us borrow his car. And I managed to get a trip to Los Angeles and I got you everything on your list except the pillowcases from Robinson's. They didn't have the exact color of the sample you gave me. They were more purple than mauve, so I didn't buy them."

"You are sweet, darling," said Daphne. "He is so sweet," she told me.

"I know," I said.

"And I got a dozen of those masks the Mexicans make out of old tin cans, and I got six silver-plated bracelets in the market. So that's the Christmas present list taken care of."

"I ordered a whole salmon for Thursday," said Daphne. "But I can't think of an extra girl for Bernard."

"I should have told you," said Dicky, turning to me. "You're invited for dinner Thursday. Are you free?"

"I imagine I am," I said. "Thanks."

"And don't worry about an extra girl for him," said Dicky. "He's having it away with one of the girls in the office." There was a note of bitterness in Dicky's voice. Daphne detected it too. She looked at him sharply, for Dicky's affections had wandered lately and Daphne had discovered it. She drained her wine glass.

"How nice," Daphne said icily, pouring herself another drink. "What's her name, Bernard?"

"Her name is Gloria," said Dicky before I replied.

"Is that the one you wanted as your secretary?" said Daphne. She stood with the bottle in her hand waiting for the reply.

"No, no, no," said Dicky. "It was Bret who wanted to foist her on to me but I wasn't having her." Having tried to appease Daphne, he turned to me and said, "No offense to you, old man. I'm sure she's a very nice girl."

"That's perfect," said Daphne. She poured me some more wine. "It will be nice to meet her. I remember Dicky saying she was a wonderful typist." I could tell that Daphne was still not totally convinced of Dicky's innocence.

"She'll come to dinner, your friend Gloria?" Dicky asked, watching me carefully.

"Gloria? Oh, of course she will," I said. "She'll go anywhere for a free meal."

"That's not very gallant of you, Bernard," said Daphne.

"We'll be here," I heard myself saying. I don't know why I say such things, except that Dicky always brings out the worst in me. I hardly knew Gloria. I'd only spoken to her twice and then it was just to tell her to hurry up with my typing.

Chapter 9

IT WAS good to be back in London again. First I opened the shutters in every room and let in the afternoon sunlight. I just couldn't get used to going home to a dark silent house. It seemed such a short time ago that it was echoing with the sound of the children, Nanny, and Fiona, my wife.

For lunch I made myself a cup of tea and balanced the contents of a tin of sardines on two very stale whole meal biscuits. It was hot and airless in the top floor room I used as a study. I opened the window and let in the sounds of London on a Sunday afternoon. I could hear the distant cries of children playing in the street, and the recorded carillon of an ice cream peddler. I phoned the office and told them I was home. The duty clerk sounded tired and bored but I resisted his attempt to engage me in conversation about the climate of Mexico at this time of year.

While eating my sardines I opened the stack of mail. Apart from bills for gas, electricity, and wine, most of the mail was colored advertising brochures: headwaiters leered at credit cards, famous chefs offered a "library" of cookbooks, pigskin wallets came free with magazine subscriptions, and there was a chance to hear all the Beethoven symphonies as I'd never heard them before. On my desk pad the Portuguese cleaning lady—Mrs. Dias—had penciled a list of people who'd phoned during her daily visits. Her handwriting was rather uncertain but I recognized no one there I felt like phoning except my mother. I called her and chatted. I had a word with the children too. They seemed happy enough, but I could hear the nanny prompting them from time to time.

"Did you like it in Mexico?" said Sally.

"It was very hot," I said.

"Grandma said you'd take us to the seaside when you got back."

"Is that where you want to go?"

"You've been away a long time, Daddy."

"I'll take you to the seaside."

"When?"

"As soon as I can."

"Billy said you'd say that."

"I'm sorry," I said. "I'm a rotten father."

"Are we coming home?"

"Yes, very soon."

IT WAS only after I'd showered and changed my clothes that I noticed the cream-colored envelope propped in front of the clock. Mrs. Dias would naturally think of the clock as the place to which the human eye most readily returned.

Phone me home or office as soon as you return. Many matters to discuss. David.

It had been delivered by hand. The envelope bore a bright red "Urgent" sticker and the message was written in ink on a heavy handmade paper that matched the envelope. I recognized the stationery even without the engraved address, and the artistic picture of the house that adorned it. The prospect of a discussion with my father-in-law, Mr. David Timothy Kimber-Hutchinson, philanthropist, philosopher, tycoon, and Fellow of the Royal Society of Arts, was not my idea of a welcome home.

But I couldn't think of any excuse for avoiding it, so I phoned and agreed to drive down to him without delay.

His house was built on a tree-covered hillside not far from the place where the ancient Roman highway of Stane Street surmounted the Downs. It was a Jacobean mansion, so restored over the ages that very little of the original sixteenth-century building remained. But priority had been given to the corporeal things of life, so that the roof never leaked and the plumbing, the heating, and the electricity supply always provided a level of comfort rarely encountered in English country houses.

Sometimes I wondered how much money went through his hands for him to be able to run this place with its desirable living accommodations for the servants, a self-contained wing for his guests, and heated stabling for his horses. I parked my battered Ford between Kimber-Hutchinson's silver Rolls and his wife's Jaguar. The Kimber-Hutchinsons wouldn't have a foreign car. It wasn't simply a matter of patriotism, the old man once told me, it would upset some of his customers. Poor fellow, he needed handmade shoes because of his "awkward feet" and Savile Row suits because he wasn't lucky enough to have the figure for ready-made ones. Cheap wines played havoc with his stomach so he drank expensive ones, and because he couldn't fit into economy-size airline seats he was forced to go everywhere first class. Poor David, he envied people like me; he was always telling me so.

David—he liked me to call him David, "father-in-law" being too specific, "father" too inaccurate, "Mr. Kimber-Hutchinson" too cumbersome, and "Kimber" a form of address reserved for his intimates—was waiting for me in the studio. The studio was a luxuriously converted barn. At one end there was a huge north-facing window and an easel where he liked to stand and paint watercolors that were snapped up at good prices by executives of the companies with which he did business. Under the skylight there was a large wooden rostrum that was said to have come from the Paris studio of Maillol, a sculptor who'd devoted his life to loving portrayals of the female nude. I'd once asked David what he used it for but got only the vaguest of answers.

"Come in and sit down, Bernard old chap." He was working on a painting when I got there, but he was not at the easel. He was seated at a small table, a drawing board resting on his knees while he penciled in the outlines of a landscape with horses. On the table there were half a dozen enlarged photos of the same view, photos of horses and a sheet of tracing paper from which he'd worked. "You've discovered my little secret," he said without looking up from his sketch. "I always start off from photographs. No sense in not using all the help you can get. Michelangelo would have used a camera when doing the Sistine Chapel ceiling had he got the chance."

Since David Kimber-Hutchinson showed no sign of revealing more about Michelangelo's frustrated technological aspirations, I grunted and sat down while he finished drawing the horse. Although it was a faithful reproduction of the horse in the photo, David's traced drawing of it looked wooden and stunted. He was obviously aware of this, for he was redrawing the outline to extend its legs but that didn't seem to improve it.

He was wearing a dark blue artist's smock over his yellow cashmere rollneck and riding breeches. His face was flushed. I guessed he'd just got back from a canter over the Downs. It was rather as if he'd arranged things so that I would see him tracing his pictures. Perhaps he thought I would admire such acquired trickery more than mere talent. A man could not take credit for talent in the way he could for cunning.

Eventually he abandoned his attempt and put the pencil down on the table in front of him. "I can never draw horses," he said. "It's just not fair. No artist loved horses as I do, or knew as much about them. But even when I use photos I can't damn well draw them. It's not fair."

I'd never heard him appeal to equity before. Usually he upheld the ultimate justice of market forces and even the survival of the fittest. "Perhaps it's because you trace photos," I said. "Maybe you should trace paintings."

He looked at me, trying to decide whether to take offense, but my face was blank and he said, "I might try that. Trace a Stubbs or something, just to get some idea of the trade secrets. Ummm. It's all tricks, you know. A Royal Academy painter admitted that to me once. Painting is just learning a set of tricks, just like playing the stock exchange."

"They are tricks I will never master," I admitted.

"Easy enough to do, Bernard. Easy enough to do." He took off his artist's smock and smiled. He liked to hear that his achievements were beyond other men; especially he liked to be praised about his skills with horses. He was up every morning grooming his horses, and he endured the long drive to his London office for the sake of seeing his horses. More than once he'd told me that he liked horses better than he liked people. "They never lie to you, horses," he said. "They never try to swindle you."

He spoke without looking up from his board. "So you're still driving that old Ford," he said. "I thought you were going to get a Volvo."

"I canceled the order," I said. "I don't need a big car now."

"And a big car costs money, more than you can afford," he said with that directness that you could always count upon. "You should see the bills I pay on that Rolls. I had to replace the fire extinguisher last month, and that cost me seventy-eight pounds."

"It might be worth that if you are on fire," I said.

"Have a drink, Bernard. It's a tiring drive from London. How did you come, Kingston bypass? Full of weekend drivers, was it? 'Murder mile' they call it, that bit south of Kingston Vale. I've seen a dozen cars crunched together on that stretch of road. The lights change at Robin Hood Gate and they go mad."

"Coming in this direction it wasn't too bad," I said.

He went over to an old cupboard that contained jars full of brushes and tubes of paint and bottles of turpentine and linseed oil for the times when he worked in oil colors. From a compartment in the cupboard he got a glass and a bottle of drink. "You're a whiskey and soda man, as I remember. Lots of soda and lots of whiskey." He laughed and poured a huge Scotch. He had me summed up nicely. "Teachers all right?" He handed it to me without waiting for a reply. "No ice over here."

"Thanks." It was a cheap tumbler, not the Waterford he used at his dinner table. This David who painted here in his studio was a different David, an artist, a plain man with earthy pleasures and simple tastes.

"Yes," he said. "A big car is no use to you now that you're on your own. The big house will be a burden too. I've scribbled out some figures to show you."

"Have you," I said.

He got a piece of paper from the table and sank down on the sofa, studying the piece of paper as if he'd never seen it before. "You bought the house four years ago and property has been sticky ever since then. I warned you about that at the time, as I remember. The way the market is now, you'll be lucky to get your money back." He looked at me.

"Really," I said.

"And when you take into account inflation and loss of earnings on capital, it's been a bad investment. But you'll have to grin and bear it, I'm afraid. The important thing is to reduce your outgoings. Get on to a house agent first thing in the morning, Bernard. Get that house on the market. And find yourself a small service flat—bedroom, sitting room, and a kitchen, that's all you need. In fact, I wonder if you really need a kitchen." When I didn't respond, he said, "I've jotted down the phone numbers of a couple of house agents I do business with. You don't want to go to the first people you happen upon. Too many Jews in that line of business." A smile. "Oh, I forgot, you like Jews, don't you."

"No more than I like Scotsmen or Saudi Arabians. But I always suspect that whatever is being done to Jews this week, is likely to be done to me next week. In any case, I've decided to hang on to the house. At least for the time being."

"That would be absurd, Bernard. You'll have only your salary in future. You won't have Fiona's trust fund, the children's trust funds, nor Fiona's salary."

"The trust funds were used solely for Fiona and the children," I pointed out to him.

"Of course, of course," said David. "But the fact remains that your household will have far less money. And certainly not enough to keep up a rather smart house in the west end."

"If I moved into a service flat there would be no room for the children."

"I was coming to that, Bernard. The children—and I think you will agree unreservedly about this—are the most important single factor in this whole tragic business."

"Yes," I said.

He looked at me. "I think I'll have a drink myself," he said. He got up and went to the cupboard and poured himself a gin and tonic with plenty of tonic. "And let me do something about yours too, Bernard." He took my glass and refilled it. After he'd sipped his drink he started again, but this time from another angle. "I'm a socialist, Bernard. You know that, I've never made a secret of it. My father worked hard all his life and died at his workbench. Died at his workbench. That is something I can't forget."

I nodded. I'd heard it all before. But I knew that the workbench was to David's father what David's easel was to him. David's father owned half of a factory that employed five hundred people.

"But I've never had any dealings with Communists, Bernard. And when I heard that Fiona had been working for the Russians all these years, I said to my wife, 'She's no daughter of ours.' I said it just like that. I said, 'She's no daughter of ours,' and I meant it. The next morning I sent for my lawyer and I disowned her. I wrote and told her so; I suppose the lawyers handling her trust fund have some sort of forwarding address . . ." He looked at me.

"I don't know," I said. "I haven't contacted them. I daresay the Department has contacted them, but I don't know anything about a forwarding address."

"Whether she'll ever get my letter or not I don't know." He came over to where I was sitting and he added in a voice lowered and throbbing with emotion, ". . . And personally, Bernard, I don't care. She's no daughter of mine. Not after this."

"I think you were going to say something about the children," I prompted him.

"Yes, I was. Fiona has gone for good, Bernard. She's never coming back. If you're holding on to the house in the hope that Fiona comes back to you, forget it."

"If she came back," I said, "she'd face a very long term in prison."

"Yes, I thought of that," he said. "Dammit, that would be the final disgrace. Her mother would die of shame, Bernard. Thank God the story was never picked up by the newspapers. As it is, I've cut back on visits to my clubs, in case I see someone who's in the know about such things. I miss a lot of my social life. I haven't had a round of golf since the news reached us."

"It hasn't exactly made life easy for me," I said.

"In the Department? I suppose they think you should have got on to her earlier, eh?"

"Yes, they do."

"But you were the one who finally worked out what was going on. You were the one who discovered she was the spy, eh?"

I didn't answer.

"You needn't worry, Bernard. I don't hold that against you. Someone had to do it. You just did your duty." He drank some of his drink and gave a grim manly smile. I suppose he thought he was being magnanimous. "But now we have to face the mess that she's left behind her. My wife and I have discussed the whole thing at great length"—a smile to share with me the difficulties that always come from discussions with women—"and we'd like to have the children. The nanny could come too so we'd preserve the essential continuity. I've spoken to a friend of mine about the schools. Billy has to change his school this year anyway . . ."

"I'm keeping the children with me," I said.

"I know how you feel, Bernard," he said. "But in practical terms it's not possible. You can't afford to keep up the mortgage payments on the house the way the interest rates are going. How would you be able to pay the nanny? And yet how could you possibly manage without her?"

"The children are with my mother at present."

"I know. But she's too old to deal with young children. And her house is too small, there's only that little garden."

"I didn't know you'd been there," I said.

"When I heard you were away in Mexico, I made it my business to see the children and make sure they were comfortable. I took some toys for them and gave your mother some cash for clothes and so on."

"That was none of your business," I said.

"They're my grandchildren," he said. "Grandparents have rights too, you know." He said it gently. He didn't want to argue; he wanted to get his way about the custody of the children.

"The children will stay with me," I said.

"Suppose Fiona sends more Russians and tries to kidnap them?"

"They have a twenty-four-hour armed guard," I said.

"For how much longer? Your people can't provide a free armed guard forever, can they?"

He was right. The guards were only there still because I'd had to go to Mexico. As soon as I got back to the office there would be pressure to withdraw that expensive facility. "We'll see," I said.

"I won't see the children's trust funds squandered on it. My lawyer is a trustee for both the children; perhaps you're overlooking that. I'll make sure you don't use that money for security guards or even for the nanny's wages. It wouldn't be fair to the children; not when we can offer them a better life here in the country with the horses and farm animals. And do it without taking their money."

I didn't answer. In a way he was right—this rural environment was better than anything I could offer them. But the bad news would be having the children grow up with a man like David Kimber-Hutchinson, who hadn't exactly made a big success of bringing up Fiona.

"Think it over," he said. "Don't say no. I don't want to find myself fighting for custody of the children through the law courts. I pay far too much money to lawyers anyway."

"You'd be wasting your money," I said. "In such circumstances a court would always give me custody."

"Don't be so sure," he said. "Things have changed a lot in the last few years. I'm advised that my chances of legal custody are good. The trouble is—and I'm going to be absolutely frank with you about this—that I don't fancy paying lawyers a lot of money to tell the world what a bad son-in-law I have."

"So leave us alone," I said. I'd feared I was heading into a confrontation like this right from the moment I saw the cream-colored envelope on the clock.

"But I wouldn't be the only loser," he continued relentlessly. "Think what your employers would say to having your name, and my daughter's name, dragged through the courts. They wouldn't keep that out of the newspapers the way they've so far been able to do with Fiona's defection."

He was right, of course. His legal advisers had earned their fees. The Department would keep this out of the courts at all costs. I'd get no support from them if I tried to hang on to my children. On the contrary; they'd press me to accept my father-in-law's sensible offer of help.

Beyond him, through the big studio windows, I could see the trees made gold by the evening sunlight and the paddock where Billy and Sally liked to explore. Money isn't everything, but for people such as him it seemed as if it could buy everything. "I'd better be getting along," I said. "I didn't get much sleep on the plane and there'll be a lot of work waiting for me on my desk tomorrow morning."

He put his hand on my shoulder. "Think about it, Bernard. Give it a couple of weeks. Take a look at some of the bills coming in and jot down a few figures. Look at your net annual income and compare it with your expenditure last year. Even if you pare your expenses right down, you still won't have enough money. Work it out for yourself, and you'll see that what I've said makes sense."

"I'll think about it," I promised, although my mind was made up already, and he could discern that from the tone of my voice.

"You could come down here anytime and see them, Bernard. I'm sure I don't have to tell you that."

"I said I'd think about it."

"And don't go reporting Fiona's Porsche as stolen. I sent my chauffeur to get it and it will be advertised for sale in next week's *Sunday Times*. Better to get rid of it. Too many unhappy memories for you to want to use it, I knew that."

"Thanks, David," I said. "You think of everything."

"I do but try," he said.

Chapter 10

DESPITE my tiredness I didn't sleep well after my return from Leith Hill. The air was warm and I left the bedroom window open. I was fully awakened by the ear-piercing screams of turbofans and the thunder of aircraft engines, throttles opening wide to compensate for flap drag. The approach controllers at London Heathrow like to send a few big jets roaring over the rooftops about six thirty each morning, just in case any inhabitants of the metropolis oversleep.

The radio alarm clock was tuned to the BBC's Third Programme so that I could hear the seven o'clock news bulletin and then spend fifteen minutes on the exercise bike to the sounds of Mozart and Bach. Since living alone I'd connected the coffee machine to a time switch so that I could come downstairs to a smell of fresh coffee. I opened a tin of Carnation milk and found a croissant in the bread bin. It was old and dried and shriveled like something discovered in a tomb with the pharaohs. I chewed it gratefully—I hadn't had a decent meal since well before getting on the plane—but I wasn't hungry. My mind was fully occupied with thoughts of the children and my conversation with my father-in-law. I didn't want to believe him, but his warnings about money worried me. He was seldom, if ever, wrong about money.

I was outside in the street, unlocking the door of my car, when the girl approached me. She was about thirty, maybe younger, dark-skinned and very attractive. She was wearing a nurse's uniform complete with dark blue cloak and a plain blue handbag. "My damned car won't start," she said. Her accent was unmistakably West Indian: Jamaica, I guessed. "And matron will kill me if I'm not at St. Mary Abbots Hospital at eight forty-five. Are you going anywhere in that direction? Or to somewhere I can get a taxi?"

"St. Mary Abbots Hospital?"

"Marloes Road near Cromwell Road, not far from where the air terminal used to be."

"I remember now," I said.

"I'm sorry to trouble you," she said. "I live across the road at number forty-seven." It was a large house that some speculator had converted into tiny apartments and then failed to sell. Now there was always a FOR RENT sign on the railings and a succession of short-term tenants. I suppose it was the sort of place that my father-in-law would like to put me. She said, "There is something wrong with the starter, I think."

I got in and leaned across and opened the passenger door for her. "The staff nurse is a bitch," she said. "I daren't be late again."

"I can go through the park," I said.

She decorously wrapped her cloak around her legs and put her handbag on her lap. "It's very kind of you. It's probably miles out of your way."

"No," I said. In fact it was a considerable detour, but the prospect of sitting next to her for twenty minutes was by no means unwelcome.

"You'd better fasten your seat belt," she said. "It's the law now, isn't it."

"Yes," I said. "Let's not break the law so early in the morning."

She fastened her own seat belt and said, "Do you follow the cricket?"

"I've been away," I said.

"I'm from Kingston, Jamaica," she explained. "I had five brothers. I had to become interested in cricket, it was all they ever talked about."

We were still talking about cricket when I came out of the park and, no right turn being permitted, continued south into Exhibition Road. As I stopped at the traffic light by the Victoria and Albert Museum she broke into my chatter about England's poor bowling against Australia last winter by saying, "I'm sorry to have to do this to you, Mr. Samson. But you're going to turn west onto Cromwell Road when we've been round this one-way system."

"Why? What do you mean?" I turned my head and found her staring at me. She didn't answer. I looked down and saw that she was holding a hypodermic on her lap. Its needle point was very close to my thigh. "Keep your eyes on the road. Just do as I say and everything will be all right."

"Who the hell are you?"

"We'll drive out along the Cromwell Road extension to London Airport. There's something I have to do. When it's done you'll be free to go wherever you have to go." She reached up with her free hand and tilted the driving mirror so that I could not see the traffic behind.

"And if I slam on the brakes suddenly?"

"Don't do that, Mr. Samson. I am a qualified nurse. My papers are in order, my story is prepared. What I have in this syringe will take effect within seconds." She still had the West Indian accent but it was less pronounced now, and there was a change in her manner too. Less of the Florence Nightingale, more of the Jane Fonda. And she didn't say "sorry" or "thank you" anymore.

I was constrained by the seat belt. I could see no alternative to driving to Heathrow. She switched on the car radio. It was tuned to Radio Four, so we both listened to a panel of experts answer questions about gardening.

"I'll say this again," she said. "No harm is intended to you."

"Why the airport?"

"You'll understand when we get there. But don't think there is any plan to abduct you. This just concerns your children and your work." We were driving behind a rusting old car that was emitting lots of black smoke; on the back window there was a sticker saying NUCLEAR POWER—NO THANKS.

When we got to the airport she directed me to Terminal Two, used by non-British airlines mostly for European services. We passed the terminal main entrance and the multi-story car-park that serves it and continued until we came to a piece of road that leads on to Terminal Three. Despite the yellow lines and NO PARKING signs there were cars parked there. "Stop here," she said. "And don't look round." Carefully, and without releasing her hold of the hypodermic or looking away from me, she reached back to unlock the near side rear door.

We were double-parked near two dark blue vans. I heard my car door open and felt the movement of the suspension as it took the weight of another passenger. "Drive on. Slowly," said the nurse. I did as I was told. "We'll go back through the tunnel. Then down to the Motorway roundabout, keep going round it, and back to Terminal Two again. Do you understand that?"

"I understand," I said.

"He's all yours," the nurse said to the person in the back-seat, but she kept her eyes on me.

"It's me, darling," said a voice. "I hope I didn't terrify you." She couldn't eliminate that trace of mockery. Some people didn't hear it, but I knew her too well to miss that touch of gloating pride. It was my wife. I was numb. I'd always prided myself on being prepared for anything—that's what being a professional agent meant—but now I was astonished.

"Fiona, are you mad?"

"To come here? There's no warrant for my arrest. I've changed my appearance and my name . . . no, don't look round. I don't want you unconscious."

"What's it all about?" To keep me driving was a good idea; it limited my chances of doing anything they didn't want me to do.

"It's about the children, darling. Billy and Sally. I went to see them. I waited on the route between your mother's house and the school. They looked so sweet. They didn't see me, of course. I had to watch out for your bloodhounds, didn't I? They both wore matching outfits—acid green with shiny yellow plastic jackets. I'm sure Daddy sent them. Only my father has that natural instinct for the sort of vulgarity that children always love."

"Have you seen your father?"

She laughed. "I'm not here on holiday, Bernard darling. And even if I were, I'm not sure that visiting my father would be on the itinerary."

"So what is all this about?"

"Don't be surly. I had to talk to you and I couldn't phone you without the risk of being recorded on that damned answering machine." She paused for a moment. I could hear the deep rapid breathing—hyperventilation almost—that was always a sign of her being excited or nervous, or both. "I don't want the children's lives made miserable, any more than you do."

"What are you proposing?"

"I'll give you an undertaking to leave the children here in

England for a year. It will give them a chance to live normal lives. It's perfectly ghastly to have them going to school in a car with two security men and having armed guards hanging around them day and night. What sort of life is that for a child?"

"For a year?" I said. "What then?"

"We'll see. But I'll promise nothing beyond a year."

"And you'd want me to leave them unguarded?"

"The Department will call them off before long anyway. You know that as well as I do. And you can't afford to pay for such security."

"I'd manage." I stopped at the roundabout until there was a break in the traffic and then moved off. It was tricky driving without the rearview mirror.

"Yes, you'd arrange some sort of protection using your old friends." She managed to imbue the word with all her distaste for them. "I can imagine what the result would be. Your pals sitting around getting drunk, and talking about what they'd do if I tried to get the children away from you."

"And you want nothing in return?"

"I'd certainly expect you to drop this absurd business with poor old Erich Stinnes."

"What has Stinnes got to do with us?"

"He's my senior assistant—that's what he's got to do with us. You won't tempt Erich with any offers of the good life waiting in the West. He's too committed and too serious for that. But I know you, and I know the Department. I know you're likely to kidnap him if all else fails."

"And that would look bad for you," I said. We were coming to the airport tunnel. I wondered if the sudden darkness would give me a chance to disable the nurse before she had a chance to jab me, but I decided it wouldn't. "Terminal Two?"

"Yes, Terminal Two," said Fiona. "If you persist with this pursuit of Erich Stinnes, I will consider any undertaking about the children null and void. Be reasonable, Bernard. I'm trying to do what's best for Billy and Sally. How do you think I feel about the prospect of not seeing them? I'm trying to prove my goodwill to you. I'm asking nothing in return except that you don't kidnap my senior assistant. Is that asking too much?"

"It won't be my decision, Fiona."

"I realize that. But you have influence. If you really want them to drop it, they'll drop it. Don't make Erich a part of your personal vendetta against me."

"I have no vendetta against you," I said.

"I did what I knew I had to do," she said. It was the nearest I'd ever heard her get to apologizing.

"You're running the KGB office over there now, are you?"

I could hear the amusement in her voice. "I'm giving it a completely new organization. It's so old-fashioned, darling. But I'll soon have it in shape. Aren't you going to wish me good luck?"

I didn't answer. At least she hadn't asked me to join her; even Fiona knew better than that. And yet it was not like her not to try. Was it because she knew there was no chance of suborning me, or because she had other plans—such as kidnapping or even removing me permanently?

"Stop behind this taxi," said the nurse. It was the first time she'd spoken since Fiona got into the car. I stopped.

"Erich Stinnes will not defect voluntarily," said Fiona. "Tell your people that."

"I've told them that already," I said.

"Then we won't quarrel. Good-bye, darling. Best not tell the children you've seen me. It will only upset them. And don't report our meeting to anyone at London Central."

"Or what?"

"Or I won't contact you again, will I? Use your brains, darling."

"Good-bye, Fiona." I still could hardly believe what had happened—I suppose she counted on the surprise—and by the time I'd said good-bye, the door had opened. It slammed loudly and she was gone. I remembered how she'd broken the hinge on the Ford by always slamming the door too hard.

"Keep your eyes this way," said the nurse. "It's not all over yet." I saw her look at her watch. She had it pinned to the shoulder strap of her apron the way all nurses do.

"What is it?" I said. "The Aeroflot flight to Moscow or the Polish Airlines flight to Warsaw? That transits in East Berlin, doesn't it?"

"We'll return on the A.4," she said, "not the Motorway, in case you get some brilliant idea about doing something very brave on the way back."

"I haven't had a brilliant idea for a long time," I said. "And you can ask anyone about that."

Chapter 11

BRET RENSSELAER sent for me that morning. I wasn't there. He sent for me again and continued to send for me until finally I arrived back from my detour to the airport. Bret was in his usual office on the top floor. It was elegantly furnished —gray carpet, glass and chrome desk, and black leather Chesterfield—in a monochrome scheme that so well suited Bret's hand-ground carbon steel personality.

Bret was a hungry-looking American in his mid-fifties, with fair hair that was turning white, and a smile that could slice diamonds. Rumors said that he had applied for British citizenship to clear the way for the knighthood he'd set his heart on. Certainly he had never had to pine for the material things of life. His family had owned a couple of small banks which had been absorbed into a bigger banking complex, and that into another, so that now Bret's shares were worth more money than he needed for his very British understated life-style.

"Sit down, Bernard." He always put the accent on the second syllable of my name. Had it not been for that and the talc he used on his chin and the ever present fraternity ring, I think I might sometimes have overlooked his American nationality, for his accent was minimal and his suits were Savile Row. "You're late," he said. "Damned late."

"Yes, I am," I said.

"Do I rate an explanation?"

"I was having this wonderful dream, Bret. I dreamed I was working for this nice man who couldn't tell the time."

Bret was reading something on his desk and gave no sign of having heard me. He was wearing a starched white Turnbull and Asser shirt with exaggerated cuffs, monogrammed pocket, and gold links. He wore a waistcoat that was unbuttoned and a gray silk bow tie. His jacket was hung on a chair that seemed to be there only so that Bret would have somewhere to hang his jacket. Finally he looked up from the very important paper he was reading and said, "You probably heard that I'm taking a little of the load off Dicky Cruyer's shoulders for the time being."

"I've been away," I said.

"Sure you have," he said. He smiled and took off his reading glasses to look at me and then put them on again. They were large, with speed-cop-style frames that made him look younger than his years. "Sure you have." So Bret had staked a claim to a chunk of Dicky's desk. I couldn't wait to see how Dicky was taking that. Bret said, "I just took on this extra work while Dicky went to Mexico. Just because I'm senior to Dicky, that doesn't mean he's not in charge of the desk. Okay?"

"Okay," I said. It was pure poetry. Just in case anyone thought Bret was assisting Dicky, he was going to precede everything he did by pointing out that he was senior to Dicky. But that was only because he wanted everyone to know that he wasn't after Dicky's job. Who could have thought of anything as Byzantine as that except helpful unassuming old Bret Rensselaer?

"So you talked with this guy Stinnes?"

"I talked with him."

"And?"

I shrugged.

Bret said, "Do I have to drag every damned word out of you? What did he say? What do you think?"

"What he said and what I think are two very different things," I said.

"I spoke with Dicky already. He said Stinnes will come over to us. He's in a dead-end job and wants to leave his wife anyway. He wants a divorce but is frightened of letting his organization know about it, in case they get mad at him."

"That's what he said."

"Does that fit in with what we know about the KGB?"

"How do I find out what 'we' know about the KGB?"

"Okay, smart-ass. Does it fit in with what you know about them?"

"Everything depends upon what his personal dossier says. If Stinnes has been sleeping around—with other men's wives, for instance—and the divorce is the result of that . . . then maybe it would blow up into trouble for him."

"And what would happen to him?"

"Being stationed outside Russia is considered a privilege for any Russian national. For instance, army regulations prevent any Jew, of any rank, serving anywhere but in the Republics. Even Latvians, Lithuanians, Estonians, Crimean Tartars, and people from the western Ukraine are given special surveillance when serving in foreign posts, even in Communist countries such as the DDR or Poland."

"But Stinnes is not in any of those categories?"

"His marriage to the German girl is unusual. Not many Russians marry foreigners; they know only too well that it will make them into second-class citizens. Stinnes is an exception, and it's worth noting the confidence he showed in doing it. His use of a German name is also curious. It made me wonder at first if he had come from one of the German communities."

"Do German communities still exist in Russia? I thought

Stalin liquidated them back in the forties." He swung his chair round and got to his feet so that he could look out of the window. Bret Rensselaer was a peripatetic man who could not think unless his body was in motion. Now he hunched his shoulders like a prizefighter and swayed as if avoiding blows. Sometimes he raised his foot to bend the knee that was said to have troubled him since he was a teenage U.S. Navy volunteer in the final months of the Pacific war. But he never complained of his knee. And it didn't give him enough trouble to interfere with his skiing holidays.

"The big German communities on the Volga were wiped out by executions and deportations back in 1941. But there are still Germans scattered across Russia from one end to the other." His back was still turned to me, but I was used to him and his curious mannerisms so I continued to talk. "Many German communities are established in Siberia and the Arctic regions. Most big cities in the U.S.S.R. have a German minority, but they keep a low profile of course."

He turned to face me. "How can you be sure that Stinnes is not from one of those German communities?" He tugged at the ends of the gray silk bow tie to make sure it was still neat and tidy.

"Because he's stationed in East Germany. The army and the KGB have an inflexible rule that no one of German extraction serves with army units in Germany."

"So if Stinnes applies for a divorce, the chances are that he'll be sent to work in Russia?"

"And probably to some remote 'new town' in Central Asia. It wouldn't be the sort of posting he'd want."

"No matter how he beefs about Berlin. Right." This thought cheered him up. "So that makes Stinnes a good prospect for our offer."

"Whatever you say, Bret," I told him.

"You're a miserable critter, Bernard." Now he took his reading glasses off and put them on the desk while he had a good look at me from head to toe.

"Forget enrolling Stinnes," I said. "The chances are it will never happen."

"You're not saying we should drop the whole business?"

"I'm not saying you should drop it. If you and Dicky have nothing better to do, go ahead. There are lots of other—even less promising—projects that the Department are putting time and money into. Furthermore I'd say it would be good for Dicky to get some practical experience at the sharp end of the business."

"Is that jibe intended for me too?"

"No reason why you shouldn't get into the act. You've never seen a Russian close to, except over the smoked salmon sandwiches at embassy tea parties," I said. "Stinnes is a real pro. You'll enjoy talking to him."

Bret didn't like comments on his lack of field experience any more than any of the others did, but he kept his anger in check. He sat down behind his desk and swung his glasses for a moment. Then he said, "We'll leave that for the time being because there's some routine stuff I have to go through with you." I said nothing. "It's routine stuff about your wife. I know you've been asked all this before, Bernard, but I have to have it from you."

"I understand," I said.

"I wish I was sure you did," said Bret. He slumped down into his chair, picked up his phone, but before using it said to me, "Frank Harrington is in town. I think it might be a good idea to have him sit in on this one. You've no objection, I take it?"

"Frank Harrington?"

"He's very much involved with all this. And Frank's very fond of you, Bernard. I guess I don't have to tell you that."

"Yes, I know he is."

"You're a kind of surrogate son for him." He toyed with the phone.

"Frank has a son," I pointed out.

"An airline pilot?" said Bret scornfully, as if that career would automatically preclude him from such paternity. He pushed a button on the phone and said, "Ask Mr. Harrington to step in." While we were waiting for Frank to arrive, he picked up a piece of paper. I could see it was a single page from his loose-leaf notebook. He turned it over, made sure there were no more of his tiny handwritten notes on the back of it, and then placed it on a pile of such pages under a glass paperweight. Bret was methodical. He ran his forefinger down the next page of notes and was still reading them when Frank came in.

Frank Harrington was the head of the Berlin Field Unit, the job my father had held long, long ago. He was a thin, bony sixty-year-old, dressed in a smooth tweed three-piece suit and highly polished Oxford shoes. Seen on the street he might have been mistaken for the colonel of a rather smart infantry regiment, and sometimes I had the feeling that Frank cultivated this resemblance. But despite the pale but weather-beaten face, the blunt-ended stubble mustache, and the handkerchief tucked into his cuff, Frank had never been in the army except on short detachments. He'd come into the Department largely on the strength of his brilliant academic record; *Literae Humaniores* was said to demand accurate speech, accurate thought, and a keen and critical intellect. Unfortunately "Greats" provides no inkling of the modern world and no clue to the mysteries of present-day politics or economics. And such classical studies could warp a young man's grasp of modern languages, so that even now Frank's spoken German had the stilted formality of a *Kaiserliche* proclamation.

Without a word of greeting Bret pointed a finger at the black leather Chesterfield. Frank smiled at me and sat down. We were both used to Bret's American style of office procedure.

"As I said, this is just a recap, Bernard, so let's get it over and done with," said Bret.

"That suits me," I said. Frank took his pipe from his pocket, fondled it, and then blew through it loudly. When Bret glanced at him, Frank smiled apologetically.

"Obviously"—Bret looked at me to see how I reacted to his

question—"you never suspected your wife of working for the KGB prior to your mission to East Berlin."

"That's correct," I said. I looked at Frank. He had brought a yellow oilskin tobacco pouch onto his knee and was rummaging through it to fill his pipe. He didn't look up.

"Even if we go back years and years?" said Bret.

"Especially if we go back years and years," I said. "She was my wife. I was in love with her."

"No suspicions? None at all?"

"She'd been cleared by the Department. She'd been cleared by Internal Security. She had been vetted regularly . . ."

"Touché," said Bret. Frank Harrington nodded to no one in particular but didn't smile.

"If you're making notes," I told Bret, "make a note of that. My failure was no greater than the Department's failure."

Bret shook his head. "Don't be stupid, Bernard. She was your wife. You brought her to me and suggested that I give her a job. You were married to her for twelve years. She's the mother of your children. How can you compare your failure to know what she truly was, with ours?"

"But finally I did know," I said. "If I hadn't flushed her out she'd still be working here, and still be passing your secrets back to Moscow."

"*Our* secrets," said Bret Rensselaer. "Let's rather say 'our' secrets, unless you are thinking of leaving us too."

I said, "That's a bloody offensive thing to say, Bret."

"Then I withdraw it," said Bret. "I'm not trying to make life more difficult for you, Bernard, really I'm not." He moved his small pages about on the desk. "You didn't ever hear any phone conversations, or find correspondence which, in the light of what we know now, has a bearing on your wife's defection?"

"Do you think I wouldn't have said so? You must have read the transcript of my formal interview. It's all there."

"I know it is, Bernard, and I've already apologized for going through all this once more. But that interview was for Internal Security. This is to go on your report." Each year a report on every member of the staff was filed to the Personnel Department by his or her immediate superior. The fact that Bret was completing mine this year was just one more sign of the way he was edging into Dicky Cruyer's department.

"To go on my report?"

"Well, you didn't imagine we'd be able to overlook your wife's defection, did you? I'm supposed to report on your"— a glance down at his notes—"judgment, political sense, power of analysis, and foresight. Almost every report has some sort of mention of an employee's wife, Bernard. There is nothing special about that. The whole British Civil Service has exactly the same system of reports, so don't get paranoid."

Frank finished filling his pipe. He leaned back and said, "The Department looks after its own, Bernard. I don't have to tell you that." He still hadn't lit his pipe but he put it into his mouth and chewed at the stem of it.

I said, "I don't think I know what you're talking about, Frank."

Frank Harrington had spent a long time in the Department and this gave him certain privileges, so that now he didn't defer to Bret Rensselaer despite Bret's senior ranking. "I'm trying to explain to you that Bret and I want this to come out well for you, Bernard."

"Thanks, Frank," I said without much warmth.

"But it's got to look right on paper too," said Bret. He stood up, put his hands in his pockets, and jingled his small change.

"And how does it look on paper now?" I said. "Without you and Frank putting all your efforts into making it come out well for me."

Bret looked at Frank with a pained expression in his eyes. He was practicing that look, so he could turn it on me if I continued to be insubordinate. Bret was standing by the window. He looked at the view across the park and without turning round said, "The Department's got a lot of enemies, Bernard. Not only certain socialist members of Parliament. The Palace of Westminster has plenty of publicity hounds who'd love to get hold of something like this so they could pontificate on 'Panorama,' get a few clips on TV news, and be interviewed on 'Newsnight.' And there are many of our colleagues in Whitehall who always enjoy the sight of us wriggling under the microscope."

"What is it we're trying to hide, Bret?" I asked.

Bret rounded on me angrily. "For Christ's sake . . ." He went across the room, picked up his jacket, and draped it over his arm. "Talk to him, Frank," he said. "I'm stepping outside for a moment. See if you can talk some sense into the man, will you?"

Frank said nothing. He held the unlit pipe in his teeth for a moment before taking it from his mouth and staring at the tobacco. It was something to do while Bret Rensselaer went out and closed the door. Even then Frank took his time before saying, "We've known each other a long time."

"That's right," I said.

"Berlin: 1945. You were just beginning to walk. You were living at the top of Frau Hennig's house. Your father was one of the first officers to get his family out to occupied Germany. I was touched by that, Bernard. So many of the other chaps preferred to be away from their families. They had the plush life of the conqueror—big apartments, servants, booze, women—everything was available for a few cigarettes or a box of rations. But your father was an exception, Bernard. He wanted you and your mother there with him, and he moved heaven and hell to get you over there. I liked him for that, Bernard. And for much more."

"What is it you want to tell me, Frank?"

"This business with your wife was a shock. It was a shock for you, and a shock for me. The whole Department was caught napping, Bernard, and they are still smarting from the blow."

"And blaming me? So that's it?"

"No one's blaming you, Bernard. As you told Bret just now, you're the one who tipped us off. No one can blame you."

"But . . . Can I hear a 'but' coming?"

Frank fiddled with his pipe. "Let's talk about this chap Stinnes," he said. "He was the officer who arrested you in East Berlin at the time of your wife's defection."

"Yes," I said.

"And he was the interrogation officer too?"

"I've been through all that with you, Frank," I said. "There was no proper interrogation. He'd had orders from Moscow to wait for Fiona to arrive."

"Yes, I remember," said Frank. "The point I'm making is that Stinnes is a senior officer with the KGB's Berlin office."

"No doubt about that," I agreed.

"Your wife is now working for the KGB in that same office?"

"The current guess is that she's in charge of it," I said.

"And Stinnes is certain to be one of her senior staff members, wouldn't you say?"

"Of course."

"So Stinnes is the one person who knows about your wife's defection and her present occupation. It's even possible that he was concerned with her debriefing."

"Don't keep going round and round in circles, Frank. Tell me what you're trying to say."

Frank brandished the pipe at me and closed his eyes while he formulated his response. It was probably a mannerism that dated all the way back to his time at Oxford. "This chap Stinnes knows all about your wife's defection and subsequent employment and he interrogated you. Since that time there has been a departmental alert for him. When he's located in Mexico City why does Dicky Cruyer—the German Stations Controller, no less—go out there to look him over?"

"We both know the answer to that one, Frank. Dicky loves free trips to anywhere. And this one got him out of the way while Bret chiseled a piece out of Dicky's little empire."

"Very well," said Frank in a way that made it clear that he didn't agree with my interpretation of those events. "So why send you?"

"Because I work with Dicky. With both of us out of the way

Bret had a better excuse for 'taking over some of the work load.' " I imitated Bret's voice.

"You're barking up the wrong tree," said Frank. "They want to enroll Stinnes. That was a decision of the steering committee, and it's been given urgent priority. They want Stinnes over here, spilling the beans to a debriefing panel."

"About Fiona?"

"Yes, about your wife," said Frank. I noticed he always said "your wife" since her defection. He couldn't bring himself to use her name anymore. "And about you."

"And about me?"

"How long before the penny drops, Bernard? How long is it going to take you to understand that you must remain a suspect until you are cleared by first-class corroborative evidence?"

"Wait a minute, Frank. Remember me? The one who tipped off the Department about Fiona's activities?"

"But she'd made mistakes, Bernard. If you hadn't raised the alarm, someone else would have done so sooner or later. So why not have you tell the Department about her. And have it done the way Moscow Centre wanted it done?"

I thought about it for a moment. "It doesn't hold water, Frank."

"The way you did it gave her a chance to escape. She got away, Bernard. You sounded the alarm but don't forget that in the event she had time enough to make her escape."

"There were a few sighs of relief at that, Frank. Some people around here would have done anything to avoid all the publicity of another spy trial. And putting Fiona on trial would have blown a hole in the Department."

"Anyone heaving such sighs of relief is a bloody fool," said Frank. "She's taken a pot full of gold with her. No secret papers as far as we know, but her experience here will be worth a lot to them. You know that."

"And people are saying that I deliberately arranged her escape?" I was both indignant and incredulous.

Frank could see how furious I was, and hastily he said, "No

one is accusing you of anything, but we must examine every possibility. *Every* possibility. That's our job, Bernard. If your wife was due to go into the bag anyway, why not arrange for you to tell us? In that way the KGB lose one highly placed agent but have another in position in the same office. And the second agent's credentials are gilt-edged; didn't he even turn in his own wife?"

"Is that why they want to enroll Stinnes?"

"I thought you'd understand that right from the start. Bringing Stinnes in for interrogation is the one way that you can prove that everything went the way you say it went."

"And if I don't bring him in?"

Frank tapped the bowl of his pipe against his thumbnail. "You're not doing yourself any good by saying that Stinnes can't be enrolled. Surely you see that."

"I'm just saying what I believe."

"Well, dammit, Bernard, stop saying what you believe. Or the Department will think you don't want us to get our hands on Stinnes."

"The Department can think what the hell they like," I said.

"That's foolish talk, Bernard. Stinnes would be a plum defector for us. But the real reason that the Department are spending all this time and money is because they think so highly of you. It's principally because they want to keep you that they are pushing the Stinnes enrollment."

Frank had the diplomatic touch, but it didn't change the underlying facts. "It makes me bloody angry, Frank."

"Don't be childish," said Frank. "No one really suspects you. It's just a formality. They haven't even put you on a restricted list for secret information. So much of the difficulty arises from the way that you and Fiona had such a happy marriage, that's the absurd thing about it. One only had to see you together to know that you were both in love. Happy marriage; promising career; delightful children. If you'd had constant arguments and separations it would be easier to see you as the wronged party—and politically uninvolved."

"And if we don't enroll Stinnes? What then if we don't enroll him?"

"It will be difficult to keep you in Operations if we don't enroll Stinnes."

"And I know what that implies." I remembered a few employees whom Internal Security considered unsuitable for employment in Operations. It was chilling to remember those people who'd had their security ratings downgraded in mid-career. The periodic routine checks were usually the cause. That's what turned up the discreet homosexuals who weekended with young Spanish waiters, and lesbians sharing apartments with ladies who turned out not to be their cousins. And there were younger people who'd conveniently forgotten being members of international friendship societies while students. Societies which had the words "freedom," "peace," and "life" in their articles so that anyone who opposed them would be associated with incarceration, war, and death. Or had joined other such innocuous-sounding gatherings that locate themselves conveniently near universities and provide coffee and buns and idealistic talk from respectably dressed foreign visitors. I knew that such downgraded rejects found themselves working the SIS end of an embassy in Central Africa or checking Aeroflot cargo manifests at London Airport.

"I wouldn't worry about having to leave Operations," said Frank. "You'll get Stinnes. Now you understand what's involved, you'll get him. I'm confident of that, Bernard."

There seemed to be nothing more to say. But as I got up from my chair Frank said, "I had a word with the D-G last night. I was having drinks at his place and a number of things came into the conversation . . ."

"Yes?"

"We're all concerned about you and the problem of looking after the children, Bernard."

"The only problem is money," I said sharply.

"We all know that, Bernard. It's money I'm talking about. The D-G has looked into the possibility of giving you a special allowance. The diplomatic service has something called 'Ac-

countable Indirect Representational Supplement.' Only a bu-
reaucrat could think up a name like that, eh? It reimburses the
cost of a nanny, so that children are taken care of while diplomats and wives attend social functions. Diplomats also have
'Boarding School Allowance.' I'm not sure how much that
would come to, but it would probably ease your financial situation somewhat. It might take a bit of time to come through,
that's the only snag."

"I'm not sending the children to boarding school."

"Relax, Bernard. You're too damned prickly these days. No
one is going to come snooping round you to find out what kind
of school your children are attending. The D-G simply wants to
find a way to help. He wants a formula that's already acceptable.
An ex-gratia payment would not be the way he'd want to do it.
If anyone discovered an ex-gratia payment going directly to an
employee it could blow up into a scandal."

"I'm grateful, Frank."

"Everyone is sympathetic, Bernard." He put his tobacco
pouch in his pocket. His pipe was still unlit. "And by the way,
Stinnes is back in Berlin. He's been in the West Sector to visit
your friends the Volkmanns . . . Mrs. Volkmann in particular.
I thought you'd like to know that."

Frank Harrington had had an affair with Zena Volkmann
and there was bad feeling between him and Werner that dated
from long before. I wondered if Frank was telling me about
Stinnes as some sort of reproach to Werner who'd not reported
it. "Yes, I'll follow that up, Frank. I will have to go to Berlin.
It's just a matter of fitting it in."

I left Frank to tell Bret that he'd done what was wanted.
He'd drawn a diagram so simple that even I could understand
it. Then he'd written detailed captions under all the component
parts.

LATER that afternoon I went to my office and sent for a young
probationer named Julian MacKenzie. "Well?" I said.

"No, the nurses at St. Mary Abbots don't wear the uniform

you described and they don't change shifts at eight forty-five. And there is no colored woman, of any age, known to the residents of the block opposite your house."

"That was very quick, MacKenzie."

"I thought it was pretty good myself, boss." MacKenzie was an impertinent little sod who'd come down from Cambridge with an honors in Modern Languages, got the A1 mark that the Civil Service Selection Board usually reserve for friends and relations, and had been a probationer with the Department for a few months. It was a record of achievement made even more remarkable by the fact that MacKenzie, despite his Scottish name, had a strong Birmingham accent. His ambition was such that he would work hard and long, and never ask questions nor expect me to give him a signed authorization for each little job. Also his insubordinate attitude to all and sundry amused me.

"I'd really like to get into fieldwork. How can I start on that? Any hints and tips, boss?" This had now become a standard inquiry.

"Yes, comb your hair now and again, change your shirt every day, and introduce an obsequious note into your social exchanges with the senior staff."

"I'm not joking."

"Neither am I," I assured him. "But while you're here. What's the last name of that girl Gloria? That typist who used to work for Mr. Rensselaer?"

"The gorgeous blonde job with the big knockers?"

"You have such a delicate way of phrasing everything, MacKenzie. Yes, that's who I mean. I haven't seen her lately. Where is she working now?"

"Her name's Kent; Gloria Kent. Her father is a dentist. She's very keen on ballroom dancing and water skiing. But she's not a typist, she's a Grade 9 Executive Officer. She's hoping to fiddle one of those departmental grants to go to university. And what's more she speaks fluent Hungarian." He grinned. "Ambition drives us all. I'd say Miss Kent is hankering after a career in the service; wouldn't you?"

"You're a mine of information, MacKenzie. Is her father Hungarian?"

"You guessed. And she lives with her parents, miles out in the sticks. No joy for you there, I'm afraid."

"You're an impertinent little sod, MacKenzie."

"Yes, I know, sir. You told me that the other day. She's working in Registry at present, the poor little thing. It's only my daily trips down there to see her among the filing cabinets that keep her sane."

"Registry, eh?" It was the most unpopular job in the Department and nearly one-third of all the staff were employed there. The theory was that the computer in the Data Centre would gradually replace the thousands of dusty files, and Registry would eventually disappear. But true to the rules of all bureaucracy, the staff at the Data Centre grew and grew but the staff in Registry did not decrease.

"She'd like working up here with you, sir. I know she'd give anything for a job with any member of the Operations staff."

"Anything?"

"Almost anything, sir," said MacKenzie. He winked. "According to what I hear."

I PHONED the old dragon who ran Registry and told her I wanted Miss Kent to work for me for a few days. When she came up to the office I showed her the great pile of papers due for filing. They'd been stacking up in the cupboard for months and my own secretary was pleased to see the task taken off her hands.

Gloria Kent was tall. She was slim and long-legged and about twenty years old. Her hair was the color of pale straw. It was wavy but loose enough to fall across her forehead, short but long enough to touch the roll neck of her dark brown sweater. She had large brown eyes and long lashes and a wide mouth. If Botticelli had painted the box top for a Barbie doll the picture would have looked like Gloria Kent. And yet she was not doll-like. There was nothing diminutive about her. And she didn't bow her head, the way so many tall women do to accommodate themselves to the egos of shorter men they find around them. And it was her straight-backed posture, for her use of makeup was minimal, that gave her the appearance of a chorus girl rather than a civil servant.

She'd been sorting out the files for about an hour when she said, "Will I be going back to work in Registry?"

"It's nothing to do with me, Miss Kent," I said. "We're both working for Mr. Cruyer. He makes all the decisions."

"He's the Controller of German Stations," she said, giving Dicky his official title. "So that's my department, is it?"

"The German desk we usually call it," I said. "Everything's in a turmoil up here at present, I'm afraid."

"I know. I was working for Mr. Rensselaer. But that only lasted ten days. Then his Economics Intelligence Committee had no more work for me. I did odd bits of typing for people on the top floor, then I was sent down to Registry."

"And you don't like Registry?"

"No one likes it. There's no daylight and the fluorescent lighting makes me so tired. And you get so dirty handling those files all day. You should see my hands when I go home at night. When I get home I can't wait to strip right off and have a bath."

I took a deep breath and said, "You won't get so dirty up here, I hope."

"It's a treat to see the daylight, Mr. Samson."

"No one round here calls me anything but Bernard," I said. "So it might be easier if you did the same."

"And I'm Gloria," she said.

"Yes, I know," I said. "And by the way, Gloria, Mr. Cruyer always likes to meet his staff socially. Every now and again he has a few members of the staff along to his house for an informal dinner and a chat."

"Well, I think that's very nice," said Gloria. She smoothed her skirt over her hips.

"It is," I said. "We all appreciate it. And the fact is that he

has one of these dinners on Thursday. And he made a special point of saying that he'd like you to be there."

"Thursday. That's rather short notice," she said. She moved her head to let her hair swing and touched it as if already calculating when to go to the hairdresser's.

"If you have something more important to do, I know he'll understand."

"It would sound terrible though, wouldn't it?"

"No, it wouldn't sound terrible. I'd explain to him that you had some other appointment that you couldn't give up."

"I'd better come," she said. "I'm sure I can rearrange things. Otherwise"—she smiled—"I might spend the rest of my life in the Registry."

"He'd like us there at seventy forty-five, for drinks. They sit down to eat at eight thirty. If you live too far away, I'm sure Mrs. Cruyer will be happy to let you have a room to change. Come to that," I said, "you could have a drink at my house and change there. Then I could drive you over. His house is rather difficult to find."

I saw a look of doubt come into her face. I feared for a moment that I'd overplayed my hand, but I busied myself with my work and said no more.

DICKY's dinner party was very successful. Daphne had worked for three days preparing the meal, and I realized that she'd not invited me for lunch the previous Sunday because she had been trying out on Dicky the same cucumber soup recipe and the same wild rice and the same gooseberry fool that she served for the dinner party. Only the boiled salmon was an experiment; its head fell on the kitchen floor as it was coming out of the fish kettle.

There were eight of us. If Gloria Kent had expected it to be a gathering of departmental staff she gave no sign of disappointment at meeting the Cruyers' new neighbors and a couple named Stephens, the wife being Liz Stephens, who was

Daphne's partner in the stripping business. Dicky couldn't resist his joke about Daphne making money from stripping, although it was clear that only Gloria had not been told it before. Gloria laughed.

The conversation at table was confined to the usual London dinner party small talk: listing foreign ski resorts, local restaurants, schools, and cars in descending order of desirability. Then there was talk about the furniture stripping. The first attempt had gone badly. No one had told them not to try it with bentwood furniture, and the first lot of chairs had disintegrated in the soda bath. The two women were able to laugh about it, but their husbands exchanged looks of mutual resignation.

The neighbors from across the road—whose schoolgirl baby-sitter had to be home very early—left after the gooseberry fool. The Stephenses left soon afterwards after just one hurried cup of coffee. This left the four of us sitting in the front room. Dicky had the hi-fi playing Chopin very quietly. Gloria asked Daphne if she could help with the washing up and, being told no, admired the primitive painting of Adam and Eve that was hanging over the fireplace. Daphne had "discovered it" in a flea market in Amsterdam. She was always pleased when someone admired it.

"A damn fine meal, darling," said Dicky as his wife brought the second pot of coffee and chocolate-covered after-dinner mints. His voice was a fruity imitation of Silas Gaunt, one of the old-timers of the Department. He pushed his cup forward for a refill.

Daphne glanced at him, smiled nervously, and poured the hot coffee onto the polished table. I had the feeling that these dinners were nightmares for Daphne. She had been a pushy self-confident career girl when Dicky married her, but she knew her limitations as a cook and she knew how critical Dicky (one-time president of Oxford University Wine and Food Society) Cruyer could be when he was playing host to people he worked with. Sometimes she seemed physically frightened of Dicky and

I knew enough about his sudden fits of bad temper to sympathize.

After a competition to see who could use the most Kleenex tissues to clean up the spilled coffee—which Daphne won by using a large handful of them to conceal and smuggle out of the room a box of very wet cigars—Gloria said, "You have such a beautiful house, Mrs. Cruyer."

"*Daphne*. Daphne, for God's sake. It's a pigsty," said Daphne with modest self-confidence. "Sometimes it gets me down."

I looked round to see any sign of the furniture that Daphne had stored in there, but it had all been removed. Poor Daphne. Their cars were parked in the street. I suppose all the furniture was now stacked in the garage.

"And lovely to see you both," said Dicky, passing coffee to Gloria. Dicky put a lot of meaning into the word "both"; it was almost carnal. She smiled nervously at Dicky and then looked at me. "Yes," said Dicky, passing a cup of coffee to me. "Bernard has talked about you so much."

"When?" said Gloria. She was no fool. She guessed immediately what was behind Dicky's remarks.

"When we were in Mexico," said Dicky.

"Mexico City," I said.

"They call it Mexico," said Dicky.

"I know," said Gloria as if her mind was on other things. "My mother and father went there two years ago, on a package holiday. They brought back a lot of home movies. That's my father's hobby. It looked awful." She turned to me and smiled; sweet smile but cold eyes. "I didn't know you were talking about me when you were in Mexico, Bernard," she said.

I drank some of my coffee.

Gloria turned her attention to Daphne. "As long as I don't have to go back to working in Registry, Mrs. Cruyer," she said. "It's absolute hell." Daphne nodded. It was brilliant of her to say it to Daphne. Had she said it to Dicky or to me, I think Daphne would have made sure Gloria went back into Registry the following morning. "Couldn't you ask your husband to let me work somewhere else?"

Daphne looked uncertain. She said, "I'm sure he'll do what he can, Gloria. Won't you, Dicky?"

"Of course I will," said Dicky. "She can work upstairs. There's always extra work to do and I've had to ask Bret Rensselaer to share his secretary with one of the deputy desk people. Gloria could help my secretary and Bernard's secretary and do the occasional job for Bret."

So Dicky was fighting back. Good old Dicky. Share his secretary—that should make Bret retire to a neutral corner and shake the tears from his eyes.

"That would be wonderful, Mr. Cruyer," said Gloria, but she smiled at Daphne. It was becoming clear to me that Gloria had a great career ahead of her. What was that joke about Hungarians going into a revolving door behind you, and coming out ahead of you?

"We're all one happy family in Dicky's department," I said.

Dicky smiled at me scornfully.

"But we'd better be moving along," I said. And to meet Dicky's gaze I added, "Gloria has left her clothes at my place."

"Oh, doesn't that sound awful," said Gloria. "Bernard let me change at his house. My parents live too far away for me to go home to change."

When we'd said our good nights and were in my old Ford, Gloria said, "What nice people they are."

"Yes," I said.

"Mr. Cruyer is a very interesting man," she said.

"Do you think so?"

"Don't you?" she said as if worried that she'd said the wrong thing.

"Very interesting," I said. "But I was surprised you got onto that so quickly."

"He was at Balliol," she said wistfully. "All the very brightest people go to Balliol."

"That's true," I said.

"Where did you go to, Bernard?"

"You can call me Mr. Samson if you like," I said. "I didn't go anywhere. I left school when I was sixteen and started work."

"Not for the Department?"

"Sort of," I said.

"You can't take the Civil Service Exam at sixteen."

"It all happened in a foreign country," I said. "My father was the Berlin Resident. I grew up in Berlin. I speak Berlin German like a native. I know the town. It was natural that I should start working for the Department. The paperwork was all done afterwards. I never took the Selection Board." It sounded more defensive than I had intended it should.

"I got five A levels," said Gloria proudly. Gone was the femme fatale, all of a sudden she was the sixth-form schoolgirl running home with her school report.

"Here we are," I said. "Should I fetch your other clothes, or do you want to come inside and have a drink?"

To my surprise she tilted her head back until it was on my shoulder. I could smell her perfume and the warmth of her body. She said, "I don't want this evening to end."

"We'll keep it going as long as possible," I said. "Come and have a drink."

She smiled lazily. She hadn't had much wine or I might have suspected that she was drunk. She put her hand on my arm and turned her face to me. I kissed her on the forehead and opened the door. "Come along then." She giggled and got out of the car. As she slid from the seat her skirt rode up to expose a lot of leg. She tugged at it and smiled modestly.

Once inside the house she sat down on the sofa and again said what a wonderful evening it had been. "Brandy?" I said. "Liqueur? Scotch and soda?"

"A very tiny brandy," she said. "But I'll miss my last train if we don't go very soon." I poured two huge Martell brandies and sat down next to her.

"Will your parents worry?" I gave her a decorous kiss on

the cheek. "If you miss your train, would they really worry?"

"I'm a big girl now," she said.

"You are indeed, Gloria," I said admiringly. "You're a wonderful girl." I put my arm round her and pulled her close. She was soft and warm and big. She was just what I wanted.

"What were you saying about me when you were in Mexico City?" Her voice was dreamy and softened by the way she was nibbling my ear.

"Mexico. You heard what Dicky said. They always call it Mexico."

She murmured, "Did you bet Dicky Cruyer that you'd get me into bed?"

"Of course not," I said.

"You said you'd already had me in bed? Ummm?"

"Good Lord, no," I said. "We were talking about staffing. We weren't talking about any one member of the staff in particular. We were talking about the office . . . the work load."

She nuzzled her face against my ear. "You're a terrible liar, Bernard. Did anyone ever tell you that? You are a completely hopeless liar. How did you ever survive as a secret agent?" She was kissing my cheek now. As I hugged her she murmured, "Admit it, you told Dicky we were lovers." As she said it she turned her head to offer me her lips and we kissed. When she broke away she purred, "You did, didn't you?"

"I might have said something that gave him the wrong impression," I admitted. "You can see what Dicky's like."

She kissed me again. "I must go home," she said.

"Must you?"

"I must. My parents *might* worry."

"You're a big girl now," I reminded her. But she pushed me away and got to her feet. "Perhaps some other time," she said. She was alert now, and I could see she had decided to leave. "I'll go upstairs and get my bag. But you . . ." She took me by the hand and pulled me to the front door. "You will go out and start the car and take me to the station."

When I showed little inclination to do this she marched upstairs to get the clothes she'd left there and, over her shoulder, said, "If I miss my train at Waterloo you'll have to drive me all the way to Epsom, Mr. Samson. And that's a miserable drive at this time of night. And my parents always wait up to see who I've been with. I hate to make them angry."

"Okay, Gloria," I said. "You talked me round." I didn't relish facing the wrath of a Hungarian dentist in the small hours of the morning.

I took her to Waterloo Station in time to catch her train and I returned to my lonely bed.

It was only next morning that I discovered that she'd used the scissors from the bathroom cupboard to cut all my underpants in two. And it was only when daylight came that I could see that she'd written "You are a bastard mister Samson" in lipstick on the bedroom window glass. I spent ages removing the lipstick marks and hiding my pieces of underwear before Mrs. Dias, the cleaning lady, arrived. I was not in a hurry to repeat that experience with Gloria. It seemed as if there might be something of deep psychological significance about the retribution she'd wreaked upon my linen for what seemed to me a harmless little joke.

Chapter 12

THAT BLOODY Werner has been seeing Stinnes," said Dicky. He was pacing up and down, chewing at the nail of his little finger. It was a sign that he was agitated. He was often agitated lately. Sometimes I wondered that Dicky had any nails left.

"So I hear," I said calmly.

"Ah," said Dicky. "I thought so. Have you been going behind my back again?"

I salaamed, a low bow in a gesture of placation. "Oh, master. I hear this only from Harrington sahib."

"Cut out the clowning," said Dicky. He sat down behind his huge rosewood table. He didn't have a real desk in his office, just a few fine pieces of antique furniture including this rosewood table that he used as a desk, a Charles Eames chair for him to sprawl in, and a couple of easy chairs for visitors. It was a big room with two windows facing across the park. At one time he'd shared this room with his secretary, but once he'd annexed the office next door for her he spread himself.

"No one tells me anything," said Dicky. He was sitting on his hard little chair, legs and knees pressed together and arms folded tight across his chest. It was an illustration from a textbook that tells you how to deal with sulking children. "Bret's determined to take over my job. Now I suppose he's going to cut off all my communications with my stations."

"Werner Volkmann doesn't officially work for the Department. You wouldn't give him any money in Mexico City. You remember I asked you, and you said over your dead body."

"He's got no right to have meetings with Stinnes without keeping me informed."

"He can't have had many meetings in Berlin," I said. "He's only been back five minutes."

"He should have asked permission," said Dicky.

"Werner doesn't owe us anything; we owe him."

"Who owes him?" said Dicky contentiously.

"The Department owes him. Werner located Stinnes for us and then you wouldn't okay a payment. What can you expect?"

"So your pal Werner is out to teach us a lesson. Is that his game?"

I sank down deep in Dicky's Charles Eames armchair; it was very relaxing. Little wonder Dicky never got any work done. "Werner is one of those strange people who like to work in intelligence. He makes a good living from his banking activities, but he wants to work for us. You put Werner back on the payroll and he'd be the most enthusiastic agent on your books. Give him a little money, and even his wife would start getting interested."

"She's mercenary. That Zena is very mercenary."

So even Dicky had noticed. "Yes, she is," I said. "But if they both are seeing Stinnes, my advice is to keep her sweet."

Dicky grunted and continued biting his nail.

"Zena keeps her ears and eyes open. And Stinnes seems to like her. She might be able to guess what's in his mind before anyone else does."

Dicky pouted. He was always like this about approving extra payments to any field agents. Normally I would have arranged any discussion about money for some day when Dicky was in one of the upward phases of his manic life-style. "If Werner Volkmann makes a complete cock-up of everything, and he's not on the payroll, I can disown him," explained Dicky, who tackled every task by deciding how he'd extricate himself from it if disaster ensued.

"I'll take personal responsibility for him," I said.

Dicky brightened at the idea. "That might be a way of doing it," he said. The wall behind Dicky was almost completely covered with framed photos of Dicky smiling and shaking hands with important people. This form of self-advertisement, more usually found in the offices of extravert American film producers, was considered bad form when Dicky first began his collection. But Dicky had made it into a prank, a droll collegiate form of fun, so that now he was able to have his joke and eat it too. One of the photos showed Dicky in Calcutta, while on a tour with Sir Henry Clevemore, the Director-General. It was a large color photo in a gold frame. The two men were standing in front of a stall displaying crude lithographic posters. By looking close you could recognize portraits of John Lennon, Napoleon, Marilyn Monroe, Lenin, and John F. Kennedy. Somehow I always thought of Dicky as that young man in the photo, smiling at his boss amid a galaxy of successful people. "I've told Berlin that I want Werner over here immediately. He'll be on the morning plane. I've sent a car to the airport so he will be here about three. We'll sit him down and find out what the hell it's all about. Okay, Bernard?"

"I hope you'll start off by offering him a proper contract," I said. "He's not your employee. He can just tell you to get stuffed and phone his lawyer."

Dicky bit his lip. "We've just been through all that. You said you'd take responsibility for him."

"Then let me offer him a proper contract," I said. Dicky looked doubtful. I said, "Distancing yourself from Werner in case everything goes wrong might be sound reasoning, but don't distance yourself from him so far that he's out of sight. Don't distance yourself so far from Werner that you'll get no credit if everything goes well."

Dicky took out a handkerchief and blew his nose. "I'm getting a cold," he said woefully. "It's coming back here after the hot weather in Mexico."

I nodded. I recognized the signs. When Dicky displayed the symptoms of the common cold it was usually because he was expecting some work he couldn't handle, or questions he didn't want to answer. "Let me see Werner," I said. "Let me draft a contract. Don't bring him up here to the office. Tell me what you want him to do and I'll keep you in touch with him. Run him through me. Then you'll have the best of both worlds."

"Very well," said Dicky. He blew his nose again, trying to conceal his relief behind his big white handkerchief.

"But I'll need money," I said. "Not a handful of small change; ten grand at least, Dicky."

"Ten grand."

"It's only money, Dicky."

"You're irresponsible, Bernard. Two thousand maybe, not ten."

"It's not your money, Dicky."

"That's just the sort of thing I'd expect you to say," said Dicky. "You think the Department has money to burn."

"Money is a part of our armory," I said. "It's what we use to do our job. We can conserve the Department's money by sitting on our asses and staring into space."

"I knew you'd have an answer," said Dicky.

I nodded. I knew it was an answer which Dicky would be noting down for future use the next time the cashier's office queried Dicky's profligate expense accounts.

"Very well then, ten thousand. On account, mind you. I shall want every penny of it accounted for."

"I think Werner should go over into East Berlin and see what he can find out about Stinnes on his home ground."

Dicky took his little finger and bit into the nail with a dedication that made our conversation a secondary matter. "Dangerous," said Dicky between nibbles. "Dangerous for all concerned."

"Let Werner be the judge of that. I won't force him to go."

"No, you'll just give him the money, and tell him he's getting a contract. And then you'll ask him if he wants to go over there. You're a ruthless bastard, Bernard. I thought Werner was your friend."

"He is my friend. Werner won't go unless he thinks he can do it without getting into trouble." But was it true, I wondered. Was I really planning to manipulate Werner in such a cynical way? If so, would I even have realized it without Dicky's rejoinder?

"Ten thousand pounds," mused Dicky. "Couldn't I use a windfall like that! I don't know how I'm going to afford the boys' school fees next year. I just had a long letter from the headmaster. I don't blame the school; their expenses are rocketing."

"The government say that inflation is down again," I said. I wondered what Dicky would say if he got to hear that I was getting a supplementary boarding school allowance and the money for the nanny.

"What do the bloody politicians care," said Dicky. "The first thing those bastards do when they get into office is to vote themselves some astronomical rise in salaries and allowances."

"Yes," I said. "To the barricades." So discontent was running through the ranks of Whitehall, despite index-linked pensions and all the rest of it.

"Yes," said Dicky. "Well, I daresay you have your own financial worries."

"Yes, Dicky. I do."

"So where shall I tell the driver to dump Werner when he brings him from the airport? You say you don't want to see him up here. And if he's in and out of the East all the time, it's just as well he stays at arm's length."

"Shall I tell your secretary to type out a chit for the money?"

"Yes, yes, yes, yes, yes," said Dicky irritably. "I said yes. I'm not going to go back on my promise to your precious Werner. Get the chit and I'll sign it."

I went back to my office with the chit. I wouldn't put it past Dicky to retrieve the signed form from his secretary's tray and start having second thoughts about it. My secretary had gone to early lunch but Gloria Kent was there. I had the feeling that she was slowing down on the filing so she could make sure she stayed upstairs.

"Take this money order along to the cashier's office. Tell them I want a check made out to cash. And I want it before lunch."

"The cashier's office is awfully busy, Bernard," she said.

"Stay there until you get it. And make yourself a nuisance while you're waiting."

"How do I do that?" said Gloria.

"Talk to them," I suggested. "Or better still, read all the paperwork you can find, and comment on what payments are going out to who. That always makes them jumpy."

"I'm never sure when you are joking," said Gloria.

"I never joke about money," I said.

No sooner had she gone down the corridor than my phone rang. It was the operator telling me there was an outside call from Mrs. Kosinski. I was always puzzled in the same way when

I heard that name Kosinski. I never thought of Fiona's sister as being Mrs. Kosinski, and I certainly never thought of dear old George, my brother-in-law, with his cockney accent and his terrible jokes as George Kosinski.

"Bernard here."

"Oh, Bernard. I've been trying to get you for ages. Your people there guard you so well, darling. How I wish I had such suspicious guardians looking after me—it's like trying to get through to Buckingham Palace. Worse in fact, because George has several customers in the Royal Household and I've seen him get through to them in no time at all." It was the breathless syntax of the gossip column.

"How are you, Tessa?" So it was my amazing, sexy, scatter-brained, wanton sister-in-law. "Is anything wrong?"

"Nothing I could possibly talk about over the telephone, darling," she said.

"Oh, really," I said, wondering if the call was being monitored by Internal Security. After everything that Frank Harrington had told me, it would have been very stupid of me to imagine I was not under some sort of surveillance, however perfunctory.

"Bernard. Are you free for lunch? Today, I mean. Right now, in fact. If you have an appointment, change it. I must see you, darling." She was able to say this with strong emphasis upon each phrase and yet not convey any note of real urgency. I had the feeling that even if her house was on fire, Tessa would shout a stylish "fire" in a manner that sounded more fashionable than desperate.

"I'm free for lunch."

"Super."

"Where would you like to go?" I knew that Tessa always had some place she wanted to go for lunch. Too many times I'd heard her acerbic descriptions of inadequate lunches in unfashionable places.

"Oh." Only the English middle class have the gliding diphthong that makes them able to say "Oh" like that. Tessa could make "Oh" into a Bach cantata. "Having had time to think," she said, "I'm too bored with all these frightfully twee little restaurants run by young male couples who've been to Bocuse on holiday. What about the Savoy, darling? When you get right down to it, it's the only place in London with any real class. Everywhere is full of advertising people these days."

"I'll see if I can get a table," I promised.

"The Restaurant, darling, not the Grill. I never see any of my friends when I go to the Grill. Shall we say one o'clock? When you phone, ask for the chef, Mr. Edelmann, George knows him awfully well. Mention George."

"Is it just social, Tessa? Or is there really something special?"

"I had dinner with Daddy last night, Bernard. I must talk to you. It's about you know who and the children, darling. I heard about your visit to Leith Hill."

"Yes, David wanted to see me."

"I know all about it. We'll have a lovely lunch and we'll talk about everything. There's so much to tell you, Bernard. It seems ages since we last had a proper talk together."

"And George is well?"

"George is always well when he's making money, darling. You know that."

"I'm glad to hear he's making money," I said.

"He has the Midas touch, darling. We've got an apartment in Mayfair now. Did you know that? No, of course you didn't, the change of address cards don't go out until next week. You'll love it, it's adorable. And so central."

"We'll talk about it over lunch," I said as I spied Dicky coming in.

"Savoy Restaurant, one o'clock sharp," said Tessa. She was muddle-headed and vague about most things, but she was making sure there would be no mistake about our lunch. I suppose anyone who had the number of illicit love affairs and assignations that Tessa enjoyed would have to be methodical and precise about appointments.

"See you there," I said.

"Who was that?" said Dicky.

I felt like saying it was none of his damn business, but I answered him truthfully. "Tessa Kosinski," I said. "My sister-in-law."

"Oh," said Dicky. As I understood it from Fiona, Tessa had had a brief mad affair with Dicky. I watched his face and decided it was probably true. "I've met her. She's a nice little woman."

Nice little woman was not the description that usually came to mind when a man met Tessa Kosinski. "Some people think she's a sex bomb," I said.

"I wouldn't say that," said Dicky very coolly.

"Was there something you wanted?"

"Werner. Where shall I send him?"

"Send him along to the Savoy Restaurant," I said. "I'm lunching there with my sister-in-law."

"I thought you were short of money," said Dicky.

"Werner is joining me for coffee," I said.

"Oh no you don't," said Dicky. "You're not going to charge that lunch. It's not on."

"The Restaurant," I said. "Not the Grill. Tessa never sees any of her friends in the Grill."

TESSA arrived looking magnificent. She was thirty-three years old, but she looked ten years younger than that. Whatever Tessa was doing, it seemed to be good for her. She had wonderful skin and light fair hair that she wore long so that it broke over her shoulders. George's income, to say nothing of the allowance she got from her father, was to be seen in every expensive stitch of the dark blue Chanel suit, the Hermès handbag, and Charles Jourdan shoes. Even the most blasé waiter turned his head to watch her as she kissed me with extravagant hugs and sighs before sitting down.

She kicked off a shoe under the table and swore softly as she rubbed her foot. "What a wonderful table you've got for us. With that lovely view of the river. They must know you."

"No," I said truthfully. "I mentioned George's name, as you suggested."

She smiled dutifully as at an oft-repeated joke. She waved away the menu without looking at it and ordered an Ogen melon and a grilled sole with a small mixed salad. When she saw me looking down the wine list she said, "Would you think me awful if I asked you to order a bottle of Bollinger, darling? My doctor has told me to avoid red wines and all other sorts of booze."

"A bottle of Bollinger," I told the waiter.

"I saw David," she said. She rubbed her foot again. "He's an absolute bastard, isn't he?"

"We've never got along very well together," I said.

"He's a bastard. You know he is. And now he's trying to get the children. I hope you told him to go straight to hell."

"I wouldn't like him to have the children," I said.

"I wouldn't allow the old bastard to run a zoo," said Tessa. "He ruined my life and I blame him for what happened to Fiona."

"Do you?"

"Well, don't they say all these spies and traitors are just reacting to the way they hate their parents?"

"It is a popular theory," I said.

"And my father is living evidence of the truth of it. Who could imagine poor old Fi working for the rotten Commies unless she'd been driven to it by David?"

"I'm keeping the children with me," I said. "It will be difficult to afford it, but no more difficult than it was for my father."

"Good for you, Bernie. I was hoping you'd say that, because I'm going to help you, if you'll let me." She looked at me with a stern expression that I found appealing. It was impossible not to compare her with the diamond-hard Zena; but despite her sophisticated life-style and smart back-chat, Tessa was insecure. Sometimes I wondered if her casual love affairs were attempts to reassure herself, just as some people use drink or mirrors. I'd always had a weak spot for her, no matter how exasperating she was. She was shallow but she was spontaneously generous. I'd find it easy to fall in love with her, but I was determined not to. She smiled demurely and then looked out of the window. The River Thames was high, the water gleaming like oil. Against the current, a string of barges, piled high with rubbish, moved very slowly and were devoured piecemeal by an arch of Waterloo Bridge.

"I'll let you, Tessa. I can use any help I can get."

"I phoned your mother. She worries about you."

"Mothers always worry," I said.

"She said the children are coming back to Duke Street. Nanny is still with them, that's one good thing. She's been wonderful, that girl. I didn't think she had it in her. It's probably very uncomfortable for her, cramped up in that little house of your mother's. Anyway, I thought I'd come over to Duke Street with my cleaning woman and get everything ready for them. Okay?"

"It's nice of you, Tessa. But I'm sure it will be all right."

"That's because you're a man and you've got no idea of what has to be done in a house when two young children are moving in. They'll need the rooms aired, clean clothes ready, beds made, food prepared, groceries in the cupboard, and some cooked meals in the freezer."

"I suppose you're right," I said.

"Well, of course I'm right, darling. You don't think all these things get done by magic, do you?"

"I've got Mrs. Dias," I explained.

"Mrs. Dias," said Tessa. She laughed, drank some champagne, eyed the waiter, and pointed to our glasses to order more. Then she laughed again at the thought of Mrs. Dias. "Mrs. Dias, darling, is about as much use as a spare whatnot at a wedding, if you know what I mean."

"I know what you mean," I said. "But Fiona always managed with Mrs. Dias."

"Because Fiona always did half the housework herself."

"Did she? I didn't know that."

"Of course you didn't. Men don't know anything. But the fact remains that you'll have to get the house properly organized if you are to hang on to your children. It won't be easy, Bernard. But I'll do everything I can."

"It's very kind of you, Tessa."

"I'm determined that David won't get his hands on them." The waiter brought the food. Tessa held up her glass and said, "I'd like more champagne, please." Leaning across the table to me, she said, "Champagne—real French champagne—is not fattening. I'm going to this perfectly wonderful doctor who's put me on a diet."

"I'm glad to hear the wonderful news about champagne," I said. "How fattening is cheap red Spanish plonk?"

"Don't start all that working-class-boy-makes-good stuff. I've heard it all before. Now let's get this straight: I'll send a car to bring your nanny and the children from your mother's house on Saturday morning. George can always find a car from one of the showrooms, and a spare driver."

"Thanks," I said. "Was there something else you wanted to talk to me about?"

"No, no, no," she said. "Just about the house. I'll get it in some sort of order. Give me your door key, I know you keep a spare one in your office desk."

"Is there anything you don't know?" I said.

She looked up and reached across the table to touch the back of my hand with her outstretched finger. Her touch made me shiver. "Quite a lot of things I don't know, Bernard," she said. "But all in good time, eh?"

Chapter 13

ERNER did not arrive at three o'clock. He did not get Dicky's message until after lunch. The plane he was due to fly out of Berlin-Tegel on had some mechanical malfunction. Since the old agreements specify that German airliners may not use the airlanes between Berlin and West Germany, there was a delay while another British Airways plane was brought into service. When eventually the plane did arrive in London, Werner was not aboard.

Werner did not arrive the following day. I phoned his apartment in Berlin-Dahlem, but the phone was unanswered.

By the third day Dicky was uttering threats and dark suspicions. "But the Berlin office sent a car," said Dicky plaintively. "And arranged his air ticket, and had one hundred pounds in sterling left with the driver. Where the hell has the bloody man gone?"

"There's probably a good explanation," I said.

"It had better be a bloody showstopper," said Dicky. "Now even the Deputy D-G has started asking about Stinnes. What am I supposed to say? Tell me that, will you?" It was not a rhetorical question; he stared at me and waited for an answer. When none came he pulled out his handkerchief and dabbed his eyes. He stood for a moment, breathing deeply as if preparing to sneeze and then finally blew his nose. "I still haven't shaken off that cold," he said.

"A couple of days at home might be the best way of curing it," I said.

He shot me a suspicious glance and then said, "It might come to that. I'm beginning to think I might be infectious."

"Give Werner until the weekend," I said. "Then perhaps we should put out some sort of alert or a contact string to find out where he is."

"Did you phone Frank Harrington?"

"Yes, but he's only just got back to Berlin. And Werner isn't one of his agents. He has no contact number for Werner."

"Only for Zena?" said Dicky sarcastically. Such caustic remarks about senior staff—let alone their misconduct—were most unusual. I began to wonder if Dicky was running a fever.

WERNER phoned me that evening, just as I was about to leave the office. The whole floor was almost empty—Dicky had gone home, Gloria Kent had gone home, my secretary had gone home. The switchboard staff had already connected the outside lines to the duty office, but luckily Werner came through on my private phone. "Where the hell have you been?" I asked him angrily. "I've had Dicky kicking my ass all around the office about you."

"I'm sorry," said Werner. He could be mournful without sounding apologetic. "But you'd better get over here right away."

"Where are you? Berlin?"

"No, I'm in England. I'm in that old safe house you used to use . . . the one near the sea at Bosham."

"Chichester? What are you doing there, Werner? Dicky will be furious."

"I can't talk. I'm using a call phone in a pub. There is someone waiting. I'll meet you at the house."

"It's about seventy miserable miles, Werner. I hate that road. It will take an hour or so."

"See you then. You remember how to find it?"

"I'll see you there," I said without enthusiasm.

BOSHAM, which the English—as a part of their chronic conspiracy to baffle foreigners—pronounce "Bozzam," is a collection of cottages, old and new, crowded onto a peninsula between two tidal creeks that give on to inland waters, and eventually to the Channel. Here are sailing boats of every shape and size, and sailing schools and sailing clubs. And here are pubs crammed with nautical junk, and clocks that chime ship's bells at closing time. And noisy men in sailor's jerseys who tow their boats behind their cars.

The safe house was not too far from Bosham's little church. It was a neat little "two up and two down," with a freshly painted weather-boarded front and bright orange roof tiles. Even in the years of depressed property prices, such little week-end cottages with their view of the boats, and sometimes even a glimpse of the water between them, had kept their value.

Summer was gone, but it had been a fine day for those lucky enough to spend it sailing. But now there was an offshore wind, and when I got out of my car the air was chilly and I needed the coat I'd thrown onto the backseat. It was twilight when I arrived. The yellow lights of the houses were reflected in the water, and there were still people on some of the boats folding their sails and trying to prolong the perfect day. Werner was waiting for me, sitting at the wheel of a Rover 2000 that was parked close up against the house. He opened the car door and I got in beside him.

"What's the story, Werner?"

"A black girl . . . woman I should say. West Indian. Was married to an American airman stationed in Germany. She's divorced. Lives in Munich; very active political worker, very vocal Communist. Then two years ago she became very quiet and very respectable. You know what I mean?"

"She was recruited by the KGB?"

"It looks that way. Last week she came to Berlin for a briefing. I followed Stinnes one evening after I'd noticed him looking at his watch all through dinner. Then I followed her. She came here." Werner smiled. He was a boy scout. He loved the whole business of espionage the way other men are obsessed with golf, women, or stamp collections.

"I believe we met," I said.

"Came here," said Werner.

"To England. Yes, I know."

"Came *here,*" said Werner. He had the car keys in his hand, and now he tapped them against the steering wheel to emphasize his words. "To this house."

"How is that possible? This is a departmental safe house."

"I know," said Werner. "I followed her here and I recognized it. You sent me here. It was a long time ago. I brought a parcel of documents for someone being held here."

"Is she in there now?"

"No, she's gone."

"Have you tried to get in?"

"I've been inside. I came out again. There's a body upstairs."

"The girl?"

"It looked like a man. I couldn't find the main switch for the electricity. You can't see much with only a flashlight."

"What sort of body?"

"The shutters were closed so there was no daylight and I didn't want to trample through the house leaving marks everywhere."

"We'd better take a look," I said. "How did you get in before?"

"Kitchen window. It's very messy, Bernard. Really messy. Blood on the floor. I've left footmarks, I'm afraid. Blood on the floor. Blood on the walls. Blood on the ceiling."

"What happened? Do you have an idea?"

"Looks like the body's been there a couple of days. Gunshot wound. High velocity head shot. You know what happens."

"We'd better take a look," I said. I got out of the car. From somewhere nearby I could hear merry holiday makers leaving the pub, their voices raised in song.

As Werner had already found, it was not difficult to get the kitchen window open, but my forced entry was not the demonstration of expertise that I'd intended. Werner did not comment on the way my shoes left mud in the sink and my elbow knocked a teacup to the floor, and for that restraint I was grateful to him.

I let Werner in through the front door and went to the cupboard under the stairs to find the fuse box and put the lights on. Nothing much had changed since I'd last visited the house. We'd had an East German scientist there for a long debriefing session. I'd taken my turn on the rota with him. To alleviate the misery of his internment, he'd been allowed some sailing trips. The house brought back happy memories for me. But since that time two Russian air force officers had been held here. One of them had eventually returned to the U.S.S.R. Despite the way in which all such internees were brought here in a closed vehicle, there had been fears about the address being compromised.

Officially the house had not been used for such defectors for some years but, such was the dogged plod of departmental housekeeping, all the arrangements about its upkeep had obviously been continued. Not only was the electricity still connected and paid for, the house was clean and tidy. There were signs of use—crockery on the draining board and fresh groceries in evidence on the shelf.

I went upstairs to the front bedroom first. I opened the doors and switched on the light. It was just as messy as Werner had described. The pale green floral wallpaper was spattered with blood; there was more on the ceiling and a sticky pool of it on the floor. Exposure to the air had discolored the blood so that it was no longer bright red but brownish and in places almost black.

It was a small room, with a single bed made up with loose covers and cushions to look like a sofa. In the corner there was a dressing table with a large mirror in which was reflected the body of a man sprawled across the cheap Indian carpet. He had been thrown forward from a small kitchen chair in which he'd been sitting. The chair was on its side; its backrest showed bare white wood where a bullet had torn a large splinter from it.

"Do you recognize him?"

"Yes," I said. "It's one of our people, a probationer. A bright kid. His name is Julian MacKenzie." The light shone on a circular disc of plastic and I picked it up from the floor. It was a watch glass with a scratch on it. I recognized it as the one from my old Omega. After it stopped I'd put the watch and the crystal in an envelope and never taken it for repair. I wondered who had found it and where.

"Did you know he was coming here?" Werner asked.

I switched off the light and pulled the door closed on the dead boy. I looked into the next room. It was another bedroom, with another single bed. "Single bed," I said, trying to keep my mind from thinking about MacKenzie's body. "No one could believe that this was a weekend cottage. Weekend cottages are always crammed with beds."

There was a dressing table in the corner, this time littered with torn pieces of wrappers, some face powder, and the smudge marks of spilled liquids. There was a large plastic box on the bed. I opened it carefully and found a set of electric hair curlers. I closed the lid again and wiped the places I'd touched. A wastepaper basket held a collection of plastic bottles—shampoo, moisturizing cream, hair conditioner, hair coloring, and a lot of screwed-up tissues and tufts of cotton wool. There was more evidence of occupation in the bathroom: long hairs in the bath where someone—probably a woman—had washed her hair, and towels draped unfolded on the rack so that they would dry easily.

"That's right," said Werner. "It's not like a weekend cottage, it's like a safe house."

He followed me downstairs. I looked round the kitchen. "Did you discover where the booze is kept when you first got in?"

"There's no booze."

"Don't be idiotic, Werner. There is always booze in a safe house."

"There's a bottle of something in the refrigerator." Werner took a chair and sat astraddle it, leaning his elbow on the chair back, his hand propped under his wide jaw. He watched me, his black eyes glowering under those bushy black eyebrows, and his forehead wrinkled in a disapproving frown. Sometimes I didn't notice what a huge bear of a man he was, but now, his shoulders hunched and feet spread wide apart, he looked almost like a Sumo wrestler.

He stared at me while I found some glasses in a cabinet and got the drink—a large square-shaped green bottle of *Bokma oude jenever*—from the refrigerator. It had no doubt come from some sailing trip to the Dutch coast. Still standing, I poured some for myself and one for Werner. He waved it away at first, but when I drank some of mine he picked it up and sniffed it suspiciously before sipping some and pulling a face.

"Poor MacKenzie," I said. I didn't sit down with him. I went round the room with bottle and glass in my hands, looking at all the pictures, the fittings, and the furniture, remembering the time I'd spent here.

"A probationer was he? He hadn't learned when to be afraid."

"The black girl was dressed as a nurse. She got a ride in my car. She said she was late for work. She pulled a hypodermic needle on me. The seat belt held me. I felt a bloody fool, Werner. But what could I do?"

"She must have slept in the second bedroom. There's a nurse's uniform in the wardrobe and a box of medical equipment including a couple of hypodermics and some drugs with labels that I don't understand."

"She said she was from Jamaica. They probably chose her because she has a British passport." I sat down and put my glass on the table with the bottle.

"Yes, I saw her go through immigration with U.K. passport holders."

"But why this house, Werner? If she was a KGB agent, why this departmental safe house? They have their own places, houses we don't know about."

Werner pulled a face to show me he didn't know the answer.

"I sent MacKenzie off to find her."

"Looks like he found her," said Werner.

"You followed the black girl here. What then?"

"I went back to London. Zena was in London, just for two days. I didn't want to leave her on her own. She frets when left alone."

"You're a bloody wonderful agent, Werner."

"I didn't know it was important," said Werner. His flushed face and the anger in his voice were indications of embarrassment. "How could I guess it was going to turn out like this?"

"But you came back. Then what?"

"The black girl's car had gone. I saw a Ford Fiesta parked down near the pub. It had a radiotelephone. I recognized the fittings and the antenna."

"MacKenzie. Yes. None of the senior staff have the standard radiotelephone fittings nowadays. It's too conspicuous."

"I climbed in here. I found the body. I phoned you. End of story."

"I appreciate it, Werner."

"Smart boy, your MacKenzie. How did he get on to her? She's not easy to follow, Bernard. What did she do that led your boy right here?"

"I don't know, Werner."

"And he didn't phone in to tell you what he was doing?"

"What are you trying to say, Werner?"

"Your MacKenzie was one of them, wasn't he? It's the only explanation that fits. He was a KGB employee. He told you nothing. He helped them do whatever they had to do, then the black girl silenced him."

"It's a tempting theory, Werner. But I don't buy it. Not yet anyway. I'd need more than that to believe that MacKenzie was a KGB employee."

"So how did he track them down? Was it just luck?"

"You saw the body upstairs, Werner. It's not pretty, is it. You and I have seen plenty of that sort of thing, but you went a bit green and I needed a drink. I don't see it as a woman's deed. She fires a gun; splashes a lot of blood. There are screams and cries and a man mortally wounded. She sees his death agonies. She fires again, more spurting blood. Then again. Then again." I rubbed my face. "No. I don't think a woman would do it that way."

"Then perhaps you don't know much about women," said Werner feelingly.

"*Crime passionel* you mean. But this is not the case of a woman who surprises her lover in bed with her rival. This was cold-blooded murder. MacKenzie was seated on a chair in the middle of the room. No evidence of any sexual motive, the bed was not even rumpled."

"If not the black woman, who?"

"It wasn't done by a woman. It was a man; men probably— a KGB hit team."

"Killing one of their own people," said Werner, resolutely holding to his theory.

"If the KGB had recruited MacKenzie at Cambridge and then he was able to get a job in the Department, they'd be keeping him in deep cover and waiting for him to get a desk for himself. They wouldn't kill him."

"So if he wasn't a KGB agent, whatever secret did your MacKenzie discover that made it necessary to kill him?"

"MacKenzie was no great detective, Werner. He was just a sharp young kid with a brilliant academic record. He wasn't even an ex-copper; no investigative experience, no training, and he wasn't a natural the way you are a natural. He'd never be able to trace an experienced KGB agent to a safe house. He was lured here, Werner. Someone was providing him with clues he had to fall over."

"Why?"

"It was our safe house, Werner. A closely guarded departmental secret. The KGB bastards wanted to show us how clever they are."

"And murder your probationer to rub salt in?" Werner was not convinced. He drank some more gin, looking at it after he sipped it as if he thought it might be poisoned. "Strange-flavored stuff this—he read the label—"*oude jenever*. It's not like real schnapps."

"Hollands; it's supposed to taste like that," I said. "It was used as a medicine when they first concocted it."

"You'd have to be damned ill to need it," said Werner, pushing it aside. "A deliberate murder?"

"He was seated in that chair in the middle of the room, Werner. His executioner was behind him. The pistol held against the top of the spine. Its the way the Okhrana executed Bolshevik revolutionaries in the time of the Czar. In the nineteen twenties the Cheka hunted down White Russian émigrés in Paris and Berlin. Some of them were killed in that fashion. In the Spanish Civil War, Stalin's NKVD went to Catalonia and executed dozens of Trotskyites like that."

"But why would a KGB hit team be so theatrical? And what did the black girl come here to do?"

"She came to see me. Or, more accurately, she saw me when she came here."

"What did she come to see you about?"

I hesitated about my reply. I poured myself another shot of gin and drank some. I'd always liked the curious malty flavor of Hollands gin, and now I welcomed the fiery path it blazed to my stomach.

"You'll have to tell me," said Werner. "We're both too deep into this one to hold back any secrets."

"Fiona sent a message. She says she'll let me keep the children here for a year but she wants me to prevent the Stinnes enrollment."

"Prevent it?"

"Not encourage it."

"Why? Did it really come from her, or is it a KGB move?"

"I don't know, Werner. I keep trying to put myself in her place. I keep trying to guess what she might do. She loves the children, Werner, but she'll want to impress her new masters. She's given her whole life to them, hasn't she—her career, her family, her marriage. She's given more of herself to Moscow than she ever gave to the children."

"Stinnes is involved," said Werner. "The black girl was briefed by Stinnes. I saw them together."

"Let's not jump to conclusions. Maybe Stinnes isn't told the whole plan. If they know he's seeing you when he comes West they might deliberately keep him in the dark." I took off my glasses and cupped my hands over my eyes to spend a moment in the dark. I felt very tired. Even the prospect of a drive back to London was daunting. Surely the existence of this safe house must have been something that Fiona had revealed to them. What else had she told them, and what else might she tell them? MacKenzie was upstairs dead, but I still had trouble believing it. My stomach was knotted with tension and even the drink didn't relax me, nor remove from my mouth the rancid taste of fear.

A sudden noise outside made me jump. I got to my feet and listened, but it was only one of the revelers falling over a rubbish bin. I sat down again and sipped my drink. I closed my eyes for a moment. Sleep was what I needed—when I woke up, it would all be different. MacKenzie would be alive, and Fiona would be at home with the children, waiting for me.

"You can't just sit here all night draining that bottle of gin, Bernard. You'll have to tell the Department."

"The trouble is, Werner, I didn't tell them about the black girl."

"But you told MacKenzie to find her."

"I kept it all unofficial."

"You're a bloody fool, Bernie." Werner had always believed that he could do my job better than I did it, and every now and again something happened to encourage him in that delusion. "A bloody fool."

"Now you tell me."

"You make trouble for yourself. Why didn't you tell them?"

"I went into the office fully intending to. Then Bret started droning on, and Frank Harrington was there to play the heavy father. I just let it slide."

"This is murder. A departmental employee, in a safe house, with KGB involvement. You can't let this one slide, Bernard."

I looked at Werner. He'd described the situation concisely, and in just the way the KGB operation planners had no doubt seen it. Well, the only thing they didn't allow for is that I might avoid the consequences by keeping my mouth tightly shut. "That's not all of it," I said. "The black girl made me drive out to London Airport. When I was there Fiona got into the back of the car. I couldn't get a look at her but it was her, no doubt of that. I'd recognize her voice anywhere. The stuff about the kids came from her direct. The black girl was with her. She heard what was said, so I suppose it was all KGB approved."

I expected Werner to be as astonished as I'd been, but he took it very calmly. "I guessed it might be something like that."

"How did you guess?"

"You saw the electric hair rollers upstairs. Rollers to change a hairstyle. There were a lot of cosmetics too. Cosmetics no black girl could use. And hair dye. When you didn't draw attention to them I realized that you knew there was another woman. It had to be Fiona. She came here to make her hair curly, and color it so she wouldn't be recognized."

"You're not just a pretty face, Werner," I said with genuine admiration.

"You don't really imagine you're going to be able to prevent all this emerging from an investigation of MacKenzie's death?"

"I don't know, Werner. But I'll try." Werner stared at me, trying to see if I was frightened. I was scared stiff but I did everything I could to conceal it.

I wished that Werner would change the subject but he persisted. "And when MacKenzie got here he'd be sure to recognize Fiona. That would be sufficient reason to kill him—they didn't want him to report her, they wanted you to do it. Or maybe wanted you *not* to report her so that the eventual consequences would be worse for you."

"Let's not get too subtle. The KGB are not noted for subtlety."

"You'd better rethink that one," said Werner. "Your wife is working for them now, and she's rewriting the book."

"Do you see evidence of that?"

"Bernie, she knows that she could never get you to defect, so she's not wasting any time trying. Instead she's doing the next best thing, she's persuading the Department that you've already changed sides. In that way she will get you removed from Operations and maybe removed from the Department completely."

"Because the KGB see me as their most dangerous enemy?" I said sarcastically.

"No, because Fiona sees you as *her* most dangerous enemy. You know her better than anyone. You know how she thinks. You're the obstacle, the one person likely to understand whatever she decides to get up to."

Perhaps Werner was right. Just as I was frightened of how Fiona could use all her knowledge of me against me, so I suppose she had that same fear of what I might do against her. The trouble was that while our marriage had left her well aware of all my weaknesses, it had taught me only that she had none. I said, "That's why I don't feel like reporting any of this to London Central. They'll say it's evidence of my being pressured and they'll keep asking me what I was under pressure about and eventually I'll find myself telling them about Fiona meeting me at the airport. And then I'll be suspended from duty pending investigation." I put the cap on the gin bottle, wiped it clean of prints, then washed up the glasses and put them back. I wanted to be active; sitting there talking to Werner was making me twitchy. "You can see this place is regularly maintained. Someone will find the body and report through the normal channels. Much better that way, Werner."

But Werner was unrelenting. "I'll do whatever you ask, Bernie. But I think you should go back to London Central and tell them everything."

"Have you left any marks anywhere?"

"A few places. But I know which places."

"Look at that," I said, holding up the watch crystal. "Some bastard planted it upstairs near the body so it would be found by the investigating officer."

"I saw you pick it up. Yours, is it?"

I nodded and put the watch glass back into my pocket. "Let's clean up and get out of here, Werner. Suppose we take the flight to Berlin tomorrow morning. Would that suit you? This will be a good time for me to be away from the office."

Werner looked at me and nodded. I was frequently complaining of the way Dicky absented himself from the office at any sign of trouble. The way in which I was now running away from trouble offended Werner's sense of duty.

"What else?" said Werner suspiciously. "I can see there's something more. You might as well tell me now." He massaged his cheek as if trying to keep awake.

It was not easy to hide my thoughts from Werner. "London Central want to put you back on their payroll. Ten thousand sterling on account, regular monthly payments plus expenses against signature. You know the score, Werner."

The sloppy cement of Werner's face set into that inscrutable concrete expression he wore to prevent anyone discovering that he was happy. "And?"

"They want you to take a short reconnaissance into the East and see what you can find out about Stinnes."

"For instance?"

"His marriage; is it really on the rocks? What is his reputation? Is he really passed over for promotion or is that just a yarn?"

"Is that all?" said Werner with heavy sarcasm. His face was very mobile now, and he moved his lips to wet them, as if his mouth had gone suddenly dry at the thought of the risks. "Any advice from London Central about how I should go about discovering all the intimate secrets of the KGB? This is not a U.S. base on visitors' day. They don't have press officers over there, handing out typewritten releases and glossy photos you can reproduce without fee, and maps of the military installations in case visitors get lost." He took a mouthful of the gin. Necessity had overcome his dislike of the flavor.

I couldn't argue with him. He knew more about the difficulties of such a job than I did, and we both knew infinitely more than those people at London Central who were going to sign the report and get the credit. "Do what you can," I said. "Take the money and do what you can."

"It won't be much," said Werner.

"The money won't be much either," I said. "So don't do anything silly." Werner emptied his glass and gave me another one of his deadpan faces. He knew I was frightened.

Chapter 14

I DROVE back to London listening to Ingrid Haebler playing Mozart piano concertos. I turned the car's tape player up very loud as I tried to disentangle the thoughts and theories whirling endlessly in my brain. Had I been less tired and less concerned with the death of MacKenzie, I might have taken reasonable precautions when entering my home. As it was, what should have been adequate warning for any man—the mortice unlocked and the letter box flap still partly open after some hand had gripped the door to push it—did not register upon my thoughts. I walked through the front door and found all the downstairs lights burning.

I walked through the hall. There was no one to be seen in the front room so I pushed the door of the kitchen and stepped back. There was a figure lost in the gloom of the tiny pantry beyond. I touched the butt of the pistol in my pocket.

"Who's there?"

"Bernard, darling. I wasn't sure if you were home or not."

"Tessa. How did you get in?"

"You gave me a door key, Bernard. Surely you remember."

"Of course."

"I'm putting frozen soup and fish fingers into the freezer, my love. Your children are coming home tomorrow. Or have you forgotten that?" She spoke over her shoulder. I could see her more clearly now in the dark shadows of the pantry. Her long fair hair was falling over her face as she stretched forward to reach into the freezer, the dark pantry ceiling made a firmament by the glittering diamond rings on her fingers. And around her there was the swirling "smoke" of frozen air.

"No," I said. But I had forgotten.

"I spoke on the phone with your nanny. She's a good girl, but she'll need food for them. You wouldn't want her to go out shopping and leave the children at home. And she won't want to drag them round the shops."

"It's very kind of you, Tessa."

She put the last packet into place and then closed the lid of the freezer chest with a loud thump. "So what about a drink?" she said. She slapped her hands to remove the crystals of ice. She was dressed in a loose-fitting button-through dress of natural cotton, and under it a shiny pink blouse that went so well with her fair hair.

I looked at my watch. It was nearly midnight. "What would you like, Tessa?"

"Did I see a bottle of champagne in the fridge? Or is that being kept for a tête-à-tête with the gorgeous Gloria?"

"News travels fast," I said, taking off my coat and getting glasses and the bottle of champagne. I put the contents of the ice tray into the champagne bucket and put the bottle into it with water.

"It's so stylish to have a proper ice bucket," said Tessa. "Did I tell you that George bought a solid silver one and someone swiped it."

"Stole it? Who?"

"We never found out, darling. It was a party we had for car people. Some bastard stole the champagne bucket. I wondered if they knew it was solid silver or if they just took it for a lark. Oh, yes, I heard all about the exotic creature you took over there to dinner. I had coffee with Daphne."

"Daphne Cruyer? I thought you and Daphne . . . That is, I thought . . ."

"Spit it out, Bernard darling. You mean you thought Daphne and I should be at each other's throats since I had a little fling with Dandy Dicky?"

"Yes." I gave all my attention to the champagne cork. After some difficulty it opened with a bang and I spilled some before pouring.

"Daphne's not like that, darling. Daphne is a lovely person. I wouldn't have done it if I'd thought that Daphne would be hurt."

"Wasn't she hurt?"

"Of course not. Daphne thinks it's all a most wonderful hoot."

"Why would Daphne think it's a hoot for you to have an affair with Dicky?"

"An affair. How romantic. It wasn't an affair, darling. No one could have an affair with Dicky, he's having an imperishable love affair with himself. What woman could compete with Dicky's first and only love?"

"So what was it?" I passed her the glass.

"It was a whim. A caprice. A sudden fancy. It was all over in a couple of weeks or so."

"Fiona said it lasted nearly three months."

"Not at all."

"Fiona had a good memory for that sort of thing. I'm sure it was three months."

"Well, three months. Don't go on about it. Three months, how long is that? I can't believe Daphne worried. She knew I wasn't going to run off with him. Could you imagine me running off with Dicky? And now Daphne has him right under her thumb."

"Does she?"

"Of course she does, darling. He's feeling as guilty as hell, and so he should. He can't do enough for Daphne nowadays; he even buys her flowers. Umm, that's delicious champagne. I told you my doctor has put me on a special diet—lots of champagne, but no other sort of alcohol and no sugar or fat." She turned the bottle so that she could read the label. "Bollinger, and vintage too. My very favorite champagne. How extravagant you are becoming. Is this something to do with Gloria?"

"I wish you'd shut up about Gloria," I said. "That bottle of Bollinger is the last bottle from the case you gave us as a present last Christmas."

"How silly I am," said Tessa. "How too too embarrassing."

"It was very kind of you, Tessa. And thank you for bringing the food for the children." I held up the glass as if in toast, and then drank to her.

"But that's not everything," said Tessa, who had a childlike need for praise. "I've had their room cleaned, and brought some new toys, and bed linen patterned with huge dragons breathing fire. Pillows, too. You should see them, Bernard. I wish they made them adult-bed size. Dragons—I would love them on my bed, wouldn't you, darling?"

"Talking of bed . . ."

"Am I keeping you up, Bernard? You look tired. I'm sorry to come over here so late, but I can't let my bridge partner down. We were playing until past eleven. And he's the one with the frozen-food wholesale place where I get all this stuff. He put it in the back of his car. It was all packed with dry ice. You needn't worry."

"I'm not worrying."

"Can I have a splash more of that champagne?" She poured it without waiting for a reply. "Oh, there's lots. More for you? Then I really must go home."

"Thanks, Tessa. Yes."

We both drank and then suddenly, as if seeing me for the first time, she said, "Bernard. Where have you been, darling? You look absolutely ghastly."

"I've been working. What do you mean?"

She stared at me. "You look positively ill, darling. You've changed. If I hadn't seen it with my own eyes, I wouldn't have believed it. In just a couple of days you've aged ten years, Bernard. Are you ill?"

"Easy does it, Tessa."

"Seriously, my love. You look frightful. You haven't had an accident in the car? You haven't run over someone or something like that?"

"Of course not."

"George had a bad accident a couple of years ago, and I remember he went quite gray-haired overnight. And he looked the way you do—green, darling. You look green and quite old."

I picked up the champagne and said, "If we're going to finish this bottle we might as well sit down and talk in comfort." I led the way into the front room, switched on the lights, and we sat down. I said, "I'm just a bit tired, that's all."

"I know. All this business with Fiona, it must be absolutely rotten for you. And now, with Daddy making himself an absolute asshole about the children, you must be having quite a time of it. And money must be a problem too. Daddy says you're selling this house. You're not, are you?" Tessa seemed tired too; at least she was not her usual high-spirited self. She let her hair swing across her face as if she wanted to hide behind it, like a child behind a curtain playing peekaboo.

"Not for the time being."

"Hang on to it, Bernard. Daddy says it's too big. But it's a sweet little house and you must have a playroom for the children as well as a bedroom. And if Nanny didn't have that large bedroom, she'd want a sitting room too."

"Your father said it was too big because he wants the children with him at Leith Hill."

"I know. I told him it was a stupid idea." Her face twitched and for a moment I wondered if she was going to cry, but she pushed her knuckles against her face and recovered her composure. "He'd never tolerate the noise the children make, and can you imagine him playing with them or reading to them at bedtime?"

"No," I said.

"He just wants the children as ornaments. Just like those suits of armor in the hall, and that ridiculous library, filled with expensive first editions that he never looks at, except when he calls a valuer in to renew the insurance. And then he goes off to tell everyone at his club what a wonderful investment he made."

"I suppose he has his good points," I said, more because of the distress she was showing than because I could think of any.

"He keeps them well hidden," she said and laughed as if shaking off her sudden bout of sadness. She got to her feet, reached for the champagne bottle, and filled her glass and mine before going back to the sofa. Then she slipped off her shoes and, leaning one elbow on the sofa end, tucked her feet under herself.

"Do you want to phone George?" I offered. "Does he know where you are?"

"The answer is no to both questions," she said. "And the answer to the next question is that he doesn't care either."

"Are things all right between you and George?"

"George doesn't love me anymore. George hates me. He's just looking for some way to get rid of me so that he can go off with someone else."

"Does George have someone else? Does he have affairs?"

"How can I be sure? Sex is like crime. Only one percent motivation and ninety-nine percent opportunity." She drank some wine. "I can't blame him, can I? I've been the worst wife any man ever had. George always wanted children." She rummaged through her handbag to get a handkerchief. "Oh, don't look so alarmed, Bernard. I'm not going to start sobbing or anything." Despite this assurance she dabbed her eyes and gave every sign of doing so. "Why did I marry him?"

"Why did you?"

"He asked me. It's as simple as that."

"I'm sure many other men asked you."

"George asked me when I was feeling low. He asked me at a time when I suddenly wanted to be married. You wouldn't understand; men never feel like that. Men just get married for peace and comfort. They never feel frightened of not being married the way women do sometimes."

I was embarrassed by the intensity of her feelings. "How do you know George has someone else? Has he told you so?"

"A wife doesn't have to be told. It's obvious that he doesn't love me. He has someone else; of course he does." She wiped her eyes with the handkerchief before looking up at me. She blinked and gave a brave little smile. "He's taking her off to South Africa."

"Women always tend to imagine men have other women," I said. "If he hasn't mentioned another woman, there possibly isn't one."

"George might have begun to hate all women. Is that what you mean? Maybe George just wants a bit of peace and quiet away from me? Away from all women. Drinking and laughing with his friends in the car business."

It was exactly what I thought. "No," I said. "Of course not. But George is very wrapped up in his work. He always has been, you know that. And the economy is still not picking up the way everyone hoped it would. Perhaps he needs to give a lot of thought to his business."

"You men always stick together."

"I hardly know George, but he always seemed a decent sort of chap. But you've led him a merry dance, Tess. It can't have been easy for him. I mean, you haven't exactly been discreet with these little affairs, have you?"

"And if you were George, the chance of being in South Africa, a few thousand miles away from me, would be a wonderful opportunity. And certainly not one to be marred by taking a wife along with you. I mean, women are everywhere, aren't they? You can rent them by the hour. Or rent them by the dozen. There are women available from the Arctic to the Pacific, from Persia to Peking."

"Women are available everywhere," I said. "But marriages, reasonably happy marriages, are extremely rare."

"I've been a fool, Bernard. George has always been a good husband. He's never made a fuss about money, and until last week I never thought of George with other women."

"What happened last week?"

"Did I tell you he went to Italy, the Ferrari factory, last week? He's been there before and I know the hotel he always stays at. So I phoned them and asked if Mrs. Kosinski was staying there. The switchboard girl said Mr. and Mrs. Kosinski were not in their room, but there was another gentleman occupying the second bedroom of the suite if I'd like to speak with him or leave a message with him."

"And did you speak with this 'him'?"

"No, I got scared and rang off."

"Who was the other man?"

"One of the people from the factory, or perhaps it was George's general manager. He goes along on these trips sometimes."

"And have you tackled George about it?"

"I tried a little test. He's going to South Africa on some business deal. I've never been to South Africa, so I said I'd go with him. He gave me a strange look and said he couldn't change the arrangements, and he's going alone."

"Is that all?"

"He's going with a woman. Surely that's obvious. He's taking her to South Africa with him."

"He's always going off on business trips. Are you saying he's always taken women with him?"

"I don't know. I've hardly ever gone with him on a business trip before. It's always so boring to meet all these car salesmen.

It was bad enough when he brought them home—all they ever talk about is delivery dates, advertising schedules, and profit margins. They never talk about motor cars unless it's rally driving or the Grand Prix. Have you ever been to a motor race, Bernard?"

"I don't think so. I don't remember it."

"Then you haven't been to one. Because if you'd been to a motor race you'd never forget it. George took me to the Monte Carlo one year. It sounded as if it might be fun. George got a suite at the Hôtel de Paris and a girl I was at school with lives in Monte Carlo with her family. Well, Bernard, I knew I'd done the wrong thing when I phoned my friend and her maid told me that they always leave town when the race is on. Because the noise is deafening and it goes on nonstop day and night. Endless, darling. I put a pillow over my head and screamed."

"You didn't stay in your hotel room all through the race?"

"I'm not a complete ninny, Bernard. George had the best seats anyone could have. But after the race has been on for ten minutes, there is no way of telling which of the wretched cars is in front and which is at the back. All you see is these stinking little machines driving past you, and you choke on the diesel fumes and get deafened by the noise. And when you try to get back to your hotel, you run into the Monaco policemen, who are just about the most asinine gorillas in the whole world. It's their big opportunity to scream and shout and push people around, and they take full advantage of it. Don't ever go, Bernard, it's absolutely ghastly."

"I take it that was the last business trip you did with George."

"And you guessed right, darling." She looked at me. Her eyes were wide and very blue.

"And now you are convinced that George has found some lady who likes the noise and diesel, and thinks the Monaco police force are wonderful."

"Well it looks that way, doesn't it? My mother always said I should go with him everywhere. Mummy never lets David out of her sight. She hated the idea of my letting George go away alone. That's always how trouble starts, my mother says." Tessa put her face into her hands and wept in a rather restrained way. I felt sorry for her. The weeping was straight out of drama school, but I could see that, beyond the abandoned-little-woman act, she was genuinely distressed.

"It's not the end of the world, Tessa."

"I've got no one to turn to," she said between sobs. "You're the only one I can talk to now that Fi has gone."

"You have a thousand friends."

"Name one."

"Don't be silly. You have so many friends."

"Is that your polite way of saying lovers, Bernard? Lovers are not friends. Not my sort of lovers, anyway. The men in my life have never been friends. My love affairs have always been jokes . . . schoolgirl jokes. Silly pranks that no one took seriously. A squeeze, a hug, a couple of hours between the sheets in a very expensive hotel room. A weekend stay in the country house of odd people I hardly knew. Passionate embraces in ski chalets and quick cuddles in parked cars. All the flushed excitement of infatuation and then it's all over. We knew it couldn't last, didn't we. Good-bye, darling, and don't look back."

"You always seemed so happy, Tessa."

"I was, darling. Happy, confident Tessa, full of fun and always making jokes about my love life. But that was while I had George to go home to. Now I don't have George to go home to."

"Do you mean . . . ?"

"Don't look so alarmed, Bernard. I don't mean literally, darling. I don't mean that I'm moving in here with you. You should see your face."

"I didn't mean that," I said. "If you leave George, you can always use the box room. There's a bed there that we've used when my mother came to stay. It's not very comfortable."

"Of course it's not comfortable, darling. It's a room made for mothers to stay. It's a horrid dark little room that would exactly suit a sister-in-law who came to stay, and who might otherwise stay too long." She gave all her attention to the bubbles rising through the champagne and ran her fingertip down the glass to trace a line through the condensation.

"Sounds like you're determined to feel sorry for yourself."

"But I am, darling. Why shouldn't I feel sorry for myself? My husband doesn't want me anymore, and the only man I've always loved keeps looking at his lovely new watch and yawning."

"Go back home and tell George you love him," I said. "You might find that everything will come out all right."

"You must be Mrs. Lonelyheart. I read your column every week."

I picked the bottle out of the bucket and divided the last of the champagne between our two glasses. The bottle dripped ice water down my arm. She smiled. This time it was a more convincing smile. "I've always adored you, Bernard. You know that, don't you?"

"We'll talk about that some other time, Tessa. Meanwhile, do you think you can drive home, or shall I phone for a cab?"

"They don't have alcohol at the bridge club, that's the worst thing about it. No, I'm as sober as a judge. I'll drive home and leave you in peace."

"Talk to George. The two of you can sort it out."

"You're a darling," she said. I helped her into her smart suede car coat and she gave me a decorous kiss. "You're the only one I can talk to." She smiled. "I'll be over here when Nanny arrives. You get on with your work. No need to worry."

"I'm flying to Berlin in the morning."

"How wretched for you, Bernard. You won't be here to welcome the children."

"No, I won't be here."

"Don't worry. I'll go to Gloriette—opposite Harrods—and get them a superb chocolate cake with 'Love from Daddy' written on the top, and I'll tell them how sorry you are to be away."

"Thanks, Tessa."

I opened the front door for her but she didn't leave. She turned to me and said, "I dreamed about Fiona the other night. I dreamed that she phoned me, and I said was she speaking from Russia, and she said never mind where she was speaking from. Do you ever dream about her, Bernard?"

"No," I said.

"It was so vivid, my dream. She said I was to meet her at London Airport. I was to tell no one. She wanted me to bring her some photos."

"Photos?"

"Photos of your children. It's so silly when you think of it —Fiona must have taken photos with her when she went. In this dream she desperately wanted these photos of the children. I dreamed she was shouting down the phone at me the way she did when we were children and she couldn't get her own way. 'Wake up,' she shouted. It was such a silly dream, but it upset me at the time. She wanted photos of you, too."

"What photos of me?"

"It was only a dream, darling. Oh, photos of you she left at my house a couple of months ago. She forgot to take them with her one night. Photos taken recently; for your passport, I should think. Awfully dull photos, and portraits of the children. Isn't it odd the way one dreams such silly trivial things?"

"Which terminal?"

"What do you mean?"

"In the dream. Which terminal at London Airport did she ask you to go to?"

"Terminal Two. Don't let it upset you, Bernard. I wouldn't have mentioned it if I'd known. Mind you, it upset me at the time. It was very early in the morning, and I dreamed I answered the phone and the operator asked me if I'd accept a reverse-charge call from Bosham. I ask you, darling, from what deep dark confines of my brain box did I dredge Bosham? I've never been there." She laughed. "George was awfully cross when I woke him up and told him. 'If the phone had really rung, I would have heard it, wouldn't I,' he said. And then I realized it was all a dream. Mind you, the phone often rings without George hearing it, especially if he's been boozing at his club the way he had been that night."

"I'd just try and forget about it," I said. "It's not unusual to get strange dreams after something like that happens."

She nodded and I squeezed her arm. Her sister's betrayal had affected her deeply. For her, as for me, it was a personal betrayal that required a fundamental rethink of their whole relationship. And that meant a fundamental rethink of oneself. Perhaps she knew what was in my mind, for she looked up at me and smiled as if at some secret we shared.

"Forget it," I said again. I didn't want Tessa to worry, and on the practical level, I didn't want her to phone the telephone exchange and check if there really had been a reverse-charge call from Bosham. It could only lead on to inquiries I was trying to avoid. I could follow Fiona's reasoning: by reversing the charges, the call didn't appear on the telephone bill of the house in Bosham and thus implicate her sister.

I kissed Tessa again and told her to look after herself. I didn't like the idea of Fiona wanting passport pictures of me. She didn't want them to set beside her bed.

I watched Tessa get into her silver VW. She lowered the car window so that she could blow me a kiss. The way the headlights flashed a couple of times and the direction indicators winked, as she backed out of the tiny parking space, made me wonder if she was telling the truth about the availability of alcohol at her bridge club.

But when I went upstairs to bed I saw MacKenzie sprawled across the floor with his brains spattered over the wallpaper. It was some sort of hallucination. Yet just for a moment, as I switched on the bedroom light, his image was as clear and as real as anything I've ever seen. It was the shock and the drink and the tiredness and the anxiety. Poor little sod, I thought, I sent him to his death. If he'd been an experienced agent, perhaps I'd not have felt so guilty about it, but MacKenzie was not much more than a child, and a novice at the spy game. As I got ready for bed, I began to suffer the delayed reaction that my body had deferred and deferred. I was shaking uncontrollably. I didn't want to admit, even to myself, that I was frightened. But that image of MacKenzie kept blurring into an image of myself, and my guilt was turning into fear. For fear is so unwelcome that it comes only in disguise, and guilt is its favorite one.

Chapter 15

THERE was a time when Lisl Hennig's house seemed gigantic. When I was a small child, each marble step of that grand staircase was a mountain. Scaling mountains had then required an exertion almost beyond me, and I'd needed a moment's rest when each summit was won. And that was how it now was for Frau Lisl Hennig. The staircase was something she tackled only when she felt at her best. I watched her as she inched her way into the "salon" and berthed in a huge gilt throne, plumped up with velvet cushions so she didn't put too much strain upon her arthritic knees. She was old, but the brown dyed hair, big eyes, and the fine features in her wrinkled face made it difficult to guess exactly how old.

"Bernd," she said, using the name by which I'd been known at my Berlin school. "Bernd. Put my sticks on the back of the chair where I can find them if I want them. You don't know what it's like to be crippled this way. Without my sticks I am a prisoner in this damned chair."

"They are there already," I said.

"Give me a kiss. Give me a kiss," she said testily. "Have you forgotten Tante Lisl? And how I used to rock you in my arms?"

I kissed her. I had been in Berlin for three days, waiting for

Werner to come back from his "short reconnaissance" to the East Sector, but every day Lisl greeted me as if seeing me after a long absence.

"I want tea," said Lisl. "Find that wretched girl Klara and tell her to bring tea. Order some for yourself if you'd like to." She had always had this same autocratic, demanding manner. She looked around her to be sure that everything was in its rightful place. Lisl's mother had chosen these hand-carved pieces of oak furniture, and the chandelier that had been hidden in the coal cellar in 1945. In Lisl's childhood this room had been softened by lacework and embroidery as befits a place to which the ladies retired after dining in the room that now contained the hotel reception desk. This salon was where Lisl's mother gave the fine ladies of Berlin afternoon tea. And on fine summer days the large windows were opened to provide a view from the balcony as the Kaiser Alexander Guard Grenadiers went marching back to their barracks behind their band.

It was Lisl who first called it a salon and entertained here Berlin's brightest young architects, painters, poets, writers, and certain Nazi politicians. To say nothing of the seven brawny cyclists from the Sports Palace who arrived one afternoon with erotic dancers from one of the city's most notorious *Tanzbars* and noisily pursued them through the house in search of vacant bedrooms. They were here still, many of those celebrities of what Berlin called the Golden Twenties. They were crowded together on the walls of this salon, smiling and staring down from sepia-toned photos that were signed with the over-wrought passions that were an expression of that reckless decade that preceded the Third Reich.

Lisl was wearing green silk, a waterfall rippling over her great shapeless bulk and cascading upon her tiny, pointed, strap-fronted shoes. "What are you doing tonight?" she asked. Klara—the "wretched girl," who was about sixty and had worked for Lisl for about twenty years—looked round the door. She nodded to me and gave a nervous smile to show that she'd heard Lisl demanding tea.

"I have to see Werner," I said.

"I was hoping you'd play cards," she said. She rubbed her painful knee and smiled at me.

"I would have liked that, Lisl," I said, "but I have to see him."

"You hate playing cards with your old Tante Lisl. I know. I know." She looked up and as the light fell on her, I could see the false eyelashes and the layers of paint and powder that she put upon her face on the days she went outside. "I taught you to play bridge. You were only nine or ten years old. You loved it then."

"I would have loved it now," I protested untruthfully.

"There is a very nice young Englishman whom I want you to meet, and old Herr Koch is coming."

"If only I didn't have to see Werner," I said, "I would have really liked to spend an evening with you." She smiled grimly. She knew I hated card games. And the prospect of meeting a "very nice young Englishman" was rivaled only by the idea of spending the evening listening to the oft-repeated reminiscences of old Mr. Koch.

"With Werner?" exclaimed Lisl, as if suddenly remembering. "There was a message for you. Werner is delayed and can't see you tonight. He'll phone you early tomorrow." She smiled. "It doesn't matter, *Liebchen*. Tante Lisl won't hold you to your word. I know you have more interesting things to do than play bridge with an ugly old crippled woman like me."

It was game, set, and match to Lisl. "I'll make up a four," I said with as much grace as I could muster. "Where was Werner phoning from?"

"*Wundervoll,*" said Lisl with a great smile. "Where was he phoning from, darling? How would I know a thing like that?" I think she'd guessed that Werner was in the East Sector, but she didn't want to admit it, not even to herself. Like so many other native Berliners, she tried not to remember that her town was now a small island in the middle of a Communist sea. She referred to the Communist world by means of jokes, half-truths, and euphemisms, the same way that three hundred years earlier the Viennese had shrugged off the besieging Ottoman Turks. "You don't really understand the bidding," said Lisl. "That's why you'll never be a good bridge player."

"I'm good enough," I said. It was stupid of me to resent her remark, since I had no ambition to become a good bridge player. I was piqued that this old woman was able to trap me into an evening's bridge, using the same obvious tactics that she'd used on me when I was an infant.

"Cheer up, Bernd," she said. "Here is the tea. And I do believe there is cake. No lemon needed, Klara, we drink it English style." The frail Klara set the tray down on the table and went through the ritual of putting out the plates, forks, and cups and saucers, and the silver bowl that held the tea strainer. "And here is my new English friend," said Lisl, "the one I was telling you about. Another cup and saucer, Klara."

I turned to see the man who'd entered the salon. It was Dicky's college chum from Mexico City. There was no mistaking this tall, thin Englishman with his brown, almost ginger, hair brushed flat against his skull. His heart-shaped face still showed the effects of the fierce Mexican sun. This ruddy complexion was marked in places by freckles that, together with his awkwardness, made him look younger than his thirty-eight years. He was wearing gray flannels and a blue blazer with large decorative brass buttons and the badge of some cricket club on the pocket. "Bernard Samson," he said. He stretched out his hand. "Henry Tiptree. Remember?" His handshake was firm but furtive, the sort of handshake that diplomats and politicians use to get through a long line of guests. "What good luck to find you here. I was talking to a chap named Harrington the other night. He said you knew more about this extraordinary town than any other ten people." His voice was cultured, throaty, and rather penetrating. The sort of voice the BBC assign to reading the news the night someone very important dies. "Extra . . . awwwrdinary town," he said again, as if practicing. This time he held the note even longer.

"I thought you worked in Mexico City."

"Und guten tag, gnädige Frau," he said to Lisl, who had been wrinkling her brow as she concentrated enough to understand this sudden onslaught of English. Henry Tiptree bent over to kiss the bejeweled hand which she lifted for him. Then he bowed again and smiled at her with that sort of sinister charm that baritones display in Hollywood musicals about old Vienna. He turned to me. "You thought I worked in Mexico City. And so did I. Haw haw. But when you've worked in the diplomatic service for a few years, you start to know that the chaps you last heard of doing the Korean language course in Seoul will next be seen working as information officers in the embassy in Paris." He scratched the side of his nose reflectively. "No, some guru in the Personnel Department considered that my school-boy German was just what was needed for me to be attached to you chaps for an undecided period of time. No explanation, no apologies, no time to get ready. Wham, bam, and here I am. Haw haw."

"Quite a surprise," I said. "I believe we're playing cards together this evening."

"I'm so pleased you're joining us," said Henry, and seemed genuinely pleased. "This is what I call the real Berlin, what? The beautiful and cultured Frau Hennig here, and this wonderful chap Koch, whom she's told me all about. These are the people one wants to meet, not the free-loading johnnies who come knocking at the door of your average embassy."

Lisl was smiling; she understood enough English to know that she was beautiful and cultured. She tapped my arm. "And wear a jacket and a tie, will you, *Liebchen?* Just to make your old Lisl happy. Just for once wear a nice suit, the one you always wear to see Frank Harrington." Lisl knew how to make me look a bloody fool. I looked at Tiptree; he smiled.

WE PLAYED cards in Lisl's study, a small room crammed with her treasures. This was where she did the accounts and collected the money from her guests. She kept her bottle of sherry here in a cupboard otherwise filled with china ornaments. And here, with its prancing angels and winged dragons, was the grotesque ormolu mantel clock that could sometimes be heard throughout the house chiming away the small hours. There was a picture of Kaiser Wilhelm over the fireplace; around it a slight brightness of the wallpaper showed it was the place where a larger signed photo of Adolf Hitler had hung for a decade that had ended with the family home becoming this hotel.

"I think the cards need a good shuffle," said Lisl plaintively as she arranged in front of her the few remaining counters for which we gave fifty pfennigs each. Lisl's losses could not possibly come to more than the price of the bottle of sherry that between us we'd almost consumed, but she didn't like losing. In that respect and many others she was very *berlinerisch*.

The four of us were arranged round the circular-topped mahogany tripod table at which Lisl usually sat to take her breakfast. The four chairs were also mahogany; superbly carved with Venetian-style figure-of-eight backs, they were all that was left of the sixteen dining chairs that her mother had so cherished. Lisl had been talking about the European royal families and the social activities of their surviving members. Despite her frequently proclaimed agnosticism, she was devoted to royalty and convinced of the divine right of kings.

But now Lothar Koch had started one of his long stories. "So what was I saying?" said Koch, who was incapable of shuffling cards and talking at the same time.

"You were telling us about this most interesting secret report on the Dutch riots," prompted Henry.

"Ah, yes," he said. Lothar Koch was a small, moth-eaten man, with dark-ringed troubled eyes and a nose far too large for his small sunken face. Mr. Koch had a large gold Rolex wristwatch and liked to wear spotted bow ties in the evening. But his expensive-looking suits were far too big for him. Lisl said that they fitted him before he lost weight, and now he refused to buy any more clothes. "I'm far too old to buy new suits," he'd told Lisl when he celebrated his seventieth birthday in a suit that was already too baggy. Now he was eighty-five, still shrinking, and he still hadn't bought any new clothes. Lisl said he stopped buying overcoats when he was sixty. "*Ja, ja, ja.* There had been riots in Amsterdam. That was the start of it. That was 1941. Brandt came into my office soon after the riots . . ."

"Rudolf Brandt," explained Lisl, "Heinrich Himmler's secretary."

"Yes," said Koch. He looked at me to be sure I was listening. He knew I'd heard all his stories before and that my attention was apt to wander.

"Rudolf Brandt," I confirmed. "Heinrich Himmler's secretary. Yes, of course."

Having confirmed that I was paying attention, Koch said, "I remember it as if it were yesterday. Brandt dumped onto my desk this report. It had a yellow front cover and consisted of forty-three typewritten pages. 'Look what that fool Bormann has come up with now,' he said. He meant Hitler, but it was customary to blame Bormann for such things. It's true Bormann had countersigned each page, but he was just the head of the party Chancellery, he had no political power. This was obviously the Führer's idea, and Brandt knew that better than anyone. But it was safer to blame Bormann; no one dared say a word against the Führer. What is it? I asked. I had enough paperwork of my own to read, I wasn't looking for another report to occupy my evening. Brandt said, 'The whole population of Holland is to be resettled in Poland.' "

"Good God," said Henry. He took a minuscule sip of his sherry and then wiped his lips with a paper napkin advertising König Pilsener. Lisl got them free. Tiptree had changed his clothes. Perhaps in response to Lisl's sartorial demands of me, he was wearing a white shirt, old school tie, and a dark gray worsted suit of the type that is issued to really sincere employees by some secret department of the Foreign Office.

"Yes," said Lisl loyally. She'd heard the story more times than I had.

"Eight and a half million people. The first three million would include 'irreconcilables,' which was Nazi jargon for anyone who wasn't a Nazi and not likely to become one. Also there would be market garden workers, farmers and anyone with agricultural training or experience. They would be sent to Polish Galicia and there create a basic economy to support the rest of the Dutch, who would arrive later."

"So what did you tell him?" said Henry. He pinched the knot of his tie between finger and thumb and shook it as if trying to remove a small striped animal that had him by the throat.

Mr. Koch looked at me. He realized that I was the "irreconcilable" part of his audience. "So what did you say, Mr. Koch?" I asked.

He looked away. My display of intense interest had not convinced him that I was listening, but he went on anyway. " 'How can we put this impossible strain upon the Reichsbahn?' I asked him. It was useless to appeal to these people on moral grounds, you understand."

"That was clever," said Henry.

"And the Wehrmacht was preparing for the attack on the U.S.S.R.," said Mr. Koch. "The work that involved was terrible . . . especially train schedules, factory deliveries, and so on. I went across to see Kersten that afternoon. It was showery, and I went out without coat or umbrella. I remember it clearly. There was a lot of traffic on Friedrichstrasse and I was drenched by the time I got back to my office."

"Felix Kersten was the personal medical adviser to Heinrich Himmler," explained Lisl.

Koch said, "Kersten was a Finnish citizen, born in Estonia. He wasn't a doctor, but he was an exceptionally skilled masseur. He'd lived in Holland before the war and had treated the Dutch royal family. Himmler thought he was a medical genius. Kersten was especially sympathetic to the Dutch, and I knew he'd listen to me."

"Why don't you deal the cards," I suggested. Koch looked at me and nodded. We both knew that if he tried to do it while continuing his story he would get his counting hopelessly muddled.

"It's a fascinating story," said Henry. "What did Kersten say?"

"He listened but didn't comment," said Koch, tapping the edges of the pack against the tabletop. "But afterwards his memoirs claimed that it was his personal intervention that saved the Dutch. Himmler suffered bad stomach cramps and Kersten warned him that such a vast scheme as resettling the entire population of Holland would not only be beyond the capabilities of the German railways but, since it would be Himmler's responsibility, it could mean a breakdown in his health."

"They dropped it?" said Henry. He was a wonderful audience, and Mr. Koch basked in the attention Henry was providing.

Koch riffled the cards so that they made a sound like a short burst of fire from a distant MG 42. He smiled and said, "Himmler persuaded Hitler to postpone it until after the war. By this time, you see, our armies were fighting in Yugoslavia and Greece. I knew there was no chance of its ever happening."

"I say, that's extraordinary," said Henry. "You should have got some sort of medal."

"He did get a medal," I said. "You did get a medal, didn't you, Herr Koch?"

Koch riffled the cards again and murmured assent.

"Mr. Koch got the *Dienstauszeichnung*, didn't you, Mr. Koch?"

Mr. Koch gave me a fixed mirthless smile. "Yes, I did, Bernd." To Henry he said, "Bernd thinks it amusing that I was given the Nazi long-service award for ten years in the Nazi Party. But as he also knows"—a finger was raised and waggled at me—"my job and my grade in the Ministry of the Interior made it absolutely necessary that I joined the party. I was never an active party worker, everyone knows that."

"Herr Koch was an irreconcilable," I said.

"You are a troublemaker, Bernd," said Mr. Koch. "If I hadn't been such a close friend of your father, I would get very angry at some of the things you say."

"Only kidding, Lothar," I said. In fact I remained convinced that old Lothar Koch was an irredeemable Nazi who read a chapter from *Mein Kampf* every night before going to sleep. But he always showed a remarkable amiability in the face of my remarks and I admired him for that.

"What's all this 'Bernd' nonsense, Samson?" said Henry, with a puzzled frown on his peeling red forehead. "You're not a German, are you?"

"Sometimes," I said, "I feel I almost am."

"This woman should have a medal," said Koch suddenly. He indicated Lisl Hennig. "She hid a family of Jews upstairs. She hid them for three years. Do you know what would have happened if the Gestapo had found them?—echhh." Mr. Koch ran his index finger across his throat. "She would have gone into a concentration camp. You were a mad fool, Lisl, my dear."

"We were all mad fools in one way or another," said Lisl. "It was a time of mad foolishness."

"Didn't your neighbors know you were hiding them?" asked Tiptree.

"The whole street knew," said Koch. "The mother of the hidden family was her cook."

"Once we had to push her into the refrigerator," said Lisl. "She was so frightened that she struggled. 'I'll suffocate,' she shouted. 'I'll suffocate.' But the kitchen maid—a huge woman, long since dead, God bless her—helped me, and we put all the food on the table and pushed Mrs. Volkmann inside."

"The Gestapo men were here, searching the house," said Mr. Koch.

"Just three of them," said Lisl. "Jumped-up little men. I took them to the bar. That is as far as they wanted to search."

"And the woman in the refrigerator?" said Henry.

"When the level of the schnapps went halfway down the bottle we decided it would be safe to get her out. She was all right. We gave her a hot-water bottle and put her to bed."

"That was Werner's mother," said Lisl to me.

"I know, Lisl," I said. "You were very brave."

OFTEN after such bridge games Lisl had provided a "nightcap" on the house, but this time she let us pay for our own drinks. I think she was still smarting because my inexpert bridge had won me five marks while she ended up losing three. She was in one of her petulant moods and complained about everything from the pain in her knees to the tax on alcohol. I was thankful that she decided to go to bed early. I knew she wouldn't sleep. She'd read newspapers and perhaps play her old records until the small hours. But we said our good nights to her, and soon after that Lothar Koch phoned for a taxi and departed.

Henry Tiptree seemed anxious to prolong the evening, and with a bottle of brandy on the table in front of us I was happy to answer his questions. "What an extraordinary old man," said Henry after Koch said good night and tottered off down the stairs to his waiting taxi.

"He saw it all," I said.

"Did he really have to become a Nazi because he worked in the Ministry?"

"It was because he was a Nazi that he got a job in the Ministry. Prior to 1933 he was working at the reception desk of the Kaiserhof. That was a hotel that Hitler used a great deal. Lothar knew most of the Nazi big shots. Some of them came in with their girl friends and the word soon went round that if you needed to rent a room by the hour, then Lothar—the one with the party badge on the lapel of his coat—was the right clerk to see."

"And for that he got a job in the Ministry of the Interior?"

"I don't know that that was the only reason, but he got the job. It wasn't, of course, the high-ranking post that Lothar now likes to remember. But he was there and he kept his ears open.

And he closed his eyes to such things as Lisl hiding Werner's parents."

"And are his stories true?"

"The stories are true. But Lothar is prone to change the cast so that the understudy plays leading man now and again."

Henry studied me earnestly before deciding to laugh. "Haw haw," he said. "This is the real Berlin. Gosh. The office wanted to put me into Kempinski or that magnificent new Steigenberger Hotel, but your friend Harrington told me to install myself in here. This is the real Berlin, he said. And, by gosh, he's right."

"Mind if I pour myself a little more of that brandy?" I said.

"Oh, I say. Let me." He poured me a generous measure while taking only a small tot for himself. "And I guess you're here for some damned cloak-and-dagger job with Dicky?"

"Wrong twice," I said. "Dicky is safely tucked up in bed in London, and I am only here to collect a bag of documents to carry back to London. It's a courier's job really, but we're short of people."

"Damn," said Henry. "And I was persuading myself that the worried look on your brow all evening was you fretting about some poor devil out there cutting his way through the barbed wire, what?" He laughed and drank some brandy. From Lisl's room I heard one of her favorite records playing. It was scratchy and muffled.

> ". . . *No one here can love and understand me,*
> *Oh, what hard luck stories they all hand me . . .*"

"I'm sorry to disappoint you," I said.

"Couldn't we compromise?" said Henry cheerfully. "Couldn't you tell me that there is at least one James Bond johnny out there risking his neck among the Russkies?"

"There probably is," I said. "But no one has told me about him."

"Haw haw," said Henry and drank some brandy. At first

he'd been drinking very sparingly but now he abandoned some of that caution.

"Tell me what you're doing here," I said.

"What am I doing here. Yes, what indeed. It's a long story, my dear chap."

"Tell me anyway." I looked at my watch. It was late. I wondered where Werner had phoned from. He was in a car with East German registration. That always made it more complicated; he wouldn't bring that car into the West. He'd planned to return through the Russian Zone and on to the autobahn that comes from Helmstedt. I'd never liked that method; the *Autobahnen* were regularly patrolled to prevent East Germans meeting West German transients at the roadside. I'd arranged for someone to be at the right place at the arranged time this morning. Now I had no idea where he was, and I could do nothing to help him. Lisl's record started again.

> "*. . . Pack up all my care and woe. Here I go, singing low,*
> *Bye bye Blackbird . . .*"

"Do you have time to hear my boring life story?" said Henry. He chuckled. We both knew that Henry Tiptree was not the sort of man who confided his life story to anyone. Never complain, never explain, is the public school canon.

"I have the time," I said. "And you have the brandy."

"I thought you were going to say, 'I have the time if you have the inclination,' as Big Ben said to the leaning tower of Pisa. What? Haw haw."

"If you're working on something secret . . ." I said.

He waved away any such suggestion. His hand knocked against his glass and spilled some of his drink, so he poured more. "My immediate boss is working on one of those interminable reports that will be called something like Western Negotiating Policy and Soviet Military Power. He will have his name on the front and get promoted on the strength of it. I'm just the chap who, after doing all the legwork, will wind up with my name lost in a long list of acknowledgments." This thought prompted him to drink more seriously.

"And what will it say, your long study?"

"I say, you are polite. You know what it will say, Samson. It will say all those things we all know only too well but that politicians are desperately keen we should forget."

"Such as?"

"That eighty percent of all armaments established in Central Europe since 1965 belong to the Warsaw Pact countries. It will say that between 1968 and 1978 American military spending was cut by forty percent, and during the same period Soviet military spending increased by seventy-five percent. It will record how Western military strength was cut by fifty thousand men, while during the same period the East increased its forces by one hundred and fifty thousand men. It will tell you nothing that you don't already know."

"So why write it?"

"Current theory has it that we must look for the motives behind the huge Soviet military buildup. Why are the Russkies piling up these enormous forces of men, and gigantic stockpiles of armaments? My master feels that an answer can be found by looking at the detailed tactical preparations made by Russian army units in the front line; units that are facing NATO ones."

"How will you do that?" I asked. Lisl's record was now playing for the third time.

"It's a long and arduous process. We have people who regularly talk with Russian soldiers—on day-to-day matters—and we interrogate deserters and we have reports from cloak-and-dagger outfits." He bared his teeth. "Have some more brandy, Samson. I heard you're quite a drinker."

"Thanks," I said. I wasn't sure I liked having that reputation, but I wasn't going to spare his brandy to disprove it. He poured a large measure for both of us and drank quite a lot of his.

"I'm mostly with your people," he said. "But I'll be spending time with other outfits too. Dicky arranged all that. Awfully good fellow, Dicky." A lock of ginger hair fell forward across his face. He flicked it back as if annoyed by a fly. And when it fell forward again, pushed it back with enough force to disarrange more hair. "Cheers."

"What will you be doing with them?" I said.

He spoke more slowly now. "Same damn thing. Soviet Military Power and Western . . . what did I say it was called?"

"Something like that," I said. I poured out more brandy for both of us. We were near the bottom of the bottle now.

"I know what you're doing, Samson," he said. His voice was pitched high, as a mother might speak to a baby, and he raised a fist in a joking gesture of anger. "At least . . . I know what you're trying to do." His words were slurred and his hair in disarray.

"What?"

"Get me drunk. But you won't do it, old chap." He smiled. "I'll drink you under the table, old fellow."

"I'm not trying to make you drunk," I said. "The less you drink, the more there is for me."

Henry Tiptree considered this contention carefully and tried to find the flaw in my reasoning. He shook his head as if baffled and drained the brandy bottle, dividing it between us drip by drip with elaborate care. "Dicky said you were cunning."

"Then here's to Dicky," I said in toast.

"Cheers to Dicky," he responded, having misheard me. "I've known him a long time. At Oxford I always felt sorry for him. Dicky's father had investments in South America and lost most of his money in the war. But the rest of Dicky's family were well off. Dicky had to watch his cousins dashing about in sports cars and flying to Paris for weekends when Dicky didn't have the price of a railway ticket to London. It was damned rotten for him; humiliating."

"I didn't know that," I said.

"Chaps at Oxford said he was a social climber . . . and he was, and still is . . . But that's what spurred Dicky into getting such good results. He wanted to show us all what he could do . . . and of course having no money meant he had a lot of time on his hands."

"He has a lot of time on his hands now," I said.

Henry Tiptree looked at me solemnly before giving a sly grin. "What about another bottle of this stuff?" he offered.

"I think we've both had enough, Henry," I said.

"On me," said Henry. "I have a bottle in my room."

"Even if it's on you, we've had enough," I said. I got to my feet. I was in no hurry. I wasn't drunk, but my response times were down and my coordination poor. What time in the morning would Werner phone, I wondered. It was stupid of me to tell Werner that he would be going on the payroll. Now he'd be determined to show London Central what they'd been missing all those years. With Werner that could be a surefire recipe for disaster. I'd seen Werner when he wanted to impress someone. When we were at school there had been a pretty girl named Renate who lived in Wedding. Her mother cleaned the floor at the clinic. Werner was so keen to impress Renate that he tried to steal an American car that was parked outside the school. He was trying to force the window open with wire when the driver, an American sergeant, caught him. Werner was lucky to get away with a punch in the head. It was ridiculous. Werner had never stolen anything in his life before. A car— Werner didn't have the slightest idea of how to drive. I wondered if he'd had trouble in the Sector or out in the Zone. If anything happened to him I'd blame myself. There'd be no one else to blame.

Henry Tiptree was sitting rigidly in his seat, his head facing forward and his body very still. His eyes flicked to see about him, like a lizard watching an unsuspecting fly. A less tidy man would not have looked so drunk. On the impeccable Henry Tiptree such slightly disarranged hair, the tie knot shifted a fraction to one side, and the jacket rumpled by his attempts to fasten the wrong button made him look comic. "You won't get away with it," he said angrily. He was going through the various stages of drunkenness from elation to depression via happiness, suspicion, and anger.

"Get away with what?" I asked.

"You know, Samson. Don't play the innocent. You know." This time his anger enabled him to articulate clearly.

"Tell me again."

"No," he said. He was staring at me with hatred in his eyes.

I knew then that Tiptree played some part in spinning the intricate web in which I was becoming enmeshed. On every side I was aware of suspicion, anger, and hatred. Was it all Fiona's doing, or was it something I had brought upon myself? And how could I fight back when I didn't know where to find my most determined enemies, or even who they were?

"Then good night," I said. I drank the rest of my brandy, got up from the chair, and nodded to him.

"Good night, Mr. bloody Samson," said Tiptree bitterly. "Champion bloody boozer and secret agent extraordinary."

I knew he was watching me as I walked across the room, so I went carefully. I looked back when I got as far as the large folding doors that divided the salon from the bar. He was struggling to get to his feet, reaching right across to grip the far edge of the table. Then, with whitened knuckles, he strained to pull himself up. He seemed well on the way to succeeding, but when I got to the stairs I heard a tremendous crash. His weight had proved too much and the table had tipped up.

I returned to the bar where Henry Tiptree had fallen full length on the floor. He was breathing very heavily and making slight noises that might have been groans, but he was otherwise unconscious. "Come along, Henry," I said. "Let's get out of here before Lisl hears us. She hates drunks." I knew if he was found there in the morning Lisl would blame me. No matter what I said, anything that happened to this "English gentleman" would be my fault. I put the table back into position and hoped that Lisl hadn't heard the commotion.

As I dragged Tiptree up onto my shoulder in a fireman's lift, I began to wonder why he'd come here. He'd been sent surely, but who had sent him? He wasn't the sort who come to stay in Tante Lisl's hotel, and go down the corridor for a bath each morning and then find there isn't any hot water. The Tiptrees of this world prefer downtown hotels, where everything works, even the staff; places where the silk-attired jet-setters of all sexes line up bottles of Louis Roederer Cristal Brut, and turn first to those columns of the newspaper that list share prices.

Henry Tiptree had the glossy polish that the best English boarding schools can sometimes provide. Such boys quickly come to terms with bullies, cold showers, corporal punishment, homosexuality, the classics, and relentless sport, but they acquire the hardness that I'd seen in Tiptree's face. He had a mental agility, plus a sense of purpose, that his friend Dicky Cruyer lacked. But of the two I'd take Dicky anytime. Dicky was just a freeloader, but behind all the haw haws and the schoolboy smiles this one was an expensively educated storm trooper.

As I crossed the salon, with Tiptree's whole weight upon me, I swayed and so did the mirror, the floor, and the ceiling, but I steadied myself again and paused before going past the door that led to Lisl's room.

"Make my bed and light the light,
I'll arrive late tonight, Blackbird bye bye."

Chapter 16

I T WAS cold. Featureless gray cloud stretched across the flat countryside as far as the horizon. Rain came down relentlessly, so that the last of those villagers who'd been huddled in cottage doorways waiting for a respite now hurried off and got wet. All the gutters were spilling and the rain gurgled down the drainpipes and overflowed the drains. Slanted sheets of it rebounded from the cobblestone village street to make a phantom field of wheat through which occasional motorcars or delivery vans slashed their way like harvesters.

The message from Werner had told me to come to the Golden Bear, and I had come here and I had waited two days. On the second day a young *Oberstabsmeister* had arrived at breakfast time. I recognized the dark green VW Passat station wagon. It bore the badge of the *Bundesgrenzschutz*. For West Germany had border guards too, and one of their jobs was investigating strangers who came to border villages and spent too much time staring eastwards at the barbed wire and the towers that marked the border where people on excursions from the German Democratic Republic got shot dead.

The border guard NCO was a white-faced youth with fair hair that covered the tops of his ears and curled out from under his uniform hat. "Papers," he said without the formality of a greeting or introduction. He knew I'd been watching him as he came in. I'd seen him check the hotel register and exchange a few words with the proprietor. "How long do you plan to stay?"

"About a week. I go back to work next Monday." I'd booked the room for seven days. He knew that. "I'm from Berlin," I said obsequiously. "Sometimes I feel I must get away for a few days."

He grunted.

I showed him my papers. I was described as a German citizen, resident in Berlin, and working as a foreman in a British army stores depot. He stood for a long time with the papers in his hand, looking from the documentation to me and then back again. I had the impression he didn't entirely believe my cover story, but plenty of West Berliners came down the autobahn and took their vacation here on the easternmost edge of West Germany. And if he contacted the army my cover story would hold up.

"Why here?" said the border guard.

"Why not here?" I countered. He looked out of the window. The rain continued relentlessly. Across the road workmen were demolishing a very old half-timbered building. They went on working despite the rain. As I watched, a wall fell with a crash of breaking laths and plaster and a shower of rubble. The bleached plaster went dark with raindrops, and the cloud of dust that rolled out of the wreckage was quickly subdued. The fallen wall revealed open fields beyond the village and a shiny strip that was a glimpse of the wide waters of the great Elbe River that divided East from West. The Elbe had always been a barrier; it had even halted Charlemagne. Throughout history it had divided the land: Lombard from Slav, Frank from Avar, Christian from barbarian, Catholic from Protestant, and now Communist from capitalist. "It's better than over there," I said.

"Anywhere is better than over there," said the guard with ill humor, as if I'd avoided his question. Beyond him I saw the proprietor's son Konrad come into the breakfast room. Konrad was a gangling eighteen-year-old in blue jeans and a cowboy shirt with fringes. He was unshaved, but I was yet to decide whether this was a deliberate attempt to grow a beard or a part of the casual indifference he seemed to show for all aspects of ordinary morning ablutions. He began setting the tables for lunch; on each he put cutlery and wine glasses, linen napkins and cruet, and finally a large blue faience pot of special mustard for which the Golden Bear was locally famous. Despite the care and attention he gave to his task, I had no doubt that he'd come into the room to eavesdrop.

"I walk," I said. "The doctor said I must walk. It's for my health. Even in the rain I walk every day."

"So I heard," said the guard. He dropped my identity papers onto the red-checked tablecloth alongside the basket containing breakfast rolls. "Make sure you don't walk in the wrong direction. Do you know what's over there?"

He was looking out of the window. One hand was in his pocket, the thumb of the other hooked into his belt. He looked angry. Perhaps it was my Berlin accent that annoyed him. He sounded like a local; perhaps he didn't like visitors from the big city, and whatever Berliners said, it could sound sarcastic to a critical ear. "Not exactly," I said. Under the circumstances it seemed advisable to be unacquainted with what was "over there."

The white-faced *Oberstabsmeister* took a deep breath. "Starting from the other side, you first come to the armed guards of the *Sperrzone*. People need a special pass to get into that forbidden zone, which is a five-kilometers-wide strip of ground, cleared of trees and bushes, so that the guards can see everything from their towers. The fields there can only be worked during daylight and under the supervision of the guards. Then comes a five-hundred-meter-deep *Schutzstreifen*. The fence there is three meters high and made of sharp expanded metal. The tiny holes are made so that you can't get a hold on it, and if your fingertips are so small that they can go into the gaps—a woman's or a child's fingers, for instance—the metal edge will cut through the finger like a knife. That marks the beginning of the 'security zone' with dog patrols—free-running dogs sometimes—and searchlights and mine fields. Then another fence, slightly higher."

He pursed his lips and closed his eyes as if remembering the details from a picture or a diagram. He was speaking as a child recites a difficult poem, prompted by some system of his own rather than because he really understood the meaning of what he said. But for me his words conjured up a vivid memory. I'd crossed such a border zone one night in 1978. The man with me had been killed. Poor Max, a good friend. He'd screamed very loudly so that I thought they'd be sure to find us, but the guards were too frightened to come into the mine field and Max took out the searchlight with a lucky shot from his pistol. It was the last thing he did; the flashes from the gun showed them where he was. Every damn gun they had was fired at him. I'd arrived safely but so shattered that they took me off the field list and I'd been behind a desk ever since. And now, listening to the guard, I did it all again. My face felt hot and there was sweat on my hands.

The guard continued. "Then a ditch with concrete sides that would stop a tank. Then barbed wire eight meters deep. Then the *Selbstschussgeräte,* which are devices that fire small sharp pieces of metal and are triggered by anyone going near them. Then there is a road for patrol cars that go up and down all the time. And on each side of that roadway there's a carefully raked strip that would show a footmark if anyone crossed it. Only then do you get to the third and final strip—the *Kontrollstreifen* with another two fences, very deep barbed wire, more mine fields, and observation towers manned by machine gunners. I don't know why they bother to man the towers in the *Kontrollstreifen;* as far as we know, no escaper along this section has ever got within a hundred meters of it." He gave a grim little chuckle.

I had gone on buttering my breakfast roll and eating it during this long litany, and this seemed to annoy him. Now that his description had finally ended I looked up at him and nodded.

"Then of course there is the river," said the guard.

"Why are you telling me all this?" I said. I drank some coffee. I desperately needed a drink, a proper drink, but the coffee would have to do.

"You might as well understand that your friend will not be coming," said the guard. He watched me. My hand trembled as I brought the cup down from my mouth and I spilled coffee on the tablecloth.

"What friend?" I dabbed at the stain.

"We've seen your sort before," said the border guard. "I know why you are waiting here at the Golden Bear."

"You're spoiling my breakfast," I said. "If you don't leave me in peace, I'll complain to the Tourist Bureau."

"Walk west in future," he said. "It will be better for your health. No matter what your doctor might prescribe." He grinned at his joke.

After the guard had departed, the proprietor's son came over to me. "He's a bastard, that one. He should be 'over there,' that one." *Drüben:* over there. No matter which side of the border it was, the other side was always "*drüben.*" The boy spread a tablecloth on the table next to mine. Then he laid out the cutlery. Only when he got to the cruet did he say, *"Are* you waiting for someone?"

"I might be," I said.

"Nagel. That's his name. Oberstabsmeister Nagel. He would make a good Communist guard. They talk to the Communists every day. Do you know that?"

"No."

"One of the other guards told me about it. They have a telephone link with the border guards on the other side. It's supposed to be used only for river accidents, floods, and forest fires. But every morning they test it and they chat. I don't like the idea of it. Some bastard like Nagel could easily say too much. Your friend won't try swimming, will he?"

"Not unless he's crazy," I said.

"Sometimes at night we hear the mines exploding," said Konrad. "The weight of a hare or a rabbit is enough to trigger them. Would you like more butter, or more coffee?"

"I've had enough, thanks, Konrad."

"Is he a close friend, the one you're expecting?"

"We were at school together," I said.

Konrad crossed himself, flicking his fingers to his forehead and to his shoulders with a quick gesture that came automatically to him.

NOTWITHSTANDING Oberstabsmeister Nagel's warning, I strolled along the river that morning. I was buttoned into my trench coat against the ceaseless rain. It is flat, this land, part of the glaciated northern lowlands. To the west is Holland, to the north an equally flat Denmark, to the south the heathland of Lüneburg. As to the east, a man could walk far into Poland before finding a decent-sized hill. Except that no man could walk very far east.

Near the river there was a battered enamel notice: HALT. ZONENGRENZE. It was an old sign that should have been replaced a long time ago. The Soviet Union's military occupation zone of Germany was now fancifully called the German Democratic Republic. But like Werner I could not stop calling it the Russian Zone. Perhaps we should have been replaced a long time ago too.

I walked on through grass so high that it soaked the legs of my trousers right up to the knees. I knew I would be no nearer to Werner out on the riverbank, but I couldn't stay cooped up in the Golden Bear. The Elbe is very wide here, meandering as great rivers do on such featureless terrain. And on both banks there are marshy fields, bright green with the tall sharp-bladed grass that flourishes in such water meadows. And although the far bank of the river had been kept clear of all obstruction, on this side there were young willow and alder, trees which are always thirsty. From across the river there came a sudden noise —the fierce rattle of a heron taking to the air. Something had flushed it out, the movement of some hidden sentry perhaps. It flew over me with leisurely beats of its great wings, its legs trailing in the soft air as a child might trail its fingers from a boat.

A light wind cut into me but did not disperse the gray mist that followed the river. The sort of morning when border guards get jumpy and desperate men get reckless. Only workingmen were abroad, and working boats too. Barges, long strings of them, brown phantoms gliding silently on the almost colorless water. They slid past, following the dredged channel that took them on a winding course, sometimes near to the east bank and sometimes near the west one. All Communist claims to half the river had faltered on the known difficulties of the deep-water channel. Even the East German patrol boats, specially built with shallow draft hulls, could not keep to the half of the river their masters claimed. There were West German boats too: a police cruiser and a high-speed customs boat put-tering along this deserted stretch of riverbank.

I spotted another heron, standing in the shallow water star-ing down. "The patient killer of the marshland," my school-book had called it. It was absolutely still, except that it swayed slightly as the reeds and rushes moved in the wind, waiting for a fish to swim into range of that spearlike beak. Now and again the wind along the water gusted enough to make the mist open like curtains. On the far bank a watchtower was suddenly vis-ible. An opened window—mirrored to prevent a clear view of the gun men—flashed as the daylight was reflected in its copper-colored glass. And then, as suddenly, the mist closed and the tower, the windows, the men—everything—vanished.

When I reached the remains of the long-disused ferry pier I saw activity on the far side of the river. Four East German workmen were repairing the fencing. The supports were tilting forwards, their foundations in the marshy riverbank softened further by the heavy rain. While the four men worked, two guards—*Kasernierte Volkspolizei*—stood by with their machine pistols ready and looked anxiously at the changing visibility lest their charges escape into the mist. Such "barracks police" were considered more trustworthy than men who went home each night to their wives and families.

More barges passed. Czech ones this time, heading down to where the river crossed the border into Czechoslovakia. Sitting on the hatch cover there was a bearded man drinking from a mug. He had a dog with him. The dog barked at a patch of undergrowth on the far side of the river and ran along the boat to continue its protest.

As I got to the place at which the dog had barked I saw what had attracted its attention. There were East German soldiers, three of them, dressed in battle order complete with camou-flaged helmets, trying to conceal themselves in the tall grass. They were *Aufklärer*, specially trained East German soldiers, who patrolled the furthermost edge of the frontier zone, and sometimes well beyond it. They had a camera, they always had cameras, to keep the capitalists observed and recorded. I waved at their blank faces and pulled my collar up across my face.

I walked for nearly two hours, looking at the river and thinking about Stinnes and Werner and Fiona, to say nothing of George and Tessa. Until ahead of me I saw a dark green VW Passat station wagon parked. Whether it was Oberstabsmeister Nagel or one of his associates I did not want to find out. I cut back across the field where the car could not follow and from there back to the village.

It was lunchtime when I arrived at the Golden Bear. I changed out of my wet shoes and trousers and put on a tie. As I was polishing the rain spots from my glasses there was a knock at my door. "Herr Samson? Konrad here."

"Come in, Konrad."

"My father asks if you are having lunch."

"Are you expecting a rush on tables?"

Konrad smiled and rubbed his chin. I suppose his unshaven face itched. "Papa likes to know."

"I'll eat the *Pinkel* and kale if that's on the menu today."

"It's always on the menu; Papa eats it. A man in this village makes the *Pinkel* sausage. He makes *Brägenwurst* and *Kochwurst* too. *Pinkel* is a Lüneburg sausage. But people come from Lüneburg, even from Hamburg, to buy them in the village. My mother prepares it with the kale. Papa says cook can't do it properly." Having heard my lunch order he didn't depart. He was looking at me, the expression on his face a mixture of curiosity and nervousness. "I think your friend is coming," he said.

I draped my wet trousers over the central heating radiator. "And some smoked eel too; a small portion as a starter. Why do you think my friend is coming?"

"Mother will press the wet trousers if you wish." I gave them to him. "Because there was a phone call from Schwanheide. A taxi is bringing someone here."

"A taxi?"

"It is a frontier crossing point," explained Konrad in case I didn't know.

"My friend would not phone to say he was coming."

Konrad smiled. "The taxi drivers phone. If they bring someone here and a room is rented, they get money from my father."

Schwanheide was a road crossing point not far away, where the frontier runs due north, away from the River Elbe. I gave the boy my trousers. "You'd better make that two lots of *Pinkel* and kale," I said.

WERNER arrived in time for lunch. The dining room was a comfortable place to be on such a damp chilly day. There was a log fire, smoke-blackened beams, polished brass, and red-checked tablecloths. I felt at home there because I'd found the same bogus interior everywhere from Dublin to Warsaw and a thousand places in between, with unashamed copies in Tokyo and Los Angeles. They came from the sort of artistic designer who paints robins on Christmas cards.

"How did it go?" I asked. Werner shrugged. He would tell me in his own good time. He always had to get his thoughts organized. He ordered a tankard of Pilsener. Werner never seemed to require a strong drink no matter what happened to him, and he still hadn't finished his beer by the time the smoked eel and black bread arrived. "Was there any trouble?"

"No real trouble," said Werner. "The rain helped."

"Good."

"It rained all night," said Werner. "It was about three o'clock in the morning when I came through Potsdam . . ."

"What the hell were you doing in Potsdam, Werner? That's to hell and gone."

"There were road repairs. I was diverted. When I came through Potsdam it was pouring with rain. There was not a soul to be seen anywhere; not one car. Not even a police car or an army truck until I got to the center of town, Friedrich Ebert Strasse . . . Do you know Potsdam?"

"I know where Friedrich Ebert Strasse is," I said. "The intelligence report I showed you said that there's a traffic checkpoint lately at the Nauener Tor after dark."

"You read all that stuff, do you?" said Werner admiringly. "I don't know how you find time enough."

"I hope you read it too."

"I did. But I remembered too late. There was a checkpoint there last night. At least there was an army truck and two men inside it. They were smoking. I only saw them because of the glow of their cigarettes."

"Were your papers okay? How did you account for being over there? That's a different jurisdiction."

"Yes, its Bezirk Potsdam," said Werner. "But I would have talked my way out of trouble. The diversion signs are not illuminated. I should think a lot of people get lost trying to find their way back to the autobahn. But the rain was very heavy and those policemen decided not to get wet. I slowed down and almost stopped, to show I was law-abiding. The driver just wound down the window of the truck and waved me through."

"It didn't used to be like that, did it, Werner? There was a time when everyone over there did everything by the book. No more, no less—always by the book. Even in hotels the staff would refuse tips or gifts. Now it's all changed. Now no one believes in the socialist revolution, they just believe in Westmarks."

"These were probably conscripts," said Werner. "Counting out their eighteen months of compulsory service. Maybe even *Kampfgruppe.*"

"*Kampfgruppen* are keen," I said. "Unpaid volunteers. They would have been all over you."

"Not any longer," said Werner. "They can't get enough volunteers. The factories pressure people to join nowadays. They make it a condition of being promoted to foreman or supervisor. The *Kampfgruppen* have gone very slack."

"Well, that suits me," I said. "And when you were coming through Potsdam with papers that say you have limited movement in the immediate vicinity of Berlin, I suppose that's all right with you too."

"It's not just the East," said Werner defensively. He regarded any criticism of Germans and Germany as a personal attack upon him. Sometimes I wondered how he reconciled this patriotism with wanting to work for London Central. "It's the same everywhere: bribery and corruption. Twenty or more years ago, when we first got involved in this business, people stole secrets because they were politically committed or patriotic. Moscow's payments out were always piddling little amounts, paid to give Moscow a tighter grip on agents who would willingly have worked for nothing. How many people are like that nowadays? Not many. Now both sides have to pay dearly for their espionage. Half the people who bring us material would sell to the highest bidder."

"That's what capitalism is all about, Werner." I said it to needle him.

"I'd hate to be like you," said Werner. "If I really believed that, I wouldn't want to work for London."

"Have you ever analyzed your obsession about working for the Department?" I asked him. "You're making enough money, you've got Zena. What the hell are you doing schlepping around in Potsdam in the middle of the night?"

"It's what I've done since I was a kid. I'm good at it, aren't I?"

"You're better at it than I am; that's what you want to prove, isn't it, Werner?" He shrugged as if he'd never thought about it before. I said, "You want to prove that you could do my job without tarnishing yourself the way that I tarnish myself."

"If you're talking about the hippies on the beach . . ."

"Okay, Werner. Here we go. Tell me about the hippies on the beach. I knew we'd have to talk about it sooner or later."

"You should have reported your suspicions to the police," said Werner primly.

"I was in the middle of doing a job, Werner. I was in a

foreign country. The job I do is not strictly legal. I can't afford the luxury of a clear conscience."

"Then what about the house in Bosham?" said Werner.

"I do things my way, Werner."

"You started this argument," said Werner. "I have never criticized you. It's your conscience that's troubling you."

"There are times when I could kill you, Werner," I said.

Werner smiled smugly, then we both looked round at the sound of laughter. A party of people were coming into the dining room for lunch. It was a birthday lunch given for a bucolic sixty-year-old. He'd been celebrating before their arrival to judge by the way he blundered against the table and knocked over a chair before getting settled. There were a dozen people in the party, all of them over fifty and some nearer seventy. The men were in Sunday suits and the women had tightly waved hair and old-fashioned hats. Twelve lunches: I suppose that's why the kitchen wanted my order in advance. "Two more Pilsener," Werner called to Konrad. "And my friend will have a schnapps with his."

"Just to clean the fish from my fingers," I said. The boy smiled. It was an old German custom to offer schnapps with the eel and use the final drain of it to clean the fingers. But like lots of old German customs it had now been conveniently discontinued.

The birthday party occupied a long table by the window, but they were too close for Werner to go on with his account. So we chatted about things of no importance and watched the celebration.

Konrad brought our *Pinkel* and kale, a casserole dish of sausage and greens, with its wonderful smell of smoked bacon and onions. And, having decided that I was a connoisseur of fine sausage, his mother sent a small extra plate with a sample of the *Kochwurst* and *Brägenwurst*.

The birthday party were eating a special order of *Schlesisches Himmelreich*. This particular "Silesian paradise" was a pork stew flavored with dried fruit and hot spices. There was a cheer when the stew, in its big brown pot, first arrived. And another cheer for the bread dumplings that followed soon after. The portions were piled high. The ladies were tackling it delicately, but the men, despite their years, were shoveling it down with gusto, and their beer was served in liter-size tankards which Konrad replaced as fast as they were emptied.

Osmund, the red-faced farmer whose birthday was being celebrated, kept proposing joke toasts to "celibacy" and "sweethearts and wives—and may they never meet" and then, more seriously, a toast for Konrad's mother, who every year cooked this fine meal of Silesian favorites.

But the party did not become more high spirited as the celebration progressed. On the contrary, everyone became more dejected, starting from the moment when Osmund proposed a toast to "absent friends." For these elderly Germans were all from Breslau. Their beloved Silesia was now a part of Poland, and they would never see it again. I'd caught their accents when they first entered the room, but now that memories occupied their minds and alcohol loosened their tongues, the Silesian accents became far stronger. There were quick asides and rejoinders using local words and phrases that I didn't know.

"Our Germany has become little more than a gathering place for refugees," said Werner. "Zena's family are just like them. They have these big family reunions and talk about the old times. They talk about the farm as if they'd left it only yesterday. They remember the furniture in every room of those vast houses, which fields never yielded winter barley and which had the earliest crop of sugar beet, and they can name every horse they've ever ridden. And they do what these people at the next table are doing, they eat the old dishes, talk about long dead friends and relatives. Eventually they'll probably sing the old songs. It's another world, Bernie. We're big-city kids. People from the country are different from us, and these Germans from the eastern lands knew a life we can't even guess at."

"It was good while it lasted."

"But when it ended it ended forever," said Werner. "Her family got out just ahead of the Red Army. The house was hit by artillery fire before they would face the reality of it and actually start moving westwards. And they came out with virtually only what they stood up in—a handful of cash, some jewelry, and a pocketful of family photos."

"But Zena is young. She never saw the family estates in East Prussia, did she?"

"Everything was blown to hell. Someone told them that there's a fertilizer factory built over it now. But she grew up listening to these fairy stories, Bernie. You know how many kids have fantasies about really being born aristocrats or film stars."

"Do they?" I said.

"Certainly they do. I grew up wondering whether I might really be the son of Tante Lisl."

"And who does Zena grow up thinking her mother might be?"

"You know what I mean, Bernie. Zena hears all these stories about her family having dozens of servants, horses and carriages . . . and about the Christmas balls, hunting breakfasts, ceremonial banquets, and wonderful parties with military bands playing and titled guests dancing outside under the stars . . . Zena is still very young, Bernard. She doesn't want to believe that it's all gone forever."

"You'd better persuade her it is, Werner. For her sake, and for your own sake too."

"She's a child, Bernie. That's why I love her so much. It's because she believes in all kinds of fairy stories that I love her."

"She doesn't really think of going back, does she?"

"Going back in time, yes. But not going back to East Prussia."

"But she has the accent," I said.

Werner looked at me as if I'd mentioned some intimate aspect of his wife that I should not have known about. "Yes, she's picked it up from her family. It's strange, isn't it?"

"Not very strange," I said. "You've more or less told me why. She's determined to hang on to her dreams."

"You're right," said Werner, who'd gone through the usual teenage dalliance with Freud, Adler, and Jung. "The desire is in her subconscious, but the fact that she chooses speech as the characteristic to imitate shows that she wants that secret desire to be known."

Oh my God, I thought, I've started him off now. Werner lecturing on psychology was among the most mind-numbing experiences known to science.

I looked across to where the birthday party was having the dessert dishes cleared away, and ordering the coffee and brandy that would be served to them in the bar. But Osmund was not to be hurried. He had his glass raised and was proposing yet another toast. He nodded impatiently at Konrad's suggestion that they retire to the next room. "The words of our immortal Goethe," said Osmund, "speak to every German soul when he says, '*Gebraucht der Zeit. Sie geht so schnell von hinnen; doch Ordnung lehrt euch Zeit gewinnen.*'"

There were murmurs of agreement and appreciation. Then they all drank to Goethe. As they all trooped off to the bar, I said to Werner, "I never feel more English than when I hear someone quoting your great German poets."

"What do you mean?" said Werner with more than a trace of indignation.

"Ideas like that would win few converts in England at any level of intellect, affluence, or political thought. Consider what our friend just proclaimed so proudly. In English it would become something like 'Employ each hour which so quickly glides away . . .' So far, so good. But then comes '. . . but, learn through order how to conquer time's swift flight.'"

"It's a rotten translation," said Werner. "In the context *gewinnen* is probably meant as 'reclaim' or 'earn.'"

"The point I'm making, my dear Werner, is the natural repulsion any Englishman would feel at the notion of inflicting order upon his time. Especially inflicting order upon his leisure time or, as is possibly implied here, his retirement."

"Why?"

"For an Englishman order does not go well with leisure. They like muddle and disarray. They like messing about in boats, or dozing in a deckchair on a beach, or pottering about in the garden, or reading the newspapers or some paperback book."

"Are you trying to persuade me that you are very English?"

"That fellow Henry Tiptree is in Berlin," I said. "He's that tall friend of—"

"I know who he is," said Werner.

"Tiptree asked me if I was German."

"And are you German?"

"I feel very German when I'm with people like Tiptree," I said. Konrad came to the table brandishing his menu. He was looking at Werner with great interest.

"So if Tiptree starts quoting Goethe at you, you'll have a nervous collapse," said Werner. "Do you want a dessert? I don't want a dessert, and you're getting too fat."

"Just coffee," I said. "I don't know what I am. I see those people from Silesia. You tell me about Zena's family. I look at myself and I wonder where I can really call home. Do you know what I mean, Werner?"

"Of course I know what you mean. I'm a Jew." He looked at Konrad. "Two coffees; two schnapps."

Konrad did not hurry us to leave the dining room after he brought our order. He poured the coffees and brought tiny glasses of clear schnapps and then left the bottle on the table. It was of local manufacture. Konrad seemed to think that anyone who'd come from "over there" would need an ample supply of alcohol. But I had to wait until we were quite alone before I could get down to business. I looked around the room to be sure there was no one who could hear us. There was no one. From the next room came the loud voices of the Silesians. "What about Stinnes?"

Werner rubbed his hands together and then sniffed at them. There was still the fishy smell of the smoked eel. He splashed some of the alcohol on his napkin and rubbed his fingers with the dampened cloth. "When I went over there I thought it would be a waste of time."

"Did you, Werner?"

"I thought if London Central wanted me to go there and cobble up some sort of report, I would oblige them. But I didn't believe I could find out very much about Stinnes. Furthermore, I was pretty well convinced that Stinnes had been leading us up the garden path."

"And now?"

"I've changed my mind on both scores."

"What happened?"

"You're concerned about him, aren't you?" said Werner.

"I don't give a damn. I just want to know."

"You identify with him."

"Don't be ridiculous," I said.

"He was born in 1943, the same year that you were born. His father was in the occupying army in Berlin, just as your father was. He went to a German civilian school, just as you did. He is a senior grade intelligence officer with a German speciality, just as you are a British one. You identify with him."

"I'm not going to argue with you, Werner, but you know as well as I do that I could prepare a list a mile long to show you that you're talking nonsense."

"For instance?"

"Stinnes has also had a Spanish language speciality for many years, and seems to be a KGB expert on Cuba and all things Cuban. I'll bet you that if Stinnes was lined up for a job in Moscow it was to be on their Cuba desk."

"Stinnes didn't originally go to Cuba just because he could speak Spanish," said Werner. "He went there primarily because he was one of Moscow's experts on Roman Catholicism. He was in the Religious Affairs Bureau; Section 44. Back in those days the Bureau was just two men and a dog. Now, with the Polish Church playing a part in politics, the Bureau is big and important. But Stinnes has not worked for Section 44 for many years. His wife persuaded him to take the Berlin job."

"That's good work, Werner. His marriage?"

"Stinnes has always been a womanizer. It's hard to believe when you look at him, but women are strange creatures, we both know that, Bernie."

"He's getting a divorce?"

"It all seems to be exactly as Stinnes described. They live in a house—not an apartment, a house—in the country, not far from Werneuchen."

"Where's that?"

"Northeast, outside the city limits. It's the last station on the S-Bahn. The electric trains only go to Marzahn, but the service continues a long way beyond."

"Damned strange place to live."

"His wife is German, Bernie. She came back from Moscow because she couldn't learn to speak Russian. She wouldn't want to live with a lot of Russian wives."

"You went out there?"

"I saw the wife. I said I was compiling a census for the bus service. I asked her how often she went into Berlin and how she traveled."

"Jesus. That's dangerous, Werner."

"It was okay, Bernie. I think she was glad to talk to someone."

"Don't do anything like that again, Werner. There are people who could do that for you, people with papers and backup. Suppose she'd sent for the police and you'd had to show your papers?"

"It was okay, Bernie. She wasn't going to send for anyone. She was nursing a bruised face that was going to become a black eye. She said she fell over, but it was Stinnes who hit her."

"What?"

"Now do you see why it's better I do these things myself? I talked to her. She told me that she was hoping to move back to Leipzig. She came from a village just outside Leipzig. She has a brother and two sisters living there. She can't wait to get back there. She hates Berlin, she told me. That's the sort of thing a wife says when she really means she hates her husband. It all fits together, Bernie."

"So you think Stinnes is on the level? He has been passed over for promotion and he does want a divorce?"

"I don't know about the promotion prospects," said Werner. "But the marriage is all but over. I went to all the houses in that little street. The neighbors are all German. They talked to me. They've heard Stinnes and the wife arguing, and they heard them shouting and things breaking the night before I saw her with the battered face. They fight, Bernie. That's an established fact. They fight because Stinnes runs around with other women."

"Let me hang this one on you. This business—the arguments with his wife, his womanizing, and his being in a dead-end job are all arranged by the KGB as part of a cover story. At best, they'll lead us on into this entrapment to see what we're going to do. At worst, they'll try to grab one of us."

"Grab one of us? They won't grab me; I've just been twice through the checkpoints. I see no reason to think they're going to grab Dicky. When you say grab one of us, you mean grab Bernie Samson."

"Well, suppose I do mean that?"

"No, Bernie. It's not just a cover story. Stinnes punched his wife in the face. You're not telling me that he did that as part of his cover story too?"

I didn't answer. I looked out of the window. Already the workmen were back from lunch and at work on the demolition. I looked at my watch; forty-five minutes exactly. That's the way it was in Germany.

Werner said, "No one would go home and hit his wife just to fit in with a story his boss invented."

"Suppose it was all part of some bigger plan. Then perhaps it would be worth while."

"Why don't you admit you are wrong, Bernie? Even if they thought they were going to get the greatest secrets in the world, Stinnes did not punch his wife for that reason."

"How can you be sure?"

"Bernie," said Werner gently. "Have you calculated the chances of me going out to that house and seeing her with a bruised face? A million to one? If we were discussing rumors, I might go along with you. If I had only the reports of the neighbors, I might go along with you. But a man doesn't smash his wife's face in on the million-to-one chance that an enemy agent would take what you describe as a dangerous chance."

"You're right, Werner."

He looked at me a long time. I suppose he was trying to decide whether to say the rest of it. Finally he said, "If you want to hear what I really think, it comes closer to home."

"What do you really think, Werner?" Now that the last remaining wall was down they had started to bulldoze the rubble into piles.

"I think Stinnes was in charge in Berlin until your wife took over his department. She told you Stinnes was her senior assistant . . ."

"That was obviously not true. If Stinnes was her senior assistant, the last person she'd tell would be me."

"I think she threw Stinnes out. I think she sent him off to Mexico to get him out of her way. It's the same when anyone takes over a new department, a new boss gets rid of all the previous top staff and their projects."

"Maybe." I looked at the workmen. I'd always thought that old buildings were better made than new ones. I'd always thought they were solid and well built, but this one was just as flimsy as any of the new ones that greedy speculators threw together.

"You know what Fiona is like. She doesn't care for competition of the sort that Stinnes would give her. It's just what Fiona would do."

"I've been giving a lot of thought to what Fiona might do," I said. "And I think you're right about her wanting to get rid of Stinnes. Maybe she's decided to get rid of him for good and all." Werner looked up and waited for the next bit. "Get rid of him to us by letting him get enrolled."

Werner closed his eyes and pinched his nose between thumb and forefinger. He said, "A bit farfetched, Bernie. She went to England to warn you off. You told me that." His eyes remained shut.

"That might be the clever part of it. She warns me to lay off Stinnes; she knows that it will have no effect on me."

"And her threats to kidnap the children?"

"There were no threats to kidnap the children. I was thinking back to the conversation. She offered to let things stay as they are for a year."

He opened his eyes and stared at me. "Providing Stinnes was left alone."

"Okay, but it was all very negative, Werner, and Fiona is not negative. Normally I would have expected her to say what I must do and she'd say what she'd do in return. That's the sort of person she is; she makes deals. I think she wants us to enroll Stinnes. I think she'd like to get rid of him permanently. If she really wanted to stop us enrolling him, she'd send him someplace where we couldn't get our hands on him."

"And killing the boy—MacKenzie. How does that fit into the theory?"

"She had a witness with her all the time—the black girl—and there were others too. That's why she was talking in riddles. She didn't want to see me alone so there would be no chance of them suspecting her of double-crossing them. I think the MacKenzie murder was a decision made by someone else: the backup team. She'd have a backup team with her. You know how they work."

Werner sat motionless for a moment as he thought about it. "She's ruthless enough for it, Bernie."

"Damn right she is," I said.

He waited a moment. "You still love her, don't you?"

"No, I don't."

"Whatever you want to call it, something prevents you

thinking about her clearly. If it came to the crunch, that something would prevent you doing what needed to be done. Maybe that wouldn't matter so much, except that you are determined to believe that she feels the same way about you. Fiona is ruthless, Bernie. Totally dedicated to doing whatever the KGB want done. Face it, she'd eliminate MacKenzie without a qualm, and if it comes to it, she'll eliminate you.''

"You're an incurable romantic, Werner," I said, making a joke of it, but the strength of his feelings had shaken me.

Now that Werner had said what he thought about Fiona, he was embarrassed. We sat silent, both looking out of the window like strangers in a railway carriage. It was still raining. "That Henry Tiptree," said Werner eventually. "What does he want?"

"He doesn't like super luxury hotels such as the Steigenberger, with private baths, and room service, disco and fancy food. He likes the real Berlin. He likes to rough it at Lisl's."

"Crap," said Werner.

"He tried to get me drunk the other night. He probably thought I was going to bare my soul to him. Why crap? I like Lisl's and so do you."

Werner didn't bother to answer my question. We both knew that Henry Tiptree was not like us and was unlikely to share our tastes in anything from music and food to cars and women. "He's spying on you," said Werner. "Frank Harrington's sent him to Lisl's to spy on you. It's obvious."

"Don't be silly, Werner." I laughed. It wasn't funny. I laughed just because I was sitting across the table from Werner and Werner was sitting there safe and sound. I said, "To hear you talk, Frank Harrington rules the world. Frank is only the Berlin Resident. All he's interested in is nursing the Berlin Field Unit along until he retires. He's not training his spies to chase me across the world from Mexico City to Tante Lisl's in order to get me drunk and see what secrets he can winkle out of me."

"You always try to make me sound ridiculous."

"Frank isn't out to get you. And he's not trying to get me either."

"So who is this Henry Tiptree?"

"Just another graduate of the Foreign Office charm school," I said. "He's helping to write one of those reports about the Soviet arms buildup. You know the sort of thing: what are the political intentions and the economic consequences."

"You don't believe any of that," said Werner.

"I believe it. Why wouldn't I believe it? The Department is buried under the weight of reports like that. Forests are set aside to provide the pulp for reports like that. Sometimes I think the entire staff of the Foreign Office does nothing else but concoct reports like that. Do you know, Werner, that in 1914 the Foreign Office staff numbered one hundred seventy-six people in London, plus four hundred fifty in the diplomatic service overseas. Now that we've lost the empire they need six thousand officials plus nearly eight thousand locally engaged staff."

Werner looked at me with heavy-lidded eyes. "Take a Valium and lie down for a moment."

"That's nearly fourteen thousand people, Werner. Can you wonder why we have Henry Tiptrees swanning round the world looking for something to occupy them?"

"I don't like him," said Werner. "He's out to make trouble. You'll see."

"I'll ask Frank who he is," I offered. "I'll have to make my peace with Frank. I'll need his help to keep London off my back." I tried to make it sound easy, but in fact I dreaded all the departmental repercussions that would emerge when I surfaced again. And I was far from sure whether Frank would be able to help. Or whether he would want to help.

"Are you driving back to Berlin? I had to leave the car in the East, of course. I'll phone Zena and say I'll be back for dinner. Are you free for dinner?"

"Zena will want you all to herself, Werner." Surely, Frank Harrington would stand by me. He'd always helped in the past.

We had a father-and-son relationship, with all the stormy encounters that so often implies, but Frank would help. Within the Department he was the only one I could always rely upon.

"Nonsense. We'll all have dinner," said Werner. "Zena likes entertaining."

"I'm not too concerned about Tiptree," I said. It wasn't true, of course, I *was* concerned about him. I was concerned about the whole bloody tangled mess I was in. And the fact that I'd denied my concern was enough to tell Werner of those fears. He stared at me; I suppose he was worried about me. I smiled at him and added, "You only have to spend ten minutes with Tiptree to know he's a blundering amateur." But was he really such a foolish amateur, I wondered. Or was he a very clever man who knew how to look like one?

"It's the amateurs who are the most dangerous," said Werner.

Chapter 17

ZENA VOLKMANN could be captivating when she was in the mood to play the gracious hostess. This evening she greeted us wearing tight-fitting gray pants with a matching shirt. And over this severe garb she'd put a loose silk sleeveless jacket that was striped with every color in the rainbow. Her hair was up and coiled round her head in a style that required a long time at the hairdresser. She had used some eye shadow and enough makeup to accent her cheekbones. She looked very pretty, but not like the average housewife welcoming her husband home for dinner, more like a girl friend expecting to be taken out to an expensive night spot. I delivered Werner to the apartment in Berlin-Dahlem ready to forget his invitation. But Zena said she'd prepared a meal for the three of us and insisted earnestly enough to convince me to stay, loudly enough for Werner to be proud of her warm hospitality.

She held his upper arms and kissed him carefully enough to preserve her lipstick and makeup and then straightened his tie and flicked dust from his jacket. Zena knew exactly how to handle him. She was an expert on how to handle men. I think she might even have been able to handle me if she'd put her mind to it, but luckily I was not a part of her planned future.

She asked Werner's advice about everything she didn't care about, and she enlisted his aid whenever there was a chance for her to play the helpless woman. He was called to the kitchen to open a tin and to get hot pans from the oven. Werner was the only one who could open a bottle of wine and decant it. Werner was asked to peer at the quiche and sniff at the roast chicken and pronounce it cooked. But since virtually all the food had come prepared by the Paul Bocuse counter of the Ka De We food department, probably the greatest array of food on sale anywhere in the world, Zena's precautions seemed somewhat overwrought. Yet Werner seemed to revel in them.

Had I read all the psychology books Werner had on his shelf, I might have started thinking that Zena was a manifestation of his desire for a daughter, or a reflection of childhood suspicions of his mother's chastity. As it was I just figured that Werner liked the dependent type and Zena was happy to play that role for him. After all, I was pretty sure that Zena hadn't read any of those books either.

But you don't have to read books to get smart, and Zena was as smart as a street urchin climbing under the flap of a circus tent. Certainly Zena could teach me a thing or two, as she did that evening. The apartment itself was an interesting indication of their relationship. Werner, despite his constant declarations of imminent bankruptcy, had always been something of a spender. But before he met Zena this apartment had been like a student's pad. It had been entirely masculine: an old piano, upon which Werner liked to play "Smoke Gets in Your Eyes," and big lumpy chairs with broken springs, their ancient floral covers perforated by carelessly held cigarettes. There'd even been a moth-eaten tiger's skin, which—like so much of Werner's furnishing—had come from the flea market in the abandoned S-Bahn station on Tauentzien-strasse. In those days the kitchen was equipped with little more than a can opener and a frying pan. And glasses outnumbered cups by five to one. Now it was different. It wasn't like a real apartment anymore; it was like one of those bare-looking sets that are photographed for glossy magazines. The lights all shone on the ceiling and walls, and the sofa had a serape draped over it. Green plants, little rugs, cut flowers, and a couple of books were strategically positioned, and the chairs were very modern and uncomfortable.

We were sitting round the dining table, finishing the main course of chicken stuffed with truffles and exotic herbs. Zena had told Werner what wonderful wine he'd chosen, and he asked her what she'd been doing while he was away.

Zena said, "The only outing worth mentioning is the evening I went to the opera." She turned to me and said, "Werner doesn't like opera. Taking Werner to the opera is like trying to teach a bear to dance."

"You didn't go alone?" asked Werner.

"That's just what I was going to tell you. Erich Stinnes phoned. I didn't tell him you weren't here, Werner. I didn't want him to know you were away. I don't like anyone to know you're away."

"Erich Stinnes?" said Werner.

"He phoned. You know what he's like. He had two tickets for the opera. One for you, Werner, and one for me. I thought it was very nice of him. He said it was in return for all the dinners he'd eaten with us."

"Not so many," said Werner glumly.

"He was just being polite, darling. So I said that you would be back late but that I would love to go."

I looked at Werner and he looked at me. In some other situation, such looks exchanged between two men in some other line of work might have been comment on a wife's fidelity. But Werner and I were thinking other thoughts. The alarm on Werner's face was registering the fear that Stinnes knew Zena was alone because he had had him followed over there in the East Sector of the city. Zena looked from one to the other of us. "What is it?" she said.

"The opera," said Werner vaguely as his mind retraced his movements from Berlin and across the dark countryside to the frontier and tried to remember any persisting headlights on the road behind, a shadow in a doorway, a figure in the street, or any one of a thousand slips that even the best of agents is prey to.

"He sent a car," said Zena. "I started worrying when it was due to arrive. I thought it might drive up to the front door with a Russian army driver in uniform, or with a hammer and sickle flag on the front of it." She giggled.

"You went to the East?"

"We saw Mozart's *Magic Flute,* darling. At the Comic Opera. It's a lovely little theater, have you never been? Lots of people from the West go over for the evening. There were British officers in gorgeous uniforms and lots of women in long dresses. I felt underdressed if anything. We must go together, Werner. It was lovely."

"Stinnes is married," said Werner.

"Don't be such a prude, Werner, I know he's married. We've both heard Erich talking enough about his failed marriage to remember that."

"It was a strange thing for him to do, wasn't it?" Werner said.

"Oh, Werner, darling, how can you say that? You heard me saying how much I liked the opera. And Erich asked you if you liked opera and you said yes you did."

"I probably wasn't listening," said Werner.

"I know you weren't listening. You almost went to sleep. I had to kick you under the table."

"You must be very careful with Erich Stinnes," said Werner. He smiled as if determined not to become angry with her. "He's not the polite gentleman that he likes to pretend to be. He's KGB, Zena, and all those Chekists are dangerous."

"I've got apple strudel, and after that I've got chocolates from the Lenotre counter at Ka De We, the ones you like. Praline. Do you want to skip the strudel? What about you, Bernard?"

"I'll have everything," I said.

"Whipped cream with the strudel? Coffee at the same time?" said Zena.

"You took the words right out of my mouth," I said.

"Stinnes is playing a dangerous game," Werner told her. "No one knows what he's really got in mind. Suppose he held you hostage over there in the East?"

Zena hugged herself, grimaced, and said, "Promises, promises."

"It's not funny," said Werner. "It could happen."

"I can handle Erich Stinnes," said Zena. "I understand Erich Stinnes better than you men will ever understand him. You should ask a woman to help if you really want to understand a man like that."

"I understand him all right," Werner called after her as she disappeared into the kitchen to get the apple strudel and switch on the coffee machine. To me in a quieter voice he added, "Perhaps I understand him too bloody well."

The phone rang. Werner answered it. He grunted into the mouthpiece in a way that was unusual for the amiable Werner. "Yes, he's here, Frank," he said.

Frank Harrington. Of the whole population of Berlin I knew of only one that Werner really disliked, and that was the Head of the Berlin Field Unit. It did not portend well for Werner's future service in the Department. For Werner's sake I hoped that Frank retired from the service soon.

I took the phone. "Hello, Frank. Bernard here."

"I've tried everywhere, Bernard. Why the hell don't you phone my office when you get into town and give me a contact number?"

"I'm at Lisl's," I said. "I'm always at Lisl's."

"You're not always at Lisl's," said Frank. He sounded angry. "You're not at Lisl's now, and you haven't been at bloody Lisl's for the last three nights."

"I haven't been in Berlin for three nights," I said. "You don't want me to phone you every night wherever I am, anywhere in the world, do you? Even my mother doesn't expect that, Frank."

"Dicky says you left London without even notifying him you were going anywhere."

"Dicky said that?"

"Yes," shouted Frank. "Dicky said that."

"Dicky's got a terrible memory, Frank. Last year he took one of those mail-order memory courses you see advertised in New York newspapers. But it didn't seem to make much difference."

"I'm not in the mood for your merry quips," said Frank. "I want you in my office, tomorrow morning at ten o'clock, without fail."

"I was going to contact you anyway, Frank."

"Tomorrow morning, my office, ten o'clock without fail," said Frank again. "And I don't want you drinking all night in Lisl's bar. Understand?"

"Yes, I understand, Frank," I said. "Give my best regards to your wife." I rang off.

Werner looked at me.

"Frank reading the riot act," I explained. "Don't get drunk in Lisl's bar, he said. It sounds as if he's been talking to that fellow Henry Tiptree."

"He's spying on you," said Werner in a voice of feigned weariness. "How long is it going to take before you start believing me?"

Zena reappeared with a tray upon which stood my slice of apple strudel, whipped cream, the coffee, and a small plate of assorted chocolates. "Who was on the phone?" she asked.

"Frank Harrington," said Werner. "He wanted Bernie."

She nodded to show she'd heard as she arranged the things from the tray on the table. Then, when she'd finished her little task, she looked up and said, "They're offering Erich a quarter of a million dollars to defect."

"What?" said Werner, thunderstruck.

"You heard me, darling. London Central are offering Erich Stinnes a quarter of a million dollars to defect." She was aware of what a bombshell she'd thrown at us. I had the impression that her main motive in persuading me to stay to dinner was to have me present when she announced this news.

"Ridiculous," said Werner. "Do you know anything about that, Bernie?"

Zena gave me no chance to steal her thunder. She said, "That is a gross sum that would include his car and miscellaneous expenses. But it wouldn't be subject to tax and it wouldn't include the two-bedroom house they'll provide for him. He'll be on his own anyway. He's decided not to ask his wife to go with him. He's not even going to tell her about the offer. He's frightened she'll report him. They don't get along together; they quarrel."

"A quarter of a million dollars," said Werner. "That's . . . nearly seven hundred thousand marks. I don't believe it."

Zena put the strudel in front of me and placed the whipped cream to hand. "Do you want whipped cream in your coffee, Werner?" She poured a cup of coffee and passed it to her husband. "Well, it's true, whether you believe it or not. That's what they've offered him."

"I haven't heard anything about it, Zena," I said. "I'm supposed to be handling the whole business, but I've heard nothing about a big lump sum. If they were going to offer him a quarter of a million dollars, I think they'd tell me, don't you?"

It was intended as a rhetorical question but Zena answered it. "No, my dear Bernard," she said. "I'm quite sure they *wouldn't* tell you."

"Why not?" I said.

"Use your imagination," said Zena. "You're senior staff at London Central, maybe more important than a man such as Stinnes . . ."

"Much more important," I said between mouthfuls of strudel.

"Exactly," said Zena. "So if Erich is worth a quarter of a million dollars to London Central, you'd be worth the same to Moscow."

It took me a moment or two to understand what she meant. I grinned at the thought of it. "You mean London Central are frightened in case I discover what I'm worth and then defect to Moscow and price myself at the same fee?"

"Of course," said Zena. She was twenty-two years old. To her it had the elegant simplicity that the world had had for me when I was her age.

"I'd need more than a quarter of a million dollars to soften the prospect of having to spend the rest of my days in Moscow," I said.

"Don't be evasive," said Zena. "Do you really think that Erich will spend the rest of his days in London?"

"You tell me," I said. I finished my strudel and sipped at my coffee. It was very strong. Zena liked strong black coffee, but I floated cream on mine. So did Werner.

Werner rubbed his face and took his coffee over to the armchair to sit down. He looked very tired. "You can see what Zena means, Bernie." He looked from me to Zena and back again, hoping to find a way of keeping the peace.

"No," I said.

"Extending this idea just for the sake of argument," he said apologetically. "Moscow would simply want to debrief you in depth. What are we talking about; six months? Twelve months at the outside."

"And after that?" I said. "Continuing to extend this for the sake of argument, what would happen to me after that?"

"A new identity. Now that the KGB have that new forgery factory near the airport at Schönefeld they can provide papers that pass damned near any sort of scrutiny. German workmanship, you see." He smiled a tiny smile; just enough to make it all a bit of a joke.

"German workmanship," I said. The Russians had been at it since 1945. They'd gathered together the scattered remnants of SS unit Amt VI F, which from Berlin's Delbruckstrasse—and using the nearby Spechthausen bei Eberswalde paper factory, and forgers housed in the equally nearby Oranienburg concentration camp—had supervised the manufacture of superb forgeries of everything from Swedish passports to British five-pound notes. "Perfect papers and a new identity. Plus an unlimited amount of forged paper money. That would be lovely, Werner."

Werner looked up from under his heavy eyelids and said, "Defectors to Moscow wind up in weird places, Bernie. You and I both know certain residents of Cape Town, Rome, and—where was that last one; some place in Bolivia?—who have changed their names and occupations suddenly and successfully since the last time we saw them."

"For a quarter of a million dollars?" I said. "And spend the rest of your life in Cape Town, Rome, or Bolivia?"

"Zena didn't mean that you'd do that for a quarter of a million dollars, Bernie."

"Didn't she? What did you mean, Zena?" I said.

Zena said, "No need to get touchy. You heard what I said, and you know it's true. I said that London Central were afraid of what you might do. I didn't say that I felt the same way. London Central trust no one. They don't trust Werner, they don't trust you, they don't trust me."

"Trust you how?" I said.

Zena touched her necklace and smoothed the collar of her silk jacket, preening herself while looking away across the room as if half occupied with other more important matters. "They don't trust me to be their contact for Stinnes. I asked Dicky Cruyer. He ignored the question. Earlier this evening I put the same idea to you. You changed the subject."

"Do you know for certain that Erich Stinnes has only the one child?" I said.

"He has just the one son, who is eighteen years old. Perhaps nineteen by now. He failed to get into Berlin University last year in spite of having very high marks. They have a system over there that gives priority to the children of manual workers. Erich was furious."

I got up from the table and went to look out of the window. It was dusk. Werner's apartment in the fashionable Berlin suburb of Dahlem looked out onto other expensive apartment blocks. But between them could be seen the dark treetops of the Grunewald—parkland that stretched some six kilometers to the wide water of the Havel. On a sunny day, with the windows open wide, the sweet warm air would endorse every claim made for that famous *Berliner Luft*. But now it was almost dark and the rain was spattering against the glass.

Zena's provocative remarks made me jumpy. Why had London not told me what they'd offered to Stinnes? I wasn't just the "file officer" on a run-of-the-mill operation. This was an enrollment—the trickiest game in the book. The usual procedure was to keep the enroller informed about everything that happened. I wondered if Dicky knew about the quarter of a million dollars. It took no more than a moment to decide that Dicky must know; as German Stations Controller he'd have to sign the chits for the payment. The quarter of a million dollars would have to be debited against his departmental outgoings, until the cashier adjusted the figures by means of a payment from Central Funding.

Street gutters overflowing with rainwater reflected the street lamps and made a line of moons that were continually shattered by passing traffic. Any one of the parked cars might have contained a surveillance team. Any of the windows of the apartment block across the street might have concealed cameras with long focal length lenses, and microphones with parabolic reflectors. At what point does sensible caution become clinical paranoia. At what point does a trusted employee become "a considered risk," and then finally a "noncritical employment only" category. I closed the curtains and turned round to face Zena. "How furious?" I said. "Is Stinnes furious enough to send his son to university in the West?"

"It's nothing to do with me," said Zena. "Ask him for yourself."

"We need all the help we can get," Werner told her gently.

"The son has gone to live with Stinnes's first wife. He's gone to live in Russia."

"You're way ahead of us there, Zena," I admitted. "There was nothing about a first wife on the computer."

She showed obvious pleasure at this. "He's had only one child. The first wife was Russian. The marriage was dissolved a long time ago. For the last year or so the son has been living with Stinnes and his second wife. He wanted to learn German. Now he's gone back to live with his mother in Moscow. She has a relative who thinks he can get the boy a place at Moscow University so the boy rushed off to Moscow immediately. He's obviously frantic to go to university."

"If you were him you'd be frantic too," I said. "Secondary-school graduates who fail to get a place in a university are sent to do manual or clerical work in any farm or factory where workers are needed. Furthermore, he'll become liable for military service; university students are exempted."

"The mother has contacts in Moscow. She'll get her son a place."

"Is Stinnes attached to the boy?" I said. I was amazed at how much she'd been able to wheedle out of the taciturn Erich Stinnes.

"They quarrel a lot," said Zena. "He is at the age when sons quarrel with their fathers. It is nature's way of making the fledglings fly from the nest."

"So you think Stinnes will come?" said Werner. His attitude to the Stinnes enrollment was still ambivalent.

"I don't know," said Zena. I could see she resented the way in which Werner had pressed her to reveal these things about

Stinnes. She felt perhaps that it was all information that London Central should pay for. "He's still thinking about it. But if he doesn't come it won't be because of his wife or his son."

"What will be the deciding factor then?" I said. I picked up the coffeepot. "Anyone else more coffee?"

Werner shook his head. Zena pushed her cup towards me but my casual attitude didn't make her any happier about providing me with free information. "He's forty years old," said Zena. "Isn't that the age when men are supposed to suffer some mid-term life crisis?"

"Is it?" I said.

"Isn't it the age at which men ask themselves what they have achieved, and wonder if they chose the right job?" said Zena.

"And the right wife? And the right son?" I said.

Zena gave a sour smile of assent.

"And don't women have the same sort of mid-term life crisis?" asked Werner.

"They have it at twenty-nine," said Zena and smiled.

"I think he'll do it," said Werner. "I've been telling Bernie that. I've changed my mind about him. I think he'll come over to us." Werner still didn't sound too happy at the prospect.

"You should offer him a proper job," said Zena. "For a man like Stinnes a quarter-million-dollar retirement plan is not much better than offering him a burial plot. You should make him feel he's coming over to do something important. You must make him feel needed."

"Yes," I said. Such psychology had obviously worked well for her with Werner. And I remembered the way in which my wife had been enrolled with the promise of colonel's rank and a real job behind a desk with people like Stinnes to do her bidding. "But what could we offer him? He's not spent the last ten years as a capitalist mole. If he comes to the West it will be because he is apolitical. He likes being a policeman."

"Policeman?" said Zena with a hoot of derision. "Is that what you all call yourselves? You think you're just a lot of fat

old cops helping old ladies across the road and telling the
tourists how to get back to the bus station?"

"That will do," said Werner in one of his rare admoni-
tions.

"You're all the same," said Zena. "You, Bernie, Stinnes,
Frank Harrington, Dicky Cruyer . . . all the ones I've ever met.
All little boys playing cowboys."

"I said cut it out," said Werner. I suspected he was angry
more because I was present to witness her outburst than because she'd said it all before many times.

"Bang, bang," said Zena, playing cowboys.

"A quarter of a million dollars," said Werner. "London
must want him awfully badly."

"I found something in Stinnes's car," said Zena.

"What did you find?" said Werner.

"I'll show you," said Zena. She went across to the glass-
fronted cabinet in which Werner used to keep his scale model
of the Dornier Do X flying boat. Now, like all his aircraft mod-
els, it was relegated to the storeroom in the basement, and Zena
had a display of china animals there. From behind them she got
a large brown envelope. "Take a look at that," she said, pulling
some typed sheets from the envelope and sliding them across
the table. I took one and passed another to Werner, who was
sitting on the sofa.

There were five sheets of gray pulp paper. Both sides were
covered with single-spaced typing. The copies were produced
on a stencil duplicator of a type seldom seen nowadays in Western countries but commonly used still in the East. I studied the
sheets under the light, for some of the lettering was broken and
on the gray paper I found it difficult to read, but such Russian
security documents were predictable enough for me to guess at
the parts I couldn't read or couldn't understand.

"What is it about?" said Zena. "I can't read Russian. Does
that mean secret?"

"Where exactly did you get this?" I asked her.

"From Stinnes's car. I was sitting in the back and so I felt inside all those pockets those old-fashioned cars have. I found old pencils and some hairpins and these papers."

"And you took it?"

"I put it in my handbag. No one saw me, if that's what's worrying you. Does that mean secret?" she asked again. She pointed to a large red-inked rubber stamp mark that had been applied to the copies.

"Yes, secret," I said. "But there's nothing here that makes it worth phoning the White House and getting the president out of bed."

"What is it?"

"The top heading says 'Group of Soviet Forces in Germany,' which is the official name for all the Russian army units there, and the reference number. The second line is the title of the document: 'Supplementary Instructions Concerning Counterintelligence Duties of State Security Organs.' Then there comes this long preamble which is standard for this sort of document. It says, 'The Communist Party of the Soviet Union traces the Soviet people's way in the struggle for the victory of communism. The Party guides and directs the forces of the nation and the organs of state security.' "

"What's it about?" said Zena impatiently.

"Its halfway down the page before it gets down to business. These numbered paragraphs are headed 'Instructions for KGB unit commanders in their relationship with commanders of army units to which they are attached.' Its says be firm and polite and cooperate . . . the sort of crap that all government clerks everywhere churn out by the ream. Then the next lot of paragraphs is headed 'Duties of Special Departments' and it instructs KGB officers about likely means that imperialist intelligence forces are currently using to obtain Russian secrets."

"What sort of methods?" said Zena.

"Two of the paragraphs give details of people discovered spying. One was in a factory and the other near a missile site. Neither example is what would normally be called espionage. One is a man who seems to have run into a forbidden zone after his dog, and the other case is a man taking photos without a permit."

"You're trying to say that this paper I've brought you is just rubbish. I don't believe you."

"Then ask Werner. Your husband knows more Russian than I do."

"Bernie has translated it perfectly," said Werner.

"So you think it's rubbish too," said Zena. Her disappointment had made her angry.

Werner looked at me, wondering how much he was permitted to say. Knowing that he'd tell her anyway, I said, "This is a regular publication; it's published every month. Copies go to the commanders of certain KGB units throughout the German Democratic Republic. You see that number at the top; this is number fifteen of what is probably a total of not more than one hundred. It's secret. London like to have copies of them if they can get them. I doubt if we've got a complete collection of them on our files, although perhaps the CIA have. The Americans like to have everything complete—the complete works of Shakespeare, a complete dinner service of Meissen, a complete set of lenses for the Olympus camera, and garages crammed with copies of the *National Geographic* going back for twenty-five years."

"And?" said Zena.

I shrugged. "It's secret, but it's not interesting."

"To you. It's not interesting to you, that's what you mean."

"It's not interesting to anyone except archive librarians."

I watched Werner getting out of the sofa. It was a very low sofa and getting out of it was no easy thing to do. I noticed that Zena never sat in it; she kneeled on it so that she could swing her legs down to the floor and get to her feet with comparative ease.

"I found it in the car," said Zena. "I guessed the stamp meant secret."

"You should have left it where it was," said Werner. "Think

what might have happened if they'd searched the car as you went through the crossing point."

"Nothing would have happened," said Zena. "It wasn't my car. It was an official car, wasn't it?"

"They're not interested in such subtle distinctions over there," said Werner. "If the border guards had found that document in the car they would have arrested you and the driver."

"You worry too much," said Zena.

Werner tossed the document pages onto the table. "It was a mad thing to do, Zena. Leave that sort of risk to the people who get paid for it."

"People like you and Bernie, you mean?"

"Bernie would never carry a paper like that through a checkpoint," said Werner. "Neither would I. Neither would anyone who knew what the consequences might be."

She had been expecting unstinting praise. Now, like a small child, she bit her red lips and sulked.

I said, "Even if the Vopos had done nothing to you, do you realize what would happen to Stinnes if they knew he'd been careless enough to leave papers in his car when it came into West Berlin? Even a KGB officer couldn't talk his way out of that one."

She looked at me evenly. There was no expression on her face, but I had the feeling that her reply was calculated. "I wouldn't cry for him," she said.

Was this callous rejection of Stinnes just something she said to please Werner, I wondered. I watched Werner's reaction. But he smiled sadly. "Do you want this stuff, Bernie?" he asked, picking up the papers.

"I don't want it," I said. It was an understatement. I didn't want to hear about Zena's crazy capers. She didn't understand what kind of dangers she was playing with, and she didn't want to understand.

It was only when Werner had gone into his study that Zena realized what he intended. But by that time we could hear the whine of the shredder as Werner destroyed the pages.

"Why?" said Zena angrily. "Those papers were valuable. They were mine."

"The papers weren't yours," I said. "You stole them."

Werner returned and said, "It's better that they disappear. Whatever we did with them could lead to trouble for someone. If Stinnes suspects you've taken them, he'll think we put you up to it. It might be enough to make him back out of the deal."

"We could have sold them to London," said Zena.

"London wouldn't be keen to have papers that were so casually come by," I explained. "They'd wonder if they were genuine, or planted to fool them. Then they'd start asking questions about you and Stinnes and so on. We don't want a lot of London deskmen prying into what we're doing. It's difficult enough to do the job as it is."

"We could have sold them to Frank Harrington," said Zena. Her voice had lost some of its assertion now.

"I'm trying to keep Frank Harrington at arm's length," I said. "If Stinnes is serious we'll do the enrollment from Mexico. If we do it from here, Frank will want to mastermind it."

"Frank's too idle," said Zena.

"Not for this one," I said. "I think Frank has already begun to see the extent of London's interest. I think Frank will want to get into the act. This would be a feather in his cap—something good for him to retire on."

"And Mexico City is a long way from London," said Werner. "Less chance of having London Central breathing down your neck if you are in Mexico. I know how your mind works, Bernie."

I smiled but said nothing. He was right—I wanted to keep London Central as far away as possible. I still felt like a mouse in a maze, every turn bringing me to another blank wall. It was difficult enough dealing with the KGB, but now I was fighting London Central too, and Fiona was thrown into the puzzle to make things even more bewildering. And what was going to be waiting at the end of the maze—a nasty trap like the one I'd sent MacKenzie to walk into?

"I still say we should have sold the papers to Frank," said Zena.

Werner said, "It might have proved dangerous. And the truth is, Zena darling, that we can't be absolutely sure that Stinnes didn't leave it there for you to find. If it all turned out that way, I wouldn't want you to be the person who took them to Frank."

She smiled. She didn't believe that Stinnes had left the papers in the car to trick her. Zena had difficulty in believing that any man could trick her. Perhaps her time with Werner had lulled her into a false sense of security.

Chapter 18

I'D KNOWN Frank Harrington for a lifetime; not his lifetime, of course, but mine. So when the car collected me from Lisl's the next morning I was not surprised that it took me to Frank Harrington's house rather than to the SIS offices at the Olympic Stadium. For when Frank said *"the* office" he meant the Stadium that Hitler had built for the 1936 Games. But *"my* office" meant the room he used as a study in the large mansion out at Grunewald that was always at the disposal of the Berlin Resident and that Frank had occupied for two long stints. It was a wonderful house that had been built for a relative of a banker named Bleichroder who'd extended to Bismarck the necessary credit for waging the Franco-Prussian War. The garden was extensive and there were enough trees to give the impression of being deep in the German countryside.

I was marched into the room by Frank's valet, Tarrant, a sturdy old man who'd been with Frank since the war. Frank was behind his desk, brandishing important-looking papers. He looked up at me from under his eyebrows, as a commanding officer looks at a recruit who has misbehaved.

Frank was wearing a dark gray three-piece suit and a starched white shirt and a tightly knotted Eton school tie. Frank's "colonel of the regiment" act was not confined to his deportment. It was particularly evident in this study. There was rattan furniture and a buttoned leather bench that was so old and worn that the leather had gone almost white in places. There was a superb camphor wood military chest, and on it an ancient typewriter that should have been in a museum. Behind him on the wall there was a large formal portrait of the Queen. It was all like a stage set for a play about the last days of the British Raj. This impression of being in an Indian army bungalow was heightened by the way in which a hundred shafts of daylight came into Frank's dark study. The louvered window shutters were closed as a precaution against sophisticated microphones that could pick up vibrations from windowpanes, but the slats of Berlin daylight that patterned the carpet might have come from some pitiless Punjab sun.

"Good God, Bernard," said Frank. "You do try my patience at times."

"Do I, Frank? I don't mean to; I'm sorry."

"What the hell were you doing at Lüneburg?"

"A meeting," I said.

"An agent?"

"You know better than to ask me that, Frank," I said.

"There's the very deuce of a fuss in London. One of your chaps was murdered."

"Who was that?"

"MacKenzie. A probationer. He worked for you sometimes, I understand."

"I know him," I said.

"What do you know about his death?"

"What you've told me."

"No more than that?"

"Is this a formal inquiry?"

"Of course not, Bernard. But it's not the right moment to conceal evidence either."

"If it was the right moment, would you tell me so, Frank?"

"I'm trying to help, Bernard. When you go back to London you'll walk into more pointed questions than these."

"For instance?"

"Don't you care about this poor boy?"

"I do care. I care very much. What would I have to do to convince you about that?" I said.

"You don't have to convince me about anything, Bernard. I've always stood behind you. Since your father died I've considered myself *in loco parentis* and I've hoped that you would come to me if in trouble in the same way that you'd have gone to your father."

Was this what Frank had been so keen to talk to me about? I couldn't decide. And now I turned the heat on Frank. "Is Henry Tiptree one of your people, Frank?" I kept my voice very casual.

"Tiptree? The chap staying at Frau Hennig's?" He touched his stubble mustache reflectively.

Frank was virtually the only person I knew who called Lisl "Frau Hennig" and it took me a moment to respond to his question. "Yes. That's the one," I said.

I'd caught Frank on the hop. He reached into a drawer of his desk and found a packet of pipe tobacco. He took his time in tearing the wrapper open and sniffing at the contents to see how fresh it had stayed in his drawer. "What did Tiptree say he's doing?"

"He gave me a lot of hogwash. But I think he's from Internal Security."

Frank became rather nervous. He stuffed tobacco into the bowl of his pipe carelessly enough to spill a lot on the otherwise very tidy desk top. "You're right, Bernard. I'm glad you tumbled to him. I wanted to tip you the wink, but the signals from London were strictly for me only. The D-G told me not to tell anyone, but now that you've guessed I might as well admit it . . ."

"What's his game, Frank?"

"He's an ambitious young diplomat who wants to have some cloak-and-dagger experience."

"In Internal Security?"

"Don't sound so incredulous. That's where they put such people. We don't want them at the sharp end, do we, Bernard?"

"And why did Internal Security send him here?"

"Internal Security never tell us lesser mortals what they are doing, or why they're doing it, Bernard. I'm sure he guesses that anything he tells me is liable to get back to you."

"And why should that matter?"

"Let me rephrase that." Frank forced a grin onto his reluctant face. "I meant that anything he told me is liable to get back to any member of the Berlin staff."

"Is that bastard investigating me?" I said.

"Now, don't get excited, Bernard. No one knows what he's doing. Internal Security are a law unto themselves, you know that. But even if he is poking his nose into your affairs, you've no cause to be surprised. We all get investigated from time to time. And you have . . ."

"I have a wife who defected. Is that what you were going to say, Frank?"

"It's not what I was going to say, but now that you've brought it into the conversation, it is a factor that Internal Security is bound to find relevant."

I didn't answer. At least I had Frank on the defensive. It was better than him giving me a hard time about MacKenzie. Now that his pipe was filled with tobacco I gave him enough time to light up. "Yes, you're sure to have them breathing down your neck for a little while," he said. "But these things eventually blow over. The service is fair-minded, Bernard. You must admit that." He sucked at his pipe in short rapid breaths that made the tobacco flare. "Do you know of even one case of a departmental employee being victimized?"

"I don't know of one," I said. "For the very good reason that the lid is kept tightly clamped upon such things."

"Couldn't have chaps writing letters to *The Times* about it, could we?" said Frank. He smiled but I looked at him blankly, and watched him as he held the matchbox over the bowl of his pipe to increase the draft. I never knew whether he was so very bad at getting his pipe lit, or whether he deliberately let it go out between puffs, to give him something to do while thinking up answers to awkward questions.

"I might not need backup on the Stinnes business, Frank," I said, choosing my words carefully. "I might want to handle it well away from the city, maybe not in Germany anywhere."

Frank recognized the remark for what it was: a departmental way of telling him to go to hell. Official notice that I was going to keep the Stinnes operation well away from him and all his doings. "It's your show, lad," said Frank. "How is it going?"

"Did you know that London have offered Stinnes a cash payment?"

Only his eyes moved. He looked up from his pipe but held it to his mouth and continued to fuss with it. "No. At least not officially."

"But you did hear?"

"The D-G told me that there might be a payment made. The old man always tells me if such things happen here on my patch. Just by way of courtesy."

"Is the D-G taking a personal interest?"

"He is indeed." An artful little grin. "That's why so many of our colleagues are giving it such close attention."

"Including you?"

"I came into the service with Sir Henry Clevemore. We trained together—although he was rather older than me—and we've become close friends. But Sir Henry is the Director-General, and I'm just the poor old Berlin Resident. He doesn't forget that, Bernard, and I make sure that I never forget it either." This was Frank's way of reminding me that I was too damned insubordinate. "Yes. If Sir Henry is taking a close personal interest in any particular enterprise, I also take an interest in it. He's no fool."

"The last time I saw him he was in bad shape."

"Sick?" said Frank as if hearing that suggestion for the first time.

"Not just sick, Frank. When I spoke to him he was rambling."

"Are you suggesting that the old man's *non compos mentis?*"

"He's completely fruitcake, Frank. You must know that if you've seen him lately."

"Eccentric, yes," said Frank cautiously.

"He's one of the most powerful men in Britain, Frank. Let's not quibble about terminology."

"I wouldn't like to think you're encouraging anyone to think the D-G is in anything but vigorous mental and physical health," said Frank. "He's been under a heavy strain. When the time is ripe he'll go, of course. But we're all very keen that it should not look like a response to the government's request."

"Are the government asking for his head?"

"There are people in the Cabinet who'd like someone else sitting in the D-G's chair," said Frank.

"You mean some particular someone else?"

"They'll put a politician in there if they get a chance," said Frank. "Virtually every government since the war has cherished the idea of having a 'reliable' man running us. Not just the socialists; the Tories also have their nominees. For all I know, the Liberals and Social Democrats have ideas about it too."

"Is it a job you'd like?"

"Me?"

"Don't say you've never thought about it."

"Berlin Resident to D-G would be a giant step for a man."

"We all know that you came back here to straighten out a mess. Had you stayed in London, you could have been the old man's deputy by now."

"Perhaps," said Frank.

"Has the idea been mentioned?" I persisted.

"With varying degrees of seriousness," admitted Frank. "But I've set my mind on retirement, Bernard. I don't think I could take on the job of running the whole Department at my age. I've said that if the old man got really sick I'd go in and hold the fort until someone permanent was appointed. It would be simply a way of keeping a political nominee out. But I couldn't do the reorganization job that is really required."

"That is desperately overdue," I said.

"That some think is desperately overdue," agreed Frank. "But the general consensus is that, if the worst came to the worst, the Department can manage better with an empty D-G's office than with no Berlin Resident."

"The D-G's office is already empty a lot of the time," I said. "And the Deputy D-G has an ailing wife and a thriving law business. It's a time-consuming combination. Not much sign of him on the top floor nowadays."

"And what does the gossip say will happen?" said Frank.

"Now that Bret Rensselaer has lost his empire, he's become one of the hopefuls."

Frank took the pipe from his mouth and grimaced. "Bret will never become D-G. Bret is American. It would be unacceptable to the government, to the Department, and to the public at large if it ever got out."

"Bret is a British subject now. He has been for some years. At least that's what I've heard."

"Bret can arrange what paperwork he likes. But the people who make the decisions regard Bret as an American, and so he's American. And he'll always remain American."

"You'd better not tell Bret."

"Oh, I don't mean he won't get his knighthood. Actors, comics, and footballers get them nowadays, so why not Bret? And that's what he really wants. He wants to go back to his little New England town and be Sir Bret Rensselaer. But he wouldn't be allowed to go back and tell them that he's just become Director-General of MI-6, would he? So what's the point?"

"You're a bit hard on Bret," I said. "He's not simply in it

for a K." I wondered whether Frank's sudden dislike of Bret had something to do with his becoming a contender for the D-G's job. I didn't believe Frank's modest disclaimers. Given a chance, Frank would fight tooth and nail for the D-G's chair.

Frank sighed. "A man has no friends in this job, Bernard. The Berlin Field Unit is the place that London send the people they want to get rid of. This is the Siberia of the service. They send you over here to handle an impossible job, with inadequate staff and insufficient funding. And all the time you're trying to hold things together, London throw shit at you. There is one thing upon which London Central Policy Committee and Controller Europe always agree. And that is that every damn cock-up in London is because of a mistake made here in the Berlin Field Unit. Bret only put me here to get me out of the way when it looked like I might be getting the Economics desk, which he later parlayed into an empire."

"All gone now, Frank," I said. "You had the last laugh on that one. Bret lost everything when they brought Brahms 4 out and closed him down. These days Bret is fighting for a piece of Dicky's desk."

"Don't write Bret off. He won't become D-G, but he's smooth, very bright, and well provided with influential supporters." Frank got up from behind his desk and went over to switch on the lamp that was balanced over his ancient typewriter. The lampshade was green glass and the light coming through it made Frank's pinched face look sepulchral. "And if you enroll Stinnes there will be a mighty reassessment of everyone's performance over the last decade." Frank's voice was more serious now and I had the feeling that he might at last tell me what had prompted this urgent meeting.

"Will there?" I said.

"You can't have overlooked that, Bernard. His interrogation will go on forever. They'll drag out every damned case file that Stinnes ever heard of. They'll read every report that any of us ever submitted."

"Looking for another mole?"

"That might well be the excuse they offer. But there is no mole. They will use Stinnes to find out how well we've all done our jobs over the past decade or so. They'll be able to see how well we guessed what was going on over the other side of the hill. They'll read our reports and predictions with all the advantage of hindsight. And eventually they will give us our end of term school reports."

"Is that what the D-G plans to do with Stinnes?" I said.

"The D-G is not quite the crackpot you like to think he is, Bernard. Personally I'm too near to retirement for it to affect me very much. But the Stinnes debriefing will leave a lot of people with egg on their face. It will take time, of course. The interrogators will have to check and double-check and then submit their reports. But eventually the exam results will arrive. And some of them might be asked to see the headmaster and discreetly told to find another school."

"But everyone at London Central seems to want Stinnes enrolled."

"Because they are all convinced that Stinnes will show how clever they are. You have to be an egomaniac to survive in the London office. You know that."

"Is that why I've survived there?" I asked.

"Yes." Frank was still standing behind me. He hadn't moved after switching on the lamp. On the wall there was a photograph—a signed portrait of Duke Ellington; it was the only picture in the room apart from the portrait of the Queen. Frank had one of the world's largest collections of Ellington recordings, and listening to them was the only leisure activity he permitted himself, apart from his sporadic love affairs with unsuitable young women. "How it will affect you I don't know," said Frank. He touched my shoulder in a gesture of paternal reassurance.

"Nothing will come to light that might affect *my* chances of becoming D-G," I said.

"You're still angry about Dicky Cruyer getting the German desk, aren't you?"

"I thought it would go to someone who really knew the job. I should have known that only Oxbridge men would be short-listed."

"The Department has always been like that. Historically it was sound. Graduates from good universities were unlikely to be regicides, agrarian reformers, or Luddites. One day it will all change, but change comes slowly in England."

"It was my fault," I said. "I knew the way it worked, but I told myself that this time it would be different. There was no reason for thinking it would."

"But you never thought of leaving the service?" said Frank.

"For a week I thought of nothing else except leaving. Twice I wrote out my resignation. I even talked to a man I used to know about a job in California."

"And what made you decide to stay?"

"I never did decide to stay. But I always seemed to be in the middle of something that had to be finished before I could leave. Then when that was done I'd already be involved with a new operation."

"You talked to Fiona about all this?"

"She never took it seriously. She said I'd never leave the Department. She said that I'd been threatening to leave since the first time she found out what I did for a living."

"You've always been like a son to me, Bernard. You know that. I daresay you're fed up with hearing me tell you. I promised your dad I would look after you, but I would have looked after you anyway. Your dad knew that, and I hope you know it too." Frank was still behind me. I didn't twist round; I stared at Duke Ellington dressed in white tails sometime back in the thirties. "So don't be angry at what I'm going to say," said Frank. "It's not easy for me." The photo was of a very young Duke, but it had been signed for Frank during Ellington's West Berlin visit in 1969. So long ago. Frank said, "If you have any doubts about what the Stinnes debriefing will turn up . . . better perhaps to get out now, Bernard."

It took me a long time to understand what he was trying to tell me. "You don't mean defect, Frank?"

"Letting Stinnes slip through our hands will be no solution," said Frank. He gave no sign of having heard my question. "Because after Stinnes there will come another and after that, another. Not perhaps as important as Stinnes, but contributing enough for Coordination to put the pieces together." His voice was soft and conciliatory as if he'd rehearsed his piece many times.

I swung round to see him. I was all ready to blow my top, but Frank looked drained. It had cost him a lot to say what he'd said and so despite my anger I spoke softly. "You think I'm a Soviet agent? You think that Stinnes will blow my cover, and so I'm deliberately obstructing his enrollment? And now you're advising me to run? Is that it, Frank?"

Frank looked at me. "I don't know, Bernard. I really don't know." He sounded exhausted.

"No need to explain to me, Frank," I said. "I lived with Fiona all those years without knowing my own wife was a Soviet agent. Even at the end I had trouble believing it. Sometimes I wake up in the middle of the night and I think it's all a nightmare, and I'm relieved it's all over. Then as I become fully awake I realize that it's not over. The nightmare is still going on."

"You must get Stinnes. And get him soon," said Frank. "It's the only way you'll prove to London that you're in the clear."

"He'll freeze if he's hurried," I said. "We've got to let him talk himself into coming. There was an old man who used to live up in Reinickendorf. He was a swimmer who'd been a competitor in the 1936 Olympics, but he'd lost a foot to frostbite in the war. He taught a lot of the kids to swim. One year I took my son, Billy, to him, and he had him swimming in no time at all. I asked him how he did it, because Billy had always been frightened of the water. The old man said he never told the kids to go into the water. He let them come along and watch the others. Sometimes it took ages before a child would summon up the courage to get into the pool, but he always let them make their own decision about it."

"And that's what you're doing with Stinnes?" Frank came back to his desk and sat down.

"He'll have to break a KGB network to prove his bona fides, Frank. You know that, I know it, and he knows it too. Stop and think what it means. He'll be turning his own people over to us. Once a network breaks, there's no telling how it will go. Scribbled notes, a mislaid address book, or some silly reply to an interrogator, and another network goes too. We both know the way it really happens, no matter what the instruction books ordain. These are his people, Frank, men and women he works with, people he knows, perhaps. He's got to come to terms with all that."

"Don't take too long, Bernard."

"If London hadn't meddled by making the big cash offer, we might have him by now. The cash will make him feel like a Judas. Mentioning the cash too early is the worst thing we could do with a man like Stinnes."

"London Central are trying to help you," said Frank. "And that's the worst thing that can happen to any man."

"It's taking a longer time than usual because we went to him, he didn't come to us. Those idiots in London are trying to compare Stinnes to the sort of defector who comes into West Berlin, picks up a phone, and says, Let's go. For them you just send a military police van and start on the paperwork. Stinnes hasn't been nursing this idea for years and waiting for a chance to jump. He's got to be tempted; he's got to be seduced. He's got to get accustomed to it."

"Surely to God he knows what he wants by now," said Frank.

"Even after he's decided, he'll want to put his hands on a few documents and so on. It's a big step, Frank. He has a wife and a grown-up son. He'll never see them again."

"I hope you don't adopt this maudlin tone with him."

"We'll get him, Frank. Don't worry. Is there anything else you wanted to talk about?"

Frank stared at me before saying, "No, I just thought it appropriate to tell you personally about the death of your man MacKenzie. The Department are keeping it all very low key."

"I appreciate it, Frank," I said. The true reason for the meeting—the suggestion that I might want to walk through Checkpoint Charlie and disappear forever—was now a closed book, a taboo subject that would probably never be mentioned again.

The door opened as if by magic. I suppose Frank must have pressed some hidden signal to summon old Tarrant, his valet and general factotum. "I appreciate it very much, Frank," I said. He'd risked what was left of his career, and a magnificent pension, to fulfill the promise he'd made to my father. I wondered if I would have shown such charity and confidence to him had our positions been reversed.

"Tarrant. Tell the driver that my guest is leaving. And have his coat ready, would you," said Frank.

"Yes, sir," said Tarrant in loud sergeant-major style.

After Tarrant had gone marching off along the hall, Frank said, "Do you ever get lonely, Bernard?"

"Sometimes," I said.

"It's a miserable affliction. My wife hates Berlin. She hardly ever comes over here nowadays," said Frank. "Sometimes I think I hate it too. It's such a dirty place. It's all those bloody coal-fired stoves in the East. There's soot in the air you breathe; I can taste it on bad days. I can't wait to get back to England. I get so damned bored."

"No outside interests, Frank?"

His eyes narrowed. I always overstepped the mark with Frank, but he always responded. Sometimes I suspected that I was the only person in the world who talked to him on an equal footing. "Women, you mean?" There was no smile; it was not something we joked about.

"That sort of thing," I said.

"Not for ages. I'm too old for philandering."

"I find that hard to believe, Frank," I said.

Suddenly the phone rang. Frank picked it up. "Hello?" He didn't have to say who he was—this phone was connected only to his private secretary here in the house. He listened for a time and said, "Just telex the usual acknowledgment and say we're sending someone, and if London want to know what we're doing, tell them that we're handling it until they give instructions otherwise. Phone me if anything develops. I'll be here."

He put the phone down and looked at me. "What is it?" I asked.

"You'd better close the door for a moment, while we sort this out," said Frank. "Paul Biedermann has been arrested by a security officer."

"What for?"

"We're not exactly sure yet. He's in Paris; Charles de Gaulle Airport. We've just had it on the printer. The signal said 'Mikado' and that's a NATO codeword for any sort of secret documents."

"What's it got to do with us?" I said.

Frank gave a grim smile. "Nothing, except that some bloody idiot in London has given Biedermann a 'sacred' tag. At present no one in London is admitting to it, but eventually they'll find out who authorized it. You can't put a tag on anyone without signing the sheet."

"That's right," I said. I went suddenly very cold. I was the idiot in question.

Frank sniffed. "And if Biedermann is carrying stolen secret papers while getting protection from someone in London, there's going to be a hell of a row." He looked at me and waited for my response.

"It doesn't sound as if he got much protection. You said he was arrested."

"A spot check. No tag could save him from a spot check. But people with sacred tags are supposed to be under some sort of surveillance, no matter how perfunctory." He smiled again at the thought of someone in London getting into hot water. "If he's got NATO secrets, they'll go mad. Do you know Paul Biedermann?"

"Of course I do. We were both on that cricket team you tried to get going for the German kids."

"Cricket team. Ah, that's going back a long time."

"And I met his sister Poppy here in this house not so long ago. The last time you had me over for dinner."

"Poppy's a darling. But Paul is a shifty bastard. Didn't you sell him that Ferrari of yours?"

"Shifty? And is that an opinion you've reached since the phone rang?" I asked. "Yes, I sold him my car. I often wish I'd kept it. He's been through half a dozen since that one, and even with my car allowance I can't afford a new Volvo."

"I've always wondered if young Biedermann was in the spy game. He's perfectly placed, with all that traveling. And he's egotistical enough to want to try it. But it sounds as if the other side got in first."

"He's a creep," I said.

"Yes, I know you hate him. I remember you lecturing me about the way he sold his father's transport yard. How would you like to go to Paris and sort this one out? It will just be a matter of a preliminary talk with the people who are holding him. By that time, London will have got hold of whoever signed the sacred tag. Whoever signed it will have to go to Paris—that's the drill, isn't it?"

"Yes, it is," I said. I had a cold feeling of foreboding. Yes, whoever had signed the sacred tag would have to go to wherever Biedermann was being held. There was no way out of that; it was mandatory. Anyone who knew I'd signed that sacred tag could make me go anywhere they wanted me to go; all they had to do was to have Biedermann arrested, and put the NATO signal on the line. I hadn't thought of that when making Biedermann sacred, and now it was too late to change anything.

"Are you all right, Bernard? You've gone a nasty shade of green."

"It was the breakfast at Lisl's," I said hastily. "I can't take those big German breakfasts anymore."

Frank nodded. Too much of an explanation. That was the trouble when dealing with Frank and Werner: they knew me too well. That was the trouble when dealing with Fiona too.

"Just hold the fort in Paris until London sends along whoever signed that tag. I'm very short of people this week, and since you're on your way back to London anyway . . . You don't mind, do you?"

"Of course not," I said. I wondered whether the person who had masterminded this one had known I'd be with Frank today, or whether that was just a lucky coincidence. Either way, the result would have been the same. Sooner or later I would have to go to Paris. I was the mouse in the maze; start running, mouse. "Can you let me have a hand gun, Frank?"

"Now? Right away? You do come up with some posers, Bernard. The army look after our hardware nowadays, and it takes a day or two to get the paperwork through channels and make an appointment with the duty armory officer. I could have it by the end of the week. What exactly do you want? I'd better write it down so that I don't get it wrong."

"No, don't bother," I said. "I just wanted to know what the score was, in case I was here and needed a gun sometime."

Frank smiled. "I thought for one moment you were thinking of taking a gun to Paris. That would mean one of those nonferrous jobs—airport guns, they call them nowadays—and I'm not sure we have any available." He was relieved, and now he placed a hand on the phone as he waited for it to ring again. "My secretary will be phoning back with all the details, and then the car can get you to the airport in time for the next plane." He consulted his gold wristwatch. "Yes, it will all fit together nicely. What a good thing you were here when it happened!"

"Yes," I said. "What a good thing I was here when it happened."

Frank must have heard the bitterness in my voice, for he looked up to see my face. I smiled.

Chapter 19

CHARLES de Gaulle is the sort of futuristic airport that you might find inside a Christmas cracker that was made in Taiwan a long time ago. Overhead the transparent plastic was discolored with brown stains, moving staircases no longer moved, carpeting was threadbare, and the imitation marble had cracked here and there to reveal a black void into which litter had been thrown. There were long lines to get coffee and even longer ones to get a drink, and travelers who liked to eat while sitting down were sprawled on the floor amid discarded plastic cups and wrappings from microwave-heated sandwiches.

I was lucky. I avoided the long lines. A uniformed CRS man met me as I stepped from the plane. He took my bag and conducted me through the customs and immigration, with no more than a perfunctory wave to the CRS officer in charge there. Now he opened a locked door that admitted me to another world. For behind the chaotic slum that the traveler knows as an airport, there is another spacious and leisurely world for the staff. Here there is an opportunity to rest and think and eat and drink undisturbed, except for the sound of unanswered telephones.

"Where are you holding him?" I asked the CRS man as he held the door open for me.

"You'll have to talk to Chief Inspector Nicol first," said the CRS man. We were in a small upper section of the main building that is used by the police. Most of the offices on this corridor were used by the Compagnie Républicaine de Sécurité, who manned the immigration desks. But the office into which I was taken was not occupied by a man who checked passports. Chief

Inspector Gerard Nicol was a well-known personality of the Sûreté Nationale. "The cardinal" they called him; he was senior enough to have his own well-furnished office in the ministry building on the rue des Saussaies. I'd met him several times before.

"Chief Inspector Nicol; I'm Samson," I said as I went into his office. I kept it very formal; French policemen demand politeness from colleagues and prisoners alike.

He looked me up and down as if deciding it.was really me. "It's a long time, Bernard," he said finally. He was dressed in that uniform that Sûreté officers wear when they aren't in uniform: dark trousers, black leather jacket, white shirt, and plain tie.

"Two or three years," I said.

"Two years. It was the security conference in Frankfurt. There was talk of you getting a big promotion."

"Someone else got it," I said.

"You said you wouldn't get it," he reminded me.

"But I didn't believe it."

He protruded his lower lip and shrugged as only a Frenchman shrugs. "So now they are sending you to charm us into letting you have custody of our prisoner?"

"What is he charged with?" I asked.

By way of answer Nicol picked up a transparent bag by the corner so that the contents fell onto the desk top. A U.S. passport crammed with immigration stamps of everywhere from Tokyo to Portugal, a bunch of keys, a wristwatch, a crocodile-skin wallet, a gold pencil, a bundle of paper money—German and French—and coins, a plastic holder containing four credit cards, a packet of paper handkerchiefs, an envelope defaced with scribbled notes, a gold lighter, and a packet of the German cigarettes—Atika—that I'd seen Biedermann smoking. Nicol picked up the credit cards. "Biedermann, Paul," he said.

"Identification, from a credit card?" I sorted quickly through Biedermann's possessions.

"It's more difficult to get a credit card these days than to get a *carte de séjour,*" said Nicol sorrowfully. "But there's a California driving license with a photo if you prefer it. We haven't charged him with anything yet. I thought we'd wait until you arrived."

"That's most considerate of you," I said. I put the packet of German cigarettes into my pocket. If Nicol saw me do so, he made no comment.

"We always try to oblige," said Nicol. There is no *habeas corpus* in French law. There is no method whereby a man unlawfully detained may be set free. The prefect of police doesn't need a formal charge or evidence that any crime has been committed, he needs no judicial authority to search houses, issue warrants, and confiscate letters in the post. He can order the arrest of anyone. He can interrogate them and then hand them over for trial, release them or send them to a lunatic asylum. No wonder French policemen look so relaxed.

"May I see what he was carrying?" I asked.

"He had that small shoulder bag containing shaving things and some underwear, a newspaper and aspirins and so on. That's over there. I found nothing of interest in it. But he was also carrying this." Nicol pointed to a hard brown leather case on the side table. It was an expensive piece of luggage without any manufacturer's labels, a one-suiter with separate spaces for shoes, shirts, and socks. I suppose the factory made it to the maximum regulation size for cabin baggage, but it was large enough to get anyone into a lot of arguments with officious check-in clerks.

One compartment inside the lid was intended for business papers. It even had special places for pens, pencils, and a notebook. Inside the zippered section there were four lots of typed pages, each neatly bound into varying-colored plastic folders. I flipped through the pages quickly. It was all in English, but it was unmistakably American in presentation and content. The way in which these reports had been prepared—with colored charts and captioned photos—made them look like the sort of elaborate pitch that an advertising agency might make to a potential client.

The introduction said, "The German yard Howaldtswerke Deutsche Werft at Kiel have dominated the market in small and medium size diesel submarines for more than 15 years. Two Type 209 (1,400t) submarines are being fitted out and Brazil has ordered two of the same displacement. Work on these will start almost immediately. Two larger (1,500t) boats are already begun for delivery to India. These will not be stretched versions of the Type 209 but specially designed to a new specification."

Soon however the detailed descriptions became more technical: "The Type 209s carry Krupp Atlas passive/active sonar in the sail but the TR 1700 also have a passive ranging sonar of French design. The fire control system made by Hollandse Signaal-apparaten is standard but modifications are being incorporated following the repeated failure of the Argentine submarine *San Luis* in attacks against the Royal Navy task force."

"It doesn't look like you've captured a master spy," I said.

"It's marked secret," said Nicol defensively.

"But so are a lot of things in the museum archives," I said.

"Never mind the archives, this is dated last month. I don't know anything about submarines, but I know the Russians give a high priority to updating their knowledge of the world's submarines. And I know that these diesel ones are the hunter killers that would have to be used to find the nuclear-powered ones."

"You've been watching too many TV documentaries," I said.

"And I've learned enough at NATO security conferences to know that a report like this which reveals secrets about submarines built in German yards for the Norwegian and Danish navies will get everyone steamed up."

"There's no denying that," I said. "We think Biedermann is a small-time KGB agent working out of Berlin. Where was he going?"

"I can't tell you."

"Can't tell me, or don't know?" I said.

"He arrived from Paris in a taxicab and hadn't yet bought a ticket. Look for yourself." Nicol indicated Biedermann's personal possessions that were still on the desk.

"So it was a tip-off?"

"A good guess," said Nicol.

"Don't give me that, Gerard," I said. "You say he hadn't bought a ticket. And he hadn't arrived by plane. So he wasn't going through customs immigration or a security check when you found the papers. Who tipped you off to search him?"

"Tip-off?"

"The only reason you know all that printed junk is secret is because you were tipped off."

"I hate policemen, don't you, Bernard? They always have such nasty suspicious minds. I never mix with them off duty."

"American passport. Have you told the embassy?"

"Not yet," he said. "Where is Biedermann resident?"

"Mexico. He has companies registered there. For tax purposes, I suppose. Is he talking?"

"He helped us a little with some preliminary questions," admitted Nicol.

"A *passage à tabac?*" I said. It was delicate police euphemism for the preliminary roughing up that was given to uncooperative prisoners under interrogation.

He looked at me blank-faced and said, "That sort of thing doesn't happen anymore. That all stopped fifty years ago."

"I was only kidding," I said, although I could have opened my shirt and showed him a few scars that proved otherwise. "What's the official policy? Are you holding on to the prisoner, or do you want me to take him away?"

"I'm waiting for instructions on that," said Nicol. "But it's been agreed that you talk to him."

"Alone?"

Nicol gave me a mirthless grin. "Providing you don't get rough with him and try and blame it on our primitive police methods."

So my taunt did find its mark. "Thanks," I said. "I'll do the same for you sometime."

"It was a tip-off. It was phoned through to my office, so it was someone who knew how the Sûreté works. The caller said a man would be at the Alitalia desk; a scarred face, walks with a limp. A clerk took the call. There's no chance of identifying the voice or tracing the call, but you can talk to the clerk if you wish. A man; perfect French, probably a Paris accent."

"Thanks," I said. "Sounds like you've already narrowed it down to eight million suspects."

"I'll get someone to take you downstairs."

THEY were holding Paul Biedermann in the specially built cell block that is one floor below the police accommodation. It is a brick-built area with a metal reinforced ceiling. In 1973—by which time airports had become a major attraction for hijackers, assassins, demonstrators, and lunatics and criminals of every kind—the cell block was tripled in size and redesigned to provide twenty-five very small solitary cells, eight cells with accommodation for three prisoners each (current penology advising that four prisoners together fight, and two get too friendly), and four rooms for interrogating prisoners in secure conditions. Three cells for women prisoners were also built at that time.

Paul Biedermann was not in a cell of any sort. They were holding him in one of the interrogation rooms. Like most such rooms, it had a small observation chamber large enough for two or three people. The door to that was unlocked and I stepped inside it and watched Paul Biedermann through the mirrored-glass panel. There was all the usual recording equipment here, but no sign of its being recently used.

The interrogation room in which Biedermann was being held had no bed; just a table and two chairs. Nothing to be broken, bent, or used as a weapon. The door was not a cell door, there was no iron grille or bolts, and it was secured only by a heavy-duty mortice lock. After I'd had a good look at him I opened the locked door and went inside.

"Bernd. Am I glad to see you." He laughed. The scars down the side of his face puckered, and his smile was so broad that his twisted face looked almost demented. "Jesus. I was hoping it would be you. They said that someone was coming from Berlin. I can explain everything, Bernd. It's all a crazy mistake." Even under stress he still had that low-pitched hoarse voice and the strong American accent.

"Easy does it, Paul," I said. I looked around the white tiled room, but I couldn't see any obvious signs of hidden microphones. If the observation chamber was not in use they were probably not recording us. Finally I decided not to worry too much about it.

"I did everything you told me to do, Bernd. Everything." He was wearing expensive linen pants and an open-neck brown shirt with a scarf tied at the neck. There was a soft brown cashmere jacket thrown carelessly onto one of the chairs. "Have you got a cigarette? They even took away my cigarettes. How do you like that."

I offered him the pack of Atika cigarettes; they were his own cigarettes from the things on Nicol's desk. He took one and I put the pack on the table. There was a tacit understanding that he'd get them if he was good. I lit his cigarette and he inhaled greedily. "Were you carrying all that secret junk I saw upstairs?"

"No," he said.

"You weren't carrying it? You never saw it before?"

"Yes. That is to say, yes and no. I was carrying it. But I don't know . . . submarines." He laughed briefly. "What do I know about submarines?"

"Sit down. Relax for a moment. Then tell me exactly how you got the papers," I said.

He exhaled smoke and waved it away with his hand as if trying to dispel the smoke in case a guard came and took the cigarette away from him. "I always travel light. I was flying to

Rome. I have a holiday place on Giglio—that's an island—"

"I know where Giglio is," I said. "Tell me about the papers."

"I travel light because a car always collects me at the airport, and the only clothes I'll need will be those I keep there."

"What a life you have, Paul. Is that what they call *la dolce vita* down there in Giglio."

He gave me a fleeting smile that was no more than a grimace. "So I just carry a little shoulder bag that's well under regulation size for cabin baggage."

"Just clothes inside it?"

"Hardly anything inside it; shaving stuff and a change of linen in case I get delayed somewhere."

"So what about the brown leather case?"

"I paid off the taxi outside the arrivals hall and went in through the main entrance, and before I got anywhere near the Alitalia desk, the taxi driver came running after me. He gave me the brown case and said I'd forgotten it. I said it wasn't mine, but he was already saying that he was illegally parked and he pushed past me and disappeared—it was very crowded—and so I thought I'd better take it to the police."

"You thought it was a genuine mistake? What did the cab driver say when he gave it to you?"

"He said, 'I'm the cab driver. Here's the bag you left behind.' "

"Give it a minute's thought, Paul. I'd really like to get it right."

"That's what he said. He said, 'I'm the cab driver, here's the bag you left behind.' " Biedermann waited, looking at my face. "What's the matter with that?"

"It could be all right, I suppose. But if I was a cab driver and someone had just paid me off, I wouldn't feel the need to say who I was, I'd be egotistical enough to think he'd know who I was. And neither would I be inclined to tell him what the bag was. I'd expect my passenger to recognize it immediately. I'd expect him to fall over with excited appreciation. And I'd hang around long enough for him to manifest that appreciation in the time-honored way. Right, Paul?"

"Yeah . . . It seemed all right at the time. But I was flustered."

"Are you quite sure that the man who gave you the case was the man you paid off in the cab?"

Paul Biedermann's face froze. Then he inhaled again and thought about it. "Jesus. You're right, Bernd. The cab driver was wearing a leather jacket the same color as one I've got, and a dark blue shirt. I noticed his sleeve while he was driving."

"And the one who gave you the case?"

"He was in shirt sleeves. I thought my driver had taken his jacket off. But the second man's shirt was white. Jesus, Bernd, you're a genius. Some bastard planted that bag on me. I was looking for the police office when they arrested me."

"You were near the Alitalia desk," I said. "Don't get careless, Paul. Who would have known you would be at the Alitalia desk?"

"Can you get me out of here?" he said. His voice had that soft whispery quality that I'd heard from other desperate men.

"I'll try," I promised. "Who'd know you'd be at the Alitalia desk?"

"Only the girl in the hotel reception. She phoned them for me. Was it your people who forced the case on me? Is it a way of getting me to work for you?"

"Don't be stupid, Paul."

"Why would the Russians do it? I mean, they could have asked me to take the bloody case and I would have taken it. I've taken other things for them, I told you that." He stubbed out his cigarette. He had that American habit of stubbing them out half-smoked.

"Yes," I said, although he hadn't told me about carrying packages for them. There was a long silence. Biedermann fidgeted.

"Why did they do that?" said Biedermann. "Why? Tell me why?"

"I don't know," I said. "I wish I did know." Nervously he reached for another cigarette and I lit it for him. "I'll go and talk to the Chief Inspector again. London have asked for you. He's waiting to hear if Paris will release you into my custody."

"I hope to God they do. Trying to sort this out in the French courts will take years."

I unlocked the door with the key Nicol had given me. Biedermann, as if anxious to do me some extra service for which I might pay in goodwill, said, "Watch out for that guy Moskvin. He's an evil old bastard. The other one is almost human at times, but Moskvin is a fink. He's really a fink."

"I'll do what I can for you, Paul," I promised.

I went out and locked the door. I went back along the corridor to the stairs to speak again with Nicol. I was at the top of the stairs when I almost bumped into a woman in a blue overall coat. She was quite young, about twenty-five, and carrying a tiny plastic tray upon which there was a coffee with froth on it and a dried-up sandwich. "With the compliments of Chief Inspector Nicol," the woman said in a shrill working-class accent. "It's for the man being held in custody. The Inspector said you had the key."

"Yes, I have. Do you want it?"

"Will you take the coffee to him?" she said nervously. "Inspector Nicol wouldn't approve of you giving the key to anyone —bad security."

"Very well," I said.

"Don't be too long. The Inspector has to go to a meeting."

"I'll be right with him," I promised.

I spent no more than a minute giving Paul Biedermann the coffee and sandwich. "They gave me lunch," he said, looking at the miserable sandwich. "But I'd love the coffee." It had that bitter smell of the high roast coffee that the French like so much.

I locked him up again and went upstairs to see Nicol. He was still behind his desk. He was speaking on the phone, but he beckoned me inside and ended his conversation abruptly. "Did you get anything out of him, Bernard?" A vase of cut flowers was now on his desk. It was the undefinable Gallic touch, that little *je ne sais quoi* that the French like to think makes them human.

"He says the case was planted on him," I said. I put the door key on Nicol's desk. I noticed that the desk had been tidied and the contents of Biedermann's pockets were now back inside the plastic bag.

"By a cab driver? He got that taxicab from a rank in the Rivoli. How would you arrange for him to select that particular cab? Not very convincing, is it?"

"I think it was another person who gave him the case. I think he might have been set up."

"Why would anyone do that? You said he was a small-time agent."

"I can't think why they'd do it," I admitted.

"Paris still hasn't replied, but they should come through any time now. Since we've got to sit here, can I send out for a drink for you?"

"A *grand crème* like the one you just sent to your prisoner would be most acceptable. Do you do that with all the prisoners, or was it just to impress me?"

"And a brandy with it? That's what I'm going to have."

"You talked me into it. Thanks."

He reached for the internal phone, but before he grasped it said, "What coffee that I sent down for him?"

"You sent a coffee and sandwich down to him, didn't you?"

"A coffee? What do you think this is, the Ritz? I don't send coffee down for prisoners. Not here; not anywhere."

"You didn't?"

"Are you mad? A prisoner can break a cup and slash his wrists. Don't they teach you anything in England?"

I stood up. "A young woman gave it to me. She was wearing a blue coverall coat. She looked like a secretary, but she spoke like a truck driver—with a very strong Paris accent. She said the coffee and sandwich came with your compliments and would I give it to the man in custody. She said you had to go to a meeting . . ."

"She wanted to get you out of the way," said Nicol. He picked up the key and shouted for the uniformed man who was sitting at a desk in the next room. He took the staircase at one leap and I was right behind him.

It was too late, of course. Paul Biedermann was on his knees in the corner, his forehead on the floor like a Muslim at prayer. But his contorted position was due to the muscular contractions that had twisted his body, put a leer on his face, and stopped his heart.

Nicol held Biedermann's wrist, trying to believe there was a pulse still beating there, but it was obvious that all signs of life had gone. "Get the doctor," Nicol told his uniformed man. A police officer may presume death but not pronounce it.

Nicol picked up the coffee cup, sniffed it, and put it down again. The sandwich was untouched. It was a miserable dried-up sandwich. It obviously wasn't part of the plan that he should eat the sandwich.

"We'll be up all night," said Nicol. He had gone white with anger. "My people will be furious when they hear. When prisoners die in custody, it's always police brutality. Everyone knows that. You told me that yourself, didn't you? Can you imagine what the Communists will make of this? There'll be hell to pay."

"The Russians?"

"Never mind the Russians," said Nicol. "I've got all the Communists I need right here in the National Assembly. I've got more than I need, in fact."

"It's my fault," I said once we were back in his office.

"You're damned right it is," said Nicol, his anger unabated by this appeasement. "And that's the way it's going to go down on paper. Don't expect me to cover up for you." He got a few sheets of lined paper from the drawer and pushed it across his desk towards me. "You'll have to give me a written statement.

I know you'll say you can't, but you'll have to write out something."

I looked at the blank paper for a long time. Statements are always on lined paper; the police don't trust anyone to write in straight lines. Nicol uncapped a ball-point pen and banged it down on the paper to hurry me along.

"You're not going to ask me to stay here?"

"Stay here? Me? Keep you here? And explain to my minister that I let some foreigner go down and murder my prisoner? Write a statement and get out of here, and stay out. The sooner I'm rid of you, the better pleased I'll be. Go and explain it all to your people in London. Although how the hell you will explain it, I can't begin to guess."

The curious rigmarole with the phony taxi driver began to make sense. The KGB were determined to frame me. It would look as if I put a sacred tag on Biedermann, when there was no real investigation in progress, to help him work as a KGB courier. And then, they'd say, the murder was done to silence him.

Now the big conundrum was finally answered. Now I knew what Stinnes had been doing in Mexico City. He'd been sent there to set up Biedermann, and Biedermann was being made ready for this murder for which I'd be blamed. Of course they hadn't let Stinnes know the whole plan—that was not the KGB way. Communism has never escaped that conspiratorial climate in which it was born, and in the field even senior KGB officers are confined to their individual tasks. But what care and attention they put into their tasks! Even while I was sitting there frozen with anxiety and twisted up with indecision, I had to admire the scheme that had trapped me. The KGB were not noted for their brilliant ideas, but their dogged planning, determination, and attention to detail could often make something out of a lousy idea.

Well, the mouse was nearing the end of the maze. Now I recognized the trap that faced me. But surely to God no one in London Central would believe that I could be a KGB agent, and certainly not one who'd murder Biedermann or MacKenzie in cold blood. And then I remembered the way that Frank had wrung out his conscience to give me a chance to run off to Moscow. There could be nothing more sincere than that; Frank had risked his job, his chances of a K, and his pension for me. Even Frank believed I might be guilty, and he'd known me since I was in my cradle. I wouldn't get the benefit of the doubt from those stony-faced Oxbridge men in London Central.

Chapter 20

ND WHEN finally I got back to London I was surprised to find a woman in my bed. Well, that's not precisely true. The woman was Tessa, my sister-in-law, and she wasn't exactly in my bed; she was sleeping in the spare room. And I wasn't surprised either; there was a note on the hall stand telling me she was sleeping there.

It was early in the morning. She came downstairs in her magnificent floral dressing gown to find me in the front room. Her long blonde hair was disheveled and her eyelids were still heavy with sleepiness. There is a curious intimacy about seeing a woman's face without makeup. Tessa looked pale, especially round her eyes where there was usually shadow and darkened eyebrows and blackened lashes. It was the face of a sleepy child, but no less attractive for that. I'd never before realized how beautiful she was; George was a lucky man, but there were too many other men equally lucky.

"Bernard. We thought you were never coming back. The children keep asking me . . ."

"I'm sorry, Tessa. I've come straight from the airport."

"Nanny gets nervous here on her own, then the children

recognize that and they get frightened too. It's stupid, but she's such a good girl with the children. She doesn't get much time to herself. I moved into the box room—you said that I could use it."

"Of course I did. Any time. Thanks for looking after them," I said. I took off my hat and coat and threw it onto an armchair. Then I sat down on the sofa.

"Did they give you breakfast on the plane?"

"Nothing fit for human consumption."

"Do you want coffee?" She fiddled with her hair as if suddenly aware that it was disarrayed.

"Desperately."

"And orange juice? It will take time for the coffee to drip through."

"Does David know I'm away so much?"

"He was furious. He threatened to come here and take the children. That was another reason why I stayed here. Nanny wouldn't be able to stand up to him." Furtively she looked at herself in the mirror and straightened the dressing gown. "I'm planning to take the children to my cousin's house on Friday . . . Perhaps you'd prefer that I didn't, now that you're home." Hastily she added, "She has three children, big garden, lots of toys. We were going to stay there over the school holiday."

"I have to go back to Mexico," I said. "Don't change your plans."

She bent over me and touched my face in a gesture of great affection. "I know you love the children. They know it too. You have to do your work, Bernard. Don't worry." She went into the kitchen and rattled bottles and glasses and cups and saucers. When she came back she was holding a tray with a half-filled bottle of champagne. There was also a jug containing water into which a can-shaped slug of frozen orange juice was trying to melt. "How do you like your orange juice?" she said. "Diluted with champagne or straight?"

"Champagne? At this time in the morning I thought they served it in ladies' slippers."

"It was in the fridge, left over from last night. I split a bottle with Nanny, but we didn't finish it. The bubbles stay if you put it straight back into the fridge after pouring. I brought a case with me when I came. I had a big bust-up with George and I thought, Why leave all the champers there?"

"A permanent bust-up?"

"Who knows? George was shouting. He doesn't often shout."

"Did he go to South Africa?"

She poured some champagne for both of us. "I told you all that, didn't I . . . phoning the hotel in Italy and asking for Mrs. Kosinski. Was it terribly tiresome of me to burden you with all that?"

"Did he go?" I stirred the frozen juice and poured some into both glasses. I was too damned puritanical to drink champagne so early in the morning, but adding the orange made it seem permissible.

"No, he sent his general manager instead. It shows that there must have been another woman."

"I don't follow the logic of that," I said. I tasted the champagne mixture.

"The other woman would have been furious if he'd turned her down and taken his wife instead. His only way out of trouble was not to go at all."

"I wish I could help," I said.

"I'm not sure that you could, Bernard." She looked at her watch. "The coffee will only take a moment or so."

"I'll speak to George."

"I'm sure you've got all sorts of worries of your own."

"No," I said resolutely. Good old Bernard, always has time to help his fellow humans no matter what threatens. Or was I just trying to convince myself?

"George is being such a fool, Bernard. I mean, he knows that I've been tempted by other men."

She paused. "Ummm," I said. I nodded and admired her choice of words. Only a woman could describe such a long

succession of reckless love affairs as being tempted, without any
clear admission that she'd submitted to the temptations.

"I didn't go to great trouble to hide it from him. You know
that, Bernard. So he's left it a bit late, hasn't he? You'd have
thought he would have said something before deciding to go
off with other women. It's not like him."

"Was it one particular relationship that might have made
George angry?"

"Oh, Bernard," she said. Her voice was loud, louder than
she intended, perhaps, for she looked round wondering if
Nanny had heard; but Nanny's room is at the top of the house
next to the children. "Bernard, really. You are exasperating."
She drank. "That's good," she said.

I hated to annoy anyone without understanding why. "What
have I done, Tessa?" I asked.

"Surely it's obvious. Even to a thick-headed idiot like you,
it must be evident."

"What?"

"Evident that I adore you, Bernard. It's you that George is
always making such a fuss about."

"But we've . . . I mean I never . . ."

She gave a short sardonic chuckle. "You've gone red, darling. I didn't know I could make you blush. You're always so
damned cool. That's what makes you so adorable."

"Now stop all this nonsense, Tessa. What is it all about?"

"It's George. He's convinced that we're having a red-hot
love affair, and nothing I tell him makes any difference."

"Oh, really. I'll have to talk to him."

"I wish you luck, darling. He takes no notice of anything I
tell him."

"And he knows you're here now?"

"Well, of course he does. That's what really got him
steamed up. He called me some horrible names, Bernard. If
you were really my lover you'd go round there and punch him
on the nose. I told him that."

"You told him what?"

"I said if Bernard was really my lover he'd come round here and give you a good thrashing."

"Oh my God, Tessa. Whatever made you say that?"

"I was angry." She laughed as she remembered the scene with her husband. But I didn't join in the laughter. "I told him you had lots of women. I told him you don't need me."

"I haven't got lots of women." I didn't want her spreading such stories. "I haven't got any women, to tell you the truth."

"Now, don't overdo it, Bernard. No one expects you to live the life of a hermit. And that Secret de Venus in the bathroom is not something you got from the supermarket to make you smell lovely."

"Secret of what?"

"Bath oil from Weil of Paris. It costs an absolute fortune and I know Fi never used it."

"I let someone from the office change here."

"Gorgeous Gloria. I know all about her from Daphne Cruyer. She left it here, did she. Her mind was on other things in store. You are a quiet one, Bernard. How many others are there?"

My inclination was to rebut her charges, but knowing that was exactly what she wanted, I let it go. "Poor George," I said. "I'll have to straighten it out."

"He won't believe you. We may as well go straight upstairs, jump into bed, and make all his suspicions come true."

"Don't joke about it," I said.

"Come over here on the sofa and I'll show you if I'm joking or not." She inched back the hem of her dressing gown to expose her thigh. It was a jokey gesture, the sort of antic she'd probably copied from some ancient film, but I could see she was naked under the dressing gown. I took a deep breath and devoted all my attention to the drink. That "sweet disorder in the dress" made it difficult to concentrate on anything but Tessa; she was disturbingly attractive.

I gulped my drink and got to my feet. "I'll go up to the children," I said. "We'll all have breakfast together." Tessa smiled. "And I'll talk to George. I'll phone him this morning."

"I'm sure you have more important things to do," she said. She stood up too. "Do you want me to clear out?"

"I thought you wanted to go back to George."

"I don't know what I want," she said. "I need time to think."

"You don't need time to think," I said. "You must either go back to George, or leave him and make a clean break. You'll both be miserable if you let things go on like this. You have to decide whether you love him or not. That's all that really matters."

"Is it? Are you still in love with Fiona?"

"No," I said. "And I never was."

"You can't just wipe out the past, Bernard. I know how happy Fi was when you asked her to marry you. She adored you, you both were happy. I don't know what happened, but don't say you never loved her."

"That Fiona I knew was only part of a person, an actress who never let me see the real person. She lived a lie and I'm glad she's gone to where she wanted to be."

"Don't be bitter. George could say the same thing about me. He could say that I've never truly given him my real self."

"I can't help you make up your mind, Tessa."

"Don't kick me out, Bernard. I'll look after the children and I'll keep out of your way. While you've been away I've been sitting upstairs watching Nanny's television with her, and I use her little kitchen to make breakfast and we eat it in the nursery. We hardly ever come down here. I won't be in the way when you bring people home."

"I have no plans for bringing people home, if by that you mean women."

"Are you going into the office this morning?"

"Eventually," I said. We stood close together. Neither of us had anything to say but we didn't want to move. We were lonely, I suppose.

She said, "I can hear the bath water running for the children. Why don't you go and say hello to them. They'll be so excited to see you."

"I'll have to have a talk with George," I warned her.

"But not right at this moment," she pleaded.

"I'll phone him when I get to the office," I said. "I hate misunderstandings."

When I got upstairs the children greeted me vociferously. I told them that Tessa was going to take them away to the country.

"Nanny too?" Billy asked.

Nanny gave a shy smile. Billy was in love with his nanny, I think. "Of course," I said.

"Aunty Tessa lets us drink champagne," said Sally. Billy glared at her because she was revealing a secret. They had never asked me about their mother. I wondered what they thought about her sudden disappearance, but it seemed better to let it go until they asked questions.

Pinned up on their board was a colored drawing of a red-faced man sitting on a pointed box strumming a guitar. Across the vivid blue sky it said WELLCOM DADDY in big letters. "Is that me?" I said.

"We copied it from a picture of Mick Jagger," Billy told me. "And then we drew your glasses on afterwards. I did the outline and Sally filled in the colors."

"And that's a pyramid in Mexico," said Sally. "We copied it from the encyclopedia."

"It's beautiful," I said. "Can I keep it?"

"No," said Billy. "Sally wants to take it to school."

I WENT into the little room where I keep my typewriter, books, and unpaid bills. I looked up "fink" in the dictionary of American slang.

> **fink** n 1 A company spy, secret informer, or strike breaker. (Orig. Pink, contraction of Pinkerton man.)

I wondered how Pavel Moskvin fitted to that definition and what else Paul Biedermann had been about to tell me about him.

Chapter 21

I KNEW what to expect. That was why I lingered over breakfast, spent a little extra time with the children, and picked
a dark suit and sober tie. Bret Rensselaer chose to see me in the
number-three conference room. It was a small top-floor room
that was normally used when the top brass wanted to have a
cozy chat far away from the noise of the typewriters, the smell
of copying machines, and the sight of the workers drinking tea
from cups without saucers.

There was a coffin-shaped table there and Bret was in the
chairman's seat at the head of it. I was at the other end. The
rest of them—Dicky Cruyer and his friend Henry Tiptree, together with Frank Harrington and a man named Morgan, who
was general factotum and hatchet man for the D-G—were
placed so that they were subject to Bret's authority. Quite apart
from anything that might happen to me, Bret was going to
stage-manage things to get maximum credit and importance.
Bret was a department head looking for a department, and
there was no more dangerous animal than that stalking through
the corridors of Whitehall. He was wearing a black worsted suit
—only a man as trim as Bret could have chosen a fabric that
would show every spot of dust and hair—and a white shirt with
stiff collar and the old-fashioned doubled-back cuffs that require cuff links. Bret's cuff links were large and made from
antique gold coins, and his blue and white tie was of a pattern
sold only to Concorde passengers.

"I've listened," said Bret. "You can't say I haven't listened.
I'm not sure I'm able to understand much of it, but I've listened
to you." He looked at his watch and noted the time in the

notebook in front of him. Bret had gone to great pains to point out to me how informal it all was: no stenographer, no recording, and no signed statements. But this way was better for Bret, for there would be no record of what had been said except what Bret wrote down. "I've got a hell of a lot of questions still to ask you," he said. I recognized the fact that Bret was ready for any sort of showdown; "loaded for bear" was Bret's elegant phrase for it.

I was trying to give up smoking, but I reached for the silver-plated cigarette box that was a permanent feature of top-floor conference rooms, and helped myself. No one else wanted a cigarette. They didn't want to be associated with me by thought, theory, or action. I had the feeling that if I'd declared abstinence they'd all have rushed out to get drunk. I lit up and smiled and told Bret that I'd be glad to do things any way he wanted.

There were no other smiles. Frank Harrington was fiddling with his gold wristwatch, pushing a button to see what time it was in Timbuktu. Henry Tiptree, having written something that was too private to say, was now showing it to Morgan. Bret seemed to have hidden away the little note pads and pencils that were always put at each place on the table. That had effectively prevented note taking except for the freckle-faced Tiptree, who'd brought his own note pad. Dicky Cruyer was wearing his blue denim outfit and a sea island cotton sports shirt open enough to reveal a glimpse of gold chain. Now it was obvious that Dicky had known all along that Henry Tiptree was an Internal Security officer. I'd never forgive him for not warning me back in Mexico City when Tiptree first came sniffing around.

Bret Rensselaer took off the big wire-frame speed-cop-style glasses that he required for reading and said, "Suppose I suggested that you were determined that Stinnes would never be enrolled? Suppose I suggested that everything you've done from the time you went to Mexico City—and maybe before that even—has been done to ensure that Stinnes stays loyal to the

KGB." He raised a hand in the air and waved it around as though he was trying to get someone to bid for it. "This is just a hypothesis, you understand."

I took my time answering. "You mean I threatened him? Are you 'suggesting' that I told him that I worked for the KGB and that I'd make sure that any attempt to defect would end in disaster for him?"

"Oh, no. You'd be far too clever for a crude approach like that. If it was you, you wouldn't tell Stinnes anything about your job with the KGB. You'd just handle the whole thing in such an incompetent fumbling way it would ensure that Stinnes got scared. You'd make sure he was too damned jumpy to make any move at all."

I said, "Is that the way you think it was handled, Bret? In an incompetent fumbling way?" No hypothesis now, I noticed. The incompetence was neatly folded in.

Mexico City had been Dicky's operation and Dicky was quick to see that Bret was out to sink him. "I don't think you have all the necessary information yet," Dicky told Bret. Dicky wasn't going to be sunk, even if it meant keeping me afloat.

"We were taking it slowly, Bret," I said. "The brief implied that London wanted Stinnes gung ho, and ready to talk. We didn't want to push hard. And you said London Debriefing Centre wouldn't want to find themselves dragging every word out of him. Frank will remember that."

Bret realized that he could get caught in the fallout. Defensively he said, "I didn't say that. What the hell would I know about what the Debriefing Centre want?"

Dicky leaned forward to see Bret and said, "Words to that effect, Bret. You definitely said that Bernard was to use his own judgment. He decided to do things slowly."

"Maybe I did," said Bret and, having pacified Dicky, turned the heat back on to me. "But how slow is slow? We don't want Stinnes to die of old age while you're enrolling him. We want to speed things up a little."

I said, "You wanted to speed things up. So you applied the

magic speed-up solution, didn't you? You offered Stinnes a quarter of a million dollars to help him make up his mind. And you did it without even informing me, despite the fact that I am the enroller. I'm going to make an official objection to that piece of clumsy meddling." I turned to the D-G's personal assistant and said, "Have you got that, Morgan? I object to that interference with my operation."

Morgan was a white-faced Welshman whose only qualifications for being in the Department were an honors degree in biology and an uncle in the Foreign Office. He looked at me as if I were an insect floating in his drink. His expression didn't change and he didn't answer. On the day I leave the Department I'm going to punch Morgan in the nose. It's a celebration I've been promising myself for a long time.

Bret continued hurriedly as if to cover up for the way I'd made a fool of myself. "We were in a hurry to debrief Stinnes for reasons that must be all too clear to you."

"To question him about Fiona's defection?" I said. "Would you push that ashtray down the table, please."

"It wasn't a defection, buddy. To defect means to leave without permission. Your wife was a KGB agent passing secret information to Moscow." He slid the heavy glass ashtray along the polished table with that violent aplomb with which bartenders shove bourbon bottles in cowboy films.

I took the ashtray, tapped ash into it, and said, "Whatever it was she did, you wanted to question Stinnes about it?"

"We wanted to question him about your role in that move. There are people downstairs who've always thought that you and your wife were working together as a team." I saw Frank edge his chair back an inch from the table, his subconscious prompting him to disassociate himself from anyone who thought that.

I said, "But when she ran I was already there. I was in East Berlin. Why would I come back here to put my head in a noose?"

Bret held one of his cuff links and twisted his wrist in the starched white cuff. His eyes were fixed on me. He said, "That was the cunning of it. What guilty man would come running back to the Department he betrayed? The fact that you came back was the most ingenious defense you could have contrived. What's more, Bernard, it's very you."

"I say, Bret. Steady on," said Frank Harrington. Bret looked at Frank for long enough to remind him who'd given him his present posting and who could no doubt get him a staff job in Iceland if he felt inclined. Frank turned his objection into a cough and Bret looked down the table to me.

"Very me?" I said.

"Yes," said Bret. "It's exactly the kind of double-think that you excel at. And you are one of the few people who could swing it. You are cool; very cool."

I inhaled on my cigarette and tried to be as cool as he said I was. I knew Bret; he worked on observation. It was his standard method to throw his weight around and then see how people reacted to him. He even did it with the office clerks. "You can invent some exciting yarns, Bret," I said. "But this particular parable leaves out one vitally important event. It leaves out the fact that I was the one who flushed Fiona out. It was my phone call to her that made her run."

"That's your version of events," said Bret. "But it conveniently overlooks the fact that she got away. I'd say that your phone call warned her in time for her to get away safely."

"But I told Dicky too."

"Only because you wanted him to stop her taking your children."

"Leaving my motivation aside," I said, "the fact is that I stampeded her into immediate flight. Even the report says that she seems to have taken no papers or anything of importance with her."

"She took nothing because she was determined to be clean for customs and immigration. The way the British law stands, there were no legal grounds for preventing her leaving the country with or without a passport. She knew that if she had nothing incriminating with her we would have had to wave good-bye with a smile on our faces when she took off."

"I don't want to be sidetracked into a discussion about the British subject's rights of exit and reentry," I said primly, as if Bret was trying to evade the subject of discussion. "I'm just telling you that she was unprepared. With proper warning she could have dealt us a bad blow."

Bret was all ready for that one. "She was a burned-out case, Bernard, and she'd run her course. The evidence that would incriminate her was there. If you hadn't stampeded her, the next agent in would have done it. But by having you do it, Moscow were going to make you a golden boy here in London. That's what chess players call a gambit, isn't it? A piece is sacrificed to gain a better position from which to attack."

"I don't know much about chess," I said.

"I'm surprised," said Bret. "I would have thought you'd be good at it. But you'll remember that next time you're playing . . . about losing a piece to get into a better position . . . won't you?"

"Since my duplicity was so bloody obvious, Bret, why didn't you arrest me as soon as I got back here?"

"We weren't sure," said Bret. He shuffled in his seat. Bret was a shirt-sleeve man. He didn't look right sitting there with his jacket on like a shop-window dummy.

"You didn't ask me to face a board. There wasn't even an inquiry."

"We wanted to see what you would do about enrolling Stinnes."

"That's not very convincing, Bret. The fact that you wanted to enroll Stinnes and question him was a measure of your doubt about my guilt."

"Not at all. This way, we could confirm or deny your loyalty and have Stinnes as a bonus. Dicky and I talked that one over. Right, Dicky?" Bret obviously felt that Dicky wasn't giving him the support he needed.

Dicky said, "I've always said that there was insufficient evidence to support any action against Bernard. I want to make that clear to everyone round this table." Dicky looked round the table, making it clear to everyone.

Well good old Dicky, so he wasn't just a pretty face either. He'd realized that this might well turn out to be the opportunity he'd been waiting for: the opportunity to dump a bucket of shit over Bret's head. Dicky was going to sit on the sidelines, but he'd be cheering for me now that Bret had adopted the role of my prosecutor. And if I proved to be guilty, Dicky would still be able to wriggle free. The present company were well equipped to understand every nuance of Dicky's carefully worded communiqué to the future. He'd said there was insufficient evidence to support any action against me. Dicky wasn't going to stick his neck out and say I wasn't guilty.

Seeing that Bret was momentarily disconcerted by his remark, Dicky followed with a quick right and left to the body. "And if Bernard didn't manage to persuade Stinnes to defect, that would prove his guilt?" Dicky asked. He used a rather high-pitched voice and a little smile. It was Dicky's idea of the droll Oxford don that he'd once hoped to be. But it fitted ill on a man in trendy faded denim and Gucci shoes. But Dicky persisted. "Is that it? It sounds like those medieval witch trials. You throw the accused into a lake and if he comes up you know he's guilty so you execute him."

"Okay, Dicky, okay," said Bret, holding up a hand and admiring his signet ring, his fraternity ring, and his manicure. "But there's still a lot more questions unanswered. Why did Bernard make Biedermann sacred?"

It was a good tactic to address the question to Dicky Cruyer, but Dicky leaped aside like a scalded cat. He knew that being cast as my counsel was just one step away from being my accessory. "Well, what about that, Bernard?" said Dicky, turning his head towards me with an expression that said he'd gone as far as any man could go to help me.

I said, "I was at school with Biedermann. I knew him all his life. He was never of any importance."

"Would you like to see a rough listing of Biedermann's business holdings?" said Bret. "Not a bad spread for a nothing."

"No, I wouldn't. I'm talking about what he did as an agent. He was of no importance."

"How can you be so sure?" said Bret.

"Biedermann's death is a red herring. He could never be anything more than a very small piece of the KGB machinery. There is nothing to suggest that Biedermann has ever had access to any worthwhile secrets." They all looked at me impassively; they all knew that I'd play down Biedermann whatever he was.

Tiptree spoke for the first time. He used his hand to smooth his well-brushed ginger hair and then fingered his thin mustache as if making sure it was still gummed on. He was like a nervous young actor just about to make his first stage appearance. He said, "Carrying secrets this time though. Eh?"

"I'll wait for the official assessment before saying anything about that," I said. "And even if it's worthwhile material, I'll bet you that it will reveal nothing about the Russians."

"Well, of course it will reveal nothing about the Russians," said Tiptree in his measured resonant voice. "This chap was a Soviet agent, what?" He looked round the table and smiled briefly.

Morgan spoke for the first time. He explained to Tiptree what I was getting at. "Samson means that we'll learn nothing about Soviet aims or intentions from the submarine construction report that was being carried by Biedermann."

"The only thing we'll learn from it," I added, "is that the KGB chose a document that will involve the maximum number of security organizations: France, Denmark, Norway, Britain, several Latin American customers, Mexico where he was Resident, and the U.S. because of his passport."

"But the material was important enough for him to be killed," said Tiptree.

"He was killed to incriminate me," I said.

"Well," said Tiptree with studied patience. "There's no avoiding the fact that you gave him the drink that poisoned him."

"But I didn't know what it was. We've been through all that. Just before we came in here Bret told me that the Sûreté have even found someone who identified the girl who gave me the poisoned coffee."

Bret fidgeted in his chair. He liked to swing round in his swivel chair in his office. This wasn't a swivel chair, but he kept throwing his weight from one side to the other as if hoping that it might become one. He corrected me. "I said the Sûreté found someone in the building who remembered seeing the girl you described. Hardly the same thing, Bernard. Hardly the same thing."

"You say that Biedermann was of no account," said Tiptree, still exhibiting that mannered patience with which great minds untangle ignorance. "I wish you could give us just one reason for believing that."

"Biedermann was so unimportant that the KGB killed him just to implicate me. Doesn't that prove something?"

Bret said, "It proves nothing, as well you know. For all we can figure, Biedermann was in this up to the neck and you were working with him. That sounds a more likely motive for his murder. That explanation shows why you made him sacred without putting his name on our copy of the filing sheets."

"I wanted a favor from him. I was preparing the way for it."

"What favor?"

"I wanted him to help me persuade Stinnes."

Bret said, "What help were you going to get from the unimportant little jerk you described?"

"Stinnes was in contact with Biedermann. I thought Stinnes would choose to work through him instead of Werner Volkmann."

"Why?"

"It's what I would have done."

"So why didn't Stinnes do it through Biedermann?"

"I think he planned to do it that way, but then the KGB began to get worried about what was happening and stopped him."

"Play that back at half speed," said Bret.

"I think Moscow encouraged Stinnes to tease us a little at first. But then Stinnes realized he had the perfect cover for coming over to us. And Moscow never trusts anyone, so I think they're monitoring Stinnes and his contacts with us. He has an assistant—Pavel Moskvin—who might be someone assigned by Moscow Centre to spy on him. It could well be that they have other people spying on him. We all know that Moscow likes to have spies who spy on spies who spy on spies. I think someone higher up told Stinnes not to use Biedermann as the go-between. They had other plans for Biedermann. He was to be murdered."

Bret fixed me with his eyes. We both knew that by "someone higher up" I meant Fiona. I half expected him to say so. Once I'd suspected him of being Fiona's lover. Even now I'd not entirely dismissed the idea. I wondered if he knew that. He said, "So you thought Biedermann would be valuable to us. That's why you made him sacred?"

"Yes," I said.

"Wouldn't it be simpler, and more logical, to think you covered for Biedermann because he was a buddy?"

"Are we looking for simplicity and logic?" I said. "This is the KGB we're talking about. Let's just stick to what is likely."

"Then how likely is this?" said Bret. "Biedermann is your KGB contact. You make him sacred to keep everyone else off his back. That way you'll be the first to hear if he attracts the attention of any NATO intelligence agency. And your excuse for contacting him, any time you want, night or day, is that you are continuing the investigation into his activities."

"I didn't like Biedermann. I've never liked him. Anyone will tell you that." It was a feeble response to Bret's convincing pattern and he ignored it.

"That sort of cover—investigation—has been used before."

"Biedermann was killed in order to frame me for his murder. And because, alive, his evidence would support everything I've told you. There's no other reason for what was otherwise a completely gratuitous killing."

"Oh, sure," said Bret. "All to get you into deep trouble."

I didn't answer. The KGB's operational staff had done their work well. Given all the facts against some other employee of the Department, I too would have been as suspicious as Bret was.

Dicky stopped biting his nail. "Shall I tell you what I think," said Dicky. His voice was high and nervous, but it wasn't a question; Dicky was determined to share his theory. "I think Stinnes never gave a damn about Biedermann. That night in Mexico, when he first made contact with the Volkmanns, he apparently went across to the table because he mistook Zena Volkmann for the Biedermann girl. I say Stinnes was after Zena Volkmann. Hell, she's a stunner, you know, and Stinnes has a reputation as a woman chaser. I think we're making too much of Biedermann's role in all this."

"Well, think about this one," I said. "Suppose Stinnes was sent to Mexico City only because Zena and Werner were already there. He told them that he'd been there a few weeks, but we have no proof of that. We've been congratulating ourselves on the way that we put out an alert and then the Volkmanns spotted him. But suppose it's the other way round. Suppose Stinnes knew exactly who the Volkmanns were that night when he went over to their table in the Kronprinz Club? Suppose the whole scenario had been planned that way by the KGB operational staff?"

I looked around. "Go on," said Bret. "We're all listening."

I said, "How could he mistake Zena Volkmann for Poppy Beidermann? No one could mistake one for the other; there's no resemblance. He pretended to mistake Zena for the Biedermann girl in order to bring Biedermann into the conversation, knowing that we'd find out Paul Biedermann was in Mexico and that we'd make contact with him. Suppose they were thinking of involving Biedermann right back when we started?"

"With what motive?" said Dicky and then regretted saying it. Dicky liked to nod things through as if he knew everything. He touched his bloodless lips as if making sure his mouth was shut.

"Well, he's not done too badly, has he?" I said. "He's got everyone here jumping up and down with excitement. You're accusing me of being a KGB agent and of murdering Biedermann on KGB instructions. Not bad. We'd be very proud to have the KGB floundering about like this trying to find out who's on which side."

Bret frowned; my accusation of floundering had found a target. Frank Harrington leaned forward and said, "So how far will they go? Send Stinnes here to give us a lot of misinformation?"

"I doubt if he could sustain a prolonged interrogation."

"Then why the hell would they bother?" said Bret.

"To get me to run, Bret," I said.

"Run to Moscow?"

"It fits. They send Stinnes to Mexico so that Volkmann will spot him because they guess that I'll be the chosen contact. And then they plan Biedermann's murder so that they can incriminate me. They might even have guessed I'd make Biedermann NATO sacred—it's been done before, we all know that—and now they want to pin his murder on me." There were all sorts of other things—from the black girl's clumsy approach to MacKenzie's murder—that supported my theory, but I had no intention of revealing those. "The whole thing adds up to a way of making me run."

"That's what physicians call a wastepaper basket diagnosis," said Bret. "You throw all the symptoms into the pot and then invent a disease."

"Then tell me what's wrong with it," I said.

"I'd want to see you completely cleared of suspicion before I started racking my brains about why they might be framing you," said Bret. "And we've still got a long way to go on that one."

Frank Harrington looked round the table and said, "It

would be worth a lot to them to have Bernard there asking for political asylum. I think we have to take into account the way that Bernard has stayed here and faced the music." Until that moment I'd wondered if Frank's offer to let me run off to Checkpoint Charlie had been in response to some directive from London. But now I decided that Frank had done it on his own. I was more than ever grateful to him. And if Frank seemed lukewarm in his contribution to this meeting, that might be because he could offer more support to me behind the scenes if he showed no partisanship.

To me Bret said, "That's your considered opinion is it—that all this evidence against you is part of a Moscow plan to have you running over there?" He paused, but no one said anything. Sarcastically Bret added, "Or could it just be your paranoia?"

"I'm not paranoid, Bret," I said. "I'm being persecuted."

Bret exploded with indignation. "Persecuted? Let me tell you . . ."

Frank put a hand on Bret's arm to calm him. "It's a joke, Bret," he said. "It's an old joke."

"Oh, I see. Yes," said Bret. He was embarrassed at losing self-control if only for a moment. "Well, it's hard to imagine KGB operations cooking that one up."

I said, "I could tell you some even stupider ideas that we've followed through on."

Bret didn't invite me to tell him any of the stupid ideas. He said, "But what you describe would be a change of style, wouldn't it? The sort of thing someone new might dream up, to show what a genius they were." Everyone round the table knew what he meant, but when he remembered there were no notes or recordings he said it anyway. "Someone like your wife?"

"Yes, Fiona. She could have had a hand in something like that."

"She makes you run. She gets you and gets your kids. Ummm," said Bret. He had a gold ball-point pen in his fist, and he clicked the top two or three times to show us he was thinking. "Would Fiona think you could be stampeded that way? She knows you well. Why would she guess wrong? Is she wrong?"

"Hold it, Bret," I said. "Just four beats to the bar."

Bret said, "Because we still have another unreported incident." He looked at Tiptree.

Tiptree continued right on cue. Maybe it hadn't been rehearsed, but this interview had obviously been discussed in detail. Tiptree looked at me and said, "A black woman asked for a lift in your car and you took her to London Airport. There you both had a brief exchange of words with a second woman."

I looked at Tiptree and then at Bret. I was shaken. They'd caught me off guard with that one. And bringing it up so late was a part of the effect it had. "That was nothing to do with the Department."

"Well, I say it *was* to do with the Department," said Bret.

"We're all allowed a private life, Bret," I reminded him. "Or are we starting a new game? We all come in on Monday mornings and discuss each others' private lives as revealed by the surveillance teams. Do you want to start right away?" Bret, who wasn't above taking some of the more shapely secretaries to his riverside mansion for a cozy weekend, was not keen to get into an exchange of confidences.

To take the pressure off Bret, Henry Tiptree said, "By that time we were checking your journeys between home and the office. You were under suspicion from the time you returned, Bernard. Surely you must have guessed that."

"No, I didn't. At least, I didn't think you were sending Internal Security teams to follow me home."

"So who was she?" said Tiptree.

"It was a neighbor. She has a friend who works at the airport and I was going to employ her to look after the children. She's a qualified nurse who wanted to earn some extra money on her days off. But the way things are now, I have to have someone full time."

It was a hasty improvisation and I was by no means sure that Tiptree believed me. Tiptree looked at me for a long time and

I stared back at him in mutual antipathy. "Well, we'll leave that for the time being," he said as if making a concession to me. I wondered if he too had been trying to trace the black girl with rather less luck than poor old MacKenzie. "Let's move on to MacKenzie," said Tiptree as if reading my thoughts. "Tell me what he was doing for you at the time of his death."

Was it a trick? "I don't know the time of his death," I said. "I just know what the doctor estimated it might have been."

Tiptree smiled grimly. "If you don't know the time of his death," he said, carefully inserting that proviso as if not believing it, "tell me about MacKenzie. You gave him quite a few errands. From what I hear of you, it's not like you to use a probationer. You're the one who's always complaining about the lack of experience around here. You're the one who won't tolerate amateurism. Why MacKenzie, then?"

I kept as near to the truth as possible. "He wanted to be a field agent," I told them. "He really wanted that." They nodded. We'd all seen lots of probationers who wanted to be field agents even though the various selection boards tried to screen out anyone with that perverted ambition. Soon even the most headstrong such probationer came to realize that his chances of being sent off to operate as a field agent were very slim. Field agents were seldom chosen from recruited staff. Field agents didn't get sent anywhere. Field agents were there already.

"You used him a lot," said Tiptree.

I said, "He would always find time to help. He'd type reports when all the bloody typing pool had refused to work overtime. He'd stand in the rain all night and never ask questions about the premises he'd watched. He'd go into municipal offices and spend hours rummaging through boxes of old birth certificates or ratings slips or voters' lists. And because he was a particularly rude and badly dressed probationer, and spoke ungrammatical English with a regional accent, he had no trouble convincing anyone that he was a reporter on one of our great national newspapers. That's why I used him."

Morgan, a man with a Welsh accent who had briefly tried his hand at being a reporter for one of our great national newspapers, allowed a ghost of a smile to haunt his face.

"That hardly explains what he was doing in a departmental safe house in Bosham," said Tiptree.

"Oh, we all know what he was doing there," I said. "He was lying there dead. He was lying there dead for seven days before anyone from that highly paid housekeeping department of ours bothered to check the premises."

"Yes, those bastards," said Bret. "Well, I shafted those lazy sons of bitches. We won't have that trouble anymore."

"That will be very comforting for me next time I walk into a safe house and sit down in a chair so that some KGB hood can put a .44 Magnum into my cranium."

"How do you know what kind of pistol it was," said Henry Tiptree as casually as he was able.

"I *don't* know what kind of pistol it was, Mr. Tiptree," I said. "I just know what kind of bullet it was: a hollow point one that mushrooms even when the muzzle velocity is high, so it blows people apart even when it's not well aimed. And before you ask me the supplementary question that I can see forming on your lips right now, I got that out of the ballistics sheet that was part of the file on MacKenzie's death. Maybe that's something you should read since you are so keen to find the culprit."

"No one is blaming you for MacKenzie's death," said Frank gently.

"Just for Biedermann's," I said. "Well, that's nice to know."

"You don't have to stand up and sing 'Rule Britannia,' " said Bret. "There's been no suggestion of opening an orange file on you. We're simply trying to get at the truth. You should be more keen than anyone that we do that."

"Then try this one on for size," I said. "Suppose everything is the way I say it is—and so far you've produced nothing to prove I'm wrong—and suppose my slow way of enrolling Stinnes is the best way. Then perhaps there are people in the Department who'd like to see my attempt to enroll Stinnes fail." I paused to let the words sink in. "Suppose those people hope that by hurrying me along and interfering with what I do, they'll keep Stinnes where he is on the other side."

"Let me hear that again," said Bret. His voice was hard and unyielding.

"You heard what I said, Bret. If Stinnes goes into London Debriefing Centre in the way I want him to go there—relaxed and cooperative—he'll sing. I'm telling you that there might be people, not a thousand miles from here, who are not musically inclined."

"It's worth thinking about, Bret," said Frank. I had voiced what Frank had already said to me in Berlin. He looked at me and gave an almost imperceptible wink.

"You're not including me?" Bret said.

"I don't know, Bret. Talk it over with your analyst. I only deal in facts."

"No one is trying to muzzle you, wise guy," said Bret. He was talking directly to me now, as if there was no one else in the room.

"You could have fooled me, Bret. The way I was hearing it, I'd handled the Stinnes enrollment with fumbling incompetence. People are throwing money at him, without even keeping me informed. I'd begun to think that perhaps I was not doing this exactly the way you wanted it done."

"Don't talk to me like that," said Bret.

"You listen to me, Bret old buddy," I said. "I'll talk to you any way I choose to talk. Because I'm the file officer on the Stinnes investigation. And, just in case you've forgotten, we have an old-fashioned system in this department: once an agent is assigned to a file he has full powers of decision. And he continues with his task until he closes the file or hands it over. Either way he does it of his own volition. Now you put me here in the hot seat and rig this kangaroo court to intimidate me, but I've been over there where intimidation is done by experts. So you don't frighten me, Bret. You don't frighten me at all. And if this pantomime was staged to make me abandon the Stinnes file, it's been a waste of time. I'll get Stinnes. And he'll come back here and talk like a rescued castaway."

They were embarrassed at my outburst. The lower ranks must not complain. That was something any decent school taught a chap in his first term. Frank coughed, Morgan tipped his head back to look at the ceiling, Tiptree stroked his hair, and Dicky had all his fingers arrayed along the edge of the table, selecting one to make a meal from.

"But if anyone present thinks the Stinnes file should be taken away from me, now is the time to stand up and say so." I waited. Bret looked at me and smiled derisively. No one spoke.

I stood up and said, "Then I'll take it as unanimously agreed that I remain file officer. And now I'm leaving you gentlemen to write up the minutes of this meeting any way you like, but don't ask me to sign them. If you want me during the next few minutes I'll be with the D-G. I'm exercising my rights under another old-fashioned rule of this department—the right to report directly to the Director-General on matters of vital concern to the service."

Bret started to get to his feet. I said, "Don't see me out, Bret. And don't try to head me off from seeing the old man. I made the appointment this morning and he's waiting for me right now."

I'd got as far as the door before Bret recovered himself enough to think of a rejoinder. "You'd better get Stinnes," he said. "You screw up on Stinnes and I'll have you working as a file clerk in Registry."

"Why not?" I said. "I've always wanted to read through the senior staff's personal files."

I TOOK a deep breath when I got out in the corridor. I'd escaped from the belly of the whale, but there was still a rough sea.

The meeting with the D-G was the sort of civilized formality that any meeting with him always was. I wasn't of course reporting anything of vital concern to the service. I was just imposing on the D-G's goodwill in order to say hello to him. I always tried to have an important appointment to escape to when I suspected that a meeting would go on too long.

His room was dim and smelled of leather chairs and dusty books that were piled upon them. The D-G sat by the window behind a small desk crowded with family photos, files, trays of paperwork, and long forgotten cups of tea. It was like entering some old Egyptian tomb to chat with an affable mummy.

"Of course I remember you," said the D-G. "Your father, Silas Gaunt, was Controller Europe when I first came here."

"No, Silas Gaunt is a distant relative, but only by marriage," I said. "My father was Colonel Samson; Berlin Resident when Silas was Controller Europe."

The D-G nodded vaguely. "Controller Europe, the Iberian desk . . . such ridiculous titles. I've always thought we sound like people running the Overseas Service of the BBC." He gave a little chuckle. It was a joke he'd made many times before. "And everything is going well, is it?"

The D-G didn't look like a man who would like to hear that anything was going less than well. I had the feeling that if I implied that all was not going well, the D-G would throw himself through the window without pausing to open it. I suppose everyone had the same protective feeling when talking with the D-G. That's no doubt why the Department was something of a shambles. "Yes, sir," I said. "Everything is going very well." A brave man that Bernard Samson, and truthful to a fault.

"I like to keep in touch with what's happening," said the D-G. "That's why I sent for you."

"Yes, sir," I said.

"The wretched doctor won't let me drink at all. But it doesn't look as if you're enjoying that lemon tea. Why don't you go and pour yourself a decent drink from my cupboard. What was that you said?"

"Thank you, sir."

"I've all the time in the world," said the D-G. "I'd love to hear what's happening in Washington these days."

"I've been in Berlin, sir. I work on the German desk."

"No matter, no matter. Tell me what's happening in Berlin. What did you say your name was again?"

"Samson, sir. Bernard Samson."

He looked at me for a long time. "Samson, yes, of course. You've had this frightful problem about your wife."

"Yes, sir."

"Mr. Harrington explained your difficulties to me. Did he tell you we're hoping to get some supplementary payment for you?"

"Yes, sir. That would be most helpful."

"Don't worry about the children. They'll come to no harm, I guarantee it." The D-G smiled. "Promise now. You'll stop worrying about the children."

"Yes, sir. I promise."

"Samson. Yes, of course. I've always had a knack for remembering names," he said.

After leaving the D-G's office I went into the toilet and found myself sharing a hot-air dryer with Frank Harrington.

"Feeling better now, Bernard?" he said humorously.

"Better than I was before? Or better than the people at that meeting of Bret's?"

"Oh, you left us in no doubt about that, my dear fellow. You made your superiority more than clear to everyone present. What did you do to the D-G, ask him for his resignation?" He saw me look round and added, "It's quite all right, there's no one else here."

"I said what needed saying," I said defensively.

"And you said it very well. Bret went home to change his underpants."

"That will be the day," I said.

"You underestimate the effect of your passionate outbursts, Bernard. Bret has only himself to blame. Your little dig about a kangaroo court went home. Bret was distressed; he even told us he was distressed. He spent ten minutes singing your praises to convince us all that it wasn't anything of the kind. But Bernard, you're inclined to the overkill."

"Is that a warning, Frank?"

"Advice, Bernard. Advice."

"To guard my tongue?"

"Not at all. I always enjoy your tantrums except when I'm on the receiving end of them. I enjoyed seeing you scare them half to death in there."

"Scared them?"

"Of course. They know how easily you can make a fool of them. Bret still hasn't forgotten that joke you made about his visit to Berlin last year."

"I've forgotten what I said."

"Well, he hasn't forgotten. You said he went up the steps at Checkpoint Charlie and looked over the Wall. He didn't like that, Bernard."

"But that's what he did do. He lined up behind a busload of tourists and went up the steps to look over the goddamned Wall."

"Of course he did. That's why he didn't join in the laughter. If Dicky had said it, or anyone else in the office without field experience, it wouldn't have mattered. But coming from you it caused Bret a loss of dignity; and dignity means a lot to Bret." All the time Frank was smiling to show me what a good joke it all was.

"But?"

"But one at a time, Bernard, old friend. Don't antagonize a whole roomful of people all at once. It's a dangerous sport, old lad. They get together when they have something in common. Just one at a time in future. Right?"

"Right, Frank."

"Your father would have enjoyed that shindig you put on for us. He wouldn't have approved of course, not your father's style, we both know that. But he would have enjoyed it, Bernard."

Why did that last remark of Frank's please me so much? Do we never shed the tyranny of our father's love?

Chapter 22

By the time I had finished my day at the office I was not in the right mood to face an aggrieved husband, even a mistakenly aggrieved one. But I'd suggested to George that we have a drink together and it was better to get it over soon. He wanted to meet at the new apartment he'd bought in Mayfair, so I went there directly from the office.

It was a huge place on two floors of a house in Mount Street towards the Hyde Park end. Although I knew that it was still unoccupied, I was unprepared for the bare floorboards and the smell of the newly plastered walls.

George was there already. He was only thirty-six years old, but he seemed to do everything he could to make himself appear at least ten years older than that. Born in Poplar, where the River Thames made a mighty loop that was the heart of London's dockland, he'd left school at fifteen to help support his crippled father. By the time he was twenty-one he was driving a Rolls Royce, albeit an old one he was trying to sell.

George's small stature contributed to the impression of restless energy as he moved from room to room in short paces, stooping, tapping, measuring, and checking everything in sight. He had heavy spectacles that constantly slipped down his nose, wavy hair that was silver gray at the temples, and a large mustache. From his appearance it was easy to believe that his parents were Polish immigrants, but the flattened vowels of his east London accent, and his frequently dropped aitches, always came as a surprise. Sometimes I wondered if he cultivated this cockney voice as some sort of asset for his car deals.

"Well, there you are, Bernard," he said. "Good to see you.

Very nice." He greeted me more like a prospect than like some-one he suspected of dalliance with his wife.

"It's quite a place you have here, George," I said.

"We'll go for a drink in a moment. I must get the measuring done before the daylight goes. There's no juice here yet, see." He clicked the electricity switch to prove it.

He was dressed in a flashy dark blue suit with a pattern of chalk stripes that made him look even shorter than he really was. It was all obviously expensive—the silk shirt and floral Cardin tie, and the black brogue shoes—for George liked ev-eryone to see immediately that he was the poor boy who'd made good. "I want to talk to you about Tessa," I said.

"Uh-huh." George could make that sound mean anything; "yes," "no," or "maybe." He was measuring the length of the room. "Hold that," he said, giving me the end of the tape measure to hold against one side of the fireplace. "Pale gold carpet in here," he said. "What do you think?"

"Very elegant," I said. I crouched to help him measure the hearth. "I'm grateful that you've let her help take care of the children while I was away," I said, in what I thought was a diplomatic approach.

"She didn't ask me," said George. "She never asks me any-thing. She just does what she wants." He wound up the tape suddenly so that it slipped from my fingers.

I stood up. "The nanny doesn't like being alone at night," I explained.

George stood up suddenly and stared into my eyes with a pained expression on his face. "Five foot six inches," he said. He rolled up the last few inches of tape, using the little handle, and then tucked it under his arm while he wrote the measure-ment on his hand in bright blue ball-point pen. "Do you mind?" he said. He gave me the end of the tape and was already backing across the room to measure the width of it.

"I thought I should have a word with you," I said.

"What about?"

"About Tessa." I reached down to hold the end of the tape

against the wall. He pulled it taut and peered closely at the tape in the fast-disappearing daylight.

"What about Tessa?" said George, writing on his hand again.

"She's been sleeping round at my place. I thought I should say thank you."

He looked at me and gave a wry smile.

"I like Tessa," I said. "But I wouldn't like you to get the wrong idea."

"What idea would be the wrong one?"

"About me and Tessa," I said.

"Your intentions are strictly honorable, are they?" said George, pronouncing the aitch as if determined to get it wrong. He walked to the other end of the room and tested a floorboard with his heel. It creaked as he put his weight on it. He pulled a face and then went to the window and looked down into the street. "I just like to make sure the car is all right," he explained.

"I don't have any intentions," I said. I was getting irritated with him, and I allowed it into my voice.

"Just talk, is it?" His voice was only a shade louder but from the other end of the room it seemed to pick up some echo and was resonant in the large empty room. "You and Tessa: you just chat together. Companionship, is it?"

"Of course we talk," I said.

"Talk about me, I suppose. You give her advice about me, I imagine. How to make our marriage work. That sort of thing."

"Sometimes," I admitted.

"Well, that's worse," he said without raising his voice. "How would you like it if it was your wife talking to other men about how to handle you? How would you like it, eh?"

"I don't know," I admitted. Put like that it made me feel bad.

"I'd rather you jumped into bed with her. A quick impersonal frolic like that can be overlooked." He came nearer and stroked the marble fireplace. "I put that fireplace in," he said.

"Marble. It came out of a beautiful old house in Bristol." Carefully he tested the newly plastered patch on the wall where the antique fireplace had been installed. And then he stepped close to say, "But she has the gall to tell me how much she likes talking with you. It's a bloody cheek, Bernard."

It was almost as if he was having two conversations with two different people. He turned to stroke the newly prepared wall. In a quieter voice he said, "Pale gray stripes this wallpaper will be, Regency pattern. It will go well with our furniture. Remember that lovely Georgian commode—the serpentine-fronted piece? It's hidden in the hall now, you can't get a proper look at it. Well, that's going in a place of honor, on that far wall. And over it there'll be an oval mirror—Georgian rococo, a great wreath of gilded leaves—a beautiful piece that I bought at Sotheby's last week. Original mirror, the frame has been restored; but really well done. I paid a damned sight too much for it, but I was bidding against a dealer. I never mind taking anything one bid beyond a dealer. After all, he's going to mark it up fifty percent, isn't he."

"I suppose so," I said.

"Of course he is."

"I'd like to be good friends with you, George," I said. "Good friends with you both."

"Why?" said George.

"Why?" I repeated.

"We're not exactly blood relations, are we? We only met because we married two birds who are sisters. You don't care about me, and I don't care about you. Why should you want to be friends with me?"

"Okay," I said angrily. "So let's not be friends. But I'm not screwing your wife and I've got no plans to try. And if you're too bloody dumb to appreciate what I'm trying to say, you can go to hell."

"Dark blue tiles in the dining room," said George, opening a sliding door and stepping through it. "Imported from Italy. Some people say tiles make a room too noisy. But in a dining room I like a bit of a rumpus. We'll keep the same dining table. It's an old piece of Victorian junk, but it was the first piece of furniture my parents ever owned. My dad bought it when they got married." He pushed his glasses up with his forefinger. "Course getting rid of the house in Hampstead won't be any picnic. The property game is tough right now. I'll lose money on it."

"I'm sure you explained that to the people you bought this place from," I said.

He gave a quick appreciative grin. "Ah, you're right. Property is always a good investment, Bernard. And when the market is depressed a sensible man should buy the most valuable things he can afford. I'll drop anything up to twenty-five grand on the Hampstead place, but I reckon I'm getting this at about eighty grand less than it would go for in normal times. And I'll do it through my own company's pension fund and save a lot on tax."

"Tessa thinks you don't love her anymore."

"She's led me a dance, Bernard. No need to tell you that. She's been a rotten wife."

It was true. What could I say to him. "Perhaps things could be different. She feels neglected, George. Perhaps you give too much time to your work."

"My business is all I've got," he said. He raised the tape and measured the dining room window for no reason except to have something to do with his hands. "She's a cruel woman. You don't know how cruel." He stepped through the doorway into the kitchen and his voice echoed in the smaller space. "I'm putting self-cleaning American ovens in here. The bloody fool who's supplying them was practically telling me the German ovens were better."

"And are the German ovens better?"

"I don't care what they're like; don't expect me to buy anything German. My dad would turn in his grave. Bad enough selling bloody Jap cars. Anyway, that idiot didn't know an oven from a vacuum cleaner. You don't think I go into a shop and ask the opinion of the people selling the goods, do you?"

"Don't you?"

"It would be like expecting someone to come into one of my showrooms asking me what's the best sort of car. The best sort of car is the one that pays me the biggest markup. No, the Americans are the only people who can design self-cleaning ovens." He sniffed. "She's suddenly decided that she can't drink anything but champagne. It's costing me a fortune, but I don't stop her—she's only doing it to make me angry. She thinks it's very funny."

"Oh, I don't know about that. She drinks champagne at my house too."

"She drinks it at a lot of houses, but it's always my champagne she drinks."

"Perhaps you're right," I said.

"She needn't have made such a show of it," he said sadly. "She could have been discreet. She didn't have to make me a laughingstock, did she?" He opened the door of the high level oven and looked inside. "She's a good cook, Tessa. She likes to pretend she's a bad cook, but she can make use of a decent kitchen."

"Perhaps she didn't realize . . ."

He closed the oven door and then studied the complicated array of dials and the clock that controlled the cooking. "She realized. Women realize everything, everything to do with love affairs and those antics. Women realize that, all right. She realized that she was hurting me. Don't make any mistake about that, Bernard." He said it without any rancor, as if discussing some particular feature of the oven.

"I didn't know you felt so bitter," I said.

"I'm not bitter. Look at this apartment. Does it look as if I'm bitter?"

"Tessa is worried that you went to Italy with someone else," I said tentatively.

"I know she is. Let her worry."

"If it's serious, George, you should tell her. It would be better for both of you."

He sighed. "My brother Stefan and his wife were on holiday in Rome. We spent a couple of days in the same hotel. Got it?"

"So when Tessa asked for Mrs. Kosinski the hotel thought she meant your sister-in-law? Why don't you tell Tessa that?"

"She never asked me," said George. "She lectures me and argues. She nevers asks me anything."

"Women are like that," I said. "You're not thinking of a divorce then?"

"No, Bernard, I'm not thinking of a divorce." He stepped into another small room that had obviously been used as a laundry room. Even the plumbing for the washing machine was still in the wall. The room was painted white with a gray tiled floor and a central drain. "This would make a nice little darkroom, wouldn't it?"

"I suppose so," I said.

"But Tessa says she'd like a little room for sewing. Sounds a funny idea to me, having a room just for sewing, but that's what she wants, so I said okay. There's a bathroom that I can make into a darkroom. In a way it's a shame to use a room with a good window for photography when I can easily make do with one of the inside rooms." He moved into the next room and tried the switch, even though he knew that there was no electricity. "The feelings I had for her have died, of course. There's no love that can survive the battering that a constantly unfaithful wife gives." The daylight was disappearing and his face was rimmed with a reddish gold line. He looked out of the window to get another glimpse of his parked car.

I said, "It sounds like a grim prospect, George, living with someone you don't love."

"Does it? It would to you, of course. But I'm a Catholic." Of course, how could I have forgotten? I felt a fool for having mentioned divorce and George must have known that for he quickly added, "No crucifix in the living room, no gold cross dangling round my neck, but I'm a Catholic and my faith is important to me. I'm up before six in the morning, so I can be at seven o'clock mass and not be late for work. My dad and mum were the same. Until Dad fell into the hold of a ship and smashed his legs and spent the rest of his days in the wheel-chair. After that she took him to a later mass. Back in Poland both my mother's brothers are priests. I wasn't brainy enough for the priesthood, but my faith is strong." He smiled. I suppose by now he knew how surprising such announcements could be to people who thought of him as a cockney capitalist who would bow only before Mammon. "It will be easier for me here. I'll go to mass at Farm Street. I am jesuitical . . ." He smiled. "Always have been. And it's only a few steps along the road. It's a wonderful little church and I'll get an extra few minutes in bed every morning." He smiled artfully but I couldn't imagine anyone for whom an extra few minutes in bed would make so little difference.

"She's insecure," I said. "Tessa is insecure."

"Is that what she told you?"

"She's very vulnerable, George. She needs reassurance. You surely realize that all that flamboyance conceals a terrible lack of self-confidence. Fiona always said it was the second-child syndrome. And now I see it happening with my own children too. Tessa grew up in the shadow of a brilliant, strong-willed sister."

"You missed out the domineering father," said George. He took his hat from the ladder where he'd left it and said, "You've thought about it a lot, I can see. Perhaps we married the wrong sisters. Perhaps you could have stopped Tessa going off the rails in a way that I failed to do." It was difficult to know if he was being sarcastic or serious.

"And you could have stopped Fiona going off the rails in a way that I failed to do. Is that what you mean?"

"Who knows," said George.

"I'm beginning to think Fiona hates me," I said. I don't know why I suddenly confided to him something I'd admitted to no one else, except that George had the dispassionate manner of the highly paid medical specialist. And of, I suppose, the confessor.

"You're a reproach to her," he said unhesitatingly. Perhaps

he'd thought it over before. "You make her feel small. You make her feel cheap."

"You think that's how she sees it?"

"Betraying your country is like betraying your partner. And when a marriage breaks up, it can't count as a success for either party; it's a mutual failure. How can Fiona bear to think of you continuing—business as normal with the job, the kids, and the home? It makes her look silly, Bernard. It makes her look like a spoiled little girl playing at politics, no better than any of these loud-mouthed film actresses who like to pretend they're political activists. Of course Fiona hates you." He had been toying with his hat but now he put it on his head, a signal that he wanted to change the subject. "Now if you'd still like a drink, let's go round to the Connaught. I prefer hotels and a comfortable place to sit down. I'm not very keen on pubs for pleasure, I see too much of them when I'm doing business. A sandwich too, if you like. I've nothing to go home for."

"It was my invitation," I reminded him. "Let me buy you dinner, George."

"That's very decent of you, Bernard. I see you're still running that old Ford. I wish you'd let me fix you up with something better."

"As a prospect, George, I'm a pushover."

"Good. Good. There's nothing I enjoy more than selling a man a car," said George, and he seemed quite serious. He was relaxed now; a changed person now that our difficult conversation was over. Perhaps he'd been dreading it as much as I had. "And I've got a set of wheels that would be right up your street, Bernard. A couple of villains bought a car from me and got her ready for a big payroll holdup. The brakes and steering are superb and she gave me a hundred and sixty up the Motorway without a murmur of complaint. She'd come cheap, Bernard. Interested?"

"Why cheap, George?"

"The bodywork's in poor condition and it's not worth my while to do anything about that. When people come to buy cars they don't want to know about brakes and steering, and not one in ten wants to look at the engine, Bernard. I buy and sell bodywork. I tell all my workpeople that."

"I'm interested."

"Of course you are. A battered-looking car that will kick sand into the face of a Mercedes 450 is just your style. Come and have a look at it sometime. I'll keep it for you."

"Thanks, George."

"I've had a funny sort of day today," he volunteered. "The police phoned up this morning and said they'd recovered a solid silver wine cooler we'd had stolen. Not so very old, but it's a lovely piece, very ornate. I thought I'd never see it again. A youngster who used to work for me as a mechanic had tried to sell it to an antique dealer at the Portobello Road market. The dealer guessed it was stolen and told the police."

Tessa's "ice bucket" was George's "wine cooler," I noticed. It was the same with so many things. They seemed to have so little in common it was a wonder they'd ever got married. "You were lucky to get it back," I said.

He took a last proud look at his new apartment before double locking the front door and then turning the mortice lock as well. "The kid thought it was silver-plated britannia metal; he didn't recognize it as solid silver. Stupid, eh? That would make anyone suspicious. He was a good little worker too, only nineteen years old, but I was paying him a very good salary. Strange thing to do; to steal something from a man's home, isn't it?"

"Yes, it is."

But the "jesuitical" George debated against himself. "On the other hand, I exposed him to temptation, didn't I? I invited him to a house with such valuable things on show. I have to bear some measure of guilt. I told the police constable that."

"What did he say?"

"He said he couldn't get into a discussion about ethics and morality, he had quite enough trouble trying to understand the law." George laughed. "Criminal activity is one percent motivation and ninety-nine percent opportunity. You must have heard me say that, Bernard."

"It sounds familiar, George," I said.

Chapter 23

THE PROSPECT of returning to Mexico—even without Dicky —was daunting. I wanted to stay here: to see more of the children, get a bellyful of home cooking and an earful of Mozart. Instead I was headed for a round of plastic hotels, "international cuisine," and Muzak.

I got home before midnight, having spent a pleasant evening dining with George. He'd gone on about what he described as exactly the right car for me: "Shabby appearance but a lot of poke under the bonnet." Was that what George felt about me, or subconscious reflections upon his own shortcomings?

I couldn't go to bed until the duty messenger arrived with my airline tickets. Feeling sorry for myself, I wandered into the nursery and fingered Sally's *Joke Book:* "How do you catch a monkey?—Hang upside down in a tree and make a noise like a banana." And in Billy's book of children's verse I found Kipling:

Five and twenty ponies
Trotting through the dark—
Brandy for the parson,
'Baccy for the Clerk;
Laces for a lady, letters for a spy,
Watch the wall, my darling, while the Gentlemen go by.

And I'd promised to get batteries for their radio-controlled racing car and try to mend Sally's Donald Duck alarm clock. I'd missed both their birthdays this year, and now they were packed off to Tessa's cousin. I felt guilty about them, but I couldn't refuse to return to Mexico. I needed the Department's backing.

If I said good-bye to the Department, I had no qualifications that would get me a comparable pay packet elsewhere. The Department wouldn't fix a job for me. On the contrary, there would be those who'd say my resignation showed I was implicated in Fiona's activities; that had been made clear enough at the meeting. There was no choice but to be an exemplary employee of the Department, a reliable professional who produced solid results while the others produced empty rhetoric. And if, as I did my job without fear or favor and cleared myself of suspicion, some of the Department's more outstanding incompetents got trampled underfoot, that would suit me fine.

The doorbell rang. Eleven forty-five. My God, but they took their time. There had been no sound of a motorcycle and that was unusual for deliveries at this time of night. Bearing in mind Werner's ominous warnings about KGB hit teams, I opened the door very cautiously and stood well back in the shadows.

"Good evening, Mr. Samson. What's the matter?" It was Gloria Kent.

"Nothing."

"You were expecting a motorcycle messenger, were you?" She was damned quick on the uptake. "Yes, I was."

"Can I come in for a moment? I'm on my way home from seeing my boyfriend."

"You've missed your last train," I said sourly. "Yes, come in."

She was wearing a fur hat and a tan suede coat, trimmed with brown leather. Its big fur collar was buttoned up to the gold-colored scarf at her throat. The coat was cut to emphasize her hips, and the flare of its hem meant you couldn't miss the shiny leather boots. I noticed the McDouglas Paris label as I took the coat from her to hang up. It was lined with some expensive-looking fur. It wasn't a coat you could afford on the salary of a Grade 9 Executive Officer. I supposed those people in Epsom must have had very well cared for teeth.

She sat down without invitation. She had a small case with her and she kept this by her side. "I wanted to say thank you," she said.

"What for?"

"For not sending me back down to Registry. For letting me stay upstairs and help your secretary. I thought you'd be angry. I thought you'd get rid of me."

"I wouldn't want you to suffer for my error of judgment," I said.

She smiled. "Could you spare a very small glass of that delicious brandy I had last time? Martell, I think it was."

"Sure." I poured small measures into two glasses and gave her one. "Did you leave some bath oil here? Secret of Venus?"

"Oh good. Did you find it?"

"My sister-in-law did."

"Oh dear." Gloria laughed and drank half of her brandy in one go, and then all but coughed. "It's cold tonight," she said. She put the glass down and got the case onto her knees. "I wanted to tell you that I'm sorry about what happened. I felt the least I could do was to make up for the damage I did." She opened the case. It contained men's undershirts and underpants, all new and in transparent wrappings.

I wasn't going to let her make a fool of me a second time. I wondered if some of the other girls in the office were in on the joke. "It's not my size," I snapped.

She looked dismayed. "But it is. 'Marks and Spencer's; Cotton, Large.' I noticed when I was . . . when I was cutting them up. I'm terribly sorry about that, Mr. Samson. It was a childish thing to do."

"We were both childish," I said. She didn't smile but I was still uncertain about her.

"But I was the one who did the damage."

"I've replaced them. I don't need them."

"I thought about that. But Marks and Sparks are very good at changing things. They even let you have cash refunds . . ." She looked at my face as she took a large manila envelope from the case. "Your tickets for Mexico City are here, and there is three hundred pounds in traveler's checks. The tickets and checks are made out in the name of Samson, but I could change them first thing in the morning if you are on some other passport. If you want to use them, the traveler's should be signed right away; the cashier's office hates letting them go out of their hands blank like this. Your secretary wasn't sure about what name or passport you'd be using. She said you preferred to keep that sort of information to yourself."

"Thanks, Gloria. Samson will be fine."

"Will you let me put these things away for you?" she said. She got to her feet, gulped the rest of her brandy, and made for the stairs. I was going to say no, but she was already on her way.

I shrugged.

She'd been upstairs about five minutes when I heard a heavy thump that made me think she'd knocked over the bedside TV set. I hurried upstairs and went into the bedroom. It was dark, but by the light of the bedside lamp I could see Gloria's clothes and silk underwear trailed across the room. Gloria was on the far side of the bed. She was stark naked. She'd just finished righting the heavy chair she'd knocked on its side. Now she stood arms akimbo as if about to do her morning gymnastics. "What the hell . . . ?" I said.

"It was the only way I could think of getting you up here," she said. "It would have been corny to call to you."

"Cut it out, Gloria. You said you've just come from your boyfriend." She had a magnificent figure and I found it impossible not to stare at her.

"There's no boyfriend. I said that in case you had some woman here already."

"What's the joke?"

"No joke. I want a second chance on what I declined the

other day. I was thinking about it. I was silly." She climbed into bed and pulled the quilt over her up to her neck. She shivered. "Hey, this bed is freezing cold. Haven't you ever heard of electric blankets? Come and warm me up."

I hesitated.

"No security risk, Bernard. I've been vetted and cleared for all categories of documents." She smiled dreamily and shook her head so that her hair shone in the lamplight. "Come along, action man. Office talk says you're impulsive and instinctive." She must have seen something in my face, for she quickly added, "No, no one at the office knows. Your secretary thinks I gave the tickets to the duty messenger. It's not a joke, I swear it."

She was irresistible. She was so young and so earnest. I undressed. She said nothing but she watched me, smiling to share the absurdity of our folly. As I got into bed she stretched right over me to switch off the light. I wanted her; I grabbed her.

AFTERWARDS, long afterwards, I found myself staring at the bedside table that stood at what had once been my wife's side of the bed. There was a glimmer of light coming from the hall. I could see a history book that Fiona had never read beyond page thirty, a comb, and a packet of aspirins. She always combed her hair as she got out of bed in the morning—it was almost a reflex action, done before she was fully awake.

"Don't go to sleep," said Gloria.

"I've never been more awake."

"Are you thinking about your wife . . . your children?"

"The children are away."

"I know that, you fool. I know everything about you, now that I work with your secretary."

"Have you been prying?" I said with pretended severity.

"Of course I have. It's what we do, isn't it?"

"Not to each other."

"Sometimes to each other," she corrected me.

"Yes, sometimes to each other," I said.

"I wish you trusted me . . . really trusted me."

"Why?"

"Because I love you," she said.

"You don't love me. I'm old enough to be your father."

"What's that got to do with love?"

"It could never come to anything, you and me . . . it could never come to anything serious, Gloria."

"Do you hate that name Gloria?"

"No, of course not."

"Because you say it as if you hated it. My family call me Zu; its short for Zsuzsa."

"Well, Zu, I don't hate the name Gloria . . ."

She laughed and hugged me, and bent her head to bite my shoulder in mock anger. Then suddenly she was serious and, stroking the blue-striped cotton quilt, she said, "Have you been in this bed with other women? Since your wife left you, have you?"

I didn't answer.

"I didn't realize that. It was insensitive of me."

"No, it's good. I can't stay celibate for the rest of my life."

"You still love her?"

"I miss her. You live with someone, you have children and watch them grow up. You worry together, you share bad times . . . she's a part of my life."

"Will she come back, do you think?"

"It's not something we should be discussing," I said. "There was an official reminder circulated in the office about her. My wife's disappearance is now covered by the Official Secrets Act."

"I don't care about the office, Bernard. I care about you . . ." A long pause. "And about me."

"She won't come back. They never come back."

"You're angry," she said. "You're not sad, you're angry. It's not the political betrayal, it's the personal betrayal that is making you so bitter."

"Nonsense," I said.

There was just a glimmer of light coming through the half-open bedroom door. She propped herself up on her elbow to see my face better. The bed covering slid from her shoulders and the light traced the lines of her nakedness. "It's not nonsense. Your wife didn't defect because she read *Das Kapital.* She must have worked on a one-to-one basis with a Soviet case officer. For years she did that. It was an assignation: a romance, a seduction. No matter how chaste the physical relationship between them, your wife was seduced."

"It's a romantic idea, Zu, but that's not exactly the way these things work."

"Women have personal relationships. They don't give loyalty to abstractions the way that men do."

"You're letting your imagination run away with you because this particular Soviet agent is a woman. Most spies are men."

"Most spies are homosexuals," she said. And that stopped me short. So many of the ones placed in Western society were homosexuals—latent or active—and it is true that the KGB depended upon regular and frequent personal contact. Our people in the East could not move so easily, and personal contact was confined to emergencies.

"Homosexuals are the most socially mobile element in Western society," I said glibly.

"Promiscuous, you mean. Cabinet minister one night, laboratory technician the next. Is that what you mean?"

"That's what I mean."

"I hope you don't think I'm promiscuous," she said, moving from the general to the personal in that way that women so often do.

"Aren't you?" I said.

"Don't be beastly, darling." She put her hand out and touched my face. "What are you thinking about?"

I remembered what Stinnes had told the clumsy Pavel Moskvin in the empty Biedermann beach house in Mexico—You scream like a rapist when we are in the middle of a seduction, he'd said. On more than one occasion I'd spoken in the same terms. I'd warned Dicky that Stinnes was not being recruited, he was being enrolled. Recruiting is a seduction, I'd told him, but enrollment is a divorce. You recruit an agent by glamorizing that innocent's future. But an enemy agent like Stinnes is not susceptible to romance. You bring him over by promises of house, motorcar, and payments of alimony. "Nothing," I answered.

"You can be so distant," she said suddenly. "You make me feel as if I was no longer here. No longer necessary."

"I'm sorry," I said. I reached out and pulled her close to me. Her body was cold as she snuggled against me, and I pulled the bedclothes up almost over our faces. She kissed me. "You're here; you're necessary," I said.

"I do love you, Bernard. I know you think I'm immature, but I love you desperately."

"I think you're very mature," I said, caressing her.

"Oh, yes," she said dreamily. And then, as the thought came to her, "You won't hide me from your children, will you?"

"No, I won't."

"Promise?"

"Of course."

"I'm good with children."

"You're good with grown-ups too," I said.

"Oh, yes," she said. She snuggled down in the bed and cuddled me. I stayed awake as long as I could. I was frightened of going to sleep in case I had another nightmare about Mac-Kenzie and woke up screaming and bathed in sweat the way I had two or three times before. But eventually I dozed off. I didn't dream at all. Gloria was good for me.

Chapter 24

IT WAS like stepping into a sauna bath to get off the plane into the heat of Mexico City. I arrived on a particularly bad day, when the humidity and temperature had reached a record-breaking high. Like a city under bombardment, the steamy streets echoed with constant rolls of distant thunder that never got louder. And black-headed cumulonimbus clouds, poised over the mountains, did not bring the threatened rainstorms. Such weather plays upon the nerves of even the most acclimatized inhabitants, and the police statistics show a pattern of otherwise unaccountable violence that peaks at this time of year.

"I'll have to talk with Stinnes," I told Werner. "I've got to see him face to face." We were in the apartment that belonged to Zena's uncle. The list of breakages hanging by the phone had grown much longer. Perhaps that was another sign of the way the oppressive weather made everyone so jumpy. I was reluctant to move away from the air conditioner, but the air coming through it was warm, and the noise of the motor was so loud that it was difficult to hear what Werner was saying in reply. I cupped my ear.

"He'll be ready to go on Friday," said Werner, raising his voice as he said it a second time. "Just as London requested. Friday; no sooner and no later." Even Werner, who seemed to enjoy the hot weather, had finally succumbed to the high humidity. He was shirtless and continually gulping deep drafts of iced lemonade. I'd told him that it wouldn't help, but he persisted. Werner could be very stubborn at times.

I said, "London will not authorize the payment of such a

large sum of money until someone on the spot checks with the recipient and okays it, and I am the someone on the spot."

Zena came into the room bringing more iced lemonade. She said, "His embassy has restricted everyone's movements. It's not so easy for them to go strolling in and out as they used to do."

"I find that difficult to believe," I said. "Stinnes is a KGB man. He doesn't have to take any notice of anything the embassy says; he can tell the ambassador to drop dead."

Zena interpreted my response as a sign of nervousness. "It will be all right," she said and smiled at me in the patronizing way she did so often with Werner.

"It won't be all right," I said. "London won't authorize the money . . . not this kind of money."

"Then tell London that they must authorize it," said Zena.

"My standing with London Central is not so good that they will take my orders so readily," I explained. "They'll want some questions answered."

"What questions?" said Werner.

"They'll ask why Stinnes is so insistent upon having the money up front."

"Why not?" said Zena, who would be surprised at anyone's wanting money any other way.

"What's the hurry?" I said. "Why won't Stinnes wait until he's in the U.K.? What's Stinnes going to do in the middle of Mexico City with a suitcase full of pound notes?"

"American dollar bills," said Zena. "That's what he asked for—used hundred-dollar bills."

Zena's manner annoyed me and I snapped at her. "Golden sovereigns, zlotys, shark teeth, or cowrie shells . . . what's the difference?" I said. "Why carry a case filled with cash through a rough town like this? What's wrong with a bank transfer or a letter of credit or even a bearer bond?"

"I wonder if Erich thought of sovereigns," said Zena. "Do you know, I think he might have preferred sovereigns or Krugerrands even to U.S. paper. How heavy would it be in gold?"

I ignored her question. "Whatever he chooses to have as a payment, he'll still have it with him when he gets into the car, won't he? So if we're acting in bad faith we could easily take it away from him. I can't see what's in his mind."

"I don't think he'll have it with him," said Zena very casually, as if wondering whether the storm would come and the rain cool the streets. "Erich is clever. He'll put it away somewhere where no one else can get their hands on it."

"Will he?" I said.

"That's what I'd do," said Zena.

"Nip into the bank, and give it to the cashier?" I said mockingly.

She rose to my bait. "Or give it to someone he trusts," said Zena.

I laughed. "He gives his money to someone he trusts, but delivers his body to people he doesn't trust? I'd say anyone who followed that line of reasoning is an imbecile." I looked at her to see what made her so sure about what Stinnes had in mind. There was no doubt that she had great influence over him. Now I began to wonder if Zena was thinking of delivering him to us and then stealing his money from him. Poor Erich Stinnes.

"No doubt you do," she said haughtily. "That's because now your wife has left you, you have no faith or trust in anything or anyone. But there are trustworthy people in this world."

"Yes," I said. "There are trustworthy people in this world, but you have to take such unacceptable risks to find out who they are."

She smiled as if pitying me and with unmuted sarcasm said, "Life is difficult, isn't it? You have to risk what you need to get what you want." She picked up the coffee cups from the table and put them on a tray, making more noise than was necessary. "I have to go out, Werner," she said, as if by her adding his name I would not be privy to this item of information.

"Yes, darling," said Werner.

"Good-bye, Mrs. Volkmann," I said. "It was nice talking with you." She glared at me. She knew I'd come back to the apartment with Werner only because I knew she had an appointment.

"I wish you and Zena got along better," said Werner after she had gone.

"You mean you wish I'd be more polite to her."

"She's not always easy to get along with," said Werner. "But you always seem to say the wrong things."

"Did you get the gun for me, Werner?"

"It wasn't easy." I followed him over to the big bookcase in which chinaware was displayed. He opened a locked drawer. Reaching into it and groping about behind the cloth-wrapped silver cutlery, he got a Colt .38 Detective Special. He handed it to me. I took it from the fancy tooled-leather holster and examined it. Its nickel finish had almost all worn off; it must have been a quarter of a century old. At some recent time it had been fitted with a hammer shroud to reduce the chance of its discharging accidentally and shooting a hole in someone's foot. "I know you wanted a small automatic with a silencer, but this is all I could get at such short notice," said Werner apologetically.

"It's fine," I said. I tried to say something nice about it other than that it might be a valuable antique. "These steel-frame guns are easier to hold against the recoil the short barrel gives. I just want it to wave about, in case Stinnes suddenly has a change of mind."

"Only one box of bullets, but they are not too ancient."

"It's Stinnes. I just don't like the feel of it, Werner," I said. I stuck the gun in the waist of my trousers and almost fell to the floor with the weight of it. I needed the box of bullets in my pocket to balance me. "It's almost as if Zena doesn't want me to see Stinnes."

"She's become protective about him. She thinks London Central are out to swindle everyone. And frankly, Bernard, you don't do very much to lessen her suspicions."

"And what about you?" I asked. "Do you share the suspicions?"

"If *you* were promising Stinnes the money, I'd be sure he was going to get it. But they're keeping you out of all that, aren't they?"

"They'll have to send me the money soon. They'll have to have it here by Friday, or they can't expect me to get him onto the plane."

Werner pinched his nose with his finger and thumb. "Well, I'm not sure London will send you the money," he said.

"What do you mean, Werner?"

"Your friend Henry Tiptree arrived here in the city. What would you bet me that he's not arranging the cash payment? They'll keep you out of it, Bernard."

"Tiptree? How do you know?"

"I know," said Werner. "Perhaps it's just as well. Let him play his secret games if that's what London wants him to do. It's right, what you said, Bernie. It's dangerous to carry a bagful of cash across this town. There are plenty of people here who'll knife you for fifty centavos. Plenty of them."

"But I still don't understand why Zena is so keen to prevent me meeting Stinnes," I said. "We can't go on with this absurd business of me talking to you and Zena, and then you bringing messages back from Stinnes. It was all right at the beginning, but now time is tight."

"What difference does it make?" said Werner. "You talking to him; me talking to him; Zena talking to him. What's the difference?"

"If Stinnes pulls out at the last moment, or if there is some other kind of cock-up—and it's quite possible that something will go wrong—then I'd like to think it was my fault rather than yours."

"It will be all right," said Werner. "But Erich is very nervous. He has enemies there in the office with him; it's dangerous for him."

He was "Erich" now to both the Volkmanns. I didn't like that, it was too personal. Better to keep a doctor-patient relationship in this sort of operation just in case it got very rough.

"He should have thought of that when he was vacillating," I said.

"It's a big step, Bernie."

"Yes, it is." I went over to the air conditioner. I held my hand in front of the outlet, but the air was still not much cooled. "It makes a lot of noise but doesn't work very well," explained Werner. "The Mexicans call them 'politicians.'"

"And if I have to finally submit to London a report about a cock-up, they are immediately going to ask me why the hell I didn't insist on seeing Stinnes for myself."

"Erich knows what's at stake," said Werner. "He's an experienced agent. It will be just as if we were doing it. We'd make sure we got it right, wouldn't we?"

"He'd better get it right," I said. "He won't be able to go back to his embassy and say he's had a change of mind afterwards."

"Why won't he?" said Werner. "We've known that to happen before, haven't we? I thought that's why London were so keen to load him onto the plane and get him away."

"London have thought of that one," I said. "As soon as they get the telex to say that we have Stinnes, they'll leak a story to one of the news agencies. It will say that we have a high-grade KGB defector who has been supplying information for some years. And the chosen reporter will even have some details of the intelligence that good old Stinnes is said to have provided to them."

Now Werner pinched the cloth of his undershirt between finger and thumb and pulled it away from his body to let some air get to him. "Erich Stinnes has never passed anything back to London, has he?"

"What do you think?"

"I'd think that's just London Central dropping him into the dirt so he doesn't dare think about going back again ever."

"Fantastic, Werner," I said with mock admiration. "You got it at first guess. But for God's sake don't let Stinnes get wind of it."

"Who came up with that nasty little idea—Bret Rens-selaer?"

"Well, we both know it couldn't be Dicky," I said. "Dicky never had an idea."

"Where do you want to meet Erich?" Werner asked.

"I'll have to see him," I said. "Face to face, and well before Friday. If he wants to confide in Zena, or anyone else for that matter, that's up to him. That's a decision I can't take for him. The information about Friday's rendezvous is for him alone, Werner."

"You're going to keep Zena out of it, are you? Are you going to keep me out of it too?"

"You've done your bit, and so has Zena. Let's get it over with. I want to get out of this city. The rain and the heat . . . and the smell. It's not my idea of a vacation."

"Zena's uncle and aunt are due back from their vacation at the weekend, so we'll also be leaving. But I won't be sorry," said Werner. "I'll never complain about Berlin weather again after this damned humidity. Three times I've had someone in to look at that air conditioner and they keep telling me it's working fine. They say it's too hot outside for the machine to cope with it."

I looked at him and nodded.

"Okay," said Werner. "I'll get you together with Erich Stinnes. He's going to phone about six. I'll bring him anywhere you want him."

"I'll need to talk to him. Somewhere safe. Angel's body shop, that car repair place out near the Shrine of Guadalupe. Remember? It's painted in very bright red and yellow."

"What time?"

"Drive straight in, through the workshop and out the back. There's a yard. I'll be parked there. Oh, say seven o'clock."

"I'll be there."

"No Zena," I said.

Werner drank some lemonade. "I've never seen her like this before," he said sadly. "She really likes Erich. She's worrying about him."

"Keep her out of it, Werner."

"Bernie. You don't think Zena could be infatuated with Erich Stinnes, do you?"

"You know her better than I do," I said to avoid the question. Or rather to avoid the answer, which was simply that I knew only one thing that Zena was infatuated with. And Erich Stinnes was about to take delivery of a quarter of a million of them.

"But do I?" said Werner as if he doubted it. "You never see the person you love, except through tinted spectacles. Sometimes I expect too much of her. I'd give her the crown jewels."

"She'd like the crown jewels, Werner."

He smiled without putting much effort into it. "I love her too much, I know that. You're a friend, you can see it better than I can."

"It's no good asking me about Zena," I said. "It's no good expecting me to understand anything about any woman. Whatever Zena feels about Erich Stinnes, there's not much chance that either of us will ever discover what it is. I thought she hated Russians."

"She talks about him a lot. She kept one of those passport photos he sent to you. She keeps it in the pages of her own passport. I noticed her remove it when we went through immigration at the airport."

"That's not very significant," I said.

"If she ran off with Stinnes I'd die," said Werner.

"She's not going to run off with Stinnes," I said. "And even in the unlikely event that she did, you wouldn't die, Werner. You'd feel miserable but you wouldn't die." I felt like grabbing him and shaking him out of his despondent mood, but I knew it wouldn't work. I'd tried such measures before.

"When we left Berlin this time, she took all her jewelry across to her sister."

Shit, I thought, don't say there's another Zena. But I smiled and said, "Has she got much jewelry?"

"Quite a bit; some diamond rings, a three-strand necklace

of pearls, and a platinum bracelet set with large diamonds. And there's a heavy gold necklace that cost me nearly ten thousand marks. Then there are things from her mother—pendants, a watch set with diamonds and pearls. She likes jewelry. You must have seen her wearing it."

"I may have done," I said. "I didn't notice."

"She took it to her sister."

"She was frightened of burglars," I said.

"She never leaves it in the apartment when we're away."

"Well, there you are. She wanted to make sure it was safe. There'd be no point in bringing it to Mexico. You'd be asking for trouble with the customs. And taking it out again they'd be even more difficult."

"But usually she asks me to put it in my safe-deposit box. This time she took it round to her sister."

"You could always ask her about it," I said, and tried to think of a way to change the subject.

"I did ask her," said Werner. "She said she thought her sister might like to wear it while we're away."

"There you are then. That's the explanation."

"Her sister never goes anywhere she could wear stuff like that."

"So why do you think she took it to her sister?"

"If Zena was going to run off with Erich Stinnes, it would be a good thing to do. She likes that jewelry better than anything in the world."

"It will be better that Zena doesn't know exactly what's happening on Friday," I said.

"You mean I refuse to tell her?" I could see Werner anticipating the fight he was going to have about it.

"Better that neither of you know," I said.

"She won't be satisfied with a refusal," said Werner. "She's followed this one through right from the beginning. She'll want to be in on the final act."

"We'll think of something to tell her," I said. "By the way, how do you know that Henry Tiptree has arrived here?"

"He phoned me. He gave me a lot of flattery about what a wonderful reputation I had. Then he arranged a meeting. He said he wanted to pick my brains. But he phoned up later and put the meeting off. He'll phone again, he said."

"Why did he cancel?"

"Is it important?"

"I'm just curious."

"I can't tell you why. Zena took the call. He didn't give any reason as far as I know. Zena said he just phoned up and canceled the meeting." I nodded. Werner said, "Don't mention the gun to Zena. She hates guns."

So Zena had been talking to Tiptree. Or he'd been talking to her. Either way I didn't like it. And I didn't like the way they'd kept Werner out of it. They were a bad combination—the tough, dedicated little Zena and Tiptree, the ambitious diplomat, trying his hand at a cloak-and-dagger job. They were amateurs. Amateurs keep their eyes on the target instead of looking over their shoulder.

Chapter 25

YOU LOOK out for the *tachería* which always has smoke from the open fire and a line of people waiting for the fresh tacos. Across the road are the buses that bring pilgrims to the Shrine of Guadalupe. Buses of all shapes and sizes and colors —huge, air-conditioned monsters that bring people from the big international hotels downtown and bone-rattling old wrecks that convey pilgrims from across the mountains. But the customers buying tacos are not all from the shrine; locals come here too.

Next door to the smoky *tachería* is the place where I was to meet Stinnes. It is a large shedlike building with a ramshackle frontage. Across the bright red overhang, "Angel—body shop" is crudely lettered in blobby script. Inside there are trucks and motorcars in various stages of repair and renovation. And always there is the intense flashing light, and the intermittent hiss of the welding torch. There is always work for skilled car repairmen in Mexico City.

I got there early, drove through the workshop, and parked in the backyard. Angel Morales, a small sad-eyed man with dark skin and a carefully trimmed mustache, came out to see who it was. "I'm meeting someone, Angel," I said. "It's business." I passed him an envelope containing money.

Angel nodded mournfully. Angel was a friend of a friend of mine, but we'd put things on a proper business footing from the time we first met. It was better than using any of the safe houses that the SIS people at the embassy would provide for me. He took the envelope and tucked it into a pocket of his oily coveralls without looking inside it. "I want no trouble," said Angel. That must have been the only English that Angel knew, for he'd said the same words to me on the two previous meetings.

"There'll be no trouble, Angel," I said, giving him the sort of wide smile that I'd seen on carefree men with easy minds.

He nodded and went back to shout abuse at an Indian youth who was bolting a new section of metal onto the back of a badly broken truck.

They arrived exactly on time. Stinnes was driving his own car. He stopped the car in the yard but didn't switch off the engine. Then Werner got into the driver's seat and—waiting only long enough for Stinnes to get clear—he gave a brief wave of the hand before reversing back. Carelessly he knocked the rear fender against the wall. Embarrassed, he swung the car round and accelerated loudly to drive away. It was arranged that Werner would return with the car in half an hour. I wondered if Werner was angry at being excluded from the meeting. But then I dismissed that idea from my mind. Werner was a pro.

Stinnes was dressed in a green tropical suit which repeated washings had faded to a very light color. The collar of his white shirt was buttoned but he wore no tie. It gave the impression of an absentminded man who'd dressed hurriedly, but I knew that Stinnes was not absentminded, and the way in which he'd dragged out the arrangements for his enrollment was the mark of a man who never hurried.

Stinnes was solemn as he got into the car. "There is nothing wrong, I hope," he said when the greetings were over.

"What sort of a game are you playing, Erich?" I said. "I wish I knew."

"What games are there?"

"There are many different ones," I said. "There is the Moscow game, in which you lead us by the nose and then say no thanks."

"I know only the Bernard Samson game," he said. "I do as you propose. I get my money and a few months of interrogation and I retire in comfort."

"What about the Erich Stinnes game? You grab the money and you take off on your own and disappear."

"You'll find a way to prevent that, I'm sure. That's your job, isn't it?"

"What have you arranged with London behind my back, Erich?" I said.

"That's what really annoys you, the way your own department have behaved. You have no complaint against me. I have kept my word all along the line."

"We haven't gone very far yet," I pointed out.

"The London game, that's what you haven't mentioned," said Stinnes.

I said nothing. He was trying to rile me in order to see what he could discover. It was to be expected; it was what I would do to him under the same circumstances.

"The London game . . ." said Stinnes. "You take the blame

for all their mistakes. Is that perhaps the London game, Mr. Samson?"

"I don't know," I said. I was tired of this silly conversation.

But Stinnes persisted. He said, "If you disappeared, it would leave your people in London with a convenient scapegoat for all their failures, wouldn't it?"

"No. They'd have a lot of explaining to do," I said with more bravado than I could spare.

"Not if the money also disappeared with you."

"What are you telling me, Erich?" I kept it light and tried to act as if I found his suggestions amusing. "That London would murder me and make the money vanish and pretend that I'd been a KGB agent for many years?"

He smiled but gave no reply.

"And how would you fit into that scenario? Me dead. Money gone. Erich Stinnes where?"

"I'll keep to my agreement. I've told you that. Do you have any reason to doubt?" I followed Stinnes's gaze. The ground sloped up at the back of the yard. On a grubby white wall a youth in faded jeans and a purple T-shirt was spraying a slogan on the tall stucco wall: *"La Revolución no tiene fronteras"*—the revolution has no frontiers. It was to be seen all over Central America, wherever they could afford the paint.

"We're still on opposing sides, Erich. On Friday we'll be meeting under different circumstances. But until then I'm treating you with great suspicion."

He turned his head to look at me. "Of course. Perhaps you're waiting for some gesture of good faith from me. Is that what you're saying?"

"It would raise my morale."

"This particular gesture of faith might not," said Stinnes. He reached into his pocket and got a Russian passport. He gave it to me. There was nothing special about it—it had been issued two years before and was convincingly marked and dog-eared —except that the photo and physical description were mine. I went cold. "Keep it," said Stinnes. "As a souvenir. But don't use it. The serial numbers are ones that will alert the frontier police. And there are invisible marks that when seen on the fluorescent light will mean a phone call to Moscow." He smiled, inviting me to join the fun.

"There was a plan to kidnap me?"

"A silly contingency plan that has long since been abandoned . . . on my instructions."

"And no one suspects you might be coming to us?"

"A frustrated fool suspects, but he has cried wolf too often with too many others."

"Take care, Erich."

"Take care? How safe is this place? Angel's body shop. Can we be sure we're not observed?"

I said, "Werner knows his job. And Angel's yard is as safe as anywhere in this dangerous town."

"Do you observe what those men over there are doing with that chisel?" he asked. "They are cutting the number from that truck engine. They are criminals. The police probably have this workshop under observation. You must be mad to bring me to such a place."

"You've got a lot to learn about the West, Erich. This fellow Angel regularly works on transforming American trucks and cars that are stolen in Texas and California. The first time I came here I walked into the office and saw him with a box of U.S. license plates that had been ripped off cars before they were resprayed."

"And?"

"Well, you don't think he can go on doing that year after year without attracting the attention of the police, do you?"

"Why isn't he in prison?"

"He bribes the police, Erich. What do they call them here —'the biting ones'—come regularly to collect their fees. This is the safest place in the whole town. No cop would dare come in here and disturb our peaceful conversation. He'd have the whole force at his throat."

"I can see I have much to learn about the West," said

Stinnes with heavy sarcasm. It was interesting that he chose to pretend that bribery and corruption were not plaguing the Eastern bloc. He took off his eyeglasses and blinked. "It was hard to say good-bye to my son," he said as if thinking aloud. "He asked me if I'd ever thought of defecting to the West . . . He'd never said such a thing before. Never. It was very strange, almost like telepathy. I had to say no, didn't I?"

For the first time I felt sorry for him, but I made sure it didn't show. "We'll meet in Garibaldi Square," I said. "Take a cab there and pretend you want to listen to the musicians. But stay in the cab. Arrive at nine o'clock. The time might change if the plane is late. Phone the number I gave you between six and seven to confirm. Whoever answers will give a time but no place. That means Garibaldi Square. No baggage. Wear something that won't look too conspicuous in England."

"I'll be there."

"And don't tell Mrs. Volkmann."

"Don't tell her where I'm meeting you?"

"Don't tell her anything."

"She's with your people, isn't she? I thought I'd be traveling on the plane with her."

"Don't tell her anything."

"Are you sure that you're in charge of this operation?"

"As one pro to another, Erich, let me admit to you that these jobs make me nervous. You will not be armed; understand? I *will* be armed. And the moment I see any sign of KGB heavies, or any other evidence of a stakeout, I will blow a hole in you so big that daylight will shine through you from the other side. No offense, Erich, but I felt it better to tell you that in advance."

"As one pro to another," said Stinnes with more than a trace of sarcasm, "I appreciate your frankness." He wasn't looking at me as he spoke. He was looking right through the open doors of the workshop to where a Jeep had stopped in the street. There were three military policemen in it, all wearing U.S. army–style equipment complete with helmets painted white. One of the MPs climbed out of the Jeep and came through into the yard where we were parked. He stared right at us for a long time. Stinnes stopped talking until the MP turned round and went back inside. We watched him go into the large crate that Angel used as an office. The outside of the crate was covered in girlie pictures, calendars, and travel posters; one said, "Sheraton Hotels let you move to the rhythm of Latin America."

After a few minutes the military policeman reappeared buttoning his top pocket. He grinned to his driver as the Jeep drove away.

"It's the same everywhere in this town. Cops even prey on the cabs taking the tourists to the airport," I said. "Everyone pays off."

Stinnes looked at his watch to see how long it would be before Werner returned. He said, "You realize how much you need my goodwill, don't you?"

"Do I?"

"London Central want to know one thing above all else. They want to know if you are Moscow's man. If I say 'yes,' you'll be finished."

"If you say I'm Moscow's man, they will discover you are lying," I said calmly.

"Perhaps they would; perhaps they wouldn't."

"The debriefing panel are not stupid," I said with more conviction than I truly felt. "They don't use thumbscrews or electric prodders or even a bread and water diet, but they'll discover the truth."

"Eventually, perhaps. But that might come too late to do you any good."

"They won't take me out and shoot me," I said.

"No, they won't. But you'd be removed from your job and discredited. If they cleared you afterwards, you wouldn't be rehabilitated and reinstated."

"If I thought this was all a KGB plot to discredit me, I'd kill you now, Stinnes."

"That would make matters worse for you. If I was killed, you would immediately be suspected. Your position would be worse than having me slander you. With me alive you could argue against me, but London Central would see my dead body as convincing proof of your guilt."

"Is that how it looks to you?"

"It's how it *is*," said Stinnes. "Is there anything else?"

"Did my wife arrange the death of the boy at Bosham?"

"Why?"

"I have to know."

"He recognized her."

"But did she kill him?"

"Your wife . . . of course not."

"Did she authorize it?"

"No, it was a local decision. Your wife was not consulted."

I looked at him, trying to see into his brain. "You'd say that anyway," I said.

I could see by his face that he could not be bothered to discuss the matter. But then he seemed to realize that from now onwards he might have to get used to doing things our way. "Pavel Moskvin, one of my people, was trying to make himself famous."

"By murdering one of our junior staff?"

"Moskvin was using my name; he was in England impersonating me. He got the idea that MacKenzie was you."

"What?"

"He knows nothing about you, except your name and that you wanted to get into contact with me. He was in England on a routine task; he was no more than a backup for your wife's team. But when MacKenzie arrived, Moskvin couldn't resist it. He pretended he was me."

"What a fiasco," I said.

"Moskvin is a meddling fool. He thinks it's all so easy. Finally he killed your man rather than have to report what a mess he'd made of everything. No, your wife was not involved. Your wife is furious about it." A workman wheeled a trailer pump from the shop and started the motor. It made a loud thumping sound until the pressure built up. Then the man began to spray a car door. The spray gun hissed loudly as clouds of pink paint came rolling across the yard.

"You came here *after* the Volkmanns arrived, didn't you?"

"I told her you'd guess that. Chronology is always the first element of deduction."

"The Volkmanns arrived here, and then you came and let them discover you here."

"Your wife was sure her scheme would make you run."

"Was she?" I had my doubts about whether she'd discuss such things with Stinnes, or with anyone else. It was not Fiona's style.

"She thought London Central would be flaying you alive by now. Instead you seem to have talked your way out of trouble there. And instead of you fleeing East, I am coming West. It will be a double defeat for her, and there are people in Moscow who'll not allow her to escape without blame. She will have within her an anger that only women know. She will take revenge upon you, Samson. I would not like to be in your shoes when she seeks retribution."

"You win some; you lose some." I could smell the paint now. It had that acrid taste of cheap boiled sweets that all such quick-drying paints have.

"You say that because you are a man," said Stinnes.

"I say it because I'm a pro. Just as you are one, and just as my wife is. Professionals don't take revenge; they have enough trouble doing their job."

"You may be a good agent," said Stinnes, "but you have a lot to learn about women."

"The only thing a man has to know about women is that he'll never know anything about them. Now let me back up the car before the radiator goes pink."

I started up the car and moved it out of the way of the mad spray man. Stinnes said, "Are you still in love with your wife?"

"No," I said. I was getting fed up with everyone concerning

themselves about how much I loved Fiona. "Are you still in love with Mrs. Volkmann?" I retorted.

Stinnes was startled. His head moved as if I'd given him a slap in the face.

"You'd better tell me," I said. "It could have a bearing on the enrollment."

"How?"

"Have you arranged to go to England with Mrs. Volkmann?"

"She arranged it. Your people approved."

"Did they, by God!"

"She told them it must be a condition. I *am* in love with her. And she's in love with me."

"Are you serious, Erich?"

"I love her. Have you never been in love?"

"Not with Zena Volkmann."

"Don't try to change anything. It's too late now. We're going to start a new life together in England. If you tell her husband or try to interfere, I will not go ahead."

"You must be a bloody fool," I said. "A man like you listening to the sweet talk of a little chiseler like Zena Volkmann. She wants to get her hands on the money. Can't you see that?"

"It's my business," he said peevishly.

"Your fight with your wife . . . her bruised face. Was that something to do with Zena Volkmann? You didn't punch her in the face just to make it all look right, did you?"

"When I told Inge there was another woman she became hysterical. I didn't want to hurt her, but she tried to kill me. She had a metal poker." He sighed. "Zena said I must tell her. Zena insisted upon a clean break. Otherwise, she said, Inge might keep trying to find me. This way perhaps she'll forget me and marry again."

"You didn't tell your wife that you were going to defect?"

"I am in love, but I am not insane. No, of course I didn't tell her."

"Then stay sane about Zena too," I said. "I'll give Zena a ticket to London, for the flight after yours. You make sure you arrive alone on Friday. Or I'll have to get rid of Zena the hard way."

Stinnes seemed not to take my threat seriously. He said, "I suppose every tourist going to London wants to see 221B Baker Street."

"What's in Baker Street?" I said. But even before I'd finished saying it I recognized it as the fictitious address of Sherlock Holmes. "Oh, yes, of course. We'll go along there together," I promised.

"It's something I've always wanted to see," said Stinnes. But before he could get started about Holmes, Werner arrived in Stinnes's car. He got out, leaving the door open, and walked over to us.

"Are you finished?" said Werner. "Or do you want me to give you a little more time?"

Stinnes looked at me. I said, "We're all through, Werner."

As Stinnes got out of the car he touched his forehead in a salutation. *"Auf Wiedersehen,"* he said with more than a trace of mockery in his voice. I noticed the way he'd abruptly introduced the subject of Sherlock Holmes; he hadn't promised not to bring Zena with him.

"Sayonara," I said. I still didn't know what to make of him.

"What's biting you?" said Werner as he got into the car alongside me. I looked in the mirror until Stinnes had got into his car and driven away. Then I gave Werner the Russian passport to look at. "Holy Christ," said Werner.

"Yes, they were going to snatch me."

"And Stinnes prevented it?"

"He's bound to want the credit," I said. "They might just have dropped it in favor of other plans."

"London would have thought you'd gone voluntarily," said Werner. "It's a smart idea."

"Yes, Moscow are having a lot of smart ideas about me lately."

"Fiona, you mean?"

"It's tempting to think it's all coming from her," I said. "But I don't want to become obsessed about it."

"Did he say anything about Zena?" said Werner.

"We've been all through that, Werner. You make sure Zena is kept busy on Friday. You tell her nothing is planned and you're taking her to Acapulco for a long weekend and swim and to get a tan. Send her off on her own on Friday morning so you can be my backup at the airport on Friday night. Then fly out on the late plane to join her."

"She won't fall for that, Bernie. She knows it's getting close."

"You convince her that you both could do with a couple of days off. Make it sound right, Werner. You know what this one means to me. I need Stinnes in London."

"And I need Zena here with me," said Werner grimly.

"Stinnes thinks Zena is eloping with him."

"Eloping?"

"You know what I mean," I said.

"Zena is just stringing him along," said Werner. "She's trying to help you, Bernie."

"She's bloody devious, Werner. She's your wife, I know. But she's too bloody devious."

Werner didn't deny it. "She's seen that man Tiptree," said Werner.

"Seen him?"

"That's where she went this afternoon when we were talking. She went to meet Henry Tiptree. She told me when she got back."

"What are London playing at?" I said wearily.

"Why put up with it?" said Werner. "Why don't you go and see Tiptree? Tell him to either take over the whole operation or stay out of it."

"I thought of that, Werner," I said. "But Tiptree is sure to say he'll take over. And we both know that Tiptree might well make a botch of it. I'm convinced that Erich Stinnes is serious. If he turns up on Friday, I'll deliver him to the bloody plane; at gunpoint, if necessary. I'll get him to London or die in the attempt. If I hand it over to Tiptree, and it all goes wrong, London will say I deliberately abandoned the operation because I didn't want Stinnes debriefed in London."

Werner turned away from me and wound down the window as if suddenly interested in something else. He was avoiding my eyes. I suppose he was upset at the prospect of losing Zena.

"Zena's not going anywhere with Stinnes," I promised him. "You'll be at the airport, Werner. You can stop her if she tries." He didn't reply. I started up the car and turned round in the yard. Then I drove through the workshop. The flashes of the acetylene torch lit up the wrecked cars like the flashguns of a thousand paparazzi. Outside a blue and white police car was parked. The driver was inside talking to Angel.

Chapter 26

GARIBALDI Square is to Mexican musicians what the Galapagos Archipelago is to wildlife. Even in the small hours of the night the square was crowded with people and the air was filled with the sound of two or three dozen groups singing and playing different songs. There is no pop, rock, soul, or punk to be heard; no Elvis, no Beatles, no Elton John. This is Mexican music and if you don't like it, you can go somewhere else.

"I've only been here before in the morning. I had no idea what it was really like. It's fantastic," said Henry Tiptree as we walked past five musicians in serape and sombrero singing ". . . life is worth nothing in Guanajuato . . ." Tiptree halted for a moment to listen. "It's not even spoiled by tourists; almost everyone here is Mexican."

"It's right for what we want," I said. "It's ill lit, noisy, and crowded." And smelly too. Trapped by the surrounding mountains, the still air was pressed down upon the city, trapping the diesel fumes and wood smoke so that the air offended the nose and stung the eyes.

"I'm not working against you, Samson," said Henry Tiptree suddenly.

"If you say so," I said. Tiptree stopped to look around the square. There was music coming from every direction and yet the effect was polyphony rather than discord. Or was I becoming inured to chaos?

Tiptree went on looking round the square. He fingered the mustache that never seemed to grow and spoke with that sort of confidential manner that people use to assert their self-importance. "You must understand," he said, "that the success of this operation will be measured according to whether we get our man to London; nothing else counts for much. That's why London Central are determined that we do everything right."

"We all are," I said. "But who knows best what's right?"

"Very philosophical," said Tiptree flatly.

"I am very philosophical," I said. "You get philosophical after London Central screw up for you a few times."

"London Central have confirmed that I'm in charge," said Tiptree. "I want that understood before we go a step farther. You will take Stinnes to London, but here in the city we're doing things my way."

"You're in charge," I agreed. London Central? Who'd put this idiot in charge—Dicky? Bret? Morgan, perhaps. Tiptree seemed to be on very good terms with Morgan, the D-G's factotum, who could have caught the D-G in a weak moment and got a signature from him.

Tiptree shot me a suspicious glance. He knew my glib pledge counted for little or nothing. I didn't risk my neck taking orders from learners. He stopped to watch another group of musicians. They were singing a song about a man who'd lost his heart to a girl from Veracruz. The men were illuminated by a hissing acetylene lamp placed at their feet. The lead singer—a very old man with a face like a walnut and a *bandido* mustache—had a fine bass voice that was racked with emotion. There is a passionate soul in every Mexican, so that love or revolution dominates his whole being; but only for a few minutes at a time. "What have you arranged about his money?" I asked.

From the corner of my eye I could see that Tiptree was looking at me, trying to decide how to answer. "Mrs. Volkmann is meeting us at the bank," he said finally. "Stinnes wants the money paid her."

Only with a great effort did I prevent myself from jumping up and down and shrieking with rage. This idiot was keeping Zena better informed than me. But very calmly I said, "What bank is open in Garibaldi Square at this hour?"

"So there are things that even you don't know, eh Samson?"

He went along the pavement to find a *pulquería* where even the barman looked drunk. The fermenting sap of the maguey plant smells like rancid nut oil, but it's the cheapest way to oblivion and, like so many such bars, this one was packed. After pushing his way between the customers right to the very back, Tiptree opened a door and held it for me. I followed him into a narrow hallway, then he started to go up a steep flight of creaking stairs.

"Wait a minute," I said. I stopped at the bottom of the stairs to look around. There was only a dim electric bulb to illuminate a passage that led out to the backyard and the urinals. "Where are we going?" My voice echoed as I closed the door behind me. The customers in the bar were kicking up so much noise that I could only faintly hear the music from Garibaldi Square. There was a lot about this place that I didn't like.

"I'm meeting Stinnes in the square," I protested.

"Don't be so nervous," said Tiptree. "The plan has been changed. Stinnes knows." He smiled to reassure me, but it only made me see what a conceited fool he was. He knew how much I resented this change of plan and the way that Zena had already been made a party to it. "It's all arranged."

I touched the butt of the old pistol to be sure it was still there and then followed him up the narrow stairs. Rat trap, fire trap, man trap; it was the sort of place I didn't like at any time. But I especially didn't like it for this sort of business. Narrow stairway with a wide well, so that a man with a Saturday night special at the top of the house could plink an army one by one.

Tiptree stopped on the second-floor landing. There was just enough light to see that the door looked new. It was the only new-looking object anywhere in sight. He rang the bell and waited for a small panel to open. It provided someone inside with a view of Tiptree's Eton tie. But he bent lower to see inside and whispered something that resulted in the sound of well-oiled bolts being slid back.

"I don't like surprises," I told Tiptree. "I arranged to meet Stinnes in the square."

"I've sent a message to him," said Tiptree. "He'll meet us here. It's too damned public, that square."

When the door was opened, by a slight Mexican boy wearing a straw hat, brim curled cowboy style, I noticed that there was a sheet of steel layered into the woodwork of the door. Another boy stood behind him, studying us warily. He recognized Tiptree and nodded.

"This is the bank," announced Tiptree. It was a large room that overlooked the square, but the blinds had been pulled down. The room, with its ornate Victorian wallpaper and brass light brackets, had the atmosphere of some Wild West saloon a century ago. Three almost identical men sat at three almost identical old tables. The men were dressed in white short-sleeved shirts with black trousers and black ties and black well-polished shoes—the uniform used throughout the world by men who wish to be entrusted with money. Each man was equipped with half a dozen ledgers, a small cash box, a scribbling pad, and a Japanese calculator. Through a half-open door I could see another room where girls were typing on the wide-platen typewriters that are required for account sheets.

"It's a money-change office," I said.

"Three partners; brothers. They used to run a loan company . . . one that was always ready to change money too. But when the government nationalized all the banks, larger horizons opened."

"Is it a legal bank?" I asked.

"Strictly speaking, it's not legal and it's not a bank," said Tiptree. "But it's right for what we want. I've spent a lot of time in Mexico, Samson. I know how things work here."

I looked at the old man sitting inside the door with a shotgun across his knees. The teenage boys who'd let us in looked like blood relations. Perhaps it was a family business.

Tiptree greeted Zena. She was sitting on a wooden bench and nodded politely to both of us. Despite the heat she was dressed in a linen suit with Paris labels, and her makeup and the low-heel shoes made her look like someone who'd prepared for a journey. There was no sign of Werner.

"Is this where the money is supposed to be?" I asked.

Tiptree smiled at the doubt he heard in my voice. "Don't be misguided by appearances. A quarter of a million dollars is bagatelle to these people, Samson. They could have ten million, in any of the world's major currencies, laid out across the floor within an hour."

"You've got it all worked out," I said.

"You're the muscle; I'm the brains," said Tiptree without expending too much energy to persuade me it was a joke.

Tiptree exchanged polite British-style greetings with one of the partners and formally introduced me. The senior partner was called Pepe, a soft-spoken man with white hair, a pockmarked face, and a pocket full of pens. Tiptree told him that Zena was the one to whom the money was to be paid. I looked at Zena and she smiled.

When they were ready to count the money, Zena went to the table to watch the man piling the hundred-dollar bills on the table. I went to watch too. They were used notes, two hundred and fifty of them in each thick bundle. They were held together by heavy-duty red rubber bands into which torn scraps of paper had been inserted with "$25,000" scrawled on each of them. There were ten bundles.

Perhaps in some other bank, in some other town, the money might then have been passed across the table. But this was Mexico, and these were men well accustomed to the mistrust that peasants show for bankers. It all had to be counted a second time note by note. Despite Pepe's fumbling, it took only a few minutes.

When he'd finished counting, Pepe opened a cupboard to get a cardboard box for the money. There were many other boxes, of all shapes and sizes, stacked in the cupboard. On the side of this box it said, "Flat fillets of anchovies 50 tins—2 oz." I wonder who first discovered that fifty tins of anchovies fit into exactly the same space as a quarter of a million dollars. Or vice versa.

Perhaps I should have given more attention to Pepe's nervous manner and to the clumsiness he showed in handling the notes, but I was too concerned with the prospect of Zena's departing with the money before Stinnes arrived. I looked at my watch and I looked at the clock on the wall. Stinnes was late. Something had gone wrong. All my professional intuition said leave, and leave right away. But I stayed.

While Pepe was putting strapping tape on the box, Zena went to the window. She was holding back the edge of the blind to see down into the square when Pepe told me and Tiptree to put our hands on our heads.

"I'm sorry," said Pepe, whose drawn white face, the stubble of tomorrow's beard already patterning his chin, bore a frown of desolate unhappiness. "I'm doing only what I must do."

Tiptree, despite his excellent Spanish, did not understand Pepe's soft instruction.

"Put your hands on your head," I said. "Do as he says." Even then I think Tiptree would not have understood except that he saw me put my hands on my head. "Someone got here ahead of us."

"Your friends?" said Tiptree, looking round the room.

"How I wish they were," I said. But I had no time for Tiptree's stupid suspicions. I was trying to decide what role the old man with the shotgun was playing in this business, and whether the two boys with him were armed.

Now Zena also had her hands on her head. She'd been pulled away from the window in case her shadow on the blind was seen by someone in the street. "What's happening?" said Zena.

It was then that a burly, dark-suited man came from the next room. Beside him there was a Mexican boy with a machine pistol. I didn't like machine pistols, especially cheap machine pistols like this one. Hoping to survive a false move against a man with a machine pistol was like shouting abuse at a man with a garden hose and hoping not to get wet. I looked at it carefully. It was a Model 25, a Czech design that dated from the time before they changed over to Soviet calibers. An old cheap gun, but the boy liked waving it around, and he kept the metal stock folded forward to make this easier to do.

I recognized the dark-suited man from the night I'd spent at Biedermann's house. It was Stinnes's companion, the man who called himself Pavel Moskvin—the "fink"—a tough-looking fifty-year-old with a cropped head and the build of a debt collector. "You," he said to me in his abominable German. "You make sure your friends know that no one will harm them if they do as they are told."

"What's it all about?" I said.

He looked at me but didn't answer. "Tell them," he said.

Zena and Tiptree had heard for themselves. Tiptree said, "Is this your doing, Samson?"

"Don't be stupid," I said. "It's a KGB stakeout. They're waiting for Stinnes. They might leave us out of it if we behave."

"What will they do?" said Tiptree. "Are they going to kill him?"

I shrugged. We could only wait and see. The door buzzer sounded and Moskvin nodded to tell Pepe to open the spy hole.

Pepe looked out and after a brief muttering through the

hatch said it was a woman who wanted to change some U.S. one-dollar bills into Mexican money. "Do you recognize her?" Moskvin asked Pepe.

"We have a lot of people asking for change—waiters, hotel workers, shop workers. I don't know. I can't see much through the hatch."

"Tell her to return tomorrow. Say you've run out of money." Moskvin's Spanish was even worse than his German. To get a job in the Soviet foreign service with so little aptitude for languages, a man would have to be a very loyal Party supporter.

Pepe sent the woman away and then we all settled down to wait. It was a nerve-racking business. Moskvin had prepared it well. It was the right place. He had all the evidence he needed to nail Stinnes, and this way he'd have the dollars too. There was nothing the KGB liked better than rubbing our noses in it. I cursed Tiptree for changing the rendezvous. It wouldn't have been so easy for Moskvin out there in the dark crowded square.

I looked at Pepe. His business made it unlikely that he had Communist Party connections. Probably the KGB had had Tiptree under observation when he came here to make arrangements about the money.

In such a situation almost everything is guesswork. I guessed the old man was the regular guard for the bank, simply because he did not look like the sort of tough whom Moskvin would bring in. And I guessed from the way he held the double-barreled gun that Moskvin had removed the shells. And the despondent expressions on the faces of the young boys and the envy with which they eyed the machine pistol convinced me that they were unarmed. I could take the old man and the kids, I could probably handle Moskvin at the same time, but the machine pistol tilted the balance.

I kept my hands on my head and tried to look very frightened. It was not difficult, especially when I saw the way the kid with the machine pistol was flourishing it and caressing the trigger lovingly. "I want everyone to remain still," said Moskvin. He said it frequently and in between saying it he was look-ing at his wristwatch. "And stay away from the windows."

Pepe took a hand from his head and got a handkerchief to blow his nose. Moskvin was angry. He punched Pepe in the back with a force that knocked him to his knees. "The next person to move without permission will be shot," he promised and gave Pepe a spiteful kick to emphasize this warning.

There were just the two of them, it seemed, and it was unlikely that they had worked together before. One machine pistol and probably some kind of hand gun in Moskvin's pocket. Yet against them, one person alone would stand little chance.

I looked round the room deciding what to do when and if Stinnes pressed the buzzer. They'd have to open the door be-cause otherwise the steel door-lining would both protect and hide him. Did they have someone downstairs in the bar, I won-dered. Or someone outside in the street to watch for Stinnes's arrival. The crowded bar would make a perfect cover.

I looked at the three partners, the three guards, and the two women clerks who'd been brought in from the next room. They all kept their hands on their heads, and they all had that patient and passive visage that makes the people of Latin America so recognizably different from the Latin people of Europe.

It was while I was musing on this question that I heard the bang of the downstairs door. Under normal circumstances the sounds of footsteps on the staircase would not have been audi-ble, but the circumstances were not normal; everyone in the room was wound up tight.

The boy with the machine pistol pulled the bolt back to cock the gun for firing. There was a click as the sear engaged the sear notch in the bolt. It was enough to snap some mechanism within Zena's mind. "You promised," she shouted. "You prom-ised not to hurt him."

She was shouting at Moskvin, but he smiled without even bothering to look back at her. So that was how it had been done: Moskvin had been monitoring the whole thing through Zena. But she wasn't KGB material; there was no need to ask what was she getting out of it—the box of money. Nice going, Moskvin.

But if my wife Fiona wasn't behind that notion, I'd eat the money bill by bill.

We could hear the footsteps as someone reached the top of the stairs and paused on the landing. "You promised," said Zena. She was almost incoherent with anger. "I love him. I told you." She stiffened as she recognized their total indifference, and her face had gone livid under the bright makeup.

Neither Moskvin nor his machine gun man bothered with Zena. Their eyes were on the door where Stinnes was expected at any moment.

There is always some damned possibility that lies beyond every probability. Perhaps the only thing I'd never considered was that Zena could be infatuated with Stinnes. There was a strong streak of romanticism in her complex personality, and there was that old Prussian rectitude that made her record every broken teacup in a notebook. Zena would allow Stinnes to be betrayed but not killed.

Ignoring the machine pistol, Zena flung herself across the room like a human cannon ball. She collided with the boy, her feet kicking and fingernails gouging. He bent and almost fell under the momentum of her attack, and there was a crash as their two bodies smashed against the wall. Trying to defend himself against her fingernails, the boy dropped his machine gun and tried to grab her hands. An ear-splitting bang echoed round the room as the bullet in the chamber was fired by the impact. But by that time Zena had her nails into the boy's face and he was yelling at her to stop. He was frightened of her and it could be heard in his shouts. Thus encouraged, she stopped only long enough to grab his long hair and use it to swing his head against a sharp corner of a filing cabinet.

Had Moskvin reached into his pocket for a pistol or stooped to pick up the machine gun, he might have regained control. But he used his huge fists. It was the reflex action of a man who'd spent his life throwing his weight around both literally and figuratively. He gave Zena's small body a mighty blow to the kidneys and followed it with a left hand to the side of her head.

The punches landed with sickening force. They took care of little Zena all right. She was only half conscious as she fell to the floor, arms flailing. Then Moskvin couldn't resist a kick at her. But it took time. There was lots of time, and I pushed my pistol back into my belt as I watched Tiptree bring a small Browning automatic from his pocket and with commendable speed fire two shots at Moskvin. The first bullet went wild—I heard it ricochet and hit a typewriter in the next room—but his second bullet hit Moskvin in the leg. Moskvin stopped kicking Zena and screamed. I had guessed he was an amateur. Now he demonstrated the way in which an amateur is only efficient while all is going well for him. Once injured, he lost interest in killing Stinnes. He lost interest in the money. He lost interest in the boy who'd had his face shredded by Zena's nails and his cranium gashed on the sharp corner of the filing cabinet. He even lost interest in the machine pistol on the floor.

The Mexicans all remained very still, hands on heads and their faces impassive. I put my hands back on my head too. There was no sense in getting killed, but I got ready for the aftermath by stepping slowly to one side so that I could plant my foot on the machine pistol. That was the trump card.

Moskvin fell back onto a chair and pressed his palm against the copious bleeding. He nursed his pain, wanting everything to stop. He clamped his hands to his wounded leg and crooned and wept with the pain of it. The pain could not have been very great, but he was frightened. He'd probably convinced himself he was going to die. Even people hardened to the sight of blood can be very deeply affected by a glimpse of their own.

Now Tiptree found time enough to look around to see where I'd gone. "Open the door," he told me with a superiority that bordered on contempt. "And take your hands off your head. It's all over." When I didn't move fast enough, he looked down to where I had my foot on the machine pistol and said, "Oh, you've got that, have you. Good."

Loudly Moskvin said, "I must go to hospital. I'm bleeding to death."

"Shut up," I said.

Despite the changed situation, the Mexicans kept their hands on their heads. They were taking no chances. I picked up the machine gun, went to the door, and slid back the hatch expecting to see Stinnes. Instead, a small child whispered, "I have a message. It is only for Señor Samson."

"I'm Señor Samson," I said.

The child looked at me for a long time before deciding to confide his very guarded message. He whispered, "Your friend is waiting for you at the place you arranged."

"Thank you," I said.

"You are to give me one hundred pesos," he said. Stinnes knew how to get his messages delivered. I passed a note through the hatch to the child, and then closed it.

"I must go to hospital," said Moskvin. His voice grew lower and more forceful as a little of his confidence returned to him.

"If he says another word about anything, shoot him," I told Tiptree in English. "They won't ask him questions in the morgue."

Tiptree nodded solemnly. I think he would have done it too; you never can be sure with enthusiasts like Tiptree.

Moskvin went suddenly quiet. He obviously understood enough English to know what was good for him.

The onetime machine gunner was sitting on the floor covered in blood. He was only half conscious and his eyes were closed with the pain. He'd discovered that a filing cabinet can be a formidable weapon.

"What's next?" said Tiptree. His voice was shrill. He was excited and overconfident and still waving his pistol around.

"You're staying here to make sure no one leaves until I phone you from you know where."

"Wait a minute," said Tiptree, his voice revealing a sudden concern. "This all has to be sorted out. This Russian shot, the Mexican boy badly hurt, and the girl unconscious. The police may come. How do I explain the guns?"

I dialed the freight office at the airport. Werner answered

immediately. "We're ready this end," he said. "Is everything all right with you?"

I looked at Zena. There was no point in alarming Werner; there was nothing he could do. "So far so good," I said, and hung up the phone. To Tiptree I said, "The success of this operation will be measured according to whether we get our man to London; nothing else counts for much. You told me that. London are relying on you, Henry—don't let them down. I'll get someone to call you at this number to tell you when we're safely airborne. Meanwhile keep them here. This is your big chance. They're very dangerous agents."

"I'll go. You stay," suggested Tiptree.

"You don't know where I arranged to meet our friend," I said.

"And you won't tell me," said Tiptree.

I didn't bother to answer. I looked at them. The stupid peasant Moskvin, with his trouser cuff rolled up, winding his tie round his leg to stop the bleeding, and frightened for his life. And the erstwhile machine gunner now sitting on the floor groaning, eyes closed, staunching blood from his lacerated face and head with a great handful of paper tissues.

And there was tiny Zena, the astounding little fireball whom I would never understand. How typical that as she began to regain consciousness her fingers were searching out the rips and torn seams in her expensive Paris suit.

Well, even Tiptree should be able to deal with these "dangerous agents." But how he'd deal with the police was something I didn't intend to stay long enough to find out.

"You're right," said Tiptree with a sudden smile. Luckily the adrenaline was marring his judgment, and his self-esteem did the rest. "I'll take care of this. Tell London that my report will follow in due course."

"I'll tell them," I said.

I WENT downstairs and out into the backyard, climbing over a tall stack of beer crates to surmount a wall and from there jumping down into the alley, just in case Moskvin had another friend waiting in the bar. Stinnes was waiting in a cab on the corner. He opened the door for me and I slid in beside him. I was expecting him to ask immediately where Zena was, but he said, "What was the delay?" He leaned forward to the driver. "Airport," he told him. The driver started the engine.

"Freight side," I said. I dropped the box of money onto Stinnes's knees, but after taking a moment to recognize what it was, he put it aside without opening it.

"I don't want the money," he said as if he'd been thinking about it for a long time. "I didn't do it for the money."

"I know you didn't," I said. "But take it anyway. You'll have no trouble getting rid of it."

The taxi pulled away from the curb, slowly at first to avoid hitting the strolling musicians and the revelers. Stinnes sank back into his seat. To think that I'd been getting ready to prevent him at pistol point from racing up there to his beloved Zena.

"Freight side," said Stinnes. "Another change of plan. And when we get to the airport freight yard, what new idea then? A bus to Los Angeles?"

"Maybe," I said.

"You're late," he said, looking at his watch.

"Your man Moskvin turned up. Apparently he couldn't bear to be parted from you."

"Moskvin," said Stinnes. "Yesterday I found him rifling through my desk. He found nothing, of course, but I should have told you about him."

"Your lady friend was reporting everything back to Moskvin. Everything."

"She was talking to Moskvin?"

"How else did she come to be there?" There were other answers to that question, but Stinnes didn't know them. And this wasn't the right time to tell him that Zena had risked her life to save him.

He was silent as we drove through Garibaldi Square. At the intersection he leaned aside and ducked his head to look at the "bank." Perhaps he needed to see the building, and the lights behind the drawn blinds, to come to terms with Zena's treachery. "You were right about her," he said sadly. "I could tell from your face when you said what a fool I was. You made me see sense."

There was heavy traffic, but I'd allowed for some delay. I'd even allowed time for the traffic jam. The traffic slowed and then came to a complete standstill. The fire-eater was still at work. He blew a fierce tongue of flame into the air. It was darker now and the flame lit up all the cars, rippled in the paintwork, and shone in all the windows. "It's fantastic the things some people do for a living," said Stinnes. He wound down the car window and gave the child collecting the money two hundred pesos.

When the traffic had started moving again, he got a small black cheroot from his pocket and put it in his mouth. When he searched his pockets for a light I watched him carefully, but it was only matches that he came up with.

"Tell me," I said. "As well as the boy with the message, did you also send that old woman?" I appreciated such extreme caution. It was what any real pro would do.

He lit the little cigar with the studied care a man might lavish upon a fine double Corona. "Yes, I sent the old woman too." He blew smoke and the car filled with a strong smell of the overfermented tobacco leaf that Stinnes seemed to like. "Yes," he said. "I wanted to know what was happening. I had no intention of going up there all on my own. The blinds were down; narrow stairs, crowded bar. It didn't look healthy. What happened?"

"Nothing much," I said. "Moskvin's a deskman, isn't he?"

"Yes," said Stinnes. "And I hate deskmen."

"So do I," I said feelingly. "They're bloody dangerous."

A Note on the Type

The text of this book was set in a digitized version of a typeface called Baskerville. The face itself is a facsimile reproduction of type cast from molds made for John Baskerville (1706–1775) from his designs. Baskerville's original face was one of the forerunners of the type style known to printers as "modern face"—a "modern" of the period A.D. 1800.

Composed, printed, and bound by
The Haddon Craftsmen, Inc., Scranton, Pennsylvania.
Designed by Virginia Tan.